D0457656

The Vampire Diaries

Books by L. J. Smith

THE VAMPIRE DIARIES:
VOL. I: THE AWAKENING

THE VAMPIRE DIARIES:
VOL. II: THE STRUGGLE

THE VAMPIRE DIARIES:
VOL. III: THE FURY

THE VAMPIRE DIARIES:
VOL. IV: DARK REUNION

THE VAMPIRE DIARIES:
THE RETURN VOL. 1: NIGHTFALL

THE VAMPIRE DIARIES:
THE RETURN VOL. 2: SHADOW SOULS

THE VAMPIRE DIARIES:
THE RETURN VOL. 3: MIDNIGHT

THE SECRET CIRCLE:
THE INITIATION AND THE CAPTIVE PART I

THE SECRET CIRCLE:
THE CAPTIVE PART II AND THE POWER

L. J. Smith

The Vampire Diaries
THE RETURN:
VOL. 3
MIDNIGHT

HARPER TEEN
An Imprint of HarperCollinsPublishers

HarperTeen is an imprint of HarperCollins Publishers.

The Vampire Diaries: The Return: Midnight

www.harperteen.com

Produced by Alloy Entertainment
151 West 26th Street, New York, NY 10001
www.alloyentertainment.com

Library of Congress Cataloging-in-Publication Data

Smith, L. J. (Lisa J.)
Midnight / L.J. Smith. — 1st ed.
p. cm. — (The vampire diaries: the return ; v. 3)
Summary: Eighteen-year-old Elena Gilbert's latest battle against the demons that have taken over her hometown of Fell's Church is complicated by the fact that Damon is a mortal since he, his brother Stefan, and Elena returned from the Dark Dimension.
ISBN 978-0-06-172085-7 (trade bdg.)
[1. Supernatural—Fiction. 2. Interpersonal relations—Fiction. 3. Brothers—Fiction. 4. Vampires—Fiction.] I. Title.
PZ7.S6537Mid 2011 *2010042677*
[Fic]—dc22

Typography by Jennifer Heuer
11 12 13 14 15 CG/RRDH 10 9 8 7 6 5 4 3 2 1
❖
First Edition

For Anne, the animal-whisperer

With thanks to the real Princess Jessalyn, and to Louise Beaudry for her help with French translations.

1

"Dear Diary,

I'm so frightened I can hardly hold this pen. I'm printing rather than writing in cursive, because that way I have more control.

What am I terrified of, you ask? And when I say "of Damon" you don't believe the answer, not if you'd seen the two of us a few days ago. But to understand, you have to know a few facts.

Have you ever heard the phrase "All bets are off"*?*

It means that anything, anything, *can happen. So that even somebody who figures out odds and takes bets from people gives them back their money. Because a wild card has entered the situation.* You can't even figure the odds to take a bet.

That's where I am. That's why my heart is pounding in my throat and head and ears and fingertips in fear.

All bets are off.

You can see how shaky even my printing is. Suppose my hands shake like this when I go in to see him*? I might drop the tray. I might annoy Damon. And then* anything *might happen.*

I'm not explaining this right. What I should be saying is that we're back: Damon and Meredith and Bonnie and me. We went to the Dark Dimension and now we're home again, with a star ball—and Stefan.

Stefan was tricked into going there by Shinichi and Misao, the brother and sister kitsune*, or evil fox-spirits, who told him that if he went to the Dark Dimension he could get the curse of being a vampire removed and become human again.*

They lied.

All they did was leave him in a stinking prison, with no food, no light, no warmth . . . until he was at the point of death.

But Damon—who was so different back then—agreed to lead us to try to find him. And, oh, I can't even begin to describe the Dark Dimension itself. But the important thing is that we finally found Stefan, and that by then we'd found the Twin Fox key we needed to release him. But—he was a skeleton, poor boy. We carried *him out of the prison on his pallet, which later Matt burned; it was so infested with creepy-crawlies. But that night we gave him a bath and put him to bed . . . and then we fed him. Yes, with our blood. All the humans did it except Mrs. Flowers, who was busy making poultices for where his poor bones were almost sticking out of his skin.*

They *had starved him to that point! I could kill* Them *with my own hands—or my Wings Powers—if only I could use them properly. But I can't. I know there is a spell for* Wings of Destruction, *but I have no idea how to summon it.*

At least I got to see how Stefan blossomed when being fed with human *blood. (I admit that I gave him a few extra feedings that weren't on his chart, and I'd have to be an idiot not to know that my blood is different from other people's—it's much richer and it did Stefan amazing amounts of good.)*

And so Stefan recovered enough that the next morning he was able to walk *downstairs to thank Mrs. Flowers for her potions!*

The rest of us, though—all the humans—were

totally exhausted. We didn't even think about what had happened to the bouquet, because we didn't know it had anything special in it. We'd gotten it just as we were leaving the Dark Dimension, from a kind white kitsune who'd been in the cell across from Stefan's before we arranged a jailbreak. He was so beautiful! I never knew a kitsune could be kind. But he had given Stefan these flowers.

Anyway, that morning Damon was up. Of course, he couldn't contribute any of his own blood, but I honestly think he would *have, if he could. That was the way he was back then.*

And that's why I don't understand how I can feel the fear I feel now. How can you be terrified of someone who's kissed you and kissed you . . . and called you his darling and his sweetheart and his princess? And who has laughed with you with his eyes dancing with mischief? And who's held *you when you were frightened, and told you there was nothing to be afraid of, not while he was there? Someone you only had to glance at to know what he was thinking? Someone who has protected you, no matter what the cost to himself, for days on end?*

I know Damon. I know his faults, but I also know what he's like inside. And he's not what he wants people to think he is. He's not cold, or arrogant, or cruel. Those are façades he puts on to cover himself, like clothes.

The problem is that I'm not sure he *knows he isn't any of these things. And right now he's all mixed-up. He might change and become all of them—because he's so confused.*

What I'm trying to say is, that morning only Damon was really awake. He was the only one who saw the bouquet. And one of the things Damon definitely is, *is curious.*

So he unwrapped all the magical wards from it and it had a single pitch-black rose in the center. Damon has been trying to find a black rose for years, just to admire it, I think. But when he saw this one he smelled it . . . and boom*! The rose disappeared!*

And suddenly he was sick and dizzy and he couldn't smell anything *and all his other senses were dulled as well. That was when Sage—oh, I haven't even mentioned Sage, but he's a tall bronze gorgeous hunk of a vampire who's been such a good friend to all of us—told him to suck in air and to hold it, to push it down into his lungs.*

Humans have to breathe that way, you see.

I don't know how long it took Damon to realize

that he really was *a human, no joke, nothing anyone could do about it. The black rose had been for Stefan; and it would have given him his dream of being human again. But when Damon realized it had worked its magic on* him . . .

That's when I saw him look at me and lump me in with the rest of my species—a species he's come to hate and scorn.

Since then I haven't dared look him in the eye again. I know *he loved me just days ago. I didn't know that love could turn to—well, to all the things he feels now about himself.*

You'd think it would be easy for Damon to become a vampire again. But he wants to be as powerful a vampire as he used to be—and there isn't anyone like that to exchange blood with him. Even Sage disappeared before Damon could ask him. So Damon is stuck like this until he finds some strong, powerful, and prestigious vampire to go through the whole process of changing him.

And every time I look into Stefan's *eyes, those jewel-green eyes that are warm with trust and gratitude—I feel terror, too. Terror that somehow he'll be snatched away again—right out of my arms. And . . . terror that he'll find out how I've come to feel about Damon. I hadn't even realized myself how much Damon has come to mean to me. And I can't . . . stop . . . my feeling . . . for him, even if he hates me now.*

And, yes, damn it, I'm crying! In a minute, I have to go take him his dinner. He must be starving, but when Matt tried to take him something earlier today, Damon threw the whole tray at him.

Oh, please, God, please *don't let him hate me!*

I'm being selfish, I know, in just talking about what's going on with Damon and me. I mean, things in Fell's Church are worse than ever. Every day more children become possessed and terrify their parents. Every day, parents get angrier with their possessed children. I don't even want to think about what's going on. If something doesn't change, the whole place will be destroyed like the last town Shinichi and Misao visited.

Shinichi . . . he made a lot of predictions about our group, about things we've kept secret from the others. But the truth is, I don't know if I want to hear any of his riddles solved.

We're lucky in one way. We have the Saitou family to help us. You remember Isobel Saitou, who pierced herself so horribly while she was possessed? Since she's gotten better, she's become a good friend, and her mother, Mrs. Saitou, and her

> *grandmother, Obaasan, too. They give us amulets—spells to keep evil away, written on Post-it Notes or little cards. We're so grateful for that kind of help. Someday maybe we can repay them all.*

Elena Gilbert put down the pen reluctantly. Shutting her diary meant having to face the things she had been writing about.

Somehow, though, she managed to make herself walk downstairs to the kitchen and take the dinner tray from Mrs. Flowers, who smiled encouragingly at her.

As she set out for the boardinghouse's storage room, she noticed that her hands were trembling so that the entire tray of food she was carrying jingled. Since there was no access to the storage room from inside, anyone who wanted to see Damon had to go out the front door and around to the addition tacked on near the kitchen garden. *Damon's lair*, people were calling it now.

As she passed the garden Elena glanced sideways at the hole in the middle of the angelica patch that was the powered-down Gateway where they'd come back from the Dark Dimension.

She hesitated at the storage room door. She was still trembling, and she knew that was not the right way to face Damon.

Just relax, she told herself. Think of Stefan.

Stefan had had a grim setback when he'd found that there was nothing left of the rose, but he had soon recovered his usual humility and grace, touching Elena's cheek and saying that he was thankful just to be there with her. That this closeness was all he asked of life. Clean clothes, decent food—*freedom*—all these were worth fighting for, but Elena was the most important. And Elena had cried.

On the other hand, she knew that Damon had no intention of remaining as he now was. He might do anything, risk anything . . . to change himself back.

It had actually been Matt who had suggested the star ball as a solution for Damon's condition. Matt hadn't understood either the rose or the star ball until it was explained that this star ball, which was probably Misao's, contained within it most or all of her Power, and that it had become more brilliant as it absorbed the lives that she took. The black rose had probably been created with a liquid from a similar star ball—but no one knew how much or whether it was combined with unknown ingredients. Matt had frowned and asked, if the rose could change a vampire to a human, could a star ball change a human to a vampire?

Elena hadn't been the only one to see the slow rising of Damon's bent head, and the glimmer in his eyes as they traveled the length of the room to the star ball filled with Power. Elena could practically hear his logic. Matt might be totally off track . . . but there was one place a human could be sure to find powerful vampires. In the Dark Dimension—to which there was a Gateway in the boardinghouse's garden. The Gateway was closed right now . . . for lack of Power.

Unlike Stefan, Damon would have absolutely no qualms about what would happen if he had to use all the star ball's liquid, which would result in the death of Misao. After all, she was one of the two foxes who had abandoned Stefan to be tortured.

So all bets were off.

Okay, you're scared; *now deal with it*, Elena told herself fiercely. Damon's been in that room for almost fifty hours now—and who knows what he's been plotting to do to get hold of the star ball. Still, somebody's got to get him to eat—and when you say "somebody," face it, it's you.

Elena had been standing at the door so long that her knees were starting to lock. She took a deep breath and knocked.

There was no answer, and no light went on inside. Damon was human. It was quite dark outside now.

"Damon?" It was meant to be a call. It came out a whisper.

No answer. No light.

Elena swallowed. He *had* to be in there.

Elena knocked harder. Nothing. Finally, she tried the knob. To her horror it was unlocked, and it swung open to reveal an interior as dark as the night around Elena, like the maw of a pit.

The fine hairs at the back of Elena's neck were standing up.

"Damon, I'm coming in," she managed in a bare whisper, as if to convince herself by her quietness that there was nobody there. "I'll be silhouetted against the very edge of the porch light. I can't see anything, so you have all the advantages. I'm carrying a tray with very hot coffee, cookies, and steak tartar, no seasonings. You should be able to smell the coffee."

It was odd, though. Elena's senses told her that there was no one standing directly in front of her, waiting for her to literally run into him. All right, she thought. Start with baby steps. Step one. Step two. Step three—I must be well into the room now, but it's still too dim to see anything. Step four . . .

A strong arm came out of the darkness and locked in an iron grip around her waist, and a knife pressed against her throat.

Elena saw blackness shot with a sudden gray network, after which the dark closed in overwhelmingly.

Elena couldn't have been out for more than a few seconds. When she came to, everything was the same—although she wondered how she hadn't lethally cut her own throat on the knife.

She knew that the tray with the dishes and cup had gone flying into the darkness in that first instant when she couldn't help flinging out her arms. But now she recognized the grip, she recognized the scent, and she understood the reason for the knife. And she was glad that she did, because she was about as proud of fainting as Sage would have been of doing it. She wasn't a fainter!

Now she willed herself to sag in Damon's arms, except for where the knife was. To *show* him that she was no threat.

"Hello, princess," a voice like black velvet said into her

ear. Elena felt an inner shiver—but not of fear. No, it was more as if her insides were melting. But he didn't change his grasp on her.

"Damon . . ." she said huskily, "I'm here to help you. *Please* let me. For your sake."

As abruptly as it had come, the iron grip was withdrawn from her waist. The knife stopped pressing into her flesh, although the sharp, stinging feeling at her throat was quite enough to remind her that Damon would have it ready. Substitute fangs.

There was a click, and suddenly the room was too bright.

Slowly, Elena turned to look at Damon. And even now, even when he was pale and rumpled and haggard from not eating, he was so gorgeous that her heart seemed to plummet into darkness. His black hair, falling every which way over his forehead; his perfect, carven features; his arrogant, sensual mouth—right now compressed into a brooding line . . .

"Where is it, Elena?" he asked briefly. Not what. *Where.* He knew she wasn't stupid, and, of course, he knew the humans in the boardinghouse were hiding the star ball from him deliberately.

"Is that all you have to say to me?" Elena whispered.

She saw the helpless softening in his eyes, and he took one step toward her as if he couldn't help himself, but the next instant he looked grim. "Tell me, and then maybe I'll have more."

"I . . . see. Well, then, we made a system, two days ago," Elena said quietly. "Everyone draws lots for it. Then the person who gets the paper with the X takes it from the center of the kitchen table and everyone goes to their rooms and stays there until the person with the star ball hides it. I didn't get the lot today, so I don't know where it is. But you can try to—test me." Elena could feel her body cringing as she said the last words, feeling soft and helpless and easily hurt.

Damon reached over and slowly slipped a hand beneath her hair. He could slam her head against a wall, or throw her across the room. He could simply squeeze her neck between knife and hand until her head fell off. Elena knew that he was in the mood to take out his emotions on a human, but she did nothing. Said nothing. Just stood and looked into her eyes.

Slowly, Damon bent toward her and brushed his lips—so softly—against hers. Elena's eyes drifted shut. But the next moment Damon winced and slid the hand back out of her hair.

That was when Elena gave another thought as to what must have become of the food she had been bringing to him. Near-scalding coffee seemed to have splashed her hand and arm and soaked her jeans on one thigh. The cup and saucer were laying in pieces on the floor. The tray and the cookies had bounced off behind a chair. The plate of steak tartar, however, had miraculously landed on the couch, right side up. There was miscellaneous cutlery everywhere.

Elena felt her head and shoulders droop in fear and pain. That was her immediate universe right now—fear and pain. Overwhelming her. She wasn't usually a crier, but she couldn't help the tears that filled her eyes.

Damn! Damon thought.

It was *her*. Elena. He'd been so certain an adversary was spying on him, that one of his many enemies had tracked him down and was setting a trap . . . someone who had discovered that he was as weak as a child now.

It hadn't even occurred to him that it might be *her*, until he was holding her soft body with one arm, and smelling the perfume of her hair as he held an ice-slick blade to her throat with the other.

And then he'd snapped on a light and saw what he had already guessed. Unbelievable! He hadn't *recognized* her. He had been outside in the garden when he'd seen the door to the storage room standing open and had known that there was an intruder. But with his senses degraded as they were he hadn't been able to tell who was inside.

No excuses could cover up the facts. He had hurt and

terrified Elena. *He* had hurt her. And instead of apologizing he had tried to force the truth out of her for his own selfish desires.

And now, her throat . . .

His eyes were drawn to the thin line of red droplets on Elena's throat where the knife had cut her when she'd jerked in fear before collapsing right onto it. Had she fainted? She could have died right then, in his arms, if he hadn't been fast enough in whipping the knife away.

He kept telling himself that he wasn't afraid of her. That he was just holding the knife absentmindedly. He wasn't convinced.

"I was outside. You know how *we humans* can't see?" he said, knowing he sounded indifferent, unrepentant. "It's like being wrapped in cotton all the time, Elena: We can't see, can't smell, can't hear. My reflexes are like a tortoise's, and I'm *starving*."

"Then why don't you try my blood?" Elena asked, sounding unexpectedly calm.

"I can't," Damon said, trying not to eye the dainty ruby necklace flowing down Elena's slim white throat.

"I already cut myself," Elena said, and Damon thought, Cut *herself*? Ye gods, the girl was priceless. As if she'd had a little kitchen accident.

"So we might as well see what human blood tastes like to you now," Elena said.

"No."

"You know that you're going to. I know you know. But we don't have much time. My blood won't flow forever. Oh, Damon—after everything . . . just last week—"

He was looking at her too long, he knew. Not just at the blood. At the glorious golden beauty of her, as if the child of a sunbeam and a moonbeam had entered his room and was harmlessly bathing him in light.

With a hiss, narrowing his eyes, Damon took hold of Elena's arms. He expected an automatic recoil like the one when he'd grabbed her from behind. But there was no movement backward. Instead there was something like the leap of an eager flame in those wide malachite eyes. Elena's lips parted involuntarily.

He knew it was involuntarily. He'd had many years to study young women's responses. He knew what it meant when her gaze went first to his lips before lifting to his eyes.

I can't kiss her again. I can't. It's a *human* weakness, the way she affects me. She doesn't realize what it is to be so young and so impossibly beautiful. She's going to learn someday. In fact, I might accidentally teach her now.

As if she could hear him, Elena shut her eyes. She let her head fall back and suddenly Damon found himself half-supporting her weight. She was surrendering all thought of herself, showing him that despite everything she still trusted him, still . . .

. . . still loved him.

Damon himself didn't know what he was going to do as he bent toward her. He *was* starving. It tore at him like a wolf's claws, the hunger. It made him feel dazed and dizzy and out of control. Half a thousand years had left him believing that the only thing that would relieve the starvation was the crimson fountain of a cut artery. Some dark voice that might have come from the Infernal Court itself whispered that he could do what some vampires did, ripping a throat like a werewolf. Warm flesh might ease the starvation of a human. What would he do, so close to Elena's lips, so close to her bleeding throat?

Two tears slipped from under the dark lashes and slid a little way down her face before dropping into golden hair. Damon found himself tasting one before he could think.

Still a maiden. Well, that was to be expected; Stefan was too weak to stand yet. But on top of the cynical thought came an image, and just a few words: a spirit as pure as driven snow.

He suddenly knew a different hunger, a different thirst. The only place to ease *this* need was close by. Desperately, urgently, he sought and found Elena's lips. And then he found himself losing all control. What he needed most was here, and Elena might tremble, but she didn't push him away.

This close, he was bathed in an aura as golden as the

hair he was touching gently at the ends. He was pleased himself when she shivered in pleasure, and he realized that he could sense her thoughts. She was a strong projector, and his telepathy was the only Power left to him. He had no idea why he still had it, but he did. And right now he wanted to tune into Elena.

The wench! She wasn't thinking at all! Elena had been offering her throat, truly surrendering herself, abandoning all thought but that she wanted to aid him, that his wishes were hers. And now she was too deeply enmeshed in the kiss to even make plans—which was extraordinary for her.

She's in love with you, the tiny part of him that could still think said.

She's never said so! She's in love with Stefan! something visceral answered.

She doesn't have to say it. She's *showing* it. Don't pretend you haven't seen it before!

But Stefan—!

Is she thinking about Stefan in the slightest right now? She opened her arms to the wolf-hunger in you. This is no one-day stand, no quick meal, not even a steady donor. This is *Elena herself.*

Then I've taken advantage of her. If she's in love, she can't protect herself. She's still a child. I have to do something.

The kisses had now gotten to the point that even the

tiny voice of reason was fading. Elena had lost her ability to stand. He was either going to have to put her down somewhere, or give her a chance to back out.

Elena! Elena! Damn it, I know you can hear me. Answer!

Damon?—faintly. *Oh, Damon, now do you understand—?*

Too well, my princess. I Influenced you, so I should *know.*

You . . . ? No, you're lying!

Why should I lie? For some reason my telepathy is as strong as ever. I still want what I want. But you might want to think a minute, maiden. I don't need to drink your blood. I'm human and right now I'm ravenous. But not for that mess of bloody hamburger you brought me.

Elena broke away from him. Damon let her go.

"I think you're lying," she said, meeting his eyes directly, her mouth kiss-swollen.

Damon locked the sight of her inside the boulder full of secrets he dragged around with him. He gave her his best opaque ebony stare. "Why should I lie?" he repeated. "I just thought you deserved a chance to make your own choice. Or have you already decided to abandon little brother while he's out of commission?"

Elena's hand flashed up, but then she dropped it. "You used Influence on me," she said bitterly. "I'm not myself. I would never abandon Stefan—especially when he needs me."

There it was, the essential fire at her core, and the fiery

golden truth. Now he could sit and let bitterness gnaw at him, while this pure spirit followed her conscience.

He was thinking this, already feeling the loss of her dazzling light receding when he realized he no longer had the knife. An instant later, horror just catching up with his hand, he was snatching it from her throat. His telepathic blast was entirely reflexive:

What in Hell are you doing? Killing yourself because of what I said? This blade is like a razor!

Elena faltered. "I was just making a nick—"

"You almost made a nick that spurted six feet high!" At least he was able to speak again, despite the constriction of his throat.

Elena was back on stable ground too. "I told you I knew you knew you'd have to try blood before you'll try to eat. It feels as if it's flowing down my neck again. This time, let's not waste it."

She was only telling the truth. At least she hadn't seriously hurt herself. He could see that fresh blood was flowing from the new cut she'd so recklessly made. To waste it would be idiotic.

Utterly dispassionate now, Damon took her again by the shoulders. He tilted up her chin to look at her soft, rounded throat. Several new ruby cuts were flowing freely.

Half a millennium of instinct told Damon that just *there* was nectar and ambrosia. Just *there* was sustenance and rest and euphoria. Just *here* where his lips were as he bent to her a second time . . . and he had only to taste it—to drink . . .

Damon reared back, trying to force himself to swallow, determined not to spit. It wasn't . . . it wasn't *utterly* revolting. He could see how humans, with their degraded senses, could make use of the animal varieties. But *this* coagulating, mineral-tasting stuff wasn't *blood* . . . it had none of the perfumed bouquet, the heady richness, the sweet, velvety, provocative, life-giving, *ineffable* attributes of blood.

It was like some sort of bad joke. He was tempted to bite Elena, just to skim a canine over the common carotid, making a tiny scratch, so he could taste the little burst that would explode onto his palate, to compare, to make sure that the *real* stuff wasn't in there somehow. In fact he was more than tempted; he was *doing* it. But no blood was coming.

His mind paused in midthought. He'd made a scratch all right—a scratch like a scuff. It hadn't even broken the outer layer of Elena's skin.

Blunt teeth.

Damon found himself pressing on a canine with his tongue, willing it to extend, willing it with all his cramped and frustrated soul to sharpen.

And . . . nothing. *Nothing.* But then, he'd spent all day doing the same thing. Miserably, he let Elena's head turn back.

"That's it?" she said shakily. She was trying so hard

to be brave with him! Poor doomed white soul with her demon lover. "Damon, you can try again," she told him. "You can bite harder."

"It's no good," he snapped. "You're useless—"

Elena almost slid to the floor. He kept her upright while snarling in her ear, "You know what I meant by that. Or would you prefer to be my dinner rather than my princess?"

Elena simply shook her head mutely. She rested in the circle of his arms, her head against his shoulder. Little wonder that she needed rest after all he'd put her through. But as for how she found his shoulder a comfort . . . well, that was beyond him.

Sage! Damon sent the furious thought out on all the frequencies he could access, just as he had been doing all day. If only he could find Sage, all his problems would be solved. *Sage,* he demanded, *where are you?*

No answer. For all Damon knew, Sage had managed to operate the Gateway to the Dark Dimension that was even now standing, powerless and useless, in Mrs. Flowers's garden. Stranding Damon here. Sage was always that blindingly fast when he took off.

And why had he taken off?

Imperial Summons? Sometimes Sage got them. From the Fallen One, who lived in the Infernal Court, at the lowest of the Dark Dimensions. And when Sage *did* get them, he was expected to be in that dimension instantly, in mid-word, in mid-caress, in mid—whatever. So far Sage had always made the deadline, Damon knew that. He knew it because Sage was still alive.

On the afternoon of Damon's catastrophic bouquet investigation Sage had left on the mantel a polite note thanking Mrs. Flowers for her hospitality, and even leaving his gigantic dog, Saber, and his falcon, Talon, for the protection of the household—a note doubtlessly pre-prepared. He had gone the way he always did, as unpredictably as the wind, and without saying good-bye. Undoubtedly he'd thought that Damon would find his way out of the problem easily. There were a number of vampires in Fell's Church. There always were. The ley lines of sheer Power in the ground drew them even in normal times.

The problem was that just now all those vampires were infested with malach—parasites controlled by the evil fox-spirits. They couldn't be lower in the vampire hierarchy.

And of course Stefan was a complete nonstarter. Even if he hadn't been so weak that trying to change Damon into a vampire would have killed him; even if his anger over Damon's "stealing his humanity" could be assuaged, he would simply never have agreed, out of his feeling that vampirism was a curse.

Humans never knew about things like the vampire hierarchy because the subjects didn't concern them—until suddenly, they did, usually because they had just been changed into a vampire themselves. The hierarchy of vampires was strict, from the useless and ignoble to the fanged aristocracy. Old Ones fit in that category, but so did others who were particularly illustrious or powerful.

What Damon wanted was to be made a vampire by the kind of women Sage knew, and he was determined to have Sage find him a vampire lady of quality, one who was really worthy of him.

Other things tormented Damon, who had spent two entire sleepless days pondering them. Was it possible that the white kitsune who had given Stefan the bouquet had engineered a rose that turned the first person to smell it *permanently* human? That would have been Stefan's greatest dream.

The white fox had listened to *days upon days* of Stefan's ramblings, hadn't he? He'd seen Elena weeping over Stefan. He'd seen the two lovebirds together, Elena hand-feeding a dying Stefan her blood through razor wire. Fortune only knew what ideas that fox had gotten into his furry white head when he'd prepared the rose that had "cured" Damon of his "curse." If it turned out to be an irreversible "cure" . . .

If Sage turned out to be unreachable . . .

It suddenly broke into Damon's thoughts that Elena was cold. It was strange, since the night was warm, but she was shivering violently. She needed his jacket or . . .

She's not *cold*, the small voice somewhere deep inside him said. And she's not shivering. She's *trembling* because of all you've put her through.

Elena?

You forgot all about me. You were holding me, but you completely forgot my existence . . .

If only, he thought bitterly. *You're branded on my soul.*

Damon was suddenly furious, but it was different from his anger at kitsune and Sage and the world. It was the kind of anger that made his throat close and his chest feel too tight.

It was an anger that made him pick up Elena's scalded hand, which was rapidly turning scarlet in patches, and examine it. He knew what he would have done as a vampire: stroked over the burns with a silky cool tongue, generating chemicals to accelerate the healing. And now . . . there was nothing he could do about it.

"It doesn't hurt," Elena said. She was able to stand now.

"You're lying, princess," he said. "The insides of your eyebrows are up. That's pain. And your pulse is jumping—"

"You can sense that without touching me?"

"I can *see* it, at your temples. *Vampires*," with vicious emphasis on what he still was, in essence, "notice things like that. I made you hurt yourself. And I can't do anything to help. Also"—he shrugged—"you're a beautiful liar. About the star ball, I mean."

"You can *always* sense when I'm lying?"

"Angel," he said wearily, "it's easy. You are either the lucky holder of the star ball today . . . or you know who is."

Again, Elena's head drooped in consternation.

"Or else," Damon said lightly, "the entire story of the drawing of the lots was a lie."

"Think what you like," Elena said, with at least some of her usual fire. "And you can clean up this mess, too."

Just as she turned to leave, Damon had a revelation. "Mrs. Flowers!" he exclaimed.

"Wrong," Elena snapped.

Elena, I wasn't talking about the star ball. I give you my word on this. You know how hard it is to lie telepathically—

Yes, and I know that therefore, if there's one thing in the world you'd . . . practice . . . at . . .

She couldn't finish. She couldn't make the speech. Elena knew how much Damon's word meant to him.

I'll never tell you where it is, she sent telepathically to Damon. *And I swear to* you *that Mrs. Flowers won't either.*

"I believe you, but we're still going to see her."

He picked Elena up easily and stepped over the smashed cup and saucer. Elena automatically grabbed his neck with both hands to balance herself.

"Darling, what are you doing—?" Elena cried, then stopped, wide-eyed, two scalded fingers flying to her lips.

Standing in the doorway, not two yards away from them, was petite Bonnie McCullough, a bottle of Black Magic wine, nonalcoholic but mystically exhilarating, held high in her hand. But as Elena watched, Bonnie's expression changed all in an instant. It *had* been triumphant joy. But now it was shock. It was disbelief that couldn't hold. Elena knew exactly what she was thinking. The whole house had devoted itself to making Damon comfortable—while Damon stole what rightfully belonged to Stefan: Elena. Plus he'd lied about not being a vampire anymore. And Elena wasn't even fighting him off. She was calling him "darling"!

Bonnie dropped the bottle and turned, running.

3

Damon leaped. Somewhere in the middle of the leap Elena felt herself left to the whims of gravity. She tried to curl into a ball to take the impact on one buttock.

What happened was strange—almost miraculous. She came down, right side up, on the opposite side of the couch from the plate of steak tartar. The plate did a little leap of its own, three or four inches, perhaps, and then settled back where it had been.

Elena was also lucky enough to get a perfect view of the end of the heroic rescue—which involved Damon diving for the floor and grabbing the bottle of precious Black Magic wine just before it hit the ground and smashed. He might not have the kind of lightning-fast reflexes he had when he was a vampire, but he was still far, far faster than an ordinary human. Leap holding girl, drop girl onto something soft, turn leap into dive, and at last instant grab bottle, just before it would hit. Amazing.

But there was another way that Damon wasn't like a vampire anymore—he wasn't invincible to falling onto hard surfaces. Elena only realized this when she heard him gasp, trying to breathe and not being able to.

She scrambled wildly in her mind for all the accidents she could remember with jocks, and—yes, recalled one when Matt had had the wind completely knocked out of him. The coach had seized him by the collar and thumped him on the back.

Elena ran to Damon and grabbed him under the arms, rolling him onto his back. She put all her strength into hauling him into a sitting position. Then she made a club of her hands. Pretending she was Meredith, who had been on the baseball team at Robert E. Lee High and had a .225 ERA, she swung as hard as she could at Damon, slamming her fists into his back.

And it worked!

Suddenly Damon was wheezing, and then breathing again. A born straightener of ties, Elena knelt and tried to rearrange his clothes. As soon as he could breathe properly, his limbs stopped being pliant under her fingers. He gently curled her hands into each other. Elena wondered if possibly they'd gone so far beyond words that they would never find them again.

How had it all happened? Damon had picked her up—perhaps because her leg was burned, or perhaps because he had decided Mrs. Flowers was the one with the star ball. She herself had said, "Damon, what are you doing?" Perfectly straightforward. And then halfway through the sentence she had heard for herself the "darling" and—but who would ever believe her?—it hadn't been connected with anything they had been doing earlier at all. It had been an accident, a slip of the tongue.

But she'd said it in front of Bonnie, the one person most likely to take it seriously and personally. And then Bonnie had been gone before she could even explain.

Darling! When they had just started fighting again.

It really was a joke. Because he had been serious about just taking the star ball. She had seen it in his eyes.

To call Damon "darling" seriously, you would have to be—have to be . . . hopelessly . . . helplessly . . . desperately in . . .

Oh, *God* . . .

Tears began to run down Elena's cheeks. But these were tears of revelation. Elena knew she wasn't in her best form today. No real sleep for going on three days—too many conflicting emotions—too much genuine terror right now.

Still, she was terrified to find that something fundamental had changed *inside* her.

It wasn't anything she had asked for. All she had asked was that the two brothers stop feuding. And she had been *born* to love Stefan; she knew that! Once, he'd been willing to marry her. Well, since then she'd been a vampire, a spirit, and a new incarnation dropped from the sky, and she could hope that one day he would be willing to marry the new Elena, too.

But the new Elena was bewildered, what with her strange new blood that to vampires was like rocket fuel compared to the gasoline most girls carried about in their veins. With her Wings Powers, such as *Wings of Redemption*, most of which she didn't understand and none of which she could control. Although lately she had seen the beginning of a stance, and she knew it was for *Wings of Destruction*. That, she thought grimly, might be quite useful someday.

Of course a number of them had already been helpful to Damon, who was no longer simply an ally, but an enemy-ally again. Who wanted to steal something that her whole town needed.

Elena hadn't asked to fall in love with Damon—but, oh God, what if she already had? What if she couldn't make the feelings stop? What could she *do*?

Silently, she sat crying, knowing that she could never say any of these things to Damon. He had a gift of farseeing and a level head in times of emotion, but not, as she knew all too well, about *this* particular issue. If she told him what was in her heart, before she knew it, he would kidnap her. He would believe she had forgotten Stefan for good, as she had forgotten him briefly tonight.

"Stefan," she whispered. "I'm sorry . . ."

She could never let Stefan know about it either—and Stefan *was* her heart.

"We've got to get rid of Shinichi and Misao *fast*," Matt was saying moodily. "I mean, I really need to get into condition soon or Kent State's gonna send me back stamped 'Reject.'" He and Meredith were sitting in Mrs. Flowers's warm kitchen nibbling on gingersnap cookies and watching her as she diligently worked at making beef carpaccio—the second of the two raw beef recipes in the antique cookbook she owned. "Stefan's doing so well that in a couple of days we could even be tossing around the old pigskin," he added, sarcasm edging his voice, "if everybody in town would just stop being crazy *possessed*. Oh, yeah, and if the cops would stop coming after me for assaulting Caroline."

At the mention of Stefan's name, Mrs. Flowers peeked into a cauldron that had been bubbling away on the stove for so long, and was now emitting such a fearsome odor that Matt didn't know who to pity more: the guy getting the huge pile of raw meat or the one who'd soon be trying to choke down whatever was in that cooking pot.

"So—assuming you're alive—you're going to be glad

to leave Fell's Church when the time comes?" Meredith asked him quietly.

Matt felt as if she had just slapped him. "You're joking, right?" he said, petting Saber with one tanned, bare foot. The huge beast was making a sort of growly purring sound. "I mean, before that, it's going to be great to throw a couple of passes to Stefan again—he's the best tight end I've ever seen—"

"Or ever will see," Meredith reminded him. "I don't think many vampires go in for football, Matt, so don't even think of suggesting that he and Elena follow you to Kent State. Besides, I'll be right beside you, trying to get them to come to Harvard with *me.* And worse, we're both checkmated by Bonnie, because that junior college—whatever—is much closer to Fell's Church and all the things around here they love."

"All the things around here *Elena* loves," Matt couldn't help correcting. "All Stefan wants is to be with Elena."

"Now, now," Mrs. Flowers said. "Let's just take things as they come, shall we, my dears? Ma*ma* says that we need to keep up our strength. She sounds worried to me—you know, she can't foresee everything that happens."

Matt nodded, but he had to swallow hard before saying to Meredith, "So, you're eager to be off for the Ivied Walls, I'm sure?"

"If it wasn't Harvard—if I could just put it off for a year

and keep my scholarship . . ." Meredith's voice trailed off, but the yearning in it was unmistakable.

Mrs. Flowers patted Meredith's shoulder, and then said, "I wonder about dear Stefan and Elena. After all, with everyone thinking that she's dead, Elena can't live here and be seen."

"I think they've given up on the idea of going somewhere far, far away," Matt said. "I'll bet that now they think of themselves as Fell's Church's guardians. They'll get by somehow. Elena can shave her head." Matt was trying for a light tone, but the words sank like lead balloons as they left his mouth.

"Mrs. Flowers was talking about *college*," Meredith said in a tone just as heavy. "Are they going to be super-heroes at night and just veg out the rest of the time? If they want to go somewhere even *next* year, they need to be thinking about it now."

"Oh . . . well, I guess there's Dalcrest."

"Where?"

"You know, that little campus in Dyer. It's small but the football team there is really—well, I guess Stefan wouldn't care how good they are. But it's only half an hour away."

"Oh, *that* place. Well, the sports may be fantastic but it's sure not an Ivy, much less Harvard." Meredith—unsentimental, enigmatic Meredith—sounded as if she had a stuffed-up nose.

"Yeah," Matt said—and just for a second took Meredith's slim, cold hand and squeezed it. He was even more surprised when she linked her chilled fingers up with his, holding his hand.

"Ma*ma* says whatever is fated to happen will happen soon," Mrs. Flowers said serenely. "The main thing, as I see it, is to save the dear, dear old town. As well as the people."

"Of course it is," Matt said. "We're going to do our best. Thank God we have somebody in town who understands Japanese demons."

"Orime Saitou," Mrs. Flowers said with a little smile. "Bless her for her amulets."

"Yeah, both of them," Matt said, thinking of the grandmother and mother who shared the name. "I think we're going to need a lot of those amulets they make," he added grimly.

Mrs. Flowers opened her mouth, but Meredith spoke, still focused on thoughts of her own.

"You know, Stefan and Elena may not have given up on their far, far away thing after all," she said sadly. "And since at this point none of us may even *live* to make it to our own colleges . . ." She shrugged.

Matt was still squeezing her hand when Bonnie dashed in the front door, keening. She tried to speed through the foyer toward the stairs, avoiding the kitchen, but Matt released Meredith and they both dashed up to block her. Instantly, everyone was in combat mode. Meredith grasped Bonnie's arm tightly. Mrs. Flowers came into the foyer, wiping her hands on a dish towel.

"Bonnie, what happened? Is it Shinichi and Misao? Are we being attacked?" Meredith asked quietly but with the intensity to cut through hysteria.

Something shot like a bolt of ice through Matt's body. No one really knew where Shinichi and Misao were right now. Perhaps in the thicket that was all that was left of the Old Woods—perhaps right here at the boardinghouse. "Elena!" he shouted. "Oh, God, she and Damon are both out there! Are they hurt? Did Shinichi get them?"

Bonnie shut her eyes and shook her head.

"Bonnie, stay with me. Stay calm. *Is* it Shinichi? Is it the police?" Meredith asked. And to Matt: "You'd better check through the curtains there." But Bonnie was still shaking her head.

Matt saw no police lights through the curtains. Nor did he see any sign of Shinichi and Misao attacking.

"If we're *not* being attacked," Matt could hear Meredith saying to Bonnie, "then what *is* happening?"

Maddeningly, Bonnie just shook her head.

Matt and Meredith looked at each other over Bonnie's strawberry curls. "The star ball," Meredith said softly, just as Matt growled, "That *bastard*."

"Elena won't tell him anything but the story," Meredith said. And Matt nodded, trying to keep from his mind a picture of Damon casually waving and Elena convulsing in agony.

"Maybe it's the possessed kids—the ones who walk around hurting themselves or acting insane," Meredith said, with a side glance at Bonnie, and squeezing Matt's hand very hard.

Matt was bewildered and fumbled the cue. He said, "If that S.O.B. is trying to get the star ball, Bonnie wouldn't have run away. She's bravest when she's scared. And unless he's killed Elena she shouldn't be like this—"

Which left Meredith the grim job of saying, "*Talk* to us, Bonnie," in her most comforting big-sister voice. "Something must have happened to get you in this state. Just breathe slowly and tell me what you saw."

And then, in a torrent, words began to spill from Bonnie's lips. "She—she was calling him *darling*," Bonnie said, gripping Meredith's other hand with both of hers. "And there was blood smeared all around on her neck. And—oh, I dropped it! The bottle of Black Magic!"

"Oh, well," Mrs. Flowers said gently. "No use crying over spilled wine. We'll just have to—"

"No, you don't *understand*," Bonnie gasped. "I heard them talking as I came up—I had to go slow because it's so hard not to trip. They were talking about the star ball!

At first I thought they were arguing, but—she had her arms around Damon's neck. And all that stuff about him not being a vampire anymore? She had blood all over her throat and he had it on his mouth! As soon as I got there he picked her up and threw her so I couldn't see but he wasn't fast enough. She must have given the star ball to him! *And she still was calling him 'darling'!*"

Matt's eyes met Meredith's and they both flushed and looked away quickly. If Damon was a vampire again—if he had somehow gotten the star ball from its hiding place—and if Elena had been "taking food" to him just to give him blood . . .

Meredith was still looking for a way out. "Bonnie—aren't you making too much of this? Anyway, what happened to Mrs. Flowers's tray of food?"

"It was—all over the place. They'd just tossed it away! But *he* was was holding her with one hand under her knees and one under her neck, and her head was way back so that her hair was falling all over his shoulder!"

There was a silence as everyone tried to imagine various positions that might correspond to Bonnie's last words.

"You mean he was holding her up to steady her?" Meredith asked, her voice suddenly almost a whisper. Matt caught her meaning. Stefan was probably asleep upstairs, and Meredith wanted to keep it that way.

"No! They—they were *looking* at each other," Bonnie

cried. "Looking. Into each other's eyes."

Mrs. Flowers spoke mildly. "But dear Bonnie—maybe Elena fell down and Damon had to just scoop her up."

Now Bonnie was speaking remorselessly and fluently. "Only if that's what's just happened to all those women on the covers of those romance books—what-d'you-call-'ems?"

"Bodice-rippers?" Meredith suggested unhappily when no one else spoke.

"That's right! Bodice-rippers. That's how he was holding her! I mean, we all knew that something was going on with the two of them in the Dark Dimension, but I thought all that would stop when we found Stefan. But it hasn't!"

Matt felt sick in the pit of his stomach. "You mean right now Elena and Damon are in there . . . kissing and stuff?"

"I don't know what I mean!" Bonnie exclaimed. "*They were talking about the star ball! He was holding her like a bride! And she wasn't fighting it!*"

With a chill of horror, Matt could see trouble, and he could see that Meredith could see it too. Even worse, they were looking in two different directions. Matt was looking upstairs, at the staircase, where Stefan had just appeared. Meredith was looking at the kitchen door, one glance at which showed Matt that Damon was entering the foyer.

What was Damon doing in the kitchen? Matt wondered. *We* were there until a minute ago. And he was, what, eavesdropping from the den side?

Matt gave the situation his best shot, anyway. "Stefan!" he said in a hearty voice that made him wince inwardly. "You ready for a little athlete's-blood nightcap?"

A tiny part of Matt's mind thought: But just look at him. Only three days out of prison and he already looks like himself again. Three nights ago he was a skeleton. Today he just looks—thin. He's even handsome enough to make the girls all go crazy over him again.

Stefan smiled faintly at him, leaning on the banister. In his pale face, his eyes were remarkably alive, a vibrant green that made them actually shine like jewels. He didn't look upset, and that made Matt's heart twist for him. How could they tell him?

"Elena is hurt," Stefan said, and suddenly there was a pause—an utter silence—as every person froze in place. "But Damon couldn't help her, so he brought her to Mrs. Flowers."

"True," Damon said coldly from behind Matt. "I couldn't help her. If I were still a vampire . . . but I'm not. Elena has burns, mainly. All I could think of was an ice pack or some kind of poultice. Sorry to disprove all your clever theories."

"Oh my heavens!" cried Mrs. Flowers. "You mean dear Elena's waiting right now in the kitchen for a poultice?" She hurried out of the foyer toward the kitchen.

Stefan was still coming down the stairs, calling, "Mrs.

Flowers, she scalded her arm and leg—she says because Damon didn't recognize her in the dark and jostled her. And that he thought it was an intruder in his room, and nicked her throat with a knife. The rest of us will be in the parlor if you need help."

Bonnie cried, "Stefan, maybe she's innocent—but *he* isn't! Even according to you, he burned her—that's *torture*—and he put a *knife* to her throat! Maybe he threatened her to make her tell us what we wanted to hear. Maybe she's still a hostage right now and we don't know it!"

Stefan flushed. "It's so hard to explain," he said very softly. "And I keep trying to tune it out. But so far—some of my Powers have been growing . . . faster than my ability to control them. Most of the time I'm asleep, so it doesn't matter. I was asleep until a few minutes ago. But I woke up and Elena was telling Damon that Mrs. Flowers doesn't have the star ball. She was upset, and injured—and I could feel *where* she'd been injured. And then suddenly I heard you, Bonnie. You're a very strong telepath. Then I heard the rest of you talking about Elena. . . ."

Oh my God. How insane, Matt was thinking. His mouth was babbling some "Sure, sure, our mistake" gibberish, and his feet followed Meredith's to the parlor as if they were attached to her Italian sandals.

But the blood on Damon's mouth . . .

There had to be some mundane reason for the blood,

too. Stefan had said that Damon had nicked Elena with a knife. As to how the blood got smeared around; well, that actually didn't sound like vampirism to Matt. He'd been a donor for Stefan at least a dozen times in the last days and the process was always very neat.

It was strange, too, he thought, that it had never occurred to any of them that, even from the top of the house, Stefan might be able to hear their thoughts directly.

Could he always do that? Matt thought, wondering at the same time whether Stefan was doing it right now.

"I try not to listen to thoughts, unless I'm invited or I have a good reason," Stefan said. "But when anybody mentions Elena, especially if they sound upset—that I can't help. It's like when you're in a noisy place and you can barely hear, but when somebody says your name you hear it instantly."

"It's called the Cocktail Party Phenomenon," Meredith said. Her voice was quiet and remorseful as she was trying to calm the mortified Bonnie. Matt felt another tug at his heart.

"Well, you can call it whatever you want," he said, "but what it means is that you can listen in on our minds any time you like."

"Not *any* time," Stefan said, wincing. "When I was drinking animal blood I wasn't strong enough unless I really worked at it. By the way, it may please my friends to know that I'm going back to hunting animals by tomorrow or the next day, depending on what Mrs. Flowers says," he added with a significant glance around the room. His eyes lingered on Damon, who was lounging against the wall by the window, looking disheveled and very, very dangerous. "But that doesn't mean I'll forget who saved my life when I was dying. For that I honor and thank them—and, well, we'll have a party sometime." He blinked hard and turned away. The two girls melted at once—even Meredith sniffled.

Damon heaved an exaggerated sigh. "Animal blood? Oh, brilliant. Make yourself as weak as you can, little brother, even with three or four willing donors around you. Then, when it comes to the final showdown with Shinichi and Misao, you'll be about as effective as a piece of damp tissue paper."

Bonnie started. "Is there going to be a showdown . . . soon?"

"As soon as Shinichi and Misao can manage it," Stefan said quietly. "I think they'd rather not give me time to get well. The whole town is supposed to go up in fire and ashes, you know. But I can't keep asking you and Meredith and Matt—and Elena—to donate blood. You've already kept me alive the last few days, and I don't know how to repay you for it."

"Repay us by getting as strong as you can," Meredith

said in her quiet, level voice. "But, Stefan, can I ask a few questions?"

"Of course," Stefan said, standing by a chair. He didn't sit himself until Meredith, with Bonnie almost in her lap, had sunk down on the love seat.

Then he said, "Fire."

"First," Meredith asked, "is Damon right? If you go back to animal blood, will you be seriously weakened?"

Stefan smiled. "I'll be the way I was when I first met you," he said. "Strong enough to do this." He bent toward the fire irons right below Damon's elbow, murmuring absently, "*Scusilo per favore*" and removed the poker.

Damon rolled his eyes. But when Stefan, in one fluid motion, bent the poker into a U shape and then straightened it immediately back and replaced it, Matt could swear that there was ice-cold envy in Damon's usual poker-player expression.

"And that was iron, which is resistant to all eldritch forces," Meredith said evenly, as Stefan stepped away from the fireplace.

"But of course he's been imbibing from you three charming girls for the past few days—not to mention the nuclear powerhouse that dear Elena has become," Damon said, clapping his hands three times slowly. "Oh . . . Mutt. *Sono spiacente*—I mean, I didn't mean to add you in with the girls. No offense meant."

"None taken," Matt said through his teeth. If he could, just once, wipe that flashing, there-and-gone smile off Damon's face, he would die happy, he thought.

"But, the truth is that you have become a very . . . willing . . . donor for Dear Brother, haven't you?" Damon added, his lips twitching slightly, as if only the strictest control kept him from smiling.

Matt took two steps toward Damon. It was all *he* could do not to get right up in Damon's face, even though something in his brain always screamed *suicide* when he had thoughts like that.

"You're right," he said as evenly as possible. "I've been donating blood to Stefan just like the girls. He's my friend, and a couple of days ago he looked like he'd just gotten out of a concentration camp."

"Of course," Damon murmured, as if chastened, but then he went on in even softer tones, "My little brother has always been popular with both—well, with ladies present, I will say *genders*. Even with male kitsune; which of course is why I am in this mess."

Matt literally saw red as if he were looking through a haze of blood at Damon.

"Speaking of which, what happened to Sage, Damon? He was a vampire. If we could find him, your problem would be over, right?" Meredith asked.

It was a good riposte, just as all Meredith's cool responses were. But Damon spoke with his fathomless black eyes fixed on Meredith's face. "The less you know and say about Sage, the better. I wouldn't speak of *him* lightly—he has friends in low places. But to answer your question: No, I would not let Sage make me into a vampire. It would just complicate things."

"Shinichi said good luck on finding out who he is," Meredith said, still calm. "Do you know what he meant by that?"

Damon shrugged fluidly. "What I know is my own business. He spends time in the lowest and darkest of the Dark Dimensions."

Bonnie burst out, "Why did Sage go? Oh, Damon, did he go because of *us*? Why did he leave Talon and Saber to watch over us, then? And, oh—oh—*oh, Damon*, I'm so *sorry*! *So, so sorry!*" She slid off the love seat and bent her head so that only strawberry curls were visible. With her small pale hands on the floor to brace her, she looked as if she were about to bow her head to the ground at his feet. "This is all my fault and everyone's angry—but it was just so horrible I had to believe the worst things I could think of!"

It was a tension-breaker. Nearly everyone laughed. It was so *Bonnie*, and so true of all of them. So human.

Matt wanted to pick her up and put her back on the love seat. Meredith was always the best medicine for Bonnie. But as Matt found himself reaching for her, he was confounded by two other pairs of hands doing the same thing. One was Meredith's own long, slender olive-skinned hands, and the other pair were male, with even longer tapering fingers.

Matt's hand clenched into a fist. Let Meredith take her, he thought, and his clumsy fist—somehow—got in the way of Damon's reaching fingers. Meredith lifted Bonnie easily and sat back on the love seat. Damon lifted his dark eyes to Matt's and Matt saw perfect comprehension there.

"You really ought to forgive her, Damon," Meredith, ever the impartial referee, said bluntly. "I don't think she'll be able to sleep tonight otherwise."

Damon shrugged, cold as an iceberg. "Maybe . . . someday."

Matt could feel his muscles clench. What kind of bastard said that to little Bonnie? Because of course she was listening.

"Damn you," Matt said under his breath.

"Excuse me?" Damon's voice was no longer languid and falsely polite, but suddenly a whiplash.

"You heard me," Matt growled. "And if you didn't, maybe we'd better go outside so I can say it louder," he added, soaring on the wings of bravado.

He left behind a wail of "No!" from Bonnie, and a gentle "Sh," from Meredith. Stefan said, "Both of you—" in a commanding voice, but then he faltered and coughed, which both Matt and Damon took as a chance to sprint for the door.

It was still very warm outside on the boardinghouse porch. "Is this the killing ground?" Damon asked lazily when they had descended the steps and stood beside the gravel path.

"It's fine by me," Matt said briefly, knowing in his bones that Damon would fight dirty.

"Yes, this is definitely close enough," Damon said, flashing an unnecessarily brilliant smile in Matt's direction. "You can yell for help while little brother is in the parlor, and he'll have plenty of time to rescue you. And now we're going to solve the problems of what you're doing in my business and why you are—"

Matt punched him in the nose.

He had no idea what Damon was trying to do. If you asked a guy to step outside, then you asked him to step outside. Then you went for the guy. You didn't stand around talking. If you tried that, you'd be stuck with the label of "coward" or worse. Damon didn't seem like the type who needed to be told that.

But then, Damon had always been able to repel any attack on him while he got as many insults as he liked . . . before.

Before, he'd have just broken every bone in my hand and gone on baiting me, Matt guessed. But now . . . I'm almost as fast as him, and he simply got taken by surprise.

Matt flexed his hand gingerly. It always hurt, of course, but if Meredith could do it to Caroline, then he could do it to . . .

Damon?

Damn, did I just take down *Damon*?

Run, Honeycutt, he seemed to hear the voice of his old coach telling him. Run. Get out of town. Change your name.

Tried that. Didn't work. Never even got a T-shirt, Matt thought sourly.

But Damon wasn't leaping up like a flaming demon from hell, with the eyes of a dragon and the strength of a raging bull to annihilate Matt. It looked and sounded more as if he were shocked and indignant from his disheveled hair to his earth-stained boots.

"You . . . ignorant . . . childish . . ." He lapsed into Italian.

"Look," Matt said. "I'm here to fight, okay? And the

smartest guy I ever knew said: 'If you're gonna fight, don't talk. If you're gonna talk, don't fight.'"

Damon tried to snarl as he knelt up and pulled spiny teasel and prickly sida out of his distressed black jeans. But the snarl didn't come out quite right. Maybe it was the new shape of his canines. Maybe it just didn't have enough conviction behind it. Matt had seen enough defeated guys to know that this fight was over. A strange exaltation came over him. He was going to keep all his limbs and organs! It was a precious, precious moment.

All right, then, should I offer him a hand? Matt wondered, to be answered instantaneously by, *Sure, if you'd offer a hand to a temporarily stunned crocodile. What do you really need ten whole fingers for, anyway?*

Oh, well, he thought, turning to go back into the front door. As long as he lived—which, conceded, might not be too long—he would remember this moment.

As he went in, he bumped into Bonnie, who was rushing out.

"Oh, Matt, oh, *Matt*," she cried. She was looking wildly around. "Did you *hurt* him? Did *he* hurt *you*?"

Matt smacked his fist into the palm of his hand, once. "He's still sitting down back there," he added helpfully.

"Oh, *no*!" Bonnie gasped, and she hurried out the door.

Okay. Less spectacular of a night. But still a pretty good one.

* * *

"They did *what*?" Elena asked Stefan. Cold poultices anchored by tight bandages were wrapped around her arm, hand, and thigh—Mrs. Flowers had cut her jeans off short—and Mrs. Flowers was wiping away the dried blood on her neck with herbs.

Her heart was pounding with more than pain. Even she hadn't realized that Stefan was tuned in to the entire house when he was awake. All she could do was to shakily thank God that he'd been asleep while she and Damon—no! She had to stop thinking about it, and right now!

"They went outside to fight," Stefan said. "It's idiotic, of course. But it's a matter of honor, too. I can't interfere."

"Well, *I* can—if you're done, Mrs. Flowers."

"Yes, dear Elena," Mrs. Flowers said, winding a bandage around Elena's throat. "Now you shouldn't get tetanus."

Elena stopped in mid-motion. "I thought you got tetanus from rusty blades," she said. "Da—this one looked brand-new."

"Tetanus comes from *dirty* blades, my dear," Mrs. Flowers corrected her. "But this"—she held up a bottle—"is *Grand*mama's own personal recipe that has kept many a wound disease-free down the cen—down the years."

"Wow," Elena said. "I never even heard of *Grand*mama before. Was she a—healer?"

"Oh, yes," Mrs. Flowers said earnestly. "She was

actually accused of being a witch. But at her trial they could prove nothing. Her accusers seemed not even to be capable of coherent speech."

Elena looked at Stefan only to find that he was looking at her. Matt was in danger of being dragged off to a kangaroo court—for allegedly assaulting Caroline Forbes while under the influence of some unknown and terrible drug. Anything to do with courts was interesting to both of them. But looking at Stefan's concerned face, Elena decided not to pursue the subject. She squeezed his hand. "We have to go now—but let's talk about *Grand*mama later. I think she sounds fascinating."

"I just remember her as a crotchety old recluse, who didn't suffer fools gladly and thought just about everyone was a fool," Mrs. Flowers said. "I suppose I was going down the same path until you children came and made me sit up and take notice. Thank you."

"We're the ones who should thank you," Elena began, hugging the old woman, feeling her heart stop pounding. Stefan was looking at her with open love. It was all going to be all right—for her.

I'm worried about Matt, she thought to Stefan, testing the waters more vigorously. *Damon's still so fast—and you know he doesn't like Matt a bit.*

I think, Stefan returned with a wry smile, *that that is a rather stunning understatement. But I also think you shouldn't worry until we see who comes back injured.*

Elena eyed that smile, and thought for a moment about impulsive, athletic Matt. After a moment, she smiled back. She was feeling both guilty and protective—and safe. Stefan always made her feel safe. And right now, she wanted to spoil him.

In the front yard, Bonnie was abasing herself. She couldn't help thinking, even now, about how handsome Damon looked, how wild and dark and ferocious and gorgeous. She couldn't help thinking about the times he'd smiled at her, laughed at her, come to save her at her urgent call. She had honestly thought that someday . . . But now she felt as if her heart were breaking in two.

"I just want to bite my tongue out," she said. "I should never have assumed anything from what I saw."

"How could you possibly have known that I *wasn't* stealing Elena away from Stefan?" Damon said wearily. "It's just the kind of thing I'd do."

"No, it isn't! You did so much to free Stefan from prison—you always faced the most danger yourself—and you kept us all from being hurt. You did all that for other people—"

Suddenly Bonnie's upper arms were being held by hands that were so strong that her mind was flooded with clichés. A grasp of iron. Strong as steel bands. An inescapable grip.

And a voice like an icy torrent was coming at her.

"You don't know anything about me, or what I want, or what I do. For all you know I could be plotting right now. So don't ever let me hear you talk again about such things, or imagine that I won't kill you if you get in my way," Damon said.

He got up and left Bonnie sitting there, staring after him. And she'd been wrong. She wasn't out of tears at all.

5

"I thought you wanted to get out so we could talk to Damon," Stefan said, still hand in hand with Elena as she made a sharp right turn onto the rickety stairway that led to the second-floor rooms and, above that, to Stefan's attic.

"Well, unless he kills Matt and runs I don't see what's to keep us from talking to him tomorrow." Elena glanced back at Stefan and dimpled. "I took your advice and thought a little about the two of them. Matt's a pretty tough quarterback and they're both only human now, right? Anyway, it's time for your dinner."

"Dinner?" Stefan's canine teeth responded automatically—embarrassingly quickly—to the word. He really needed to have a word with Damon later and make sure Damon understood his place as a guest at the boardinghouse—nothing more—but it was true, he could do that tomorrow. It might even be more effective tomorrow, when Damon's own pent-up rage was spent.

He pressed his tongue against his fangs, trying to force them back down, but the small stimulation caused them to sharpen, nicking his lip. Now they were aching pleasantly. All in response to a single word: *dinner.*

Elena threw him a teasing glance over her shoulder and giggled. She was one of those lucky females with a beautiful laugh. But this was a clearly mischievous giggle, straight from her wicked, scheming childhood. It made Stefan want to tickle her to hear more; it made him want to laugh with her; it made him want to grab her and demand to know the joke. Instead he said, "What's up, love?"

"Someone has sharp teeth," she responded innocently, and giggled again. He lost himself in admiration for a second and also suddenly lost hold of her hand. Laughing like a musical cascade of white water over rock, she ran up the stairs ahead of him, both to tease and to show him what good shape she was in, he thought. If she had stumbled, or faltered, she knew he would decide that her donation of blood was harming her.

So far it didn't seem to be damaging any of his friends, or he would have insisted on a rest for that person. But even Bonnie, as delicate as a dragonfly, hadn't seemed to be the worse for it.

* * *

Elena raced up the stairs knowing that Stefan was smiling behind her, and there was no shadow of mistrust in his mind. She didn't deserve it, but that only made her more anxious to please him.

"Have you had *your* dinner?" Stefan asked as they reached his room.

"Long ago; roast beef—cooked." She smiled.

"What did Damon say when he finally realized it was you and looked at the food you'd brought?"

Elena made herself giggle again. It was all right to have tears in her eyes; her burns and cuts hurt and the episode with Damon justified any amount of weeping.

"He called it bloody hamburger. It was steak tartar. But, Stefan, I don't want to talk about him now."

"No, of course you don't, love." Stefan was immediately contrite. And he was trying so hard not to seem eager to feed—but he couldn't even control his canines.

And Elena was in no mood to dally either. She perched on the bed, carefully unwinding the bandage Mrs. Flowers had just wound on it. Stefan suddenly looked troubled.

Love— He stopped abruptly.

What? Elena finished with the bandage, studying Stefan's face.

Well—shall I take it out of your arm instead? You're

already in pain and I don't want to fool with Mrs. Flowers's anti-tetanus treatment.

There's still plenty of room around it, Elena said cheerfully.

But a bite on top of those cuts . . . He stopped again.

Elena looked at him. She knew her Stefan. There was something he wanted to say. *Tell me,* she pressed him.

Stefan finally met her eyes directly, and then put his mouth close to her ear. "I can heal the cuts," he whispered. "But—it would mean opening them again so they can bleed. That will hurt."

"And it might poison you!" Elena said sharply. "Don't you see? Mrs. Flowers put heaven knows what on them—"

She could feel his laughter, which sent warm tingles down her spine. "You can't kill a vampire so easily," he said. "We only die if you stake us through the heart. But I don't want to hurt you—even to help you. I could Influence you not to feel anything—"

Once again, Elena cut him off. "No! No, I don't mind if it hurts. As long as you get as much blood as you need."

Stefan respected Elena enough to know that he shouldn't ask the same question twice. And he could hardly restrain himself any longer. He watched her lie down and then stretched out beside her, bending to get to the green-stained cuts. He licked gently, at first rather tentatively, at the wounds, and then ran a satiny tongue over them. He had no idea how the process worked or what chemicals he was stroking over Elena's injuries. It was as automatic as breathing was to humans. But after a minute, he chuckled softly.

What? What? Elena demanded, smiling herself as his breath tickled.

Your blood's laced with lemon balm, Stefan replied. Grand*mama's healing recipe has lemon balm and alcohol in it! Lemon balm wine!*

Is that good or bad? Elena asked uncertainly.

It's fine—for a change. But I still like your blood straight the best. Does it hurt too much?

Elena could feel herself flush. Damon had healed her cheek this way, back in the Dark Dimension, when Elena had, with her own body, protected a bleeding slave from a whiplash. She knew Stefan knew the story, and must know, each time he saw her, that the almost-invisible white line on her cheekbone had been stroked just this gently into healing.

Compared to that, these scratches are nothing, she sent. But a sudden chill went through her.

Stefan! I never begged your pardon for protecting Ulma at the risk of not being able to save you. Or, worse—for dancing while you were starving—for keeping up the society pretense so we could get the Twin Fox key—

Do you think I care about that? Stefan's voice was mock-angry as he gently sealed one cut at her throat. *You did what you had to in order to track me—find me—save me—after*

I'd left you alone here. Don't you think I understand? I didn't deserve the saving—

Now Elena felt a small sob choke her. *Never say that! Never! And I suppose—I suppose I knew you would forgive me—or I would have felt every jewel I wore burning like a brand. We had to chase you down like a fox with hounds—and we were so scared that a single misstep could mean you'd be hanged . . . or we would be.*

Stefan was holding her tightly now. *How can I make you understand?* he asked. *You gave up everything—even your freedom—for me. You became slaves. You—you—were "Disciplined"* . . .

Elena asked wildly, *How do you know that? Who told you?*

You told me, beloved. In your sleep—in your dreams.

*But, Stefan—*Damon *took the pain for me. Did you know that?*

Stefan was silent a moment, then responded, *I . . . see. I didn't know that before.*

Scenes strewn from the Dark Dimension bubbled in Elena's mind. That city of tarnished baubles—of illusive glitter, where a whiplash that spread blood across a wall was as much celebrated as a handful of rubies strewn on the sidewalk. . . .

Love, don't think about it. You followed me, and you rescued me, and now we're here together, Stefan said. The last cut closed, he lay his cheek on hers. *That's all I care about. You and I—together.*

Elena was almost dizzily glad to be forgiven—but there was something inside her—something that had grown and grown and *grown* during the weeks she was in the Dark Dimension. A feeling for Damon that was not just the result of her need for his help. A feeling that Elena had thought Stefan understood. A feeling that might even change the relations between the three of them: her, Stefan, and Damon. But now Stefan seemed to assume that everything would return to the way it was before his kidnapping.

Oh, well, why fret about tomorrow when tonight was enough to make her weep with joy?

This was the best feeling in the world, the knowledge that she and Stefan were *together*, and she made Stefan promise her over and over that he would not ever leave her on another quest again, no matter how briefly, no matter what the cause.

By now, Elena could not even focus on what she had been worried about before. She and Stefan had always found heaven in each other's arms. They were meant to be together forever. Nothing else mattered now that she was home.

"Home" was where she and Stefan were together.

6

Bonnie couldn't get to sleep after Damon's words to her. She wanted to talk to Meredith, but there was an unseeing, unhearing lump in Meredith's bed.

The only thing she could think of was to go down to the kitchen and huddle up with a cup of cocoa in the den, alone with her misery. Bonnie wasn't good at being alone with herself.

But as it turned out, when she got to the bottom floor, she didn't head for the kitchen after all. She went straight to the den. Everything was dark and strange-looking in the silent dimness. Turning on one light would just make everything else even darker. But she managed, with shaking fingers, to twist the switch of the standing lamp beside the couch. Now if only she could find a book or something . . .

She was holding on to her pillow as if it were a teddy

bear, when Damon's voice beside her said, "Poor little redbird. You shouldn't be up so late, you know."

Bonnie started and bit her lip.

"I hope you're not still hurting," she said coldly, very much on her dignity, which she suspected was not very convincing. But what was she supposed to do?

The truth was that Bonnie had absolutely no chance of winning a duel of wits with Damon—and she knew it.

Damon wanted to say, "Hurting? To a vampire, a human fleabite like that was . . ."

But unfortunately *he* was a human too. And it did hurt.

Not for long, he promised himself, looking at Bonnie.

"I thought you never wanted to see me again," she said, chin trembling. It almost seemed too cruel to make use of a vulnerable little redbird. But what choice did he have?

I'll make it up to her somehow, someday—I swear it, he thought. And at least I can make it pleasant now.

"That wasn't what I said," he replied, hoping that Bonnie wouldn't remember exactly what he *had* said. If he could just Influence the trembling woman-child before him . . . but he couldn't. He was a human now.

"You told me you would kill me."

"Look, I'd just been knocked down by a human. I don't suppose you know what that means, but it hasn't happened to me since I was twelve years old, and still an original human boy."

Bonnie's chin kept trembling, but the tears had stopped. You *are* bravest when you're scared, Damon thought.

"I'm more worried about the others," he said.

"Others?" Bonnie blinked.

"In five hundred years of life, one tends to make a remarkable amount of enemies. I don't know; maybe it's just me. Or maybe it's the simple little fact of being a vampire."

"Oh. Oh, *no*!" Bonnie cried.

"What does it matter, little redbird? Long or short, life seems all too brief."

"But—Damon—"

"Don't fret, kitten. Have one of Nature's remedies." Damon pulled out of his breast pocket a small flask that smelled unquestionably of Black Magic.

"Oh—you saved it! How clever of you!"

"Try a taste? Ladies—strike that—young women first."

"Oh, I don't know. I used to get awfully silly on that."

"The world is silly. Life is silly. Especially when you've been doomed six times before breakfast." Damon opened the flask.

"Oh, all right!" Clearly thrilled by the notion of "drinking with Damon," Bonnie took a very dainty sip.

Damon choked to cover a laugh. "You'd better take bigger swigs, redbird. Or it's going to take all night before I get a turn."

Bonnie took a deep breath, and then a deep draft. After

about three of those, Damon decided she was ready.

Bonnie's giggles were nonstop now. "I think . . . Do I think I've had enough now?"

"What colors do you see out here?"

"Pink? Violet? Is that right? Isn't it nighttime?"

"Well, perhaps the Northern Lights are paying us a visit. But you're right, I should get you into bed."

"Oh, no! Oh, yes! Oh, no! Nonono*yes*!"

"Shh."

"SHHHHHH!"

Terrific, Damon thought; I've overdone it.

"I meant, get *you* into a bed," he said firmly. "*Just* you. Here, I'll walk you to the first-floor bedroom."

"Because I might fall on the stairs?"

"You might say that. And this bedroom is much nicer than the one you share with Meredith. Now you just go to sleep and don't tell anyone about our rendezvous."

"Not even *Elena*?"

"Not even anybody. Or I might get angry at you."

"Oh, no! I won't, Damon: I swear on your life!"

"That's—pretty accurate," Damon said. "Good night."

Moonlight cocooned the house. Fog misted the moonlight. A slender, hooded dark figure took advantage of shadows so skillfully that it would have passed unnoticed even if someone had been watching out for it—and no one was.

Bonnie was in her new first-floor bedroom, and was feeling very bewildered. Black Magic always made her feel giggly, and then very sleepy, but somehow tonight her body refused to sleep. Her head hurt.

She was just about to turn the bedside light on, when a familiar voice said, "How about some tea for your headache?"

"Damon?"

"I made some from Mrs. Flowers's herbs and I decided to make you a cup as well. Aren't you the lucky girl?" If Bonnie had been listening closely, she might have heard something almost like self-loathing behind the light words—but she wasn't.

"Yes!" Bonnie said, meaning it. Most of Mrs. Flowers's

teas smelled and tasted good. This one was especially nice, but grainy on her tongue.

And not only was the tea good, but Damon stayed to talk to her while she drank it all. That was sweet of him.

Strangely, this tea made her feel not exactly sleepy, but as if she could only concentrate on one thing at a time. Damon swam into her field of view. "Feeling more relaxed?" he asked.

"Yes, thank you." Weirder and weirder. Even her voice sounded slow and dragging.

"I wanted to make sure nobody was too hard on you for the silly mistake about Elena," he explained.

"They weren't, really," she said. "Actually everybody was more interested in seeing you and Matt fight—" Bonnie put a hand over her mouth. "Oh, no! I didn't mean to say that! I'm so sorry!"

"It's all right. It should heal by tomorrow."

Bonnie couldn't imagine why anyone would be so afraid of Damon, who was so nice as to pick up her mug of tea and say he'd put it in the sink. That was good because she was feeling as if she couldn't get up to save her life. That cozy. That comfy.

"Bonnie, can I ask you just one little thing?" Damon paused. "I can't tell you why, but . . . I have to find out where Misao's star ball is kept," he said earnestly.

"Oh . . . that," Bonnie said fuzzily. She giggled.

"Yes, that. And I am truly sorry to ask you, because you're so very young and innocent . . . but I know you'll tell me the truth."

After this praise and comfort, Bonnie felt she could fly. "It's been in the same place all the time," she said with sleepy disgust. "They tried to make me think they'd moved it . . . but when I saw him chained and going down to the root cellar I knew they hadn't really." In the dark, there was a short shake of curls and then a yawn. "If they were really going to move it . . . they should have sent me away or something."

"Well, maybe they were concerned for your life."

"Wha'? . . ." Bonnie yawned again, not sure what he meant. "I mean, an old, old safe with a combination? I told them . . . that those old safes . . . could be . . . really be . . . easy to . . . to . . ." Bonnie let out a sound like a sigh and her voice stopped.

"I'm glad we had this talk," Damon murmured in the silence.

There was no answer from the bed.

Pulling Bonnie's sheet up as high as it would go, he let it drift down. It covered most of her face. "Requiescat in pace," Damon said softly. Then he left her room, not forgetting to take the mug.

Now . . . *"him chained and going down to the root cellar."* Damon mused as he washed out the mug carefully and put it back in the cupboard. The line sounded strange but he had almost all the links now, and it was actually simple. All he needed were twelve more of Mrs. Flowers's sleeping cachets and two plates heaped with raw beef. He had all the ingredients . . . but he'd never heard of a root cellar.

Shortly thereafter, he opened the door to the basement. Nope. Didn't match the criteria for "root cellar" he'd looked up on his mobile. Irritated and knowing that any moment someone was likely to wander downstairs for something, Damon turned around in frustration. There was an elaborately carved wooden panel across from the basement, but nothing else.

Curse it, he would *not* be thwarted at this point. He would have his life as a vampire back, or he didn't want any life at all!

To punctuate the sentiment, he slammed a fist against the wooden panel in front of him.

The knock sounded hollow.

Immediately all frustration vanished. Damon examined the panel very carefully. Yes, there were hinges at the very edge, where no sane person would expect them. It wasn't a panel but a door—undoubtedly to the root cellar where the star ball was.

It didn't take long for his sensitive fingers—even his human fingers were more sensitive than most—to find a place that clicked—and then the whole door swung open.

He could see the stairs. He tucked his parcel under one arm and descended.

By the illumination of the small flashlight he'd taken from the storage room, the root cellar was just as described: a damp, earthy room to store fruit and vegetables before refrigerators had been invented. And the safe was just as Bonnie had said: an ancient, rusty combination safe, which any whiz cracker could have opened in about sixty seconds. It would take Damon about six minutes, with his stethoscope (he'd heard once that you could find *anything* in the boardinghouse if you looked hard enough and it seemed to be true) and every atom of his being concentrating on hearing the tumblers quietly click.

First, however, there was the Beast to conquer. Saber the black hellhound had unfolded, awake and alert from the moment the secret door had opened. Undoubtedly, they had used Damon's clothes to teach him to howl madly at his scent.

But Damon had his own knowledge of herbs and had ransacked Mrs. Flowers's kitchen to find a handful of witch hazel, a small amount of strawberry wine, aniseed, some peppermint oil, and a few other essential oils she had in stock, sweet and sharp. Mixed, this created a pungent lotion, which he had gingerly applied to himself. The concoction formed for Saber an impossible tangle of strong smells. The only thing the now-sitting dog knew was that it was surely *not* Damon sitting on the steps and tossing him hearty balls of hamburger and delicate strips of filet mignon—each of which he gulped down whole. Damon watched with interest as the animal devoured the mix of sleeping powder and raw meat, tail whisking on the floor.

Ten minutes later Saber the hellhound was sprawled out happily unconscious.

Six minutes after that, Damon was opening an iron door.

One second later he was pulling a pillowcase out of Mrs. Flowers's antique safe.

In the glow of the flashlight he found that he did indeed have a star ball, but that it was just a little more than half full.

Now what did that mean? There was a very neat hole drilled and corked at the top so that not one precious droplet more need be wasted.

But who had used the rest of the fluid—and why? Damon himself had seen the star ball brimful of opalescent, shimmering liquid just days ago.

Somehow between that time and now someone had used about a hundred thousand individuals' life energy.

Had the others tried to do some remarkable deed with it and failed, at the cost of burning so much Power? Stefan was too kind to have used so much, Damon was certain of that. But . . .

Sage.

With an Imperial Summons in his hand, Sage was likely to do anything. So, sometime after the sphere had been brought into the boardinghouse, Sage had poured out almost exactly half the life force from the star ball and then, undoubtedly, left the rest behind for Mutt or someone to cork.

And such a colossal amount of Power could only have been used for . . . opening the Gate to the Dark Dimensions.

Very slowly, Damon let out his breath and smiled. There were only a few ways to get into the Dark Dimensions, and as a human he obviously could not drive to Arizona and pass through a public Gateway as he had the first time with the girls. But now he had something even better. A star ball to open his own private Gateway. He knew of no other way to cross, unless one was lucky enough to hold one of the almost-mythical Master Keys that allowed one to roam the dimensions at will.

Doubtless, someday in the future, in some nook, Mrs. Flowers would find another thank-you note: this time along with something that was literally invaluable—something exquisite and priceless and probably from a dimension quite far from Earth. That was how Sage operated.

All was quiet above. The humans were relying on their animal companions to keep them safe. Damon gave the root cellar a single look around and saw nothing more than a dim room completely empty except for the safe, which he now closed. Dumping his own paraphernalia into the pillowcase, he patted Saber, who was gently snoring, and turned toward the steps.

That was when he saw that a figure was standing in the doorway. The figure then stepped smoothly behind the door, but Damon had seen enough.

In one hand the figure had been holding a fighting stave almost as tall as it was.

Which meant that it was a hunter-slayer. Of vampires.

Damon had met several hunter-slayers—briefly—in his time. They were, in his consideration, bigoted, unreasonable, and even more stupid than the average human, because they'd usually been brought up on legends of vampires with fangs like tusks who ripped out the throats of their victims and killed them. Damon would be the first to admit that there were some vampires like that, but most were more restrained. Vampire hunters usually worked in groups, but Damon had a hunch that this one would be alone.

He now ascended the steps slowly. He was fairly certain of the identity of this hunter-slayer, but if he was wrong he was going to have to dodge a stave launched straight down at him like a javelin. No problem—if he were still a vampire. Slightly more difficult, unarmed as he was and at a severe tactical disadvantage.

He reached the top of the stairs unharmed. This was really the most dangerous part of climbing steps, for a weapon of just the right length could send him crashing all the way back down. Of course a vampire wouldn't be permanently injured by that, but—again—he was no longer a vampire.

But the person in the kitchen allowed him to climb all the way out of the root cellar unhindered.

A killer with honor. How sweet.

He turned slowly to measure up his vampire hunter. He was immediately impressed.

It wasn't the obvious strength that allowed the hunter to be able to whip off a figure eight with the fighting stave that impressed him. It was the weapon itself. Perfectly balanced, it was meant to be held in the middle, and the designs picked out in jewels around the handhold showed that its creator had had excellent taste. The ends showed that he or she had a sense of humor as well. The two ends of the stave were made of ironwood for strength—but they were also decorated. In shape, they were made to resemble one of humankind's oldest weapons, the flint-tipped spear. But there were tiny spikes extruding from each of these "spear flakes," set firmly into the ironwood. These tiny spikes were of different materials: silver for werewolves, wood for vampires, white ash for Old Ones, iron for all eldritch creatures, and a few that Damon couldn't quite work out.

"They're refillable," the hunter-slayer explained. "Hypodermic needles inject on impact. And of course different poisons for different species—quick and simple for humans, wolfsbane for those naughty puppies, and so on. It really is a jewel of a weapon. I wish I had found it before we met Klaus."

Then she seemed to shake herself back into reality.

"So, Damon, what's it going to be?" asked Meredith.

8

Damon nodded thoughtfully, glancing back and forth between the fighting stave and the pillowcase in his hand.

Hadn't he suspected something like this for a long time? Subconsciously? After all, there had been that attack on the grandfather, which had failed to either kill him or to erase his memory completely. Damon's imagination could fill in the rest: her parents seeing no reason to blight their tiny daughter's life with this gruesome business—a whole new change of scenery—and then giving up the practice in the provincial, protected little town of Fell's Church.

If they had only known.

Oh, doubtless they had made sure that Meredith had had self-defense and various martial arts training since she was a child, while swearing her to absolute secrecy—even from her best friends.

Well, now, Damon thought. The first of Shinichi's riddles was already solved. *"One of you has a lifetime secret kept from everyone."* I always knew there was something about this girl . . . and this is it. I'd bet my life that she's a black belt.

There had been a long silence. Now Damon broke it.

Your ancestors were hunters too? he asked, as if she were telepathic. He waited a moment—still silence. Okay—no telepathy. That was good. He nodded at the magnificent stave. "That was certainly made for a lord or lady."

Meredith wasn't stupid. She spoke without glancing away from his eyes. She was ready, at any instant, to go into killing mode. "We're just ordinary folk, trying to get a job done so innocent humans will be safer."

"By killing the odd vampire or two."

"Well, so far in recorded history saying 'Naughty, naughty, Mama spank' has failed to convert a single vampire to vegetarianism."

Damon had to laugh. "Pity you weren't born early enough to convert Stefan. He could have been your grand triumph."

"You think that's funny. But we do have converts."

"Yes. People will say anything while you're holding a pointed stick at them."

"People who feel that it's *wrong* to Influence other

people into believing they're getting something for nothing."

"That's it! Meredith! Let me Influence you!"

This time it was Meredith who laughed.

"No, I'm serious! When I'm a vampire again, let me Influence you not to be so much afraid of a bite. I swear I won't take more than a teaspoon. But that would give me time to show you—"

"A nice big house of candy that never existed? A relative who died ten years ago and who would have abhorred the thought of you taking my memory of her and using it as a lure? A dream of ending world hunger that doesn't put food into one mouth?"

This girl, thought Damon, is dangerous. It's like a Counter-Influence that they've taught to their members. Wanting her to see that vampires, or ex-vampires, or Once and Future Vampires had some good qualities—like courage—he let go of the pillowcase and grasped the end of the fighting stave with both hands.

Meredith raised an eyebrow. "Did I not just recently tell you that a number of those spikes you've just driven into your flesh are poisonous? Or were you not listening?"

She had automatically grabbed the stave as well, above the dangerous zone.

"You told me," he said inscrutably—he hoped.

"I particularly said 'poisonous to humans as well as to

werewolves and other things'—recall it?"

"You told me that, too. But I'd rather die than live as a human, so: Let the games begin." And with that, Damon began to push the two-headed stave toward Meredith's heart.

She immediately clamped down on the stave as well, pushing it back toward him. But he had three advantages, as they both soon realized. He was slightly taller and more strongly muscled even than lithe, athletic Meredith; he had a longer reach than hers; and he had taken up a much more aggressive position. Even though he could feel poisoned little spikes biting into his palms, he thrust forward and up until the killing point was once again near her heart. Meredith pushed back with an amazing amount of strength and then suddenly, somehow, they were even again.

Damon glanced up to see how that had happened, and saw, to his shock, that she also had grasped the stave in the killing zone. Now her hands were dripping blood onto the floor just as his were.

"Meredith!"

"What? I take my job seriously."

Despite her gambit, he was stronger. Inch by inch, he forced his torn palms to hang on, his arms to exert pressure. And inch by inch she was forced backward, refusing to quit—until there was no more room to back up.

And there they stood, the entire length of the stave

between them, and the refrigerator flat against Meredith's back.

All Damon could think of was Elena. If he somehow survived this—and Meredith did not—then what would those malachite eyes say to him? How would he live with what they said?

And then, with infuriating timing, like a chess player knocking over her own king, Meredith let go of the spear, conceding Damon's superior strength.

After which, seeming to have no fear of turning her back on him, she took a jar full of salve from a kitchen cupboard, scooped out a dollop of the contents, and motioned for Damon to hold out his hands. He frowned. He'd never heard of a poison that got into the blood that could be cured by external measures.

"I didn't put real poison in the human needles," she said calmly. "But your palms will be torn and this is an excellent remedy. It's ancient, passed down for generations."

"How kind of you to share,"—at his most sharply ironic.

"And now what are we going to do? Start all over again?" he added as Meredith calmly began to rub salve into her own hands.

"No. Hunter-slayers have a code, you know. You won the sphere. I assume you're planning to do what Sage seems to have done. Open the Gate to the Dark Dimension."

"Open the Gate to the Dark *Dimensions*," he corrected.

"Probably I should have mentioned—there's more than one. But all I want is to become a vampire again. And we can talk as we go, since I see we're both wearing our cat burglar costumes."

Meredith was dressed much as he was, in black jeans and a lightweight black sweater. With her long shining dark hair she looked unexpectedly beautiful. Damon, who had considered running her through with the stave, just as his obligation to vampire-kind, now found himself wavering. If she gave him no trouble on his way to the Gate, he would let her go, he decided. He was feeling magnanimous—for the first time he had faced down and conquered the fearsome Meredith, and besides, she had a code as he did. He felt a sort of kinship with her.

With ironic gallantry, he waved her on before him, retaining possession of the pillowcase and the fighting stave himself.

As Damon quietly shut the front door he saw that dawn was about to break. Perfect timing. The stave caught the first rays of light. "I have a question for you," he said to Meredith's long, silky dark hair. "You said that you didn't find this gorgeous stave until after Klaus—that wicked Old One—was dead. But if you're from a hunter-slayer family you might have been more help in getting him dispatched. Like mentioning that only white ash could kill him."

"It was because my parents didn't actively pursue the family business—they didn't know. They were both from hunter families, of course—you have to be, to keep it out of the tabloids and—"

"—police files—"

"Do you want me to talk, or can you do your stand-up routine alone?"

"Point taken"—hefting the *extremely* pointed stave. "I'll listen."

"But even though they chose not to be active, they knew that a vampire or werewolf might decide to pick on their daughter if they found out her identity. So during school, I took 'harpsichord lessons' and 'riding lessons' one day a week each—have done since I was three. I'm a Black Belt Shihan, and a Taekwondo Saseung. I might start Dragon Kung Fu—"

"Point taken once more. But then how exactly did you find that gorgeous killing stick?"

"After Klaus was dead, while Stefan was babysitting Elena, suddenly Grandpa started talking—just single words—but it made me go look in our attic. I found this."

"So you *really* don't know how to use it?"

"I'd just started practicing when Shinichi turned up. But, no, I don't really have a clue. I'm pretty good with a bo staff, though, so I just use it like that."

"You didn't use it like a bo staff on me."

"I was hoping to *persuade* you, not kill you. I couldn't think of how to explain to Elena that I'd broken all your bones."

Damon kept himself from laughing—barely.

"So how did a couple of *inactive* hunter-slayers end up moving to a town on top of a few hundred crossing ley lines?"

"I'm guessing they didn't know what a line of natural Power was. And Fell's Church *looked* small and peaceful—back then."

They found the Gateway just as Damon had seen it before, a neat rectangular piece sliced out of the earth, about five feet deep.

"Now sit down there," he adjured Meredith, putting her on the opposite corner from where he lay the stave.

"Have you given a thought—even the briefest—as to what will happen to Misao if you pour out *all* the liquid in there?"

"Actually, not one. Not one microsecond's worth," Damon said cheerfully. "Why? Do you think she would for me?"

Meredith sighed. "No. That's the problem with both of you."

"She's certainly *your* problem at the moment, although I may stop by sometime after the town's destroyed to have a little tête-à-tête with her brother about the concept of keeping an oath."

"After you've gotten strong enough to beat him."

"Well, why don't *you* do something? It's your town they've devastated, after all," Damon said. "Children attacking themselves and each other, and now adults attacking children—"

"They're either scared to death or possessed by those malach the foxes are still spreading everywhere—"

"Yes, and so fear and paranoia keep spreading too. Fell's Church may be little by the standards of other genocides they've caused, but it's an important place because it's sitting on top—"

"Of all those ley lines full of magical power—yes, yes, I know. But don't *you* care at all? About us? Their future plans for us? Doesn't *any* of it matter to you?" Meredith demanded.

Damon thought of the still, small figure in the first-floor bedroom and felt a sick qualm. "I told you already," he snapped. "I'm coming back for a talk with Shinichi."

After which, carefully, he began to pour liquid from the uncorked star ball at one corner of the rectangle. Now that he was actually at the Gate, he realized he had no idea what he should do. The proper procedure might be to jump in and pour out the star ball's entire liquid in the middle. But four corners seemed to dictate four different places to pour, and he was sticking to that.

He expected Meredith to try to foul things up somehow.

Make a run for the house. Make some noise, at least. Attack him from behind now that he had dropped the stave. But apparently her code of honor forbade this.

Strange girl, he thought. But I'll leave her the stave, since it really belongs to her family, and, anyway, it's going to get me killed the instant I land in the Dark Dimension. A slave carrying a weapon—especially a weapon like that—won't have a chance.

Judiciously, he poured out *almost* all of the liquid left into the final corner and stepped back to see what would happen.

SSSS-bah! White! Blazing white light. That was all his eyes or his mind could take in at first.

And then, with a rush of triumph he thought: I've done it! The Gateway is open!

"The center of the upper Dark Dimension, please," he said politely to the blazing hole. "A secluded alley would probably be the best, if you don't mind." And then he jumped into the hole.

Except that he didn't. Just as he was starting to bend his knees, something hit him from the right. "Meredith! I thought—"

But it wasn't Meredith. It was Bonnie.

"You tricked me! You can't go in there!" She was sobbing and screaming.

"Yes, I can! Now let go of me—before it disappears!"

He tried to pry her off, while his mind whirled uselessly. He'd left this girl—what?—an hour or so ago, so deeply asleep that she had looked dead. Just how much could that little body take?

"*No!* They'll kill you! And *Elena* will kill *me*! But I'll get killed first because I'll still be here!"

Awake, and actually capable of putting together puzzles.

"Human, I told you to *let go*," he snarled. He bared his teeth at her, which only caused her to bury her head in his jacket and cling on koala-bear style, wrapping both her legs around one of his.

A couple of really hard slaps should dislodge her, he thought.

He lifted his hand.

9

Damon dropped his hand. He simply couldn't make himself do it. Bonnie was weak, light-headed, a liability in combat, easy to confuse—

That's it, he thought. I'll use that! She's so naive—

"Let go for a *second*," he coaxed. "So I can get the stave—"

"No! You'll jump if I do! What's a stave?" Bonnie said, all in one breath.

—and stubborn, and impractical—

Was the brilliant light beginning to flicker?

"Bonnie," he said in a low voice, "I am deadly serious here. If you don't let go, I'll *make* you—and you won't like that, I promise."

"Do what he says," Meredith pleaded from somewhere

quite close. "Bonnie, he's going into the Dark Dimension! But you're going to end up going with him—and you'll *both* be human slaves this time! Take my hand!"

"Take her hand!" Damon roared, as the light definitely flickered, for an instant becoming less blinding. He could feel Bonnie shifting and trying to see where Meredith was, and then he heard her say, "I can't—"

And then they were falling.

The last time they had traveled through a Gate they had been totally enclosed in an elevator-like box. This time they were simply flying. There was the light, and there were the two of them, and they were so blinded that somehow speaking didn't seem possible. There was only the brilliant, fluctuating, beautiful light—

And then they were standing in an alley, so narrow that it just barely allowed the two of them to face each other, and between buildings so high that there was almost no light down where they were.

No—that wasn't the reason, Damon thought. He remembered that blood-red perpetual light. It wasn't coming directly from either side of the narrow slit of alley, which meant that they were basically in deep burgundy twilight.

"Do you realize where we are?" Damon demanded in a furious whisper.

Bonnie nodded, seeming happy about having figured

that out already. "We're basically in deep burgundy—"

"Crap!"

Bonnie looked around. "I don't smell anything," she offered cautiously, and examined the soles of her feet.

"We are," Damon said slowly and quietly, as if he needed to calm himself between every word, "in a world where we can be flogged, flayed, and decapitated just for stepping on the ground."

Bonnie tried a little hop and then a jump in place, as if diminishing her ground-interaction time might help them in some manner. She looked at him for further instructions.

Quite suddenly, Damon picked her up and stared at her hard, as revelation dawned. "You're drunk!" he finally whispered. "You're not even awake! All this while I've been trying to get you to see sense, and you're a drunken sleepwalker!"

"I am not!" Bonnie said. "And . . . just in case I am, you ought to be nicer to me. You made me this way."

Some distant part of Damon agreed that this was true. He was the one who'd gotten the girl drunk and then drugged her with truth serum and sleeping medicine. But that was simply a fact, and had nothing to do with how he felt about it. How he felt was that there was no possible way for him to proceed with this all-too-gentle creature along.

Of course, the sensible thing would be to get away from her very quickly, and let the city, this huge metropolis of evil, swallow her in its great, black-fanged maw, as it would most certainly do if she walked a dozen steps on its streets without him. But, as before, something inside him simply wouldn't let him do it. And, he realized, the sooner he admitted that, the sooner he could find a place to put her and begin taking care of his own affairs.

"What's that?" he said, taking one of her hands.

"My opal ring," Bonnie said proudly. "See, it goes with everything, because it's all colors. I always wear it; it's casual or dress-up." She happily let Damon take it off and examine it.

"These are real diamonds on the sides?"

"Flawless, pure white," Bonnie said, still proudly. "Lady Ulma's fiancé Lucen made it so that if we ever needed to take the stones out and sell them—" She came up short. "You're going to take the stones out and sell them! No! No no no no no!"

"Yes! I have to, if you're going to have any chance of surviving," Damon said. "And if you say one more word or fail to do exactly as I tell you, I *am* going to leave you alone here. And then you will *die*." He turned narrowed, menacing eyes on her.

Bonnie abruptly turned into a frightened bird. "All right," she whispered, tears gathering on her eyelashes. "What's it for?"

Thirty minutes later, she was in prison; or as good as.

Damon had installed her in a second-story apartment with one window covered by roller blinds, and strict instructions about keeping them down. He had pawned the opal and a diamond successfully, and paid a sour, humorless-looking landlady to bring Bonnie two meals a day, escort her to the toilet when necessary, and otherwise forget about her existence.

"Listen," he said to Bonnie, who was still crying silently after the landlady had left them, "I'll try to get back to see you within three days. If I don't come within a week it'll mean I'm dead. Then you—don't cry! Listen!—*then* you need to use these jewels and this money to try to get all the way from *here* to *here*; where Lady Ulma will still be—we hope."

He gave her a map and a little moneybag full of coins and gems left over from the cost of her bread and board. "*If* that happens—and I can pretty well promise it won't, your best chance is to try walking in the daytime when things are busy; keep your eyes down, your aura small, and don't talk to *anyone.* Wear this sacking smock, and carry this bag of food. Pray that nobody asks you anything, but try to look as if you're on an errand for your master. Oh, yes." Damon reached into his jacket pocket and pulled out two small iron slave bracelets, bought when he had gotten the map. "*Never* take them off, not when you're sleeping, not when you're eating—*never.*"

He looked at her darkly, but Bonnie was already on the threshold of a panic attack. She was trembling and crying, but too frightened to say a word. Ever since entering the Dark Dimension she'd been keeping her aura as small as possible, her psychic defenses high; she didn't need to be told to do that. She was in danger. She knew it.

Damon finished somewhat more leniently. "I know it sounds difficult, but I can tell you that I personally have no intention whatsoever of dying. I'll try to visit you, but getting across the borders of the various sectors is dangerous, and that's what I may have to do to come here. Just be patient, and you'll be all right. Remember, time passes differently here than back on Earth. We can be here for weeks and we'll get back practically the instant we set out. And, look"—Damon gestured around the room—"dozens of star balls! You can watch all of them."

These were the more common kind of star ball, the kind that had, not Power in them, but memories, stories, or lessons. When you held one to your temple, you were immersed in whatever material had been imprinted on the ball.

"Better than TV," Damon said. "Much."

Bonnie nodded slightly. She was still crushed, and she was so small, so slight, her skin so pale and fine, her hair such a flame of brilliance in the dim crimson light that seeped through the blinds, that as always Damon found himself melting slightly. "Do you have any questions?" he asked her finally.

Bonnie said slowly, "And—you're going to be . . . ?"

"Out getting the vampire versions of *Who's Who* and the *Book of Peers*," Damon said. "I'm looking for a lady of quality."

After Damon had left, Bonnie looked around the room.

It was horrible. Dark brown and just horrible! She had been trying to save Damon from going back into the Dark Dimension because she remembered the terrible way that slaves—who were mostly humans—were treated.

But did he appreciate that? Did he? Not in the slightest! And then when she'd been falling through the light with him, she'd thought that at least they would be going to Lady Ulma's, the Cinderella-story woman whom Elena had rescued and who had then regained her wealth and status and had designed beautiful dresses so that the girls could go to fancy parties. There would have been big beds with satin sheets and maids who brought strawberries and clotted cream for breakfast. There would have been sweet Lakshmi to talk to, and gruff Dr. Meggar, and . . .

Bonnie looked around the brown room and the plain rush-filled pallet with its single blanket. She picked up a star ball listlessly, and then let it drop from her fingers.

Suddenly, a great sleepiness filled her, making her head

swim. It was like a fog rolling in. There was absolutely no question of fighting it. Bonnie stumbled toward the bed, fell onto it, and was asleep almost before she had settled under the blanket.

"It's my fault far more than yours," Stefan was saying to Meredith. "Elena and I were—deeply asleep—or he'd never have managed any part of it. I'd have noticed him talking with Bonnie. I'd have realized he was taking *you* hostage. Please don't blame yourself, Meredith."

"I should have tried to warn you. I just never expected Bonnie to come running out and grab him," Meredith said. Her dark gray eyes shimmered with unshed tears. Elena squeezed her hand, sick in the pit of her stomach herself.

"You certainly couldn't be expected to fight off Damon," Stefan said flatly. "Human or vampire—he's trained; he knows moves that you could never counter. You *can't* blame yourself."

Elena was thinking the same thing. She was worried about Damon's disappearance—and terrified for Bonnie. Yet at another level of her mind she was wondering at the lacerations on Meredith's palm that she was trying to warm. The strangest thing was that the wounds appeared to have been treated—rubbed slick with lotion. But she wasn't going to bother Meredith about it at a time like this. Especially when it was really Elena's own fault. She was the one who had enticed Stefan the night before. Oh, they had been deep, all right—deep in each other's minds.

"Anyway, it's Bonnie's fault if it's anyone's," Stefan said regretfully. "But now I'm worried about her. Damon's not going to be inclined to watch out for her if he didn't want her to come."

Meredith bowed her head. "It's *my* fault if she gets hurt."

Elena chewed her lower lip. There was something wrong. Something about Meredith, that Meredith wasn't telling her. Her hands were really damaged, and Elena couldn't figure out how they could have gotten that way.

Almost as if she knew what Elena was thinking, Meredith slipped her hand out of Elena's and looked at it. Looked at both her palms, side by side. They were equally scratched and torn.

Meredith bent her dark head farther, almost doubling over where she sat. Then she straightened, throwing back her head like someone who had made a decision. She said, "There's something I have to tell you—"

"Wait," Stefan whispered, putting a hand on her shoulder. "Listen. There's a car coming."

Elena listened. In a moment she heard it too. "They're coming to the boardinghouse," she said, puzzled.

"It's so early," Meredith said. "Which means—"

"It has to be the police after Matt," Stefan finished. "I'd

better go in and wake him up. I'll put him in the root cellar."

Elena quickly corked the star ball with its meager ounces of fluid. "He can take this with him," she was beginning, when Meredith suddenly ran to the opposite side of the Gate. She picked up a long, slender object that Elena couldn't recognize, even with Power channeled to her eyes. She saw Stefan blink and stare at it.

"This needs to go in the root cellar too," Meredith said. "And there are probably earth tracks coming *out* of the cellar, and blood in the kitchen. Two places."

"Blood?" Elena began, furious with Damon, but then she shook her head and refocused. In the light of dawn, she could see a police car, cruising like some great white shark toward the house.

"Let's go," Elena said. "Go, go, go!"

They all dashed back to the boardinghouse, crouching to stay low to the ground as they did it. As they went, Elena hissed, "Stefan, you've got to Influence them if you can. Meredith, you try to clean up the soil and blood. I'll get Matt; he's less likely to punch me when I tell him he has to hide."

They hastened to their appointed duties. In the middle of it all, Mrs. Flowers appeared, dressed in a flannel nightgown with a fuzzy pink robe over it, and slippers with bunny heads on them. As the first hammering knock on the door sounded, she had her hand on the door handle, and the police officer, who was beginning to shout, "POLICE! OPEN THE—" found himself bawling this directly over the head of a little old lady who could not have looked more frail or harmless. He ended almost in a whisper, "—door?"

"It is open," Mrs. Flowers said sweetly. She opened it to its widest, so that Elena could see two officers, and the officers could see Elena, Stefan, and Meredith, all of whom had just arrived from the kitchen area.

"We want to speak to Matt Honeycutt," the female officer said. Elena noted that the squad car was from the Ridgemont Sheriff's Department. "His mother informed us that he was here—after serious questioning."

They were coming inside, shouldering their way past Mrs. Flowers. Elena glanced at Stefan, who was pale, with tiny beads of sweat visible on his forehead. He was looking intently at the female officer, but she just kept talking.

"His mother says he's been virtually living at this boardinghouse recently," she said, while the male officer held up some kind of paperwork.

"We have a warrant to search the premises," he said flatly.

Mrs. Flowers seemed uncertain. She glanced back toward Stefan, but then let her gaze move on to the other teenagers. "Perhaps it would be best if I made everyone a nice cup of tea?"

Stefan was still looking at the woman, his face looking

paler and more drawn than ever. Elena felt a sudden panic clutch at her stomach. Oh, God, even with the gift of her blood tonight, Stefan was weak—far too weak to even use Influence.

"May I ask a question?" Meredith said in her low, calm voice. "Not about the warrant," she added, waving the paper away. "How is it out there in Fell's Church? Do you know what's going on?"

She was buying time, Elena thought, and yet everyone stopped to hear the answer.

"Mayhem," the female sheriff replied after a moment's pause. "It's like a war zone out there. Worse than that because it's the kids who are—" She broke off and shook her head. "That's not our business. Our business is finding a fugitive from justice. But first, as we were driving toward your hotel we saw a very bright column of light. It wasn't from a helicopter. I don't suppose you know anything about what it *was*?"

Just a door through space and time, Elena was thinking, as Meredith answered, still calmly, "Maybe a power transmitter blowing up? Or a freak shaft of lightning? Or are you talking about . . . a UFO?" She lowered her already soft voice.

"We don't have time for this," the male sheriff said, looking disgusted. "We're here to find this Honeycutt man."

"You're welcome to look," Mrs. Flowers said. They were already doing so.

Elena felt shocked and nauseated on two fronts. *"This Honeycutt man." Man, not boy.* Matt was over eighteen. Was he still a juvenile? If not, what would they do to him when they eventually caught up to him?

And then there was Stefan. Stefan had been so certain, so . . . convincing . . . in his announcements about being well again. All that talk about going back to hunting animals—but the truth was that he needed much more blood to recover.

Now her mind spun into planning mode, faster and faster. Stefan obviously wasn't going to be able to Influence both of those officers without a very large donation of human blood.

And if Elena gave it . . . the sick feeling in her stomach increased and she felt the small hairs on her body stand up . . . if she gave it, what were the chances that she would become a vampire herself?

High, a cool, rational voice in her mind answered. Very high, considering that less than a week ago, she had been exchanging blood with Damon. Frequently. Uninhibitedly.

Which left her with the only plan she could think of. These sheriffs wouldn't find Matt, but Meredith and Bonnie had told her the whole story of how another Ridgemont sheriff had come, asking about Matt—and about Stefan's girlfriend. The problem was that she, Elena Gilbert, had "died" nine months ago. She shouldn't *be* here—and she had a feeling that these officers would be inquisitive.

They needed Stefan's Power. Right now. There was no other way, no other choice. Stefan. Power. Human blood.

She moved to Meredith, who had her dark head down and cocked to one side as if listening to the two sheriffs clomping above on the stairs.

"Meredith—"

Meredith turned toward her and Elena almost took a step back in shock. Meredith's normally olive complexion was gray, and her breath was coming fast and shallowly.

Meredith, calm and composed Meredith, already knew what Elena was going to ask of her. Enough blood to leave her out of control as it was being taken. And fast. That terrified her. More than terrified.

She can't do it, Elena thought. We're lost.

10

Damon was making his way up the beautiful rose-covered trellis below the window of the bedchamber of M. le Princess Jessalyn D'Aubigne, a very wealthy, beautiful, and much-admired girl who had the bluest blood of any vampire in the Dark Dimension, according to the books he'd bought. In fact, he'd listened to the locals and it was rumored that Sage himself had changed her two years ago, and had given her this bijoux castle to live in. Delicate gem that it appeared, though, the little castle had already presented Damon with several problems. There had been that razor-wire fence, on which he ripped his leather jacket; an unusually dexterous and stubborn guard whom it had really been a pity to strangle; an inner moat that had almost taken him unawares; and a few dogs that he had treated with the

Saber-tranquilizer routine—using Mrs. Flowers's sleeping powder, which he'd brought with him from Earth. It would have been easier to poison them, but Jessalyn was reputed to have a very soft heart for animals and he needed her for at least three days. That should be long enough to make him a vampire—if they did nothing else during those days.

Now, as he pulled himself silently up the trellis, he mentally added long rose thorns to the list of inconveniences. He also rehearsed his first speech to Jessalyn. She had been—was—would forever be—eighteen. But it was a *young* eighteen, since she had only two years' experience at being a vampire. He comforted himself with this as he climbed silently into a window.

Still silently, moving slowly in case the princess had guardian animals in her bedchamber, Damon parted layer after layer of filmy, translucent black curtains that kept the blood-red light of the sun from shining into the chamber. His boots sank into the thick pile of a black rug. Making it out of the enfolding curtains, Damon saw that the entire chamber was decorated in a simple theme by a master of contrast. Jet-black and off-black.

He liked it a lot.

There was an enormous bed with more billowing filmy black curtains almost encasing it. The only way to approach it was from the foot, where the diaphanous curtains were thinner.

Standing there in the cathedral-like silence of the great chamber, Damon looked at the slight figure under the black silk sheets, among dozens of small throw pillows.

She was a jewel like the castle. Delicate bones. A look of utter innocence as she slept. An ethereal river of fine, scarlet hair spilling about her. He could see individual hairs straying on the black sheets. She looked a little like Bonnie.

Damon was pleased.

He pulled out the same knife he had put to Elena's throat, and just for a moment hesitated—but no, this was no time to be thinking of Elena's golden warmth. Everything depended on this fragile-shouldered child in front of him. He put the point of the knife to his chest, deliberately placing it wide of his heart in case some blood had to be spilled . . . and coughed.

Nothing happened. The princess, who was wearing a black negligee that showed frail-looking arms as fine and pale as porcelain, went on sleeping. Damon noticed that the nails on her small fingers were lacquered the exact scarlet of her hair.

The two large pillar candles set in tall black stands were giving off an enticing perfume, as well as being clocks—the farther down they burned, the easier to tell time. The lighting was perfect—everything was perfect—except that Jessalyn was still asleep.

Damon coughed again, loudly—and bumped the bed.

The princess woke, starting up and simultaneously bringing two sheathed blades out of her hair.

"Who is it? Is someone there?" She was looking in every direction but the right one.

"It's only me, your highness." Damon pitched his voice low, but fraught with unrequited need. "You don't have to be afraid," he added, now that she'd at last gotten the right direction and seen him. He knelt by the foot of her bed.

He'd miscalculated a bit. The bed was so large and high that his chest and the knife were far below Jessalyn's line of sight.

"Here I will take my life," he announced, very loudly to make sure that Jessalyn was keeping up with the program.

After a moment or two the princess's head popped up over the foot of the bed. She balanced herself with hands spread wide and narrow shoulders hunched close to her. At this distance he could see that her eyes were green—a complicated green consisting of many different rings and speckles.

At first she just hissed at him and lifted her knives held in hands whose fingers were tipped with nails of scarlet. Damon bore with her. She would learn in time that all this wasn't really necessary; that in fact it had gone out of fashion in the real world decades ago and was only kept alive by pulp fiction and old movies.

"Here at your feet I slay *myself*," he said again, to make sure she didn't miss a syllable, or the entire point, for that matter.

"You—yourself?" She was suspicious. "Who are you? How did you get here? Why would you do such a thing?"

"I got here through the road of my madness. I did it out of what I know is madness I can no longer live with."

"What madness? And are you going to do it now?" the princess asked with interest. "Because if you're not, I'll have to call my guards and—wait a minute," she interrupted herself.

She grabbed his knife before he could stop her and licked it. "This is a metal blade," she told him, tossing it back.

"I know." Damon let his head fall so that hair curtained his eyes and said painfully: "I am . . . a human, your highness."

He was covertly watching through his lashes and he saw that Jessalyn brightened up. "I thought you were just some weak, useless vampire," she said absently. "But now that I look at you . . ." A rose petal of a pink tongue came out and licked her lips. "There's no point in wasting the good stuff, is there?"

She *was* like Bonnie. She said exactly what she thought, when she thought it. Something inside Damon wanted to laugh.

He stood again, looking at the girl on the bed with all

the fire and passion of which he was capable—and felt that it wasn't enough. Thinking about the real Bonnie, alone and unhappy, was . . . well, passion-quenching. But what else could he do?

Suddenly he knew what he could do. Before, when he'd stopped himself from thinking of Elena, he had cut off any genuine passion or desire. But he was doing this *for* Elena, as much as for himself. Elena couldn't be his Princess of Darkness if he couldn't be her Prince.

This time, when he looked down at M. le Princess, it was differently. He could feel the atmosphere change.

"Highness, I have no right even to speak to you," he said, deliberately putting one booted foot on the metal scrollwork that formed the frame of the bed. "You know as well as I that you can kill me with a single blow . . . say, here"—pointing to a spot on his jaw—"but you have already slain me—"

Jessalyn looked confused, but waited.

"—with love. I fell in love with you the moment I saw you. You could break my neck, or—as I would say if I were permitted to touch your perfumed white hand—you could curl those fingers around my throat and strangle me. I beg you to do it."

Jessalyn was beginning to look puzzled but excited. Blushing, she held out one small hand to Damon, but clearly without any intention of strangling him.

"Please, you must," Damon said earnestly, never taking his eyes off hers. "That is the only thing I ask of you: that you kill me yourself instead of calling your guards so that the last sight I see will be your beautiful face."

"You're ill," Jessalyn decided, still looking flustered. "There have been other unbalanced minds who have made their way past the first wall of my castle—although never to my chambers. I'll give you to the doctors so that they can make you well."

"Please," said Damon, who had forged his way through the last of the filmy black hangings and was now looming over the sitting princess. "Grant me instant death, rather than leaving me to die a little each day. You don't know what I've done. I can't stop dreaming of you. I've followed you from shop to shop when you went out. I am already dying now as you ravish me with your nobility and radiance, knowing that I am no more than the paving stones you walk on. No doctor can change that."

Jessalyn was clearly considering. Obviously, no one had ever talked to her like *this.*

Her green eyes fixed on his lips, the lower of which was still bleeding. Damon gave an indifferent little laugh and said, "One of your guards caught me and very properly tried to kill me before I could reach you and disturb your sleep. I'm afraid I had to kill him to get here," he said, standing between one pillar candle and the girl on the bed so that his shadow was thrown over her.

Jessalyn's eyes widened in approval even as the rest of her seemed more fragile than ever. "It's still bleeding," she whispered. "I could—"

"You can do anything you want," Damon encouraged her with a wry quirk of a smile on his lips. It was true. She could.

"Then come here." She thumped a place by the nearest pillow on the bed. "What are you called?"

"Damon," he said as he stripped off his jacket and lay down, chin propped on one elbow, with the air of one not unused to such things.

"Just that? Damon?"

"You can cut it still shorter. I am nothing but Shame now," he replied, taking another minute to think of Elena and to hold Jessalyn's eyes hypnotically. "I was a vampire—a powerful and proud one—on Earth—but I was tricked by a kitsune . . ." He told her a garbled version of Stefan's story, omitting Elena or any nonsense about wanting to be human. He said that when he managed to escape the prison that had taken his vampire self, he decided to end his own human life.

But at that moment, he had seen Princess Jessalyn and thought that, serving her, he would be happy with his sorry lot. Alas, he said, it only fed his disgraceful feelings for her highness.

"Now my madness has driven me to actually accost you in your own chambers. Make an example of me, your highness, that will cause other evildoers to tremble. Burn me, have me flogged and quartered, put my head on a pike to cause those who might do you ill to cast themselves into a fire first." He was now in bed with her, leaning back a little to expose his bare throat.

"Don't be silly," Jessalyn said, with a little catch in her voice. "Even the meanest of my servants wants to live."

"Perhaps the ones that never see you do. Scullions, stable boys—but *I* cannot live, knowing that I can never have you."

The princess looked Damon over, blushed, gazed for a moment into his eyes . . . and then she bit him.

"I'll get Stefan to go down to the root cellar," Elena said to Meredith, who was angrily thumbing tears out of her eyes.

"You know we can't do that. With the police right here in the house—"

"Then *I'll* do it—"

"You *can't*! You *know* you can't, Elena, or you wouldn't have come to me!"

Elena looked at her friend closely. "Meredith, you've been donating blood all along," she whispered. "You never seemed even slightly bothered . . ."

"He only took a tiny bit—always less from me than

anyone. And always from my arm. I just pretended I was having blood drawn at the doctor's. No problem. It wasn't even bad with Damon back in the Dark Dimension."

"But now . . ." Elena blinked. "Now—what?"

"Now," Meredith said with a faraway expression, "Stefan *knows* that I'm a hunter-slayer. That I even have a fighting stave. And now I have to . . . to submit to . . ."

Elena had gooseflesh. She felt as if the distance from her to Meredith in the room was getting larger. "A hunter-slayer?" she said, bewildered. "And what's a fighting stave?"

"There's no time to explain now! Oh, Elena . . ."

If Plan A was Meredith and Plan B was Matt, there was really no choice. Plan C *had* to be Elena herself. Her blood was much stronger than anyone else's anyway, so full of Power that Stefan would only need a—

"No!" Meredith whispered right in Elena's ear, somehow managing to hiss a word without a single sibilant. "They're coming down the stairs. We have to find Stefan *now*! Can you tell him to meet me in the little bedroom behind the parlor?"

"Yes, but—"

"Do it!"

And I still don't know what a fighting stave is, Elena thought, allowing Meredith to take her arms and propel her toward the bedroom. But I know what a "hunter-slayer" sounds like, and I definitely don't like it. And that weapon—it makes a stake look like a plastic picnic knife. Still, she sent to Stefan, who was following the sheriffs downstairs: *Meredith is going to donate as much blood as you need to Influence them. There's no time to argue. Come here fast and for God's sake look cheerful and reassuring.*

Stefan didn't sound cooperative. *I can't take enough from her for our minds to touch. It might—*

Elena lost her temper. She was frightened; she was suspicious of one of her two best friends—a horrible feeling—and she was desperate. She needed Stefan to do just as she said. *Get here fast!* was all she projected, but she had the feeling that she'd hit him with all of the feelings full force, because he suddenly turned concerned and gentle. *I will, love,* he said simply.

While the female police officer was searching the kitchen and the male the living room, Stefan stepped into the small first-floor guest room, with its single rumpled bed. The lamps were turned off but with his night vision he could see Elena and Meredith perfectly well by the curtains. Meredith was holding herself as stiffly as an acrophobic bungee jumper.

Take all you need without permanently harming her—and try to put her to sleep, too. And don't invade her mind too deeply—

I'll take care of it. You'd better get out in the hallway, let them see at least one of us, love, Stefan replied soundlessly. Elena was obviously simultaneously frightened for and defensive about her friend and had sped right into micromanagement mode. While this was usually a good thing, if there was one thing Stefan knew about—even if it was the only thing he knew—it was taking blood.

"I want to ask for peace between our families," he said, reaching one hand toward Meredith. She hesitated and Stefan, even trying his hardest, could not help but hearing her thoughts, like small, scuttling creatures at the base of her mind. What was she committing herself to? In what sense did he mean family?

It's really just a formality, he told her, trying to gain ground on another front: her acceptance of the touch of his thoughts to hers. *Never mind it.*

"No," Meredith said. "It's important. I want to trust you, Stefan. Only you, but . . . I didn't get the stave until after Klaus was dead."

He thought swiftly. "Then you didn't know what you were—"

"No. I knew. But my parents were never active. It was Grandpa who told me about the stave."

Stefan felt a surge of unexpected pleasure. "So your grandfather's better now?"

"No . . . sort of." Meredith's thoughts were confusing. *His voice changed,* she was thinking. *Stefan was truly happy that Grandpa's better. Even most* humans *wouldn't care—not really.*

"Of course I care," Stefan said. "For one thing, he helped save all our lives—and the town. For another, he's a very brave man—he must have been—to survive an attack by an Old One."

Suddenly, Meredith's cold hand was around his wrist and words were tumbling from her lips in a rush that Stefan could barely understand. But her thoughts stood bright and clear under those words, and through them he got the meaning.

"All I can know about what happened when I was very young is what I've been told. My parents told me things. My parents changed my birthday—they actually *changed the day* we celebrate my birthday on—because a vampire attacked my grandpa, and then my grandpa tried to kill me. They've always said that. But how do they know? They weren't there—that's part of what they say. And what's more likely, that my grandpa attacked me or that the vampire did?" She stopped, panting, trembling all over like a white-tailed doe caught in the forest. Caught, and thinking she was doomed, and unable to run.

Stefan put out a hand that he deliberately made warm around Meredith's cold one. "I won't attack you," he said simply. "And I won't disturb any old memories. Good enough?"

Meredith nodded. After her cathartic story Stefan knew she wanted as few words as possible.

"Don't be afraid," he murmured, just as he had thought the soothing phrase into the mind of many an animal he'd chased through the Old Wood. *It's all right. There's no reason to fear me.*

She couldn't help being afraid, but Stefan soothed her as he soothed the forest animals, drawing her into the darkest shadow of the room, calming her with soft words even as his canines screamed at him to bite. He had to fold down the side of her blouse to expose her long, olive-skinned column of neck, and as he did the calming words turned into soft endearments and the kind of reassuring noises he would use to comfort a baby.

And at last, when Meredith's breathing had slowed and evened and her eyes had drifted shut, he used the greatest of care to slide his aching fangs into her artery. Meredith barely quivered. Everything was softness as he easily skimmed over the surface of her mind, too, seeing only what he already knew about her: her life with Elena and Bonnie and Caroline. Parties and school, plans and ambitions. Picnics. A swimming hole. Laughter. Tranquility that spread out like a great pool. The need for calm, for control. All this stretching back as far as she could remember . . .

The farthest depths that she could remember were here at the center . . . where there was a sudden plunging dip.

Stefan had promised himself he would not go deeply into her mind, but he was being pulled, helpless, being dragged down by the whirlpool. The waters closed over his head and he was drawn at tremendous speed to the very depths of a second pool, this one not composed of tranquility, but of rage and fear.

And then he saw what had happened, what was happening, what would forever be happening—there at Meredith's still center.

11

When M. le Princess Jessalyn D'Aubigne had drunk her fill of Damon's blood—and she was thirsty for such a fragile thing—it was Damon's turn. He forced himself to remain patient when Jessalyn flinched and frowned at the sight of his ironwood knife. But Damon teased her and joked with her and played chasing games up and down the enormous bed, and when he finally caught her, she scarcely felt the knife's sting at her throat.

Damon, though, had his mouth on the dark red blood that welled out immediately. Everything he'd done, from pouring Black Magic for Bonnie to pouring out the star ball's liquid at the four corners of the Gate to making his way through the defenses of this tiny gem of a castle had been for *this*. For this moment, when his human palate could savor the nectar that was vampire blood.

And it was . . . heavenly!

This was only the second time in his life that he'd tasted it as a human. Katerina—Katherine, as he thought of her in English—had been the first, of course. And how she could have crept off after *that* and gone, wearing just her short muslin shift, to the wide-eyed, inexperienced little *boy* who was his brother, he would never understand.

His disquiet was spreading to Jessalyn. That mustn't happen. She had to stay calm and tranquil as he took as much as he could of her blood. It wouldn't hurt her at all, and it meant all the difference to him.

Forcing his consciousness away from the sheer elemental pleasure of what he was doing, he began, very carefully, very delicately, to infiltrate her mind.

It wasn't difficult to get to the nub of it. Whoever had wrenched this delicate, fragile-boned girl from the human world and had endowed her with a vampire's nature hadn't done her any favors. It wasn't that she had any moral objections to vampirism. She'd taken to the life easily, enjoying it. She would have made a good huntress in the wild. But in this castle? With these servants? It was like having a hundred snooty waiters and two hundred condescending sommeliers staring her down as soon as she opened her mouth to give an order.

This room, for instance. She had wanted some color in

it—just a splash of violet here, a little mauve there—naturally, she realized, a vampire princess's bedchamber had to be *mostly* black. But when she'd timidly mentioned the subject of colors to one of the parlor maids, the girl had sniffed and looked down her nostrils at Jessalyn as if she'd asked for an elephant to be installed just beside her bed. The princess had not had the courage to bring up the matter with the housekeeper, but within a week three baskets full of black-and-off-black throw pillows had arrived. There was her "color." And in the future would her highness be so good as to consult her housekeeper before querying the staff as to her household whims?

She actually said that about my "whims," Jessalyn thought as she arched her neck back and ran sharp fingernails through Damon's thick soft hair. *And—oh, it's no good.* I'm *no good. I'm a vampire princess, and I can* look *the part, but I can't* play *it.*

You're every bit a princess, your highness, Damon soothed. *You just need someone to enforce your orders. Someone who has no doubts about your superiority. Are your servants slaves?*

No, they're all free.

Well, that makes it a little trickier, but you can always yell louder at them. Damon felt swollen with vampire blood. Two more days of this and he would be, if not his old self, then at least almost his old self: a full vampire, free to walk about the city as he liked. And with the Power and status of a vampire prince. It was *almost* enough to balance out the horrors he'd gone through in the last couple of days. At least, he could tell himself that and try to believe it.

"Listen," he said abruptly, letting go of Jessalyn's slight body, the better to look her in the eye. "Your glorious highness, let me do one favor for you before I die of love or you have me killed for impudence. Let me bring you 'color'—and then let me stand beside you if any of your menials grumble about it."

Jessalyn wasn't used to this kind of sudden decision, but couldn't help but be carried along with Damon's fiery excitement. She arched her head back again.

When he finally left the bijoux palace, Damon went out the front door. He had with him a little of the money left over from pawning the gems, but this was more than enough for the purpose he had in mind. He was quite certain that the *next* time he went out, it would be from the flying portico.

He stopped at a dozen shops and spent until his last coin was gone. He'd meant to sneak in a visit to Bonnie as well while doing his errands, but the market was in the opposite direction from the inn where he'd left her, and in the end there just wasn't time.

He didn't worry much as he walked back to the bijoux castle. Bonnie, soft and fragile as she seemed, had a wiry core that he was sure would keep her inside the room for three days. She could take it. Damon knew she could.

He banged on the little castle's gate until a surly guard opened it.

"What do you want?" the guard spat.

Bonnie was bored out of her mind. It had only been a day since Damon had left her—a day she could only count by the number of meals brought to her, since the enormous red sun stood forever on the horizon and the blood-red light never varied unless it was raining.

Bonnie wished it was raining. She wished it was snowing, or that there would be a fire or a hurricane or a small tsunami. She had given one of the star balls a try, and found it a ridiculous soap opera that she couldn't understand in the least.

She wished, now, that she had never tried to stop Damon from coming here. She wished that he had pried her off before they had both fallen into the hole. She wished that she had grabbed Meredith's hand and just let go of Damon.

And this was only the first day.

Damon smiled at the surly guard. "What do I want? Only what I already have. An open gate." He didn't go inside, however. He asked what M. le Princess was doing and heard that she was at a luncheon. On a donor.

Perfect. Soon there came a deferential knock at the gate, which Damon demanded be opened wider. The guards clearly didn't like him; they had properly put together the disappearance of what turned out to be their captain of guard and the intrusion of this strange human. But there was something menacing about him even in this menacing world. They obeyed him.

Soon after that there came another quiet knock and then another, and another and so on until twelve men and women with arms full of damp and fragrant brown paper had quietly followed Damon up the stairs and into M. le Princess's black bedchamber.

Jessalyn, meanwhile, had had a long and stuffy post-luncheon meeting, entertaining some of her financial advisors, who both seemed very old to her, although they had been changed in their twenties. Their muscles were soft with lack of use, she found herself thinking. And, naturally, they were dressed in full-sleeved, wide-legged black except for a frill at their throats, white inside by gaslight, scarlet outside by the eternal blood-red sun.

The princess had just seen them bow out of her presence when she inquired, rather irritably, where the human Damon was. Several servants with malice behind their smiles explained that he had gone with a dozen . . . humans . . . up to her bedchamber.

Jessalyn almost flew to the stairs and climbed very

quickly with the gliding motion that she knew was expected of proper female vampires. She reached the Gothic doors, and heard the hushed sounds of indignant spite as her ladies-in-waiting all whispered together. But before the princess could even ask what was going on, she was engulfed in a great warm wave of scent. Not the luscious and life-sustaining scent of blood, but something lighter, sweeter, and at the moment, while her bloodlust was sated, even headier and more dizzying. She pushed open the double doors. She took a step into her bedchamber and then stopped in astonishment.

The cathedral-like black room was full of flowers. There were banks of lilies, vases full of roses, tulips in every color and shade, and riots of daffodils and narcissus, while fragrant honeysuckle and freesia lay in bowers.

The flower peddlers had converted the gloomy, conventional black room into this fanciful extravaganza. The wiser and more farsighted of M. le Princess's retainers were actively helping them by bringing in large, ornate urns.

Damon, upon seeing Jessalyn enter the room, immediately went to kneel at her feet.

"You were gone when I woke!" the princess said crossly, and Damon smiled, very faintly.

"Forgive me, your highness. But since I am dying anyway, I thought that I should be up and securing these flowers for you. Are the colors and scents satisfactory?"

"The scents?" Jessalyn's whole body seemed to melt. "It's . . . like . . . an orchestra for my nose! And the colors are like nothing I've ever seen!" She burst into laughter, her green eyes lightening, her straight red hair a waterfall around her shoulders. Then she began to stalk Damon back into the gloom in one corner. Damon had to control himself or he would have laughed; it was so much like a kitten stalking an autumn leaf.

But once they got into the corner, tangled in the black hangings and nowhere near a window, Jessalyn assumed a deadly serious expression.

"I'm going to have a dress made, just the color of those deep, dark purple carnations," she whispered. *"Not black."*

"Your highness will look wonderful in it," Damon whispered in her ear. "So striking, so daring—"

"I may even wear my corsets on the *inside* of my dress." She looked up at him through heavy lashes. "Or—would that be too much?"

"Nothing is too much for you, my princess," Damon whispered back. He stopped a moment to think seriously. "The corsets—would they match the dress or be black?"

Jessalyn considered. "Same color?" she ventured.

Damon nodded, pleased. He himself wouldn't be caught dead in any color other than black, but he was willing to put up with—even encourage—Jessalyn's oddities. They might get him made a vampire faster.

"I want your blood," the princess whispered, as if to prove him right.

"Here? Now?" Damon whispered back. "In front of all your servants?"

Jessalyn surprised him then. She, who had been so timid before, stepped out of the curtains and clapped her hands for silence. It fell immediately.

"Everyone out!" she said peremptorily. "You have made me a beautiful garden in my room, and I am grateful. The steward"—she nodded toward a young man who was dressed in black, but who had wisely placed a dark red rose in his buttonhole—"will see to it that you're all given food—and drink—before you go!" At this there was a murmur of praise that made the princess blush.

"I'll ring the bell pull when I need you"—to the steward.

In fact, it wasn't until two days later that she reached up and, a little reluctantly, rang the bellpull. And that was merely to give the order that a uniform be made for Damon as quickly as possible. The uniform of captain of her guard.

By the second day, Bonnie had to turn to the star balls as her only source of entertainment. After going through her twenty-eight orbs she found that twenty-five of them were soap operas from beginning to end, and two were full of experiences so frightening and hideous that she labeled them in her own mind as *Never Ever.* The last one was called *Five Hundred Stories for Young Ones*, and Bonnie quickly found that these immersion stories could be useful, for they specified the names of things a person would find around the house and the city. The sphere's connecting thread was a series about a family of werewolves named the Düz-Aht-Bhi'iens. Bonnie promptly christened them the Dustbins. The series consisted of episodes showing how the family lived each day: how they bought a new slave at the market to replace one who had died, and where they went to hunt human prey, and how Mers Dustbin played in an important *bashik* tournament at school.

Today the last story was almost providential. It showed little Marit Dustbin walking to a Sweetmeat Shop and getting a sugarplum. The candy cost exactly five soli. Bonnie got to experience eating part of it with Marit, and it was good.

After reading the story, Bonnie very carefully peeked through the edge of the window blind and saw a sign on a shop below that she'd often watched. Then she held the star ball to her temple.

Yes! Exactly the same kind of sign. And she knew not only what she wanted, but how much it should cost.

She was dying to get out of her tiny room and try what she had just learned. But before her eyes, the lights in the sweetshop went dark. It must be closing time.

Bonnie threw the star ball across the room. She turned the gas lamp down to just the faintest glow, and then flung herself on her rush-filled bed, pulled the covers up . . . and discovered that she couldn't sleep. Groping in ruby twilight, she found the star ball with her fingers and put it to her temple again.

Interspersed with clusters of stories about the Dustbin family's daily adventures were fairy tales. Most of them were so gruesome that Bonnie couldn't experience them all the way through, and when it was time to sleep, she lay shivering on her pallet. But this time the story seemed different. After the title, *The Gatehouse of the Seven Kitsune Treasures*, she heard a little rhyme:

Amid a plain of snow and ice
There lies kitsune paradise.
And close beside, forbidden pleasure:
Six gates more of kitsune treasure.

The very word *kitsune* was frightening. But, Bonnie thought, the story might prove relevant somehow.

I can do this, she thought and put the star ball to her temple.

The story didn't start with anything gruesome. It was about a young girl and boy kitsune who went on a quest to find the most sacred and secret of the "seven kitsune treasures," the kitsune paradise. A treasure, Bonnie learned, could be something as small as a single gem or as large as an entire world. This one, going by the story, was in the middle range, because a "paradise" was a kind of garden, with exotic flowers blooming everywhere, and little streams bubbling down small waterfalls into clear, deep pools.

It was all wonderful, Bonnie thought, experiencing the story as if she were watching a movie all around her, but a movie that included the sensations of touch, taste, and smell. The paradise was a bit like Warm Springs, where they sometimes had picnics back at home.

In the story, the boy and girl kitsune had to go to "the top of the world" where there was some kind of fracture in the crust of the highest Dark Dimension—the one Bonnie was in right now. They managed somehow to travel down, and even farther down, and passed through various tests of courage and wit before they got into the next lowest dimension, the Nether World.

The Nether World was completely different from the Dark Dimension. It was a world of ice and slippery snow, of glaciers and rifts, all bathed in a blue twilight from three moons that shone from above.

The kitsune children almost starved in the Nether World because there was so little for a fox to hunt. They made do with the tiny animals of the cold: mice and small white voles, and the occasional insect (Oh, yuck, Bonnie thought). They survived until, through the fog and mist, they saw a towering black wall. They followed the wall until finally they came to a Gatehouse with tall spires hidden in the clouds. Written above the door in an old language they could hardly read were the words: *The Seven Gates.*

They entered a room in which there were eight doorways or exits. One was the door through which they had just entered. And as they watched, each door brightened so they could see that the other seven doors led to seven different worlds, one of which was the kitsune paradise. Yet another gate led to a field of magical flowers, and another showed butterflies flittering around a splashing fountain. Another dropped to a dark cavern filled with bottles of the mystical wine Clarion Loess Black Magic. One gate led to a deep mine, with jewels the size of a fist. And then there was a gate which showed the prize of all flowers: the Royal Radhika. It changed its shape from moment to moment, from a rose to a cluster of carnations to an orchid.

Through the last door they could see only a gigantic tree, but the final treasure was rumored to be an immense star ball.

Now the boy and girl forgot all about the kitsune paradise. Each of them wanted something from another of the gates, but they couldn't agree on what. The rule was that any party or group who reached the gates could enter one and then return. But while the girl wanted a sprig of the Royal Radhika, to show that they'd completed their quest, the boy wanted some Black Magic wine, to sustain them on the way back. No matter how they argued they couldn't reach an agreement. So finally they decided to cheat. They would simultaneously open a door and jump through, snatch what they wanted, and then jump back out and be out of the Gatehouse before they could be caught.

Just as they were about to do so, a voice warned them against it, saying, "One gate alone may you twain enter, and then return from whence you came."

But the boy and the girl chose to ignore the voice. Immediately, the boy entered the door that led to the bottles of Black Magic wine and at the same instant the girl stepped into the Royal Radhika door. But when each turned around there was no longer any sign of a door or gate behind them. The boy had plenty to drink but he was left forever in the dark and cold and his tears froze upon his cheeks. The girl had the beautiful flower to look at but nothing to eat or drink and so under the glowing yellow sun she wasted away.

Bonnie shivered, the delicious shiver of a reader who had gotten what she expected. The fairy tale, with its moral of "don't be greedy" was like the stories she'd heard from the Red and the Blue Fairy Books when she was a child sitting on her grandmother's lap.

She missed Elena and Meredith, badly. She had a story to tell, but no one to tell it to.

"Stefan. Stefan!" Elena had been too nervous to stay out of the bedroom for longer than the five minutes it had taken to show herself to the sheriffs. It was Stefan the officers really wanted and couldn't find, not seeming to consider that someone might backtrack and hide in a room that had already been searched.

And now Elena couldn't get a response out of Stefan, who was locked in an embrace with Meredith, mouth pressed tightly over the two little wounds he'd made. Elena had to shake him by the shoulders, to shake both of them, in order to get any response.

Then Stefan reared back suddenly, but held on to Meredith, who would otherwise have fallen. He hastily licked blood from his lips. For once, though, Elena wasn't focused on him, but on her friend—her friend whom she'd allowed to do this.

Meredith's eyes were shut, but they had dark, almost plum-colored circles under them. Her lips were parted, and her dark cloud of hair was wet where tears had fallen into it.

"Meredith? Merry?" The old nickname just slipped out of Elena's lips. And then, when Meredith gave no sign of having heard her: "Stefan, what's wrong?"

"I Influenced her at the end to sleep." Stefan lifted Meredith and put her on the bed.

"But what happened? Why is she crying—and what's wrong with *you*?" Elena couldn't help but notice that despite the healthy flush on Stefan's cheeks his eyes were shadowed.

"Something I saw—in her mind," Stefan said briefly, pulling Elena behind his back. "Here comes one of them. Stay there."

The door opened. It was the male sheriff, who was red-faced and panting, and who had clearly just lapped himself, returning to this room after starting from it to search the entire first floor.

"I have them all in a room—all but the fugitive," the sheriff said into a large black mobile. The female sheriff made some brief reply. Then the red-faced male turned to speak to the teenagers. "Now what's going to happen is that I'm going to search *you*"—he nodded at Stefan—"while my partner searches *you two*." His head jerked, ear-first, at Meredith. "What's wrong with her, anyway?"

"Nothing that you could understand," Stefan replied coolly.

The sheriff looked as if he couldn't believe what had just been said. Then, suddenly, he looked as if he could, and did, and he took a step toward Meredith.

Stefan snarled.

The sound made Elena, who was right behind him, jump. It was the low savage snarl of an animal protecting its mate, its pack, its territory.

The ruddy-faced policeman suddenly looked pale and panicked. Elena guessed that he was looking at a mouth full of teeth much sharper than his own, and tinged with blood as well.

Elena didn't want this to turn into a pi—that was, a . . . snarling match.

As the sheriff gabbled to his partner, "We may need some of them silver bullets after all," Elena poked her beloved, who was now making a noise like a very big buzz saw that she could feel in her teeth, and whispered, "Stefan, Influence him! The other one's coming, and she may already have called for backup."

At her touch, Stefan stopped making the sound, and when he turned she could see his face changing from that of a savage animal baring its teeth back to his own dear, green-eyed self. He must have taken a *lot* of blood from Meredith, she thought, with a flutter in her stomach. She wasn't sure how she felt about that.

But there was no denying the after-effects. Stefan turned back to the male sheriff and said crisply, "You will go into the front hallway. You will remain there, silent, until I tell you to move or speak." Then, without looking up to see if the officer was obeying or not, he tucked the blankets more tightly around Meredith.

Elena was watching the sheriff, though, and she noticed that he didn't hesitate an instant. He made an about-face and marched off to the front foyer.

Then Elena felt safe enough to look at Meredith again. She couldn't find anything wrong in her friend's face, except her unnatural pallor, and those violet shadows around her eyes.

"Meredith?" she whispered.

No response. Elena followed Stefan out of the room.

She had just made it to the foyer when the female sheriff ambushed them. Coming down the stairs, pushing the fragile Mrs. Flowers before her, she shouted, "On the ground! All of you!" She gave Mrs. Flowers a hard shove forward. "Get down now!"

When Mrs. Flowers almost fell sprawling on the floor, Stefan leaped and caught her, and then turned back to the other woman. For a moment Elena thought that he would snarl again, but instead, in a voice tight with self-control, he said, "Join your partner. You can't move or speak without my permission."

He took the shaken-looking Mrs. Flowers to a chair on the left side of the foyer. "Did that—person—hurt you?"

"No, no. Just get them out of my house, Stefan, dear, and I'll be most grateful," Mrs. Flowers replied.

"Done," Stefan said softly. "I'm sorry we've caused you so much trouble—in your own home." He looked at each of the sheriffs, his eyes piercing. "Go away and don't come back. You have searched the house, but none of the people you were looking for were here. You think further surveillance will yield nothing. You believe that you would do more good by helping the—what was it? Oh, yes, the *mayhem* in the town of Fell's Church. You will never come here again. Now go back to your car and leave."

Elena felt the tiny hairs on the back of her neck stand up. She could feel the Power behind Stefan's words.

And, as always, it was satisfying to see cruel or angry people become docile under the power of a vampire's Influence. These two stood for another ten seconds quite still, and then they simply walked out the front door.

Elena listened to the sound of the sheriff's car driving away and such a strong feeling of relief washed over her that she almost collapsed. Stefan put his arms around her, and Elena hugged him back tightly, knowing that her heart was pounding. She could feel it in her chest and her fingertips.

It's all over. All done now, Stefan thought to her and Elena suddenly felt something different. She felt pride. Stefan had simply taken charge and chased the officers away.

Thank you, she thought to Stefan.

"I guess we'd better get Matt out of the root cellar," she added.

Matt was unhappy. "Thanks for hiding me—but do you know how long that was?" he demanded of Elena when they were upstairs again. "And no light except what was in that little star ball. And no sound—I couldn't hear a thing down there. And what is *this*?" He held out the long, heavy wooden staff, with its strangely shaped, spiked ends.

Elena felt sudden panic. "You didn't cut yourself, did you?" She snatched up Matt's hands, letting the long staff fall to the ground. But Matt didn't seem to have a single scratch.

"I wasn't dumb enough to hold it by the ends," he said.

"Meredith did, for some reason," Elena said. "Her palms were covered with wounds. And I don't even know what it is."

"I do," Stefan said quietly. He picked up the stave.

"But it's Meredith's secret really. I mean it's Meredith's property," he added hastily as all eyes fixed on him at the word *secret*.

"Well, I'm not blind," Matt said in his frank, straightforward way, flipping back some fair hair in order to look more closely at the thing. He raised blue eyes to Elena. "I know what it *smells* like, which is vervain. And I know what it *looks* like with all those silver and iron spikes coming out of the sharp ends. It looks like a giant staff for exterminating every kind of Godawful Hellacious monster that walks on this earth."

"And vampires, too," Elena added hastily. She knew that Stefan was in a funny mood and she definitely didn't want to see Matt, for whom she still cared deeply, lying on the floor with a crushed skull. "And even humans—I think these bigger spikes are for injecting poison."

"Poison?" Matt looked at his own palms hastily.

"You're okay," Elena said. "I checked you, and besides it would be a very quick-acting poison."

"Yes, they would want to take you out of the fight as fast as possible," Stefan said. "So if you're alive now, you're likely to stay that way. And now, this Godawful Hellacious monster just wants to get back up to bed." He turned to go to the attic. He must have heard Elena's swift, involuntarily indrawn breath, because he turned around and she could see that he was sorry. His eyes were dark emerald, sad but blazing with unused Power.

I think we'll have a late morning, Elena thought, feeling pleasurable thrills ripple through her. She squeezed Stefan's hand, and felt him return the pressure. She could see what he had in mind; they were close enough and he was projecting pretty clearly what he wanted—and she was as eager to get upstairs as he was.

But at that moment Matt, eyes on the wickedly spiked staff, said, "Meredith has something to do with *that*?"

"I should never have said anything at all about it," Stefan replied. "But if you want to know more, you'd really better ask Meredith herself. Tomorrow."

"All right," Matt said, finally seeming to understand. Elena was way ahead of him. A weapon like that *was*—could only be—for killing all sorts of monsters walking the earth. And Meredith—Meredith who was as slim and athletic as a ballerina with a black belt, and *oh*! Those lessons! The lessons that Meredith had always put off if the girls were doing something at that exact moment, but that she always somehow managed to make time for.

But a girl could hardly be expected to carry a harpsichord around with her and nobody else had one. Besides, Meredith had said she hated to play, so her BFFs had let it go at that. It was all part of the Meredith mystique.

And riding lessons? Elena would bet some of them were genuine. Meredith would want to know how to make a quick escape mounting anything available.

But if Meredith wasn't practicing for a little light music in the drawing room, or for starring in a Hollywood Western—then what would she have been doing?

Training, Elena guessed. There were a lot of dojos out there, and if Meredith had been doing this since that vampire attacked her grandfather she must be pretty darn good. And when we've fought grisly things, whose eyes have ever been on her, a soft gray shadow that kept out of the limelight? A lot of monsters probably got knocked out but good.

The only question that needed to be answered was why Meredith hadn't shown them the Godawful Hellacious monster staker or used it in any fights—say against Klaus—until now. And Elena didn't know, but she could ask Meredith herself. Tomorrow, when Meredith was up. But she trusted that it had some simple answer.

Elena tried to stifle a yawn in a ladylike way. *Stefan?* she asked. *Can you get us out of here—without picking me up—and to your room?*

"I think we've all had enough stress this morning," Stefan said in his own gentle voice. "Mrs. Flowers, Meredith is in the first-floor bedroom—she'll probably sleep very late. Matt—"

"I know, I know. I don't know where the schedule went but I might as well make it my night." Matt presented an arm to Stefan.

Stefan looked surprised. *Darling, you can never have too much blood,* Elena thought to him, seriously and straightforwardly.

"Mrs. Flowers and I will be in the kitchen," she said aloud.

When they were there, Mrs. Flowers said, "Don't forget to thank Stefan for defending the boardinghouse for me."

"He did it because it's our home," Elena said, and went back into the hall, where Stefan was thanking a flushing Matt.

And then Mrs. Flowers called Matt into the kitchen and Elena found herself swooped up in lithe, hard arms and then they were gaining altitude rapidly, with the wood staircase emitting little creaks and groans of protest. And finally they were in Stefan's room and Elena was in Stefan's arms.

There was no better place to be, or anything else either of them really wanted now, Elena thought and turned her face up as Stefan turned his down and they began with a long slow kiss. And then the kiss went molten, and Elena had to cling to Stefan, who was already holding her with arms that could have cracked granite, but only squeezed her exactly as tightly as she wanted them to.

Elena, sleeping serenely with one hand locked onto Stefan's, knew she was having an extraordinary dream. No, not a dream—an out-of-body experience. But it wasn't like her previous out-of-body visits to Stefan in his cell. She was skimming through the air so quickly that she couldn't really make out what was below her.

She looked around and suddenly, to her astonishment, another figure appeared beside her.

"Bonnie!" she said—or rather tried to say. But of course there was no sound. Bonnie looked like a transparent edition of herself. As if someone had created her out of blown glass, and then put in just the faintest tint of color in her hair and eyes.

Elena tried telepathy. *Bonnie?*

Elena! Oh, I miss you and Meredith so much! I'm stuck here in a hole—

A hole? Elena could hear the panic in her own telepathy. It made Bonnie wince.

Not a real hole. A dive. An inn, I guess, but I'm locked in and they only feed me twice a day and take me to the toilet once—

My God! How did you get there?

Well . . . Bonnie hesitated. *I guess it was my own fault.*

It doesn't matter! How long have you been there, exactly?

Um, this is my second day. I think.

There was a pause. Then Elena said, *Well, a couple of days in a bad place can seem like forever.*

Bonnie tried to make her case clearer. *It's just that I'm so bored and lonely. I miss you and Meredith so much!* she repeated.

I was thinking of you and Meredith, too, Elena said.

But Meredith's there with you, isn't she? Oh my God, she didn't fall, too? Bonnie blurted.

No, no! She didn't fall. Elena couldn't decide whether to tell Bonnie about Meredith or not. Maybe not just yet, she thought.

She couldn't see what she was rushing toward, although she could feel that they were slowing down. *Can you see anything?*

Hey, yeah, below us! There's a car! Should we go down?

Of course. Can we hold hands?

They found that they couldn't, but that just trying to kept them closer together. In another moment they were sinking through the roof of a small car.

Hey! It's Alaric! Bonnie said.

Alaric Saltzman was Meredith's engaged-to-be-engaged boyfriend. He was about twenty-three now, and his sandy-blond hair and hazel eyes hadn't changed since Elena had seen him almost ten months ago. He was a parapsychologist at Duke, going for his doctorate.

We've been trying to get hold of him for ages, Bonnie said.

I know. Maybe this is the way we're supposed to contact him.

W*here is he supposed to be again?*

Some weird place in Japan. I forget what it's called, but look at the map on the passenger seat.

She and Bonnie intermingled as they did, their ghostly forms passing right through each other.

Unmei no Shima: The Island of Doom, was written at the top of an outline of an island. The map beside him had a large red X on it with the caption: *The Field of Punished Virgins.*

The what? Bonnie asked indignantly. *What's that mean?*

I don't know. But look, this fog is real fog. And it's raining. And this road is terrible.

Bonnie dove outside. *Ooh, so weird. The rain's going right through me. And I don't think this is a road.*

Elena said, *Come back in and look at this. There aren't*

any other cities on the island, just a name. Dr. Celia Connor, forensic pathologist.

What's a forensic pathologist?

I think, Elena said, *that they investigate murders and things. And they dig up dead people to find out why they died.*

Bonnie shuddered. *I don't think I like this very much.*

Neither do I. But look outside. This was a village once, I think.

There was almost nothing left of the village. Just a few ruins of wooden buildings that were obviously rotting, and some tumbledown, blackened stone structures. There was one large building with an enormous bright yellow tarp over it.

When the car reached this building, Alaric skidded to a stop, grabbed the map and a small suitcase, and dashed through the rain and mud to get under cover. Elena and Bonnie followed.

He was met near the entrance by a very young black woman, whose hair was cut short and sleek around her elfin face. She was small, not even Elena's height. She had eyes dancing with excitement and white, even teeth that made for a Hollywood smile.

"Dr. Connor?" Alaric said, looking awed.

Meredith isn't going to like this, Bonnie said.

"Just Celia, please," the woman said, taking his hand. "Alaric Saltzman, I presume."

"Just Alaric, please—Celia."

Meredith really *isn't going to like this,* Elena said.

"So you're the spook investigator," Celia was saying below them. "Well, we need you. This place has spooks—or did once. I don't know if they're still here or not."

"Sounds interesting."

"More like sad and morbid. Sad and *weird* and morbid. I've excavated all sorts of ruins, especially those where there's a chance of genocide. And I'll tell you: This island is unlike any place I have ever seen," Celia said.

Alaric was already pulling things from his case, a thick stack of papers, a small camcorder, a notebook. He turned on the camcorder, and looked through the viewfinder, then propped it up with some of the papers. When he apparently had Celia in focus, he grabbed the notebook too.

Celia looked amused. "How many ways do you need to take down information?"

Alaric tapped the side of his head and shook it sadly. "As many as possible. Neurons are beginning to go." He looked around. "You're not the only one here, are you?"

"Except for the janitor and the guy who ferries me back to Hokkaido, yes. It started out as a normal expedition—there were fourteen of us. But one by one, the others have died or left. I can't even re-bury the specimens—the girls—we've excavated."

"And the people who left or died from your expedition—"

"Well, at first people died. Then that and the other spooky stuff made the rest leave. They were frightened for their lives."

Alaric frowned. "Who died first?"

"Out of our expedition? Ronald Argyll. Pottery specialist. He was examining two jars that were found—well, I'll skip that story until later. He fell off a ladder and broke his neck."

Alaric's eyebrows went up. "That was spooky?"

"From a guy like him, who's been in the business for almost twenty years—yes."

"Twenty years? Maybe a heart attack? And then off the ladder—boom." Alaric made a downward gesture.

"Maybe that's the way it was. You may be able to explain all our little mysteries for us." The chic woman with the short hair dimpled like a tomboy. She was dressed like one too, Elena realized: Levi's and a blue and white shirt with the sleeves rolled up over a white camisole.

Alaric gave a little start, as if he'd realized he was guilty of staring. Bonnie and Elena looked at each other over his head.

"But what happened to all the people who lived on the island in the first place? The ones who built the houses?"

"Well, there never were that many of them in the first

place. I'm guessing the place may even have been named the Island of Doom before this disaster my team was investigating. But as far as I could find out it was a sort of war—a civil war. Between the children and the adults."

This time when Bonnie and Elena looked at each other, their eyes were both wide. *Just like home*—Bonnie began, but Elena said, *Sh. Listen.*

"A civil war between kids and their parents?" Alaric repeated slowly. "Now that is spooky."

"Well, it's a process of elimination. You see, I like graves, constructed or just holes in the ground. And here, the inhabitants don't appear to have been invaded. They didn't die of famine or drought—there was still plenty of grain in the granary. There were no signs of illness. I've come to believe that *they all killed one another*—parents killing children; children killing parents."

"But how can you tell?"

"You see this square-ish area on the periphery of the village?" Celia pointed to an area on a larger map than Alaric's. "That's what we call *The Field of Punished Virgins.* It's the only place that has carefully constructed actual graves, so it was made early in what became a war. Later, there was no time for coffins—or no one who cared. So far we've excavated twenty-two female children—the eldest in her late teens."

"Twenty-two girls? All girls?"

"All girls in this area. Boys came later, when coffins were no longer being made. They're not as well preserved, because the houses all burned or fell in, and they were exposed to weathering. The girls were carefully, sometimes elaborately, buried; but the markings on their bodies indicate that they were subjected to harsh physical punishment at some time close to their deaths. And then—they had stakes driven through their hearts."

Bonnie's fingers flew to her eyes, as if to ward off a terrible vision. Elena watched Alaric and Celia grimly.

Alaric gulped. "They were staked?" he asked uneasily.

"Yes. Now I know what you'll be thinking. But Japan doesn't have any tradition of vampires. Kitsune—foxes—are probably the closest analog."

Now Elena and Bonnie were hovering right over the map.

"And do kitsunes drink blood?"

"Just kitsune. The Japanese language has an interesting way of expressing plurals. But to answer your question: no. They are legendary tricksters, and one example of what they do is possess girls and women, and lead men to destruction—into bogs, and so on. But here—well, you can almost read it like a book."

"You make it sound like one. But not one I'd pick up for pleasure," Alaric said, and they both smiled bleakly.

"So, to go on with the book, it seems that this disease

spread eventually to all the children in the town. There were deadly fights. The parents somehow couldn't even get to the fishing boats in which they might have escaped the island."

Elena—

I know. At least Fell's Church isn't on an island.

"And then there's what we found at the town shrine. I can show you that—it's what Ronald Argyll died for."

They both got up and went farther into the building until Celia stopped beside two large urns on pedestals with a hideous thing in between them. It looked like a dress, weathered until it was almost pure white, but sticking through holes in the clothing were bones. Most horribly, one bleached and fleshless bone hung down from the top of one of the urns.

"This is what Ronald was working on in the field before all this rain came," Celia explained. "It was probably the last death of the original inhabitants and it was suicide."

"How can you possibly know that?"

"Let's see if I can get this right from Ronald's notes. The priestess here doesn't have any other damage than that which caused her death. The shrine was a stone building—once. When we got here we found only a floor, with all the stone steps tumbled apart every which way. Hence Ronald's use of the ladder. It gets quite technical, but Ronald Argyll was a great forensic pathologist and I trust *his* reading of the story."

"Which is?" Alaric was taking in the jars and the bones with his camcorder.

"Someone—we don't know who—smashed a hole in each of the jars. This is before the chaos started. The town records make note of it as an act of vandalism, a prank done by a child. But long after that the hole was sealed and the jars made almost airtight again, except where the priestess had her hands plunged in the top up to the wrist."

With infinite care, Celia lifted the top off the jar that did not have a bone hanging from it—to reveal another pair of longish bones, slightly less bleached, and with strips of what must have been clothing on it. Tiny finger bones lay inside the jar.

"What Ronald thought was that this poor woman died as she performed a last desperate act. Clever, too, if you see it from their perspective. She cut her wrists—you can see how the tendon is shriveled in the better-preserved arm—and then she let the entire contents of her bloodstream flow into the urns. We do know that the urns show a heavy precipitation of blood on the bottom. She was trying to lure something in—or perhaps something *back* in. And she died trying, and the clay that she had probably hoped to use in her last conscious moments held her bones to the jars."

"Whew!" Alaric ran a hand over his forehead, but

shivered at the same time.

Take pictures! Elena was mentally commanding him, using all her willpower to transmit the order. She could see that Bonnie was doing the same, eyes shut, fists clenched.

As if in obedience to their commands, Alaric was taking pictures as fast as he could.

Finally, he was done. But Elena knew that without some outside impetus there was no way that he was going to get those pictures to Fell's Church until he himself came to town—and even Meredith didn't know when that would be.

So what do we do? Bonnie asked Elena, looking anguished.

Well . . . my tears were real when Stefan was in prison.

You want us to cry on him?

No, Elena said, not quite patiently. *But we look like ghosts—let's act like them. Try blowing on the back of his neck.*

Bonnie did, and they both watched Alaric shiver, look around him, draw his windbreaker closer.

"And what about the other deaths in your own expedition?" he asked, huddling, looking around apparently aimlessly.

Celia began speaking but neither Elena nor Bonnie was listening. Bonnie kept blowing on Alaric from different directions, herding him to the single window in the building that wasn't shattered. There Elena had written with her finger on the darkened cold glass. Once she knew that Alaric was looking that way she blew her breath across the sentence: *send all pix of jars 2 meredith now!* Every time Alaric approached the window she breathed on it to refresh the words.

And at last he saw it.

He jumped backward nearly two feet. Then he slowly crept back to the window. Elena refreshed the writing for him. This time, instead of jumping, he simply ran a hand over his eyes and then slowly peeked out again.

"Hey, Mr. Spook-chaser," said Celia. "Are you all right?"

"I don't know," Alaric admitted. He passed his hand over his eyes again, but Celia was coming and Elena didn't breathe on the window.

"I thought I saw a—a message to send copies of the pictures of these jars to Meredith."

Celia raised an eyebrow. "Who is Meredith?"

"Oh. She—she's one of my former students. I suppose this would interest her." He looked down at the camcorder.

"Bones and urns?"

"Well, you were interested in them quite young, if your reputation is correct."

"Oh, yes. I loved to watch a dead bird decay, or find bones and try to figure out what animal they were from," Celia said, dimpling again. "From the age of six. But I wasn't like most girls."

"Well—neither is Meredith," Alaric said.

Elena and Bonnie were eyeing each other seriously now. Alaric had implied that Meredith was special, but he hadn't *said* it, and he hadn't mentioned their engagement to be engaged.

Celia came closer. "Are you going to send her the pictures?"

Alaric laughed. "Well, all this atmosphere and everything—I don't know. It might just have been my imagination."

Celia turned away just as she reached him and Elena blew once more across the message. Alaric threw his hands up in a gesture of surrender.

"I don't suppose the Island of Doom has satellite coverage," he said helplessly.

"Nope," Celia said. "But the ferry will be back in a day, and you can send pictures then—if you're really going to do it."

"I think I'd *better* do it," Alaric said. Elena and Bonnie were both glaring at him, one from each side.

But that was when Elena's eyelids started to droop. *Oh, Bonnie, I'm sorry. I wanted to talk to you after this, and make sure you're okay. But I'm falling . . . I can't . . .*

She managed to pry her lids open. Bonnie was in a fetal position, fast asleep.

Be careful, Elena whispered, not even sure who she was whispering it to. And as she floated away, she was aware of Celia and the way Alaric was talking to this beautiful, accomplished woman only a year or so older than he was. She felt a distinct fear for Meredith, on top of everything else.

The next morning Elena noticed that Meredith still looked pale and languid, and that her eyes slid away if Stefan happened to glance at her. But this was a time of crisis, and as soon as the breakfast dishes were washed, Elena called a meeting in the parlor. There she and Stefan explained what Meredith had missed during the visit from the sheriffs. Meredith smiled wanly when Elena told how Stefan had banished them like stray dogs.

Then Elena told the story of her out-of-body experience. It proved one thing, at least, that Bonnie was alive and relatively well. Meredith bit her lip when Mrs. Flowers said this, for it only made her want to go and get Bonnie out of the Dark Dimension personally.

But on the other hand, Meredith wanted to stay and

wait for Alaric's photographs. If that would save Fell's Church . . .

No one at the boardinghouse could question what had happened on the Island of Doom. It was happening here, on the other side of the world. Already a couple of parents in Fell's Church had had their children taken away by the Virginia Department of Child Protective Services. Punishments and retaliations had begun. How much longer would it be before Shinichi and Misao turned all the children into lethal weapons—or let loose those already turned? How long before some hysterical parent killed a kid?

The group sitting in the parlor discussed plans and methods. In the end, they decided to make jars identical to those Elena and Bonnie had seen, and prayed that they could reproduce the writing. These jars, they were sure, were the means by which Shinichi and Misao were originally sealed off from the rest of the Earth.

Therefore Shinichi and Misao had once fit into the rather cramped accommodations of the jars. But what did Elena's group have now that could lure them back inside?

Power, they decided. Only an amount of Power so great that it was irresistible to the kitsune twins. That was why the priestess had tried to lure them back with her own blood. Now . . . it meant either the liquid in a full star ball . . . or blood from an extraordinarily powerful vampire.

Or two vampires. Or three.

Everyone was sober, thinking of this. They didn't know how much blood would be needed—but Elena feared that it would be more than they can afford to lose. It had certainly been more than the priestess could afford.

And then there was a silence that only Meredith could fill. "I'm sure you've all been wondering about this," she said, producing the staff thing from thin air, as far as Elena could see. How did she *do* that? Elena wondered. She didn't have it with her and then she did.

They all stared in the bright sunlight at the sleek beauty of the weapon.

"Whoever made that," Matt said, "had a twisted imagination."

"It was one of my ancestors," Meredith said. "And I won't contest that."

"I have a question," Elena said. "If you'd had that from the beginning of your training; if you'd been raised in that kind of world, would you have tried to kill Stefan? Would you have tried to kill *me* when I became a vampire?"

"I wish I had a good answer to that," Meredith said, her dark gray eyes pained. "But I don't. I have nightmares about it. But how can I ever say what I *would* have done if I'd been a different person?"

"I'm not asking that. I'm asking you, the person you are, if you'd had the training—"

"The training is brainwashing," Meredith said harshly. Her composed façade seemed about to break.

"Okay, forget that. Would you have tried to kill Stefan, if you'd just had that staff?"

"It's called a fighting stave. And *we're* called—people like my family, except that my parents dropped out—hunter-slayers."

There was a sort of gasp around the table. Mrs. Flowers poured Meredith more herbal tea from the pot sitting on a trivet.

"Hunter-slayers," repeated Matt with a certain relish. It wasn't hard to tell who he was thinking about.

"You can just call us one or the other," Meredith was saying. "I've heard that out west they've got hunter-killers. But we hang on to tradition here."

Elena suddenly felt like a lost little girl. This was Meredith, her big sister Meredith, saying all of this. Elena's voice was almost pleading. "But you didn't even tell on Stefan."

"No, I didn't. And, no, I don't think I'd have had the courage to kill anyone—unless I'd been brainwashed. But I *knew* Stefan loved you. I *knew* he would never make you into a vampire. The problem was—I didn't know enough about Damon. I didn't know that you were fooling around so much. I don't think *anybody* knew that." Meredith's voice was anguished, too.

"Except me," Elena said, flushing, with a lopsided smile. "Don't look so sad, Meredith. It worked out."

"You call having to leave your family and your town because everyone knows you're dead, working out?"

"I do," Elena replied desperately, "if it means I get to be with Stefan." She did her best not to think about Damon.

Meredith looked at her blankly for a moment, then put her face in her hands. "Do you want to tell them or should I?" she asked, coming up for air and facing Stefan.

Stefan looked startled. "You remember?"

"Probably as much as you got from my mind. Bits and pieces. Stuff I don't *want* to remember."

"Okay." Now Stefan looked relieved, and Elena felt frightened. Stefan and Meredith had a secret together?

"We all know that Klaus made at least two visits to Fell's Church. We know that he was—completely evil—and that on the second visit he planned to be a serial murderer. He killed Sue Carson and Vickie Bennett."

Elena interrupted quietly. "Or at least he helped Tyler Smallwood to kill Sue, so that Tyler could be initiated as a werewolf. And then Tyler got Caroline pregnant."

Matt cleared his throat as something occurred to him. "Uh—does Caroline have to kill somebody to be a full werewolf, too?"

"I don't think so," Elena said. "Stefan says that having

a werewolf litter is enough. Either way, blood is spilled. Caroline will be a full werewolf when she has her twins, but she'll probably begin changing involuntarily before that. Right?"

Stefan nodded. "Right. But getting back to Klaus: What was it he was supposed to have done on his first visit? He attacked—without killing—an old man who was a full hunter-slayer."

"My grandfather," Meredith whispered.

"And he supposedly messed with Meredith's grandfather's mind so much that this old man tried to kill his wife and his three-year-old granddaughter. So what is wrong with this picture?"

Elena was truly frightened now. She didn't want to hear whatever was coming. She could taste bile, and she was glad that she'd only had toast for breakfast. If only there had been someone to take care of, like Bonnie, she would have felt better.

"I give up. So what *is* wrong?" Matt asked bluntly.

Meredith was staring into the distance again.

Finally Stefan said, "At the risk of sounding like a bad soap opera . . . Meredith had, or has, a twin brother."

Dead silence fell over the group in the parlor. Even Mrs. Flowers's Ma*ma* didn't put in a word.

"*Had or has*?" Matt said finally, breaking the silence.

"How can we know?" Stefan said. "He may have been

killed. Imagine Meredith having to watch that. Or he could have been kidnapped. To be killed at a later time—or to become a vampire."

"And you really think her parents wouldn't tell her?" Matt demanded. "Or would try to make her forget? When she was—what, three already?"

Mrs. Flowers, who had been quiet a long time, now spoke sadly. "Dear Meredith may have decided to block out the truth herself. With a child of three it's hard to say. If they never got her professional help . . ." She looked a question at Meredith.

Meredith shook her head. "Against the code," she said. "I mean, strictly speaking, I shouldn't be telling any of you this, and especially not Stefan. But I couldn't stand it anymore . . . having such good friends, and constantly deceiving them."

Elena went over and hugged Meredith hard. "We understand," she said. "I don't know what will happen in the future if you decide to be an active hunter—"

"I can promise you my friends won't be on my list of victims," Meredith said. "By the way," she added, "Shinichi knows. I'm the one who's kept a secret from my friends all my life."

"Not any longer," Elena said, and hugged her again.

"At least there are no more secrets now," Mrs. Flowers said gently, and Elena looked at her sharply. Nothing was ever that simple. And Shinichi had made a whole handful of predictions.

Then she saw the look in the mild blue eyes of the old woman, and she knew that what was important right then was not truth or lies, or even reckonings, but simply comforting Meredith. She looked up at Stefan while still hugging Meredith and saw the same look in his eyes.

And that—made her feel better somehow. Because if it was *truly* "no secrets" then she would have to figure out her feelings about Damon. And she was more afraid of that than of facing Shinichi, which was saying quite a lot, really.

"At least we've got a potter's wheel—somewhere," Mrs. Flowers was saying. "And a kiln in the back, although it's all grown over with Devil's Shoestring. I used to make flowerpots for outside the boardinghouse, but children came and smashed them. I think I could make an urn like the ones you saw if you can draw one for me. But perhaps we'd better wait for Mr. Saltzman's pictures."

Matt was mouthing something to Stefan. Elena couldn't make it out until she heard Stefan's voice in her mind. *He says Damon told him once that this house is like a swap meet, and you can find* anything *here if you look hard enough.*

Damon didn't make that up! I think Mrs. Flowers said it first, and then it sort of got around, Elena returned heatedly.

"When we get the pictures," Mrs. Flowers was saying

brightly, "we can get the Saitou women to translate the writing."

Meredith finally moved back from Elena. "And until then we can pray that Bonnie doesn't get into any trouble," she said, and her voice and face were composed again. "I'm starting now."

Bonnie was sure she could stay out of trouble.

She'd had that strange dream—the one about shedding her body, and going with Elena to the Island of Doom. Fortunately, it had seemed to be a real out-of-body experience, and not something she had to ponder over and try to find hidden meanings in. It didn't mean *she* was doomed or anything like that.

Plus, she'd managed to live through another night in this brown room, and Damon *had* to come and get her out soon. But not before she had a sugarplum. Or two.

Yes, she had gotten a taste of one in the story last night, but Marit was such a good girl that she had waited for dinner to have any more. Dinner was obtained in the next story about the Dustbins, which she'd plunged into this morning. But that contained the horror of little Marit tasting her first hand-caught piece of raw liver, fresh from the hunt. Bonnie had hastily pulled the little star ball off her temple, and had determined not to do anything that could possibly get her on a human hunting range.

But then, compulsively, she had counted up her money. She had money. She knew where a shop was. And that meant . . . shopping!

When her bathroom break came around, she managed to get into a conversation with the boy who usually led her to the outdoor privy. This time she made him blush so hard and tug at his earlobe so often that when she begged him to give her the key and let her go by herself—it wasn't as if she didn't know the way—he had relented and let her go, asking only that she hurry.

And she did hurry—across the street and into the little store, which smelled so much of melting fudge, toffee being pulled by hand, and other mouth-watering smells that she would have known where she was blindfolded.

She also knew what she wanted. She could picture it from the story and the one taste Marit had had.

A sugarplum was round like a real plum, and she'd tasted dates, almonds, spices, and honey—and there may have been some raisins, too. It should cost five soli, according to the story, but Bonnie had taken fifteen of the small coppery-looking coins with her, in case of a confectionary emergency.

Once inside, Bonnie glanced warily around her. There were a lot of customers in the shop, maybe six or seven. One brown-haired girl was wearing sacking just like Bonnie and looked exhausted. Surreptitiously, Bonnie inched toward her, and pressed five of her copper soli into the girl's chapped hand, thinking, there—now she can get a sugar-plum just like me; that ought to cheer her up. It did: the girl gave her the sort of smile that Mother Dustbin often gave to Marit when she had done something adorable.

I wonder if I should talk to her?

"It looks pretty busy," she whispered, ducking her head.

The girl whispered back, "It has been. All yesterday I kept hoping, but at least one noble came in as the last one left."

"You mean you have to wait until the shop's empty to—?"

The brown-haired girl looked at her curiously. "Of course—unless you're buying for your mistress or master."

"What's your name?" Bonnie whispered.

"Kelta."

"I'm Bonnie."

At this Kelta burst into silent but convulsive giggles.

Bonnie felt offended; she'd just given Kelta a sugar-plum—or the price of one, and now the girl was laughing at her.

"I'm sorry," Kelta said when her mirth had died down. "But don't you think it's funny that in the last year there are so many girls changing their names to Alianas and Mardeths, and Bonnas—some slaves are even being *allowed* to do it."

"But why?" Bonnie whispered with such obvious genuine bewilderment that Kelta said, "Why, to fit into the story, of course. To be named after the ones who killed old Bloddeuwedd while she was rampaging through the city."

"That was such a big deal?"

"You really don't know? After she was killed all her money went to the fifth sector where she lived and there was enough left over to have a holiday. That's where I'm from. And I used to be so frightened when I was sent out with a message or anything after dark because she could be right above you and you'd never know, until—" Kelta had put all her money into one pocket and now she mimed claws descending on an innocent hand.

"But you really are a Bonna," Kelta said, with a flash of white teeth in rather dingy skin. "Or so you said."

"Yeah," Bonnie said feeling vaguely sad. "I'm a Bonna, all right!" The next moment she cheered up. "The shop's empty!"

"It is! Oh, you're a good-luck Bonna! I've been waiting two days."

She approached the counter with a lack of fear that was very encouraging to Bonnie. Then she asked for something called a blood jelly that looked to Bonnie like a small mold of strawberry Jell-O, with something darker deep inside. Kelta smiled at Bonnie from under the curtain of her long, unbrushed hair and was gone.

The man who ran the sweetshop kept looking hopefully

at the door, clearly hoping a free person—a noble—would come in. No one did, however, and at last he turned to Bonnie.

"And what is it you want?" he demanded.

"Just a sugarplum, please?" Bonnie tried hard to make sure her voice didn't quaver.

The man was bored. "Show me your pass," he said irritably.

It was at that point that Bonnie suddenly knew that everything was going to go horribly wrong.

"Come on, come on, snap it up!" Still looking at his accounting books, the man snapped his fingers.

Meanwhile Bonnie was running a hand over her sackcloth smock, in which she knew perfectly well there was no pocket, and certainly no pass.

"But I thought I didn't need a pass, except to cross sectors," she babbled finally.

The man now leaned over the counter. "Then show me your freedom pass," he said, and Bonnie did the only thing she could think of. She turned and ran, but before she could reach the door she felt a sudden stinging pain in her back and then everything went blurry and she never knew when she hit the ground.

15

Bonnie woke slowly, coming up from some dark place.

Then she wished she hadn't. She was in some out-of-doors place—only buildings blocked the horizon where the sun hung forever. Around her were a lot of other girls, all approximately her own age. That was puzzling, first of all. If you took a random sampling of females off the street there would be little girls crying for their mothers, and there would be mother-aged women taking care of them. There might be a few older women. This place looked more like—

—oh, God, it looked like one of those slave warehouse places that they had had to pass the last time they had come to the Dark Dimension. The ones that Elena had ordered them not to look at or listen to. But now Bonnie felt sure she was inside one herself, and there was no way not to look at the still faces, at the terrified eyes, at the quivering mouths around her.

She wanted to speak, to find the way—there would *have* to be a way, Elena would insist—to get out. But first she gathered all the Power at her command, wrapped it into a cry, and soundlessly screamed *Damon! Damon! Help! I really need you!*

All she heard in return was silence.

Damon! It's Bonnie! I'm at a slave warehouse! Help!

Suddenly she had a hunch, and lowered her psychic barriers. She was instantly crushed. Even here, at the edge of the city, the air was choked full of long messages and short: cries of impatience, or camaraderie, of greeting, of solicitation. Longer, less impatient conversations about things, instructions, teasings, stories. She couldn't keep up with it. It turned into a menacing wave of psychic sound that was curled like a wave about to break over her head, to crush her into a million pieces.

And then, all of a sudden, the telepathic melee vanished. Bonnie was able to focus her eyes on a blond girl, a little older than her and about four inches taller.

"I said, are you okay?" the girl was repeating—obviously she'd been saying it for a while.

"Yes," Bonnie said automatically. No! Bonnie thought.

"You might want to get ready to move. They've sounded

the first dinnertime whistle, but you looked so out of it, I waited for the second one."

What am I supposed to say? *Thank you* seemed safest. "Thanks," Bonnie said. Then her mouth said all on its own, "Where am I?"

The blond girl looked surprised. "The depot for runaway slaves, of course."

Well, that was that. "But I didn't run away," she protested. "I was going right back after I got a sugarplum."

"I don't know about that. I *was* trying to run away, but they finally caught me." The girl slammed one fist into an open hand. "I knew I shouldn't have trusted that litter carrier. Carried me right to the authorities and me blind and without a clue."

"You mean you had the litter curtains down—?" Bonnie was asking, when a shrill whistle interrupted her. The blond girl took hold of her arm and began dragging her away from the fence. "That's the second service dinnertime whistle—we don't want to miss that, because after that they shut us up for the night. I'm Eren. Who're you?"

"Bonnie."

Eren snorted and grinned. "All right by me."

Bonnie allowed herself to be led up a dirty stairway and into a dirty cafeteria. The blond girl, who seemed to regard herself as Bonnie's keeper, handed her a tray, and pushed her along. Bonnie didn't get any choice in what she was to have, not even to veto the noodles that were squirming slightly, but she did manage to snatch an extra bread roll in the end.

Damon! Nobody was telling her not to send a message, so she kept on doing it. If she was going to be punished, she thought defiantly, she was going to be punished for trying to get out of here. *Damon, I'm in a slave warehouse! Help me!*

Blond Eren grabbed a spork, so Bonnie did too. There were no knives. There were thin napkins, which relieved Bonnie, because that was where the Squirmy Noodles were going to end up.

Without Eren, Bonnie would never have found a place at the tables, which were crammed with young girls eating. "Shove over, shove over," Eren kept saying, until there was room for Bonnie and her.

Dinner was a test of Bonnie's courage—and also of how loud she could scream. "Why are you doing all this for me?" she shouted into Eren's ear, when a lull in the deafening conversation gave her a chance.

"Oh, well, you being a redhead and all—it put me in mind of Aliana's message, you know. To the real Bonny." She pronounced it oddly, sort of swallowing the y, but at least it wasn't Bonna.

"Which of them? Which message, I mean?" Bonnie screamed.

Eren gave her an *are you kidding* look. "Help when you can, shelter when you have room, guide when you know where to go," she said in a sort of impatient chant, then looked chagrined and added, "And be patient with the slow." She attacked her food with an air of having said everything there was to say.

Oh, boy, Bonnie thought. Somebody had really taken the ball and run with it. Elena had never said any of those things.

Yeah, but—but maybe she'd *lived* them, Bonnie thought, a tingling breaking out all over her body. And maybe somebody had seen her and made up the words. For instance, that crazy-looking guy she'd given her ring or bracelet or something to. She'd given her earrings away to people with signs, too. Signs that said: POETRY FOR FOOD.

The rest of dinner was a matter of picking up food with the spork and not looking at it, crunching it once, and then deciding whether to spit into her still-writhing napkin, or to try to swallow without tasting.

Afterward the girls were marched into another building, this one filled with pallets, smaller and not so comfortable-looking as Bonnie's at the inn. She was now horrified at herself for leaving that room. There she had had safety, she had had food that she could actually eat, she had had entertainment—even the Dustbins were clothed in a golden glow of remembrance now—and she had had the chance of Damon finding her. Here she had nothing.

But Eren seemed to have some mesmeric influence on the girls around, or else they all were Aliana-ites too, because when she shouted "Where's a pallet? I've got a new girl in my bedroom. Think she's gonna sleep on the bare floor?" And eventually, a dusty pallet was passed hand over hand into Eren's "bedroom"—a group of pallets all spread with the heads together in the middle. In exchange, Eren handed over the wriggling napkin Bonnie had given her. "Share and share alike," she said firmly, and Bonnie wondered if she thought Aliana had said that, too.

A whistle shrilled. "Ten minutes until lights-out," a hoarse voice shouted. "Every girl not on her pallet in ten minutes will be punished. Tomorrow section C goes up."

"All right! We're going to be bloody deaf before we're sold," Eren muttered.

"Before we're sold?" Bonnie repeated stupidly, even though she had known what would happen from the first moment she had recognized this as a warehouse for slaves.

Eren turned and spat. "Yeah," she said. "So you can have one more breakdown and then that's it. Only two per customer, and by tomorrow you may wish you'd saved one up."

"I wasn't going to have a breakdown," Bonnie said, with all the courage at her command. "I was going to ask how we're going to be sold. Is it at one of those horrible public places, where you have to stand in front of a crowd in just a shift?"

"Yeah, that's what most of us will be doing," a young girl, who had been crying quietly through dinner and the pallet-arranging time, spoke up in a soft voice. "But the ones they pick out as special items will have to wait. They'll give us a bath and special clothes, but it's all just so we look more presentable for the clients. So the clients can *inspect* us more closely." She shuddered.

"You're frightening the new girl, Mouse," Eren scolded. "We call her Mouse, because she's always so scared," she told Bonnie.

Bonnie silently screamed, *Damon!*

Damon was decked out in his new captain of the guard suit. It was nice, being black on black, with lighter black piping (even Damon recognized the necessity of contrast). It had a cloak.

And he was a full vampire again, as powerful and prestigious as even he could have imagined. For a moment he simply luxuriated in the feeling of a job well done. Then he flexed his vampire muscles more strongly, urging Jessalyn, who was upstairs, into deeper sleep, while he sent tendrils of Power all over the Dark Dimension, sampling what was going on in different districts.

Jessalyn . . . now there was a dilemma. Damon had the

feeling that he should leave her a note or something, but he wasn't quite sure what to say.

What could he tell her? That he was gone? She would see that for herself. That he was sorry? Well, obviously he wasn't so sorry that he'd chosen not to go. That he had duties elsewhere?

Wait. That might actually work. He could tell her that he needed to check up on her territory and that if he were to stay here in the castle he doubted he'd ever get anything done. He could tell her he'd be back . . . soon. Soonish. Soonishly.

Damon pressed his tongue against a canine and felt the prompt rewarding sharpness and length. He really wanted to try out those legendary Black Ops vs. vampires programs. He wanted to hunt, period. Of course, there was so much Black Magic wine about the place that when he stopped a male servant and asked for some, the servant had brought a magnum. Damon had been having flutes every now and then, but what he really *wanted* was to go hunting. And not to hunt a slave and certainly not an *animal*, and it hardly seemed fair to wander the streets on the chance that there was a noblewoman to get to know better.

It was at that moment that he remembered Bonnie.

In a matter of three more minutes he had everything he needed to do wrapped up, including the annual delivery of dozens of roses to the princess in his name. Jessalyn had given him a *very* liberal allowance, and already advanced for the first month.

In a matter of five minutes he was flying, though that was very bad manners on the street, and doubly so in a market district.

In a matter of fifteen minutes he had his hands around the landlady's neck, the one whom he had paid very well to make sure that exactly what had happened never happened.

In sixteen minutes, the landlady was grimly offering him the life of her young and not very intelligent slave as recompense. He was still wearing his captain of guard suit. He could have the boy to kill, to torture, whatever . . . he could have the money back . . .

"I don't want your filthy slave," he snarled. "I want my own back! She's worth . . ." Here he came to a stop, trying to calculate how many ordinary girls Bonnie was worth. A hundred? A thousand? "She is worth *infinitely* more—" he began, when the landlady surprised him by interrupting.

"Why'd you leave her in a dump like this, then?" she said. "Oh, yes, I know what my own lodgings are like. If she was so damn precious, why'd you leave her *here*?"

Why *had* he left her in this place? Damon couldn't think now. He'd been panicked, half out of his mind—that was what being human had done to him. He'd been thinking only about himself, while little Bonnie—fragile Bonnie, his little redbird—had been shut up in this filthy place. He didn't want to keep thinking about it. It made him feel searing hot and icy cold at once.

He demanded that a search be made of all the neighborhood buildings. Someone had to have seen something.

Bonnie had been awakened too early and parted from Eren and Mouse. She immediately had an urge to lose control, to have a breakdown at once. She was shivering all over. *Damon! Help me!*

Then she saw a girl who couldn't seem to get up off her pallet and saw a woman with arms like a man's go over with a white ash rod to administer punishment.

And then something seemed to go blank in Bonnie's mind. Elena or Meredith might have tried to stop the woman, or even this huge machine they were caught in, but Bonnie couldn't. The only thing she could do was try not to have a breakdown. She had a song stuck in her head, not even a song she liked, but it repeated endlessly over and over as the slaves around her were dehumanized, broken into mechanical, but clean, mindless bodies.

She was being scrubbed mercilessly by two muscular women whose whole life doubtless consisted of scrubbing grimy street girls into pink cleanliness—at least for a night. But finally her protests led the women to actually look at her—with her fair, almost translucent skin scrubbed raw—and concentrate instead on washing her hair, which felt as if it were being pulled out at the roots. Finally, though, she was done and was given an adequate towel with which to dry off. Next, in what she was realizing was a giant assembly line, were kinder plump women who stripped off the towel and proceeded to put her on a couch and massage her with oil. Just when she was starting to feel better she was hustled up to have the oil removed, except that which had soaked into her skin. Women then appeared who measured her, calling out the numbers as they did, and by the time Bonnie had tramped to the wardrobe station, three dresses were waiting for her on a bar. There was a black one, a green one, and a gray one.

I'll get the green for sure because of my hair, Bonnie thought blankly, but after she had tried all three on, a woman took the green and gray away, leaving Bonnie in a little black bubble dress, strapless, with a glittery touch of white material at the neck.

Next was a giant sanitary room, where her dress was carefully covered with a white paper robe that kept ripping. She was led to a chair with a hair dryer and the rudiments of makeup, which a white-shirted woman used to put too much on Bonnie's face. Then the hair dryer was swung over her head, and Bonnie, with a stolen tissue, took off as much makeup as she dared. She didn't want to look good, didn't want to be sold. When she finished she had silvery eyelids, a touch of blush, and velvety rose-red lipstick that wouldn't wipe off.

After that she just sat and finger-combed her hair until it was dry, which the ancient machine announced with a *ping.*

The next station was a bit like the day after Thanksgiving at a big shoe store. The stronger or more determined girls managed to wrench shoes away from their weaker sisters and jammed them on one foot, only to start the process again the next minute. Bonnie was lucky. She saw a tiny black shoe that had a faintly silvery bow coming down the ramp and kept her eye on it while it passed from girl to girl until someone dropped it and then she swooped in and tried it on. She didn't know what she would have done if it hadn't fit. But it did fit, and she went to the next station to get its mate. As she sat waiting, other girls were trying on perfume. Bonnie saw two entire bottles go down the bodices of girls and wondered if they meant to sell them or try to poison themselves with them. There were also flowers. Bonnie was already dizzy with perfume and had decided not to wear any, but a tall woman bellowed over her head and a garland of freesia was pinned to frame her curls, without anyone asking her permission.

The last station was the hardest to bear. She had on no jewelry and would have worn only one bracelet with the dress. But she was given two: slim unbreakable plastic bracelets, each with a number on it—her identity from now on, she was told.

Slave bracelets. She had now been washed, packaged, and stamped, so that she could be conveniently sold.

Damon! she cried voicelessly, but something had died inside her, and she knew now that her calls would not be answered.

"She was picked up as a runaway slave and confiscated," the sweetshop man told Damon impatiently. "And that's all I know."

Damon was left with a feeling he didn't often have. Sickening terror. He was really beginning to believe that this time he had cut it too fine; that he would be too late to save his redbird. That any of several dreadful scenarios might have played out before he got to her.

He couldn't stand to visualize them in detail. What he would do if he didn't find her in time . . .

He reached out and without the slightest effort gripped the sweetshop man around the throat, lifting him off the floor.

"We need to have a little chat," he said, turning the full force of his menacing dark eyes on the bulging ones of his prey. "About just *how* she got confiscated. Don't struggle. If you haven't hurt the girl, you've got nothing to fear. If you have . . ."

He pulled the terrified man completely across the

counter and said very softly, "If you have, then, by all means struggle. It won't make any difference in the end—if you know what I mean?"

The girls were put into the largest carriages Bonnie had yet seen in the Dark Dimension, three slim girls to a seat and two sets of seats in a carriage. She got a nasty jolt, though, when instead of going forward like a carriage, the whole thing was lifted straight up by sweaty male slaves straining at poles. It was a giant litter and Bonnie immediately snatched off her freesia garland and buried her nose in it. It had the added function of hiding her tears.

"Do you have any idea of how many homes and dancing rooms and halls and theaters there are where girls are being sold tonight?" The golden-haired Guardian looked at him sardonically.

"If I knew that," Damon said with a cold and ominous smile, "I wouldn't be here asking you."

The Guardian shrugged. "Our job is really only to try to keep the peace here—and you can see how well we succeed. It's a matter of too few of us; we're insanely understaffed. But I can give you a list of the venues where girls are being sold. Still, as I said, I doubt you'll be able to find your runaway before morning. And by the way, we'll have an eye on you, because of your little query. If your runaway wasn't a slave, she's Imperial property—no humans are free here. If she was, and you freed her, as reported by the baker across the street—"

"Sweet-seller."

"Whatever. Then he had a right to use a stun gun when she ran. Better for her, really, than being Imperial property; they tend to char, if you get my drift. That level's a long way down."

"But if she was a slave—*my* slave . . ."

"Then you can have her. But there's a certain mandatory punishment set *before* you can have her. We want to discourage this kind of thing."

Damon looked at her with eyes that made her shrink and look away, abruptly losing her authority. "Why?" he demanded. "I thought you claimed to be from the other Court. You know. The Celestial one?"

"We want to discourage runaways because there've been so many since some girl named Alianna came around," the Guardian said, her frightened pulse visible in her temple. "And then they get caught and have even more reason to try it again . . . and it wears out the girl, eventually."

There was no one in the Great Hall when Bonnie and the others were hustled off the giant litter and into the building.

"It's a new one, so it's not on the lists," Mouse said, unexpectedly at her shoulder. "Not that many people will know about it, so it doesn't fill up till late, when the music gets loud."

Mouse seemed to be clinging to her for comfort. That was fine, but Bonnie needed some comfort of her own. The next minute she saw Eren and, dragging Mouse behind her, headed for the blond girl.

Eren was standing with her back against the wall. "Well, we can stand around like wallflowers," she said, as a few men came in, "or we can look like we're having the best time of any of them right here by ourselves. Who knows a story?"

"Oh, I do," Bonnie said absently, thinking of the star ball with its *Five Hundred Stories for Young Ones.*

Instantly there was a clamor. "Tell it!" "Yes, please tell!"

Bonnie tried to think of the fairy tales that she had experienced.

Of course. The one about the kitsune treasure.

16

"Once upon a time," began Bonnie, "there were a young girl and boy . . ."

She was immediately interrupted. "What were their names?" "Were they slaves?" "Where did they live?" "Were they vampires?"

Bonnie almost forgot her misery and laughed. "Their names were . . . Jack and . . . Jill. They were kitsune, and they lived way up north in the kitsune sector around the Great Crossings . . ." And she proceeded, albeit with many excited interruptions, to tell the story she had gotten from the star ball.

"So," Bonnie concluded nervously, as she opened her eyes and realized that she'd attracted quite a crowd with her story, "that's the tale of the Seven Treasures, and—and I suppose the moral is—don't be too greedy, or you won't end up with anything."

There was a lot of laughter, the nervous giggling of the girls and the "Haw! Haw haw!" kind of laughter from the crowd behind them. Which Bonnie now noticed was entirely male.

One part of her mind started unconsciously to go into flirt mode. Another part immediately squashed it. These weren't boys looking for a dance; these were ogres and vampires and kitsune and even men with mustaches—and they wanted to *buy* her in her little black bubble dress, and as nice as the dress might be for some things, it wasn't like the long, jeweled gowns that Lady Ulma had made for them. Then they had been princesses, wearing a fortune's worth of jewels at their throats and wrists and hair—and besides, they had had fierce protection with them at all times.

But now, she was wearing something that felt a lot like a baby-doll nightgown and delicate little shoes with silvery bows. And she wasn't protected because this society said you had to have men to be protected, and, worst of all . . . she was a slave.

"I wonder," said a golden-haired man, moving through the girls around her, all of whom hurried out of his way except Mouse and Eren, "I wonder if you would go upstairs with me and perhaps tell *me* a story—in private."

Bonnie tried to swallow her gasp. Now she was the one

hanging on to Mouse and Eren.

"All such requests must go through me. No one is to take a girl out of the room unless I approve," announced a woman in a full-length dress, with a sympathetic, almost Madonna-like face. "That will be treated as theft of my mistress's property. And I'm sure we don't all want to be arrested as if we'd been caught carrying off the silverware," she said and laughed lightly.

There was equally light laughter among the guests as well, and movement toward the woman—at a sort of mannerly run.

"You tell really good stories," Mouse said in her soft voice. "It's more fun than using a star ball."

"Mouse, here, is right," Eren said, grinning. "You do tell good stories. I wonder if that place really exists."

"Well, I *got* it out of a star ball," Bonnie said. "One that the girl—um, Jill, put her memories in, I think—but then how did it get out of that tower? How did she know what happened to Jack? And I read a story about a giant dragon and *that* felt real too. How do they do it?"

"Oh, they trick you," Eren said, waving a dismissive hand. "They have somebody go someplace cold for the scenery—an ogre probably, because of the weather."

Bonnie nodded. She'd met mauve-skinned ogres before. They only differed from demons in their level of stupidity. At this level, they tended to be stupid in society, and she'd heard Damon say with a curled lip that the ones that were out of society were hired muscle. Thugs.

"And the rest they just fake somehow—I don't know. Never really thought about it." Eren looked up at Bonnie. "You're an odd one, aren't you, Bonny?"

"Am I?" Bonnie asked. She and the two other girls had revolved, without letting go of hands. This meant that there was some space behind Bonnie. She didn't like that. But, then, she didn't like anything about being a slave. She was starting to hyperventilate. She wanted Meredith. She wanted Elena. She wanted *out of here.*

"Um, you guys probably don't want to associate with me anymore," she said uncomfortably.

"Huh?" said Eren.

"Why?" asked Mouse.

"Because I'm running through that door. I have to get out. I have to."

"Kid, calm down," Eren said. "Just keep breathing."

"No, you don't understand." Bonnie put her head down, to shade out some of the world. "I can't *belong* to somebody. I'm going crazy."

"Sh, Bonny, they're—"

"I can't *stay* here," Bonnie burst out.

"Well, that's probably all to the good," a terrible voice, right in front of her, said.

No! Oh, God. No, no, no, no, no!

"When we're in a new business we work hard," the Madonna-like woman's voice said. "We look up at prospective customers. We don't misbehave or we are punished." And even though her voice was sweet as pecan pie, Bonnie somehow knew that the harsh voice in the night shouting at them to find a pallet and stay on it, had been this same woman.

And now there was a strong hand under her chin and Bonnie couldn't keep it from forcing her head up, or from covering her mouth when she screamed.

In front of her, with the delicate pointed ears of a fox, and the long sweeping black tail of a fox but otherwise looking human, looking like a regular guy wearing jeans and a sweater, was Shinichi. And in his golden eyes she could see, twisting and turning, a little scarlet flame that just matched the red on the tip of his tail and the hair that fell across his forehead.

Shinichi. He was here. Of course he could travel through the dimensions; he still had a full star ball that none of Elena's group had ever found as well as those magical keys Elena had told Bonnie about. Bonnie remembered the horrible night when trees, actual trees, had turned into something that could understand and obey him. About how four of them each grabbed one of her arms and legs and pulled, as if they were planning to pull her apart. She could feel tears leaking out behind her shut eyelids.

And the Old Wood. He'd controlled every aspect of it, every creeper to trip you, every tree to fall in front of your car. Until Elena had blasted all but that one thicket of the Old Wood, it had been full of terrifying insect-like creatures Stefan called malach.

But now Bonnie's hands were behind her back and she heard something fasten with a very final-sounding click.

No . . . oh, please no . . .

But her hands were definitely fixed in place. And then someone—an ogre or a vampire—picked her up as the lovely woman gave Shinichi a small key off a key ring full of identical keys. Shinichi handed this to a big ogre whose fingers were so large that they eclipsed it. And then Bonnie, who was screaming, was quickly whisked up four flights of stairs and a heavy door thunked shut behind her. The ogre carrying her followed Shinichi, whose sleek scarlet-tipped tail swung jauntily from a hole in his jeans, back and forth, back and forth. Bonnie thought: That's satisfaction. He thinks he's won this already.

But unless Damon really had forgotten her completely, he would hurt Shinichi for this. Maybe he would kill him. It was an oddly comforting thought. It was even ro—

No, it's not romantic, you nitwit! You have to find a way to get out of this mess! Death is not romantic, it's horrible!

They had reached the final doors at the end of the hall.

Shinichi turned right and walked all the way down a long corridor. There the ogre used the key to open a door.

The room had an adjustable overhead gaslight. It was dim but Shinichi said, "Can we have a little illumination, please?" in a false polite voice, and the other ogre hurried and turned the light up to interrogation-lamp-in-your-face level.

The room was a sort of bedroom-den combination, the kind you'd get at a decent hotel. It had a couch and some chairs on the upper level. There was a window, closed, on the left side of the room. There was also a window on the right side of the room, where all the other rooms should be in a line. This window had no curtains or blinds that could be drawn and it reflected Bonnie's pale face back at her. She knew at once what it was, a two-way mirror, so that people in the room behind it could see into this room but not *be* seen. The couch and chairs were positioned to face it.

Beyond the sitting room, off to her left, was the bed. It wasn't a very fancy bed, just white covers that looked pink, because there was a real window on that side that was almost in a line with the sun, sitting as it always was, on the horizon. Right now, Bonnie hated it more than ever before because it turned every light-colored object in the room pink, rose, or outright red. The bow at her own bodice was deep pink now. She was going to die saturated with the color of blood.

Something on some deeper level told her that her mind was thinking of such things as distractions, that even thinking about hating to die in such a juvenile color was running away from the bit in the middle, the dying bit. But the ogre holding her moved her around as if she weighed nothing, and Bonnie kept having little thoughts—were they premonitions? Oh, God, let them not be premonitions!—about going out of that red window in a sitting position, the glass no impediment to her body being thrown at a tremendous force. And how many stories up were they? High enough, anyway, that there was no hope of landing without . . . well, dying.

Shinichi smiled, lounging by the red window, playing with the cord to the blinds.

"I don't even know what you want from me!" Bonnie found herself saying to Shinichi. "I've never been able to hurt you. It was you hurting other people—like me!—all the time."

"Well, there were your friends," murmured Shinichi. "Although I seldom wreak my dread revenge against lovely young women with red-gold hair." He lounged beside the window and examined her, murmuring, "Hair of red-gold; heart true and bold. Perhaps a scold . . ."

Bonnie felt like screaming. Didn't he remember her? He certainly seemed to have remembered their group, since he'd mentioned revenge. "What do you *want*?" she gasped.

"You are a hindrance, I'm afraid. And I find you very suspicious—and delicious. Young women with red-gold hair are always so elusive."

Bonnie couldn't find anything to say. From everything she'd seen, Shinichi was a nutcase. But a very dangerous psychopathic nutcase. And all he enjoyed was destroying things.

In just one moment there could be a crash through the window—and then she'd be sitting on air. And then the fall would begin. What would that feel like? Or would she already be falling? She only hoped that at the bottom it was quick.

"You seem to have learned a lot about *my* people," Shinichi said. "More than most."

"Please," Bonnie said desperately. "If it's about the story—all I know about kitsune is that you're destroying my town. And—" She stopped short, realizing that she could never let him know what had happened in her out-of-body experience. So she could never mention the jars or he'd know that they knew how to catch him. "And you won't stop," she finished lamely.

"And yet you found an ancient star ball with stories about our legendary treasures."

"About what? You mean from that kiddy star ball?

Look, if you'll just leave me alone I'll *give* it to you." She knew exactly where she'd left it, too, right beside her sorry excuse for a pillow.

"Oh, we'll leave you alone . . . in time, I assure you," Shinichi said with an unnerving smile. He had a smile like Damon's, which wasn't meant to say "Hello; I won't hurt you." It was more like "Hullo! Here's my lunch!"

"I find it . . . curious," Shinichi went on, still fiddling with the cord. "Very curious that just in the middle of our little dispute, you arrive here in the Dark Dimension again, alone, apparently without fear, and manage to bargain for a star ball. An orb that just happens to detail the location of our most priceless treasures that were stolen from us . . . a long, long time ago."

You don't care about anybody but yourself, Bonnie thought. You're suddenly acting all patriotic and stuff, but in Fell's Church you didn't pretend to care about anything but hurting people.

"In your little town, as in other towns throughout history, I had orders to do what I did," Shinichi said, and Bonnie's heart plunged right down to her shoes. He was telepathic. He knew what she was thinking. He'd heard her thinking about the jars.

Shinichi smirked. "Little towns like the one on Unmei no Shima have to be wiped off the face of the earth," he said. "Did you see the number of ley lines of Power under *it*?" Another smirk. "But of course you weren't *really* there, so you probably didn't."

"If you can tell what I'm thinking, you know that story about treasures was just a story," Bonnie said. "It was in the star ball called *Five Hundred Stories for Young Ones*. It's not *real*."

"How strange then that it coincides so exactly with what the Seven Kitsune Gates are supposed to have behind them."

"It was in the middle of a bunch of stories about the—the Düz-Aht-Bhi'iens. I mean the story right before it was about a kid buying candy," Bonnie said. "So why don't you just go get the star ball instead of trying to scare me?" Her voice was beginning to tremble. "It's at the inn right across the street from the shop where I was—arrested. Just go and *get* it!"

"Of course we've tried that," Shinichi said impatiently. "The landlady was quite cooperative after we gave her some . . . compensation. There is no such story in that star ball."

"That's not possible!" Bonnie said. "Where did I get it, then?"

"That's what *I'm* asking *you*."

Stomach fluttering, Bonnie said, "How many star balls did you look at in that brown room?"

Shinichi's eyes went blurry briefly. Bonnie tried to

listen, but he was obviously speaking telepathically to someone close, on a tight frequency.

Finally he said, "Twenty-eight star balls, exactly."

Bonnie felt as if she'd been clubbed. She *wasn't* going crazy—she *wasn't*. She'd experienced that story. She knew every fissure in every rock, every shadow in the snow. The only answers were that the real star ball had been stolen, or—or maybe that they hadn't looked hard enough at the ones they had.

"The story is there," she insisted. "Right before it is the story about little Marit going to a—"

"We probed the table of contents. There is the story about a child and"—he looked scornful—"a sweetshop. But not the other."

Bonnie just shook her head. "I *swear* I'm telling the truth."

"Why should I believe you?"

"Why does it *matter*? How could I make something like that up? And why would I tell a story I *knew* would get me in trouble? It doesn't make any sense."

Shinichi stared at her hard. Then he shrugged, his ears flat against his head. "What a pity you keep saying that."

Suddenly Bonnie's heart was pounding in her chest, in her tight throat. "Why?"

"Because," Shinichi said coolly, pulling the blinds completely open so that Bonnie was abruptly drenched in the color of fresh blood, "I'm afraid that now we have to kill you."

The ogre holding her strode toward the window. Bonnie screamed. In places like this, she knew screams went unheard.

She didn't know what else to do.

17

Meredith and Matt were sitting at the breakfast table, which seemed sadly empty without Bonnie. It was amazing how much space that slight body had seemed to fill, and how much more serious everyone was without her. Meredith knew that if Elena had done her best, she could have offset it. But she also knew that Elena had one thing on her mind above all others, and that was Stefan, who was stricken with guilt for allowing his brother to abduct Bonnie. And meanwhile Meredith knew that both she and Matt were feeling guilty too, because today they would be leaving the other three, even if only for the evening. They each had been summoned home by parents who demanded to see them for dinner.

Mrs. Flowers clearly didn't want them to feel too badly.

"With the help you've given, I can make our urns," she said. "Since Matt has found my wheel—"

"I didn't exactly find it," Matt said under his breath. "It was there in the storage room all the time and it fell on me."

"—and since Meredith has received her pictures—along, I'm sure, with an email from Mr. Saltzman—perhaps she could get them enlarged or whatever."

"Of course, and show them to the Saitous, too, to make sure that the symbols say the things we want them to," Meredith promised. "And Bonnie can—"

She broke off short. Idiot! She was an idiot, she thought. And, as a hunter-slayer, she was supposed to be clear-minded and at all times maintain control. She felt terrible when she looked at Matt and saw the naked pain in his face.

"Dear Bonnie will surely be home soon," Mrs. Flowers finished for her.

And we all know that's a lie, and I don't have to be psychic to detect it, Meredith thought. She noticed that Mrs. Flowers hadn't weighed in with anything from Ma*ma*.

"We'll all be just fine here," Elena said, finally picking up the ball as she realized that Mrs. Flowers was looking at her with ladylike distress. "You two think we're some kind of babies who need to be taken care of," she said, smiling at Matt and Meredith, "but you're just babies too!

Off you go! But be careful."

They went, Meredith giving Elena one last glance. Elena nodded very slightly, then turned stiffly, mimicking holding a bayonet. It was the changing of the guard.

Elena let Stefan help her clean up the dishes—they were all letting him do little things now because he looked so much better. They spent the morning trying to contact Bonnie in different ways. But then Mrs. Flowers asked if Elena could board up the last few of the basement windows, and Stefan couldn't stand it. Matt and Meredith had already done a far more dangerous job. They'd hung two tarps from the house's ridgepole, each one hanging down one side of the main roof. On each tarp were the characters that Isobel's mother put on the Post-it Note amulets she always gave them, painted at an enormous scale in black paint. Stefan had been allowed only to watch and give suggestions from the widow's walk above his attic bedroom. But now . . .

"We'll nail up the boards together," he said firmly, and went off to get a hammer and nails.

It wasn't really such a hard job anyway. Elena held the boards and Stefan wielded the hammer and she trusted him not to hit her fingers, which meant that they got on very quickly.

It was a perfect day—clear, sunny, with a slight breeze.

Elena wondered what was happening to Bonnie, *right* now, and if Damon was taking care of her properly—or at all. She seemed unable to shake off her worries these last days: over Stefan, over Bonnie, and over a curious feeling that she *had* to know what was going on in town. Maybe she could disguise herself . . .

God, no! Stefan said voicelessly. When she turned he was spitting out nails and looking both horrified and ashamed. Apparently she'd been projecting.

"I'm sorry," he said before Elena could get the nails out of *her* mouth, "but you know better than anyone why you can't go."

"But it's *maddening* not knowing what's happening," Elena said, having gotten rid of *her* nails. "We don't know anything. What's happening to Bonnie, what state the town's in—"

"Let's finish this board," Stefan said. "And then let me hold you."

When the last board was secure, Stefan raised her from the lower embankment where she was sitting, not bride-style, but kid-style, putting her toes on top of his feet. He danced her a little, whirled her a couple of times in the air, and then nabbed her coming down again.

"I know your problem," he said soberly.

Elena looked up quickly. "You do?" she said, alarmed.

Stefan nodded, and to her further alarm said, "It's

Love-itis. Means the patient has a whole slew of people she cares about, and she can't be happy unless each and every one of them is safe and happy themselves."

Elena deliberately slipped off his shoes and looked up at him. "Some more than others," she said hesitantly.

Stefan looked down at her and then he took her in his arms. "I'm not as good as you," he said while Elena's heart pounded in shame and remorse for ever having touched Damon, ever having danced with him, ever having kissed him. "If *you* are happy, that's all I want, after that prison. I can live; I can die . . . peacefully."

"If *we're* happy," Elena corrected.

"I won't tempt the gods. I'll settle for *you*."

"No, you can't! Don't you see? If you disappeared again, I'd worry and fret and follow you. To Hell if I had to."

"I'll take you with me wherever I go," Stefan said hastily. "If you'll take me with *you*."

Elena relaxed slightly. That would do, for now. As long as Stefan was with her she could stand anything.

They sat and cuddled, right under the open sky, even with a maple tree and a clump of slender waving beeches nearby. She extended her aura a little and felt it touch Stefan's. Peace flooded into her, and all the dark thoughts were left behind. *Almost* all.

"Since I first saw you, I loved you—but it was the wrong kind of love. See how long it took me to figure that out?" Elena whispered into the hollow of his throat.

"Since I first saw you, I loved *you*—but I didn't know who you really were. You were like a ghost in a dream. But you put me straight pretty quickly," Stefan said, obviously glad that he could brag about her. "And we've survived—everything. They say long-distance relationships can be pretty difficult," he added, laughing, and then he stopped, and she could feel all his faculties fixed on her suddenly, breath stopping so he could hear her better.

"But then, there's Bonnie and Damon," he said before she could say or think a word. "We have to find them soon—and they'd damn well better be together—or it had better have been Bonnie's decision to part."

"There's Bonnie and Damon," agreed Elena, glad that she could share even her darkest thoughts with someone. "I can't think about them. I can't *not* think about them. We *do* have to find them, and *very* fast—but I pray that they're with Lady Ulma now. Maybe Bonnie is going to a ball or gala. Maybe Damon is hunting with that Black Ops program."

"As long as nobody's really hurt."

"Yes." Elena tried hard to tuck herself closer to Stefan. She wanted to—be closer to him, somehow. The way they had when she had been out of her body and she had just sunk into him.

But of course, with regular bodies, they couldn't . . .

But of course they *could*. Now. Her blood . . .

Elena really didn't know which of them thought of it first. She looked away, embarrassed at even having considered it—and caught the tail end of Stefan looking away too.

"I don't think we have the right," she whispered. "Not to—be that happy—when everyone else is miserable. Or doing things for the town or for Bonnie."

"Of course we don't," Stefan said firmly, but he had to gulp a little first.

"No," Elena said.

"No," Stefan said firmly, and then right in the middle of her echoing "no," he went and pulled her up and kissed her breathless.

And of course, Elena couldn't let him do that and not get even. So she demanded, still breathless, but almost angry, that he say "no" again, and when he did it she caught *him* and kissed him.

"You were happy," she accused a moment later. "I felt it."

Stefan was too much of a gentleman to accuse her of being happy because of anything she might do. He said, "I couldn't help it. It just happened by itself. I felt our minds together, and that made me happy. But then I remembered about poor Bonnie. And—"

"Poor Damon?"

"Well, somehow I don't think we need to go so far as to call him 'poor Damon.' But I did remember him," he said.

"Well done," Elena said.

"We'd better go inside now," Stefan said. And then hastily, "Downstairs, I mean. Maybe we can think of something more to do for them."

"Like *what*? There's not a thing *I* can think of. I did meditation and Attempt to Contact by Out-of-Body Experience—"

"From nine thirty to ten thirty A.M.," Stefan said. "And meanwhile I was trying all frequency telepathic calls. No response."

"Then we tried with the Ouija board."

"For half an hour—and all we got was nonsense."

"It did tell us the clay was coming."

"I think that was me bumping it toward 'yes.' "

"Then I tried to tap into the ley lines below us for Power—"

"From eleven to around eleven thirty," Stefan recited. "While I tried to go into hibernation to have a prophetic dream. . . ."

"We *really* tried hard," Elena said grimly.

"And then we nailed the last few boards up," Stefan added. "Bringing us to a little after twelve thirty P.M."

"Can you think of a single Plan—we're down to G or H now—that might allow us to help them any more?"

"I can't. I just honestly can't," Stefan said. Then he added, hesitantly, "Maybe Mrs. Flowers has some housework for us. Or"—even more hesitantly, testing the waters—"we could go into town."

"No! You're definitely not strong enough for that!" Elena said sharply. "And there's no more housework," she added. Then she threw everything to the wind. Every responsibility. Every rationality. Just like that. She began to tow Stefan to the house so they could get there quicker.

"Elena—"

I'm burning my bridges! Elena thought stubbornly, and suddenly she didn't care. And if Stefan cared she would *bite* him. But it was as if some spell had suddenly come over her so that she felt she would die without his touch. She wanted to touch him. She wanted him to touch her. She wanted him to be her mate.

"Elena!" Stefan could hear what she was thinking. He was torn, of course, Elena thought. Stefan was always torn. But how dare he be torn about *this*?

She turned around to face him, blazing. "You don't want to!"

"I don't want to do it and then find out I've Influenced you into it!"

"You were *Influencing* me?" shouted Elena.

Stefan threw out his hands and yelled, "How can I know when I want you so much?"

Oh. Well, that was better. There was a little glitter in Elena's side-eye and she looked at it and realized that Mrs. Flowers had quietly shut a window.

Elena darted a glance at Stefan. He was trying not to blush. She doubled over, trying not to laugh. Then she stood on his shoes again.

"Maybe we *deserve* an hour alone"—dangerously.

"A whole hour?" Stefan's conspiratorial whisper made an hour sound like eternity.

"We *do* deserve it," Elena said, enthralled. She began to tow him again.

"No." Stefan pulled her back, lifted her—bridal-style—and suddenly they were going straight up, fast. They shot up three stories and a little more and landed on the platform of the widow's walk above his room.

"But it's locked from inside—"

Stefan stomped on the trapdoor—hard. The door disappeared.

Elena was impressed.

They floated down into Stefan's room amid a shaft of light and motes of dust that looked like fireflies or stars.

"I'm a little nervous," Elena said.

She heeled her sandals off and slid out of her jeans and top and into bed . . . only to find Stefan already there.

They're faster, she thought. As fast as you think you are, they're always faster.

She turned toward Stefan in the bed. She was wearing a camisole and underwear. She was scared.

"Don't," he said. "I don't even have to bite you."

"You do so. It's all that weird stuff about my blood."

"Oh, yeah," he said, as if he'd forgotten. Elena would bet that he hadn't forgotten a word about her blood . . . allowing vampires to do things they couldn't otherwise. Her life energy gave them back all their human abilities, and he wouldn't forget that.

They're smarter, she thought.

"Stefan, it's not supposed to be like this! I'm supposed to parade in front of you in a golden negligee designed by Lady Ulma, with jewels by Lucen and golden stilts—which I don't own. And there are supposed to be scattered flower petals on the bed and roses in little round bubble bowls and white vanilla candles."

"Elena," Stefan said, "come here."

She went into his arms, and let herself breathe in the fresh smell of him, warm and spicy, with a trace of rusty nails.

You're my life, Stefan told her silently. *We're not going to do anything today. There's not much time, and you deserve your golden negligee and your roses and candles. If not from Lady Ulma, from the finest Earth designers that money can provide. But . . . kiss me?*

Elena kissed him willingly, so glad that he was willing

to wait. The kiss was warm and comforting and she didn't mind the slight taste of rust. And it was wonderful to be with someone who would provide exactly what she needed, whether that was a slight mind probe, just to make her feel safer, or . . .

And then sheet lightning hit them. It seemed to come from both of them at once, and then Elena involuntarily clamped her teeth on Stefan's lip, drawing blood.

Stefan locked his arms around her, and barely waited for her to back off a little, before deliberately taking her lower lip in his own teeth and . . . after a moment of tension that seemed to last forever . . . biting down hard.

Elena almost cried out. She almost then and there unleashed the still-undefined *Wings of Destruction* on him. But two things stopped her. One, Stefan had never, ever hurt her before. And, two, she was being drawn into something so ancient and mystical that she *couldn't* stop now.

A minute of finessing and Stefan had the two little wounds aligned. Blood surged from Elena's bleeding lip and, in direct connection with Stefan's less serious wound, caused a backflow. Her blood into his lip.

And the same thing happened with Stefan's blood; some of it, rich with Power, rushed into Elena.

It wasn't perfect. A bead of blood swelled and stood gleaming on Elena's lip. But Elena couldn't have cared less. A moment later the bead dropped down into Stefan's mouth and she felt the sheer staggering power of how much he loved her.

She herself was concentrating on one single tiny feeling, somewhere in the center of this storm they'd called up. This kind of exchange of blood—she was sure as she could be—this was the old way, the way that two vampires could share blood and love and their souls. She was being drawn into Stefan's mind. She felt his soul, pure and unconstrained, swirling around her with a thousand different emotions, tears from his past, joy from the present, all open without a trace of a shield from her.

She felt her own soul lift to meet his, herself unshielded and unafraid. Stefan had long ago seen any selfishness, vanity, over-ambition in her—and forgiven it. He'd seen all of her and loved all of her, even the bad parts.

And so she saw him, as darkness as tender as rest, as gentle as evensong, wrapping black protective wings around her . . .

Stefan, I . . .

Love . . . I know . . .

That was when someone knocked on the door.

18

After breakfast Matt went online to find two stores, neither in Fell's Church, that had the amount of clay Mrs. Flowers said she'd need and that said they'd deliver. But after that there was the matter of driving away from the boardinghouse and by the last lonely remains of where the Old Wood had been. He drove by the little thicket where Shinichi often came like a demonic Pied Piper with the possessed children shuffling behind him—the place where Sheriff Mossberg had gone after them and hadn't come out. Where, later, protected by magical wards on Post-it Notes, he and Tyrone Alpert had pulled out a bare, chewed femur.

Today, he figured the only way to get past the thicket was to work his wheezing junk car up by stages, and it was actually going over sixty when he flew by the thicket, even managing to hit the turn perfectly. No trees fell on him, no swarms of foot-long bugs.

He whispered "Whoa," in relief and headed for home. He dreaded that—but simply driving through Fell's Church was so horrible it glued his tongue to the top of his mouth. It looked—this pretty, innocent little town where he had grown up—as if it were one of those neighborhoods you saw on TV or on the Internet that had been bombed, or something. And whether it was bombs or disasterous fires, one house in four was simply rubble. A few were half-rubble, with police tape enclosing them, which meant that whatever had happened had happened early enough for the police to care—or dare. Around the burned-out bits the vegetation flourished strangely: a decorative bush from one house grown so as to be halfway across a neighbor's grass. Vines dipping from one tree to another, to another, as if this were some ancient jungle.

His home was right in the middle of a long block of houses full of kids—and in summer, when grandchildren inevitably came to visit, there were even *more* kids. Matt just hoped that that part of summer vacation was done . . . but would Shinichi and Misao let the youngsters go home? Matt had no idea. And, if they went home, would they keep spreading the disease in their own hometowns? Where did it stop?

Driving down his block, though, Matt saw nothing

hideous. There were kids playing out on the front lawns, or the sidewalks, crouching over marbles, hanging out in the trees. There was no single overt thing that he could put his finger on that was weird.

He was still uneasy. But he'd reached his house now, the one with a grand old oak tree shading the porch, so he had to get out. He coasted to a stop just under the tree and parked by the sidewalk. He grabbed a large laundry bag from the backseat. He'd been accumulating dirty clothes for a couple of weeks at the boardinghouse and it hadn't seemed fair to ask Mrs. Flowers to wash them.

As he got out of the car, pulling the bag out with him, he was just in time to hear the birdsong stop.

For a moment after it did, he wondered what was wrong. He knew that something was missing, cut short. It made the air heavier. It even seemed to change the smell of the grass.

Then he realized. Every bird, including the raucous crows that lived in the oak trees, had gone silent.

All at once.

Matt felt a twisting in his belly as he looked up and around. There were two kids in the oak tree right beside his car. His mind was still stubbornly trying to hang on to: Children. Playing. Okay. His body was smarter. His hand was already in his pocket, pulling out a pad of Post-it

Notes: the flimsy bits of paper that usually stopped evil magic cold.

Matt hoped Meredith would remember to ask Isobel's mother for more amulets. He was running low, and . . .

. . . and there were two kids playing in the old oak tree. Except they weren't. They were staring at him. One boy was hanging upside down by his knees and the other was gobbling something . . . out of a garbage bag.

The hanging kid was staring at him with strangely acute eyes. "Have you ever wondered what it's like to be dead?" he asked.

And now the head of the gobbling boy came up, thick bright red all around his mouth. Bright red—

—*blood.* And . . . whatever was in the garbage bag was moving. Kicking. Thrashing weakly. Trying to get away.

A wave of nausea washed over Matt. Acid hit his throat. He was going to puke. The gobbling kid was staring at him with stony black-as-a-pit eyes. The hanging kid was smiling.

Then, as if stirred by a hot breath of wind, Matt felt the fine hairs on the back of his neck stand up. It wasn't just the birds that had gone quiet. Everything had. No child's voice was raised in argument or song or speech.

He whirled around and saw why. They were staring at *him*. Every single kid on the block was silently watching him. Then, with a chilling precision, as he turned back to look at the boys in the tree, all the others came toward him.

Except they weren't walking.

They were creeping. Lizard-fashion. That's why some of them had seemed to be playing with marbles on the sidewalk. They were all moving in the same way, bellies close to the ground, elbows up, hands like forepaws, knees splaying to the side.

Now he could taste bile. He looked the other way down the street and found another group creeping. Grinning unnatural grins. It was as if someone was pulling their cheeks from behind them, pulling them *hard*, so that their grins almost broke their faces in half.

Matt noticed something else. Suddenly they'd stopped, and while he stared at them, they stayed still. Perfectly still, staring back at him. But when he looked away, he saw the creeping figures out of the corner of his eye.

He didn't have enough Post-it Notes for all of them.

You can't run away from this. It sounded like an outside voice in his head. Telepathy. But maybe that was because Matt's head had turned into a roiling red cloud, floating upward.

Fortunately, his body heard it and suddenly he was up on the back of his car, and had grabbed the hanging kid. For a moment he had a helpless impulse to let go of the boy. The kid still stared at him but with eerie, uncanny eyes that were half rolled back in his head. Instead of dropping him, Matt slapped a Post-It Note on the boy's forehead, swinging him at the same time to sit on the back of the car.

A pause and then wailing. The kid must be fourteen at least, but about thirty seconds after the Ban Against Evil (pocket-size) was smacked on him he was sobbing real kid sobs.

As one, the crawling kids let out a hiss. It was like a giant steam engine. *Hsssssssssssssssssssssss.*

They began to breathe in and out very fast, as if working up to some new state. Their creeping slowed to a crawl. But they were breathing so hard Matt could see their sides hollow and fill.

As Matt turned to look at one group of them, they froze, except for the unnatural breathing. But he could feel the ones behind him getting closer.

By now Matt's heart was pounding in his ears. He could fight a group of them—but not with a group on his back. Some of them looked only ten or eleven. Some looked almost his age. Some were girls, for God's sake. Matt remembered what possessed girls had done the last time he'd met them and felt violent revulsion.

But he knew that looking up at the gobbling kid was going to make him sicker. He could hear smacking, chewing sounds—and he could hear a thin little whistle of helpless pain and weak struggling against the bag.

He whirled quickly again, to keep off the other side

of crawlers, and then made himself look up. With a quiet crackle, the garbage bag fell away when he grabbed it but the kid held on to what was in—

Oh my God. He's eating a baby! A baby! A—

He yanked the kid out of the tree and his hand automatically slapped a Post-It onto the boy's back. And then—then, thank God, he saw the fur. It wasn't a baby. It was too small to be a baby, even a newborn. But it was eaten.

The kid raised his bloody face to Matt's, and Matt saw that it was Cole Reece, Cole who was only thirteen and lived right next door. Matt hadn't even recognized him before.

Cole's mouth was wide open in horror now, and his eyes were bulging out of his head with terror and sorrow, and tears and snot were streaming down his face.

"He made me eat Toby," he started in a whisper that became a scream. "He made me eat my guinea pig! He made me—*why why why did he do that*? *I ATE* TOBY*!*"

He threw up all over Matt's shoes. Blood-red vomit.

Merciful death for the animal. *Quick*, Matt thought. But this was the hardest thing he'd ever tried to do. How to do it—a hard stomp on the creature's head? He couldn't. He had to try something else first.

Matt peeled off a Post-It Note and put it, trying not to look, on the fur. And just like that it was over. The guinea pig went slack. The spell had undone whatever had been keeping it alive up to this point.

There was blood and puke on Matt's hands, but he made himself turn to Cole. Cole had his eyes shut tight and little choking sounds came from him.

Something in Matt snapped.

"You want some of *this*?" he shouted, holding out the Post-it pad as if it were the revolver he'd left with Mrs. Flowers. He whirled again, shouting, "*You* want some? How about *you*? You, Josh?" He was recognizing faces now. "You, Madison? How 'bout you, Bryn? Bring it on! *You all bring it on! BRING IT—*"

Something touched his shoulder. He spun, Post-it Note ready. Then he stopped short and relief bubbled up in him like Evian water at some fancy restaurant. He was staring right into the face of Dr. Alpert, Fell's Church's own country doctor. She had her SUV parked beside his car, in the middle of the street. Behind her, protecting her back, was Tyrone, who was going to be next year's quarterback at Robert E. Lee High. His sister, a sophomore-to-be, was trying to get out of the SUV too, but she stopped when Tyrone saw her.

"*Jayneela!*" he roared in a voice only the Tyre-minator could produce. "You get back in and buckle up! You know what Mom said! You do it *now*!"

Matt found himself clutching at Dr. Alpert's chocolate

brown hands. He *knew* she was a good woman, and a good caretaker, who had adopted her daughter's young children when their divorced mother had died of cancer. Maybe she would help him, too. He began babbling. "Oh, God, I've gotta get my mom out. My mom lives here alone. And I have to get her away from here." He knew he was sweating. He hoped he wasn't crying.

"Okay, Matt," the doctor said in her husky voice. "I'm getting my own family out this afternoon. We're going to stay with relatives in West Virginia. She's welcome to come."

It couldn't be this easy. Matt knew he had tears in his eyes now. He refused to blink, though, and let them come down. "I don't know what to say—but if you would—you're an adult, you see. She won't listen to me. She *will* listen to you. This whole block is infected. This kid Cole—" He couldn't go on. But Dr. Alpert saw it all in a flash—the animal, the boy with blood on his teeth and his mouth, still retching.

Dr. Alpert didn't react. She just had Jayneela throw her a packet of Wet Wipes from the SUV and held the heaving kid with one hand, while vigorously scrubbing his face clean. "Go home," she told him sternly.

"You have to let the infected ones go," she said to Matt, with a terrible look in her eyes. "Cruel as it seems, they only pass it on to the few who're still well." Matt started to tell her about the effectiveness of the Post-it Note amulets, but she was already calling, "Tyrone! Come over here and you boys bury this poor animal. Then you be ready to move Mrs. Honeycutt's things into the van. Jayneela, you do what your brother says. I'm going in for a little talk with Mrs. Honeycutt right now."

She didn't raise her voice much. She didn't need to. The Tyre-minator was obeying, backing up to Matt, watching the last of the creeping children that Matt's explosion hadn't scattered.

He's quick, Matt realized. Quicker than me. It's like a game. As long as you watch them they can't move.

They took turns being the watcher and handling the shovel. The earth here was hard as rock, heavy with weeds. But somehow they got a hole dug and the work helped them mentally. They buried Toby, and Matt walked around like some foot-dragging monster, trying to get the vomit off his shoes in the grass.

Suddenly beside them there was the noise of a door banging open and Matt ran, ran to his mother, who was trying to heft a huge suitcase, much too heavy for her, through the door.

Matt took it from her and felt himself encompassed in her hug even though she had to stand on tip-toes to do it. "Matt, I can't just leave you—"

"He'll be one of those to get the town out of this mess," Dr. Alpert said, overriding her. "He'll clean it up. Now *we've* got to get out so we don't drag him down. Matt, just so you know, I heard that the McCulloughs are getting out too. Mr. and Mrs. Sulez don't seem to be going yet, and neither do the Gilbert-Maxwells." She said the last two words with a distinct emphasis.

The Gilbert-Maxwells were Elena's aunt Judith, her husband Robert Maxwell, and Elena's little sister, Margaret. There was no real reason to mention them. But Matt knew why Dr. Alpert had. She *remembered* seeing Elena when this whole mess had started. Despite Elena's purification of the woods where Dr. Alpert had been standing, the doctor remembered.

"I'll tell—Meredith," Matt said, and looking her in the eyes, he nodded a little, as if to say, I'll tell Elena, too.

"Anything else to carry?" Tyrone asked. He was encumbered by a canary birdcage, with the little bird frantically beating its wings inside, and a smaller suitcase.

"No, but how can I thank you?" Mrs. Honeycutt said.

"Thanks later—now, everybody in," said Dr. Alpert. "We are taking *off*."

Matt hugged his mother and gave her a little push toward the SUV, which had already swallowed the birdcage and small suitcase.

"Good-bye!" everyone was yelling. Tyrone stuck his head out of the window to say, "Call me whenever! I want to help!"

And then they were gone.

Matt could hardly believe it was over; it had happened so fast. He ran inside the open door of his house and got his other pair of running shoes, just in case Mrs. Flowers couldn't fix the smell of the ones he was wearing.

When he burst out of the house again he had to blink. Instead of the white SUV there was a different white car parked beside his. He looked around the block. No children. None at all.

And the birdsong had come back.

There were two men in the car. One was white and one was black and they both were around the age to be concerned fathers. Anyway they had him cut off, the way their car was parked. He had no choice but to go up to them. As soon as he did they both got out of the car, watching him as if he was as dangerous as a kitsune.

The instant they did that, Matt knew he'd made a mistake.

"You're Matthew Jeffrey Honeycutt?"

Matt had no choice but to nod.

"Say yes or no, please."

"Yes." Matt could see inside the white car now. It was a stealth police car, one of those with lights inside, all ready to be fixed outside if the officers wanted to let you in on the secret.

"Matthew Jeffrey Honeycutt, you are under arrest for

assault and battery upon Caroline Beula Forbes. You have the right to remain silent. If you give up this right, anything you say can and will be used against you in a court of law—"

"Didn't you see those kids?" Matt was shouting. "You had to have seen one or two of them! Didn't that mean *anything* to you?"

"Lean over and put your hands on the front of the car."

"It's going to destroy the whole town! You're *helping* it!"

"Do you understand these rights—?"

"Do *you* understand what is going *on* in Fell's Church?"

There was a pause this time. And then, in perfectly even tones, one of the two said, "We're from Ridgemont."

19

Bonnie decided, with seconds precious and seeming to stretch for hours, that what was going to happen was going to happen no matter what she did. And there was a matter of pride here. She knew that there were people who would laugh at that, but it was true. Despite Elena's new Powers, Bonnie was the one most used to confronting stark darkness. She was somehow alive after all that. And very soon she would not be. And the way she went was the only thing left up to her.

She heard a glissando of screams and then she heard them come to a halt. Well, that was all she could do for the moment. Stop screaming. The choice was made. Bonnie would go out, unbroken, defiant—and silent.

The moment she stopped shrieking Shinichi made a gesture and the ogre who had hold of her stopped carrying her to the window.

She'd known it. He was a bully. Bullies wanted to *hear* that things hurt or that people were miserable. The ogre lifted her so her face was level with Shinichi's. "Excited about your one-way trip?"

"Thrilled," she said expressionlessly. Hey, she thought, I'm not so bad at this brave thing. But everything inside her was shaking at double time in order to make up for her stony face.

Shinichi opened the window. "Still thrilled?"

Now *that* had done something, opening the window had. She was not going to be smashed against glass until she broke it with her face and went sailing through the jagged bits. There wasn't going to be pain until she hit the ground and nobody would know about that, not even her.

Just *do it* and get it over with, Bonnie thought. The warm breeze from the window told her that this—place—this slave-selling place—where customers were allowed to sift through the slaves until they found just the right one—was too highly air-conditioned.

I'll be warm, even if it's just for a second or so, she thought.

When a door near them banged, Bonnie nearly jumped out of the ogre's arms, and when the door to their own room banged open, she nearly jumped through her own skin.

You see? Something surged wildly through her. *I'm*

saved! It only took a little of that brave stuff and now . . .

But it was Shinichi's sister, Misao. Misao, looking gravely ill, her skin ashen, holding on to the door to hold herself up. The only thing about her that wasn't grayed-out was her brilliant black hair, tipped with scarlet at the ends, just like Shinichi's.

"Wait!" she said to Shinichi. "You never even asked about—"

"You think a little airhead like her would know? But have it your own way." Shinichi seated Misao on the couch, rubbing her shoulders comfortingly. "I'll ask."

So *she* was the one inside the two-way mirror room, Bonnie thought. She looks really bad. Like dying bad.

"What happened to my sister's star ball?" Shinichi demanded and then Bonnie saw how this thing formed a circle, with a beginning and an ending, and how, understanding this, she could die with true dignity.

"It was my fault," she said, with a faint smile as she remembered. "Or half of it was. Sage opened it up the first time to open the Gate back on Earth. And then . . ." She told them the story, as if it were one she'd never heard before, putting an emphasis on how it was *she* who had given Damon the clues to find Misao's star ball, and it was Damon who then had used it to enter the top level of the Dark Dimensions.

"It's all a circle," she explained. "What you do comes

back to *you*." Then despite herself, she started to giggle.

In two strides, Shinichi was across the room and slapping her. She didn't know how many times he did it. The first was enough to make her gasp and stop her giggling. Afterward her cheeks felt as swollen as if she had a very painful case of the mumps, and her nose was bleeding.

She kept trying to wipe it on her shoulder, but it wouldn't stop. At last Misao said, "Ugh. Unfasten her hands and give her a towel or something."

The ogres moved just as if Shinichi had given the order.

Shinichi himself was now sitting beside Misao, talking to her softly, as if he were speaking to a baby or a beloved pet. But Misao's eyes, with their tiny flicker of fire in them, were clear and adult as she looked at Bonnie.

"Where is my star ball now?" she asked with dreadful gray intensity.

Bonnie, who was wiping her nose, feeling the bliss of not being handcuffed behind her back, wondered why she wasn't even trying to think of a lie. Like, let me free and I'll lead you to it. Then she remembered Shinichi and his damn kitsune telepathy.

"How could I know?" she pointed out logically. "I was just trying to pull Damon away from the Gate when we both fell in. It didn't come with us. As far as I know, it got kicked in the dust and all the liquid spilled out."

Shinichi got up to hurt her again, but she was only

telling the truth. Misao was already speaking. "We know that didn't happen because I am"—she had to pause to breathe—"still alive."

She turned her ashen, sunken face toward Shinichi and said, "You're right. She's useless now, and full of information she shouldn't have. Throw her out."

An ogre picked Bonnie up, towel and all. Shinichi came around the other side. "Do you *see* what you've done to my sister? Do you *see*?"

No more time now. Just a second to wonder if she really was going to be brave or not. But what should she say to show she was brave? She opened her mouth, honestly not sure whether what was coming out was a scream or words.

"She's going to look even worse when my friends are done with her," she said, and saw in Misao's eyes that she'd hit her target.

"Throw her *out*," Shinichi shouted, livid with fury.

And the ogre threw her out the window.

Meredith was sitting with her parents, trying to figure out what was wrong. She had finished her errands in record time: getting enlarged versions of the writing on the front of the jars made; calling the Saitou family to find that they would all be home at noon. Then she had examined and numbered the individual blow-ups of each character in the pictures that Alaric had sent.

The Saitous had been . . . tense. Meredith hadn't been surprised since Isobel had been a prime, if entirely innocent, carrier of the kitsune's deadly possessing malach. One of the worst casualties was Isobel's own steady boyfriend, Jim Bryce, who had gotten the malach from Caroline and spread it to Isobel without knowing what he was doing. He himself had been possessed by Shinichi's malach and had demonstrated all the hideous symptoms of Lesch-Nyhan Syndrome, eating away at his own lips and fingers, while poor Isobel had used dirty needles—sometimes the size of a child's knitting needles—to pierce herself in more than thirty places, besides forking her tongue with scissors.

Isobel was out of the hospital and on the mend now. Still, Meredith was bewildered. She had gotten approval of the cards with enlarged, individual characters off the jars from the older Saitous—Obaasan (Isobel's grandmother) and Mrs. Saitou (Isobel's mother)—not without a good deal of argument in Japanese over each character. She was just getting into her car when Isobel had come running out of the house with a bag of Post-it Notes in her hand. "Mother did them—in case you needed," she gasped in her new, soft, slurring voice. And Meredith had taken the notes from her gratefully, murmuring something awkward about repayment.

"No, but—but may I have a look at the blow-ups?" Isobel had panted. Why was she panting so hard? Meredith wondered. Even if she'd run from the top floor all the way following Meredith—that wouldn't account for it. Then Meredith remembered: Bonnie had said Isobel had a "jumpy" heart.

"You see," Isobel said with what looked like shame and a plea for understanding, "Obaasan is really almost blind now—and it's been so long since Mother was in school . . . but *I* take Japanese classes right *now*."

Meredith was touched. Obviously, Isobel had felt it bad manners to contradict an adult when they were in earshot. But there, sitting in the car, Isobel had gone through every card with a blown-up character, writing a similar, but definitely different character on the back. It had taken twenty minutes. Meredith had been awed. "But how do you remember them all? How do you ever write to each other?" she had blurted, after seeing the complicated symbols that differed only by a few lines.

"With dictionaries," Isobel had said, and had for the first time given a little laugh. "No, I'm serious—to write a very proper letter, say, don't you use Thesaurus and Spell Check and—"

"I need those to write *anything*!" Meredith had laughed.

It had been a nice moment, both of them smiling together, relaxed. No problems. Isobel's heart had seemed just fine.

Then Isobel had hurried away and when she was gone

Meredith was left staring at a round circle of moisture on the passenger seat. A tear. But why should Isobel be crying?

Because it reminded her of the malach, or of Jim?

Because it would take several plastic surgeries before her ears would have flesh on them again?

No answer that Meredith could think of made sense. And she had to hurry to get to her own home—late.

It was only then that Meredith was stricken by a fact. The Saitou family knew that Meredith, Matt, and Bonnie were friends. But none of them had asked about either Bonnie or Matt.

Strange.

If she had only known how much stranger her visit with her own family would be . . .

Meredith usually found her parents funny and silly and dear. They were solemn about all the wrong things like, "Make sure, honey, that you really get to know Alaric—before—before—" Meredith had no doubts about Alaric at all, but he was another of those silly, dear, gallant people, who talked all around things without getting to the point.

Today, she was surprised to see that there was no cluster of cars around the ancestral home. Maybe people had to stay home to fight it out with their own children. She locked the Acura, conscious of the precious contents given by Isobel, and rang the doorbell. Her parents believed in chain locks.

Janet, the housekeeper, looked happy to see her but nervous. Aha, Meredith thought, they have discovered that their dutiful only child has ransacked the attic. Maybe they want the stave back. Maybe I should have left it back at the boardinghouse.

But she only realized that things were truly serious when she came into the family room and saw the big La-Z-Boy deluxe lounging chair, her father's throne: empty. Her father was sitting on the couch, holding her mother, who was sobbing.

She had brought the stave with her, and when her mother saw it, she broke into a fresh burst of tears.

"Look," Meredith said, "this doesn't have to be so tragic. I've got a pretty good idea of what happened. If you want to tell me about how Grandma and I really got hurt, that's your business. But if I was . . . contaminated in some way . . ."

She stopped. She could hardly believe it. Her father was holding out an arm to her, as if the somewhat rank condition of her clothes didn't matter. She went to him slowly, uncomfortably, and let him hug her regardless of his Armani suit. Her mother had a glass with a few sips left of what looked like Coke in front of her, but Meredith would bet it wasn't all Coke.

"We'd hoped that this was a place of peace," her father orated. Every sentence her father spoke was an oration. You got used to it. "We never dreamed . . ." And then he stopped. Meredith was stunned, Her father didn't stop in the middle of an oration. He didn't pause. And he certainly didn't *cry.*

"Dad! Daddy! What is it? Have kids been around here, crazy kids? Did they hurt somebody?"

"We have to tell you the whole story from that time long ago," her father . . . said. He spoke with such despair that it wasn't anything like an oration. "When you were . . . all attacked."

"By the vampire. Or Grandfather. Or do you know?"

Long pause. Then her mother drained the contents of her glass and called, "Janet, another one, please."

"Now, Gabriella—" her father said, chiding.

"'Nando—I can't bear this. The thought that *mi hija inocente* . . ."

Meredith said, "Look, I think I can make this easier for you. I already know . . . well, first, that I had a twin brother."

Her parents looked horrified. They clung together, gasping. "Who told you?" her father demanded. "At that boardinghouse, who could know—?"

Calming down time. "No, no. Dad, I found out—well, Grandpa talked to me." That was true enough. He had. Just not about her brother. "Anyway, that was how I got the stave. But the vampire that hurt us is dead. He was the serial killer, the one who killed Vickie and Sue. His name was Klaus."

"You thought that there was only one *vampire*?" her mother got out. She pronounced the word the Hispanic way, which Meredith always found more scary. *Vahm-peer.*

The universe seemed to start moving slowly around Meredith.

"That's just a guess," her father said. "We don't really know that there was more than the very strong one."

"But you know about Klaus—how?"

"We saw him. He was the strong one. He killed the security guards at the gate with one blow each. We moved to a new town. We hoped you would never have to know you had a brother." Her father brushed his eyes. "Your grandfather spoke to us, right after the attack. But the next day . . . nothing. He couldn't talk at all."

Her mother put her face in her hands. She only lifted it to call, "Janet! Another, *por favor*!"

"Right away, ma'am." Meredith looked to the housekeeper's blue eyes for the solution to this mystery and found nothing—sympathy, but no help. Janet walked away with the empty glass, blond French braid receding.

Meredith turned back to her parents, so dark of eye and hair, so olive of skin color. They were huddling together again, eyes on her.

"Mom, Dad, I know that this is really hard. But I'm going after the kind of people who hurt Grandpa, and Grandma, and my brother. It's dangerous, but I have to do it." She dropped into a Taekwondo stance. "I mean you *did* have me trained."

"But against your own family? You could do that?" her mother cried.

Meredith sat down. She had reached the end of the memories that she and Stefan had found. "So Klaus didn't kill him like Grandmother. He took my brother with him."

"Cristian," wailed her mother. "He was just *un bebé.* Three years old! That was when we found the two of you . . . and the blood . . . oh, the blood . . ."

Her father got up, not to orate, but to put his hand on Meredith's shoulder. "We thought it would be easier not to tell you—that you wouldn't have any memories of what was happening when we came in. And you don't, do you?"

Meredith's eyes were filling with tears. She looked to her mother, trying to silently tell her she couldn't understand this.

"He was drinking my blood?" she guessed. "Klaus?"

"No!" cried her father as her mother whispered prayers.

"He was drinking Cristian's, then." Meredith was kneeling on the floor now, trying to look up into the face of her mother.

"No!" cried her father again. He choked.

"*La sangre!*" gasped her mother, covering her eyes. "The blood!"

"*Querida—*" her father sobbed, and went to her.

"Dad!" Meredith went after him and shook his arm. "You've ruled out all the possibilities! I don't understand! Who was drinking blood?"

"You! You!" her mother almost screamed. *"From your own brother! Oh,* el aterrorizar*!"*

"Gabriella!" moaned her father.

Meredith's mother subsided into weeping.

Meredith's head was whirling. "I'm not a vampire! I hunt vampires and kill them!"

"*He* said," her father whispered hoarsely: "'Just see she gets a tablespoon a week. If you want her to live, that is. Try a blood pudding.' He was laughing."

Meredith didn't need to ask if they had obeyed. At her house, they had blood sausage or pudding at least once a week. She had grown up with it. It was nothing special.

"Why?" she whispered hoarsely now. "Why didn't he kill me?"

"I don't know! We still don't know! That man with his front all dripping with blood—your blood, your brother's blood, we didn't know! And then at the last minute he grabbed for the two of you but you bit his hand to the bone," her father said.

"He laughed—laughed!—with your teeth clamped in him and your little hands pushing him away, and said, 'I'll just leave you this one, then, and you can worry about what she will turn out to be. The boy I'm taking with me.' And then suddenly I seemed to come out of a spell, for I was reaching for you again, ready to fight him for both of you. But I couldn't! Once I had you, I couldn't move another inch. And he left the house still laughing—and took your brother, Cristian, with him."

Meredith thought. No wonder they didn't want to hold any kind of celebration on the anniversaries of that day. Her grandmother dead, her grandfather going crazy, her brother lost, and herself—what? No wonder they celebrated her birthday a week early.

Meredith tried to stay calm. The world was falling to pieces around her but she had to stay calm. Staying calm had kept her alive all her life. Without even having to count, she was breathing out deep, and in through her nostrils, and out through her mouth. Deep, deep, cleansing breaths. Soothing peace throughout her body. Only part of her was hearing her mother:

"We came home early that night because I had a headache—"

"Sh, *querida*—" her father was beginning.

"We got home early," her mother keened. "*O Virgen Bendecida,* what would we have found if we had been late? We would have lost you, too! My baby! My baby with blood on her mouth—"

"But we got home early enough to save her," Meredith's father said huskily, as if trying to wake her mother from a spell.

"Ah, *gracias, Princesa Divina, Vigen pura y impoluto . . .*" Her mother couldn't seem to stop crying.

"Daddy," Meredith said urgently, aching for her mother but desperately needing information. "Have you ever seen him again? Or heard about him? My brother, Cristian?"

"Yes," her father said. "Oh, yes, we have seen something."

Her mother gasped. "'Nando, no!"

"She has to learn the truth sometime," her father said. He rummaged among some cardboard file folders on the desk. "Look!" he said to Meredith. "Look at this."

Meredith stared in utter disbelief.

In the Dark Dimension Bonnie shut her eyes. There was a lot of wind at the top of a tall building's window. That was all her mind had a thought for when she was out of the window and then back into it and the ogre was laughing and Shinichi's terrible voice saying, "You don't really think we'd let you go without questioning you *thoroughly*?"

Bonnie heard the words without them making sense, and then suddenly they did. Her captors were going to hurt her. They were going to torture her. They were going to take her bravery away.

She thought she screamed something at him. All she knew, though, was that there was a soft explosion of heat behind her, and then—*unbelievably*—all dressed up in a cloak with badges that made him look like some kind of military prince, there was Damon.

Damon.

He was so late she'd long ago given up on him. But now he was flashing a there-and-gone brilliant smile at Shinichi, who was staring as if he'd been stricken dumb.

And now Damon was saying, "I'm afraid Ms. McCullough has another engagement at that moment. But *I* will be back to kick your ass—*immediately.* Move from this room and I'll kill you all, slowly. Thank you for your time and consideration."

And before anyone could even recover from their first shock at his arrival, he and Bonnie were blasting off through the windows. He went, not out of the building backward as if retreating, but straight ahead forward, one hand in front of him, wrapping them both in a black but ethereal bundle of Power. They shattered the two-way mirror in Bonnie's room and were almost all the way through to the next room before Bonnie's mind tagged the first "empty." Then they were crashing through an elaborate videoset-window—made to let people think they had a view of the outdoors, and flying over someone lying on a bed. Then . . . it was just a series of crashes, as far as Bonnie was concerned. She barely got a glimpse of what was going on in each room. Finally . . .

The crashing stopped. This left Bonnie holding on to Damon koala-style—she wasn't stupid—and they were very, very high in the air. And mobilizing in front of them, and off to the sides, and as far as Bonnie could see, were women who were also flying, but in little machines that looked like a combination of a motorcycle and a Jet Ski. No wheels, of course. The machines were all gold, which was also the color of each driver's hair.

So the first word Bonnie gasped to her rescuer, after he had blasted a tunnel through the large slave-owner's building to save her, was, *"Guardians?"*

"Indispensable, considering the fact that I didn't have the first idea where the bad guys might have taken you and I suspected that there might be a time limit. This was actually the very last of the slave-sellers we were due to check. We finally . . . lucked out." For someone who had lucked out, he sounded a little strange. Almost . . . choked up.

Water was on Bonnie's cheeks but it was being flicked away too fast for her to wipe it. Damon was holding her so that she couldn't see his face, and he was holding her very, very tightly.

It really was Damon. He had called out the cavalry and, despite the city-wide mind-gridlock, he had found her.

"They hurt you, didn't they, little redbird? I saw . . . I saw your face," Damon said in his new choked-up voice. Bonnie didn't know what to say. But suddenly she didn't mind how hard he squeezed her. She even found herself squeezing back.

Suddenly, to her shock, Damon broke her koala-grip and pulled her up and kissed her on the lips very gently. "Little redbird! I'm going to go now, and make them pay for what they did to you."

Bonnie heard herself say, "No, don't."

"No?" Damon repeated, bewildered.

"No," Bonnie said. She needed Damon with her. She didn't care what happened to Shinichi. There was a sweetness unfolding inside her, but there was also a rushing in her head. It really was a pity, but in a few moments she would be unconscious.

Meanwhile, she had three thoughts in mind and all of them were clear. What she was afraid of was that they would be less clear later, after she had fainted. "Do you have a star ball?"

"I have twenty-eight star balls," Damon said, and looked at her quizzically.

That wasn't what Bonnie meant at all; she meant one to record onto. "Can you remember three things?" she said to Damon.

"I'd gamble on it." This time Damon kissed her softly on the forehead.

"First, you ruined my very brave death."

"We can always go back and you can have another try." Damon's voice was less choked now; more his own.

"Second, you left me at that horrible inn for a week—"

As if she could see inside his mind, she saw this slice into him like some kind of wooden sword. He was holding her so tightly that she really couldn't breathe. "I . . . I didn't mean to. It was really only four days, but I never should have done it," he said.

"Third." Bonnie's voice dropped to a whisper. "I don't

think any star ball was ever stolen at all. What never existed can't be stolen, can it?"

She looked at him. Damon was looking back in a way that normally would have thrilled her. He was obviously, blatantly distressed. But Bonnie was just barely hanging on to consciousness at this point.

"And . . . fourth . . ." She puzzled out slowly.

"Fourth? You said three things." Damon smiled, just a little.

"I have to say this—" She dropped her head down on Damon's shoulder, gathered all of her energy, and concentrated.

Damon loosened his grip a little. He said, "I can hear a faint murmuring sound in my head. Just tell me normally. We're well away from anyone."

Bonnie was insistent. She scrunched her whole tiny body together and then explosively sent out a thought. She could tell that Damon caught it.

Fourth, I know the way to the seven legendary kitsune treasures, Bonnie sent to him. *That includes the biggest star ball ever made. But if we want it, we have to get to it—fast.*

Then, feeling that she had contributed enough to the conversation, she fainted.

21

Someone was *still* knocking on Stefan's door.

"It's a woodpecker," Elena said when she could speak. "They knock, don't they?"

"On doors inside houses?" Stefan said dazedly.

"Ignore it and it will go away."

A moment later the knocking resumed.

Elena moaned, "I don't *believe* this."

Stefan whispered, "Do you want me to bring you its head? Unattached from its neck, I mean?"

Elena considered. As the knocking continued, she was getting more worried and less confused. "Better see if it *is* a bird, I guess," she said.

Stefan rolled away from her, somehow got on his jeans, and went reeling to the door. In spite of herself, Elena pitied whoever was on the other side.

The knocking started again.

Stefan reached the door and nearly wrenched it off its hinges.

"What the—" He stopped, suddenly moderating his voice. *"Mrs. Flowers?"*

"Yes," Mrs. Flowers said, deliberately not seeing Elena, who was wearing a sheet and directly in her line of vision.

"It's poor dear Meredith," Mrs. Flowers said. "She's in such a state, and she says she has to see you *now*, Stefan."

Elena's mind switched tracks as suddenly and smoothly as a train. Meredith? In a *state*? Demanding to see Stefan, even if, as Elena was sure she must have, Mrs. Flowers had delicately indicated just how . . . busy Stefan was at the moment?

Her mind was still solidly linked with Stefan's. He said, "Thank you, Mrs. Flowers. I'll be down in just a moment."

Elena, who was slipping into her clothes as fast as she could, while crouching on the far side of the bed, added a telepathic suggestion.

"Maybe you could make her a nice cup of tea—I mean, a cup of tea," Stefan added.

"Yes, dear, what a good idea," Mrs. Flowers said gently. "And if you should see Elena, perhaps you could say that dear Meredith is asking for her, too?"

"We will," Stefan said automatically. Then he turned around and hastily shut the door.

Elena gave him time to put his shirt and shoes on, and then they both hurried down to the kitchen, where Meredith was not having a nice cup of tea, but pacing around like a caged leopard.

Stefan began, "What's—"

"I'll tell you what's wrong, Stefan Salvatore! No—you tell me! You were in my mind before, so you must know. You *must* have been able to see—to tell—about me."

Elena was still mindlocked with Stefan. She felt his dismay. "To tell what about you?" he asked gently, pulling out a chair at the kitchen table so Meredith could sit.

The very simple act of sitting down, of pausing to respond to civility, seemed to calm Meredith slightly. But still Elena could feel her fear and pain like the taste of a steel sword on her tongue.

Meredith accepted a hug and became a little calmer yet. A little more herself and less like a caged animal. But the struggle was so visceral and so clear within her that Elena couldn't bear to leave her, even when Mrs. Flowers deposited four mugs of tea around the table and took another chair Stefan offered.

Then Stefan sat down. He knew Elena would stand or sit or share a chair with Meredith, but whatever it was, she would be the one to decide.

Mrs. Flowers was gently stirring honey into her mug of tea and then passing the honey along to Stefan who gave it to Elena who put just the little bit that Meredith liked into Meredith's mug and stirred it gently, too.

The ordinary, civilized sounds of two spoons quietly clinking seemed to relax Meredith still further. She took the mug Elena gave her and sipped, then drank thirstily.

Elena could feel Stefan's mental sigh of relief as Meredith floated down another few levels. He politely sipped his own tea, which was hot but not burning hot and made from naturally sweet berries and herbs.

"It's good," Meredith said. She was almost a human now. "Thank you, Mrs. Flowers."

Elena felt lighter. She relaxed enough to pull over her own cup of tea and squeeze lots of honey in and stir it and take a gulp. Good! Calming down tea!

That's chamomile and cucumber, Stefan told her.

"Chamomile and cucumber," Elena said, nodding wisely, "for calming down." And then she blushed, for Mrs. Flowers's bright smile had knowledge in it.

Elena hastily drank more tea and watched Meredith have more tea and everything began to feel *almost* all right. Meredith was completely Meredith now, not some fierce animal. Elena squeezed her friend's hand tightly.

There was just one problem. Humans were less frightening than beasts but they could cry. Now Meredith, who never wept, was shaking and tears were dripping into the tea.

"You know what *morcillo* is, right?" she asked Elena at last.

Elena nodded hesitantly. "We had it sometimes in stew at your house?" she said. "And for *tapas*?" Elena had grown up with the blood sausage as a meal or a snack at her friend's house, and she was used to the bite-sized pieces as a delicious food only Mrs. Sulez made.

Elena felt Stefan's heart sinking. She looked back and forth from him to Meredith.

"It turns out my mother didn't always make it," Meredith said, looking at Stefan now. "And my parents had a very good reason for changing my birthday."

"Just tell it all," Stefan suggested softly. And then Elena felt something she hadn't before. A surge, like a wave—a long gentle swell that spoke right into the center of Meredith's brain. It said: *Just tell it and be calm. No anger. No fear.*

But it wasn't telepathy. Meredith felt the thought in her blood and bones, but didn't hear it with her ears.

It was Influence. Before Elena could brain her beloved Stefan with her mug for using Influence on one of her friends, Stefan said, just to her, *Meredith's hurting, feeling scared and angry. She has reason to, but she needs peace. I probably won't be able to hold her anyway, but I'll try.*

Meredith wiped her eyes. "It turns out that nothing was like what I thought happened—that night when I was three." She described what her parents had told her, about everything that Klaus had done. Telling the story, even quietly, was undoing all the calming influences that had helped Meredith maintain herself. She was beginning to shake again. Before Elena could grab her, she was up and striding around the room. "He laughed and said that I'd need blood every week—animal blood—or I'd die. I didn't need much. Just a tablespoon or two. And my poor mother didn't want to lose another child. She did what he told her to. But what happens if I have more blood, Stefan? What happens if I drink *yours*?"

Stefan was thinking, desperately trying to see if in all his years of experience he'd come across anything like this. Meanwhile he answered the easy part.

"If you drank enough of my blood you'd become a vampire. But so would anyone. With you—well, it might take less. So don't let any vampire trick you into blood exchange. Once might be enough."

"So I'm *not* a vampire? Now? Not any kind? *Are* there different kinds?"

Stefan answered seriously. "I've never heard of 'different kinds' of vampires in my life, except for Old Ones. I can tell you that you don't have a vampire's aura. What about your teeth? Can you make your canines sharp? Usually it's best to test over human flesh. Not your own."

Elena promptly stuck out her arm, wrist vein-side

up. Meredith, eyes closed in concentration, made a great effort, which Elena felt through Stefan. Then Meredith opened her eyes, mouth also open for a dental inspection. Elena stared at her canines. They looked a little bit sharp, but so did anybody's, didn't they?

Carefully Elena reached a fingertip in. She touched one of Meredith's canines.

Tiny pinch.

Startled, Elena pulled back. She stared at her finger where a very small drop of blood was welling up.

Everyone watched it, mesmerized. Then Elena's mouth said without pausing to consult her brain, "You have kitten teeth."

The next moment Meredith had brushed Elena aside and was pacing wildly all around the kitchen. "I won't be one! I won't be! I'm a hunter-slayer, not a vampire! I'll *kill myself* if I'm a vampire!" She was deadly serious. Elena felt Stefan feeling it, the quick thrust of the stave between her ribs and into the heart. She would go on the Internet to find the right area. Ironwood and white ash piercing her heart, stilling it forever . . . sealing off the evil that was Meredith Sulez.

Be calm! Be calm! Stefan's Influence flooded into her.

Meredith was not calm.

"But before that I have to kill my brother." She flung down a photograph on Mrs. Flowers's kitchen table. "It turns out that Klaus or someone has been sending these since Cristian was four—on my real birthday. *For years!* And in every picture you could see his vampire teeth. *Not* 'kitten teeth.' And then they stopped coming when I was about ten. But they had shown him growing up! With pointed teeth! And last year this one came."

Elena leaped for the photo, but it was closer to Stefan and he was faster. He stared in astonishment. "Growing up?" he said. She could feel how shaken he was—and how envious. No one had given him that option.

Elena looked at the pacing Meredith and around at Stefan. "But it's impossible, isn't it?" she said. "I thought that if you were bitten, that was it, right? You never got any older—or bigger."

"That's what I thought too. But Klaus was an Old One and who knows what they can do?" Stefan answered.

Damon will be furious when he finds out, Elena told Stefan privately, reaching for the picture even though she'd already seen it through Stefan's eyes. Damon was very bitter about Stefan's height advantage—about *anyone's* height advantage.

Elena brought the picture to Mrs. Flowers and looked at it with her. It showed an extremely handsome boy, with hair that was just Meredith's dark color. He looked like Meredith in his facial structure and olive skin. He was wearing a motorcycle jacket and gloves, but no helmet, and he was laughing merrily with a full set of very white teeth. You could easily see that the canines were long and pointed.

Elena looked back and forth from Meredith to the picture. The only difference she could see was that this boy's eyes seemed lighter. Everything else screamed "twins."

"First I kill him," Meredith repeated tiredly. "Then I kill myself." She stumbled back to the table and sat, almost knocking over her chair.

Elena hovered near her, snatching two mugs from the table, to prevent Meredith's clumsy arm from sweeping them to the floor.

Meredith . . . clumsy! Elena had never seen Meredith ungraceful or clumsy before. It was frightening. Was it somehow due to being—at least partly—a vampire? The kitten teeth? Elena turned apprehensive eyes on Stefan, felt Stefan's own bewilderment.

Then both of them, without consultation, turned to look at Mrs. Flowers. She gave them an apologetic little-old-lady smile.

"Gotta kill . . . find him, kill him . . . first," Meredith was whispering as her dark head lowered to the table, to the pillow of her arms. "Find him . . . where? Grandpa . . . where? Cristian . . . my brother . . ."

Elena listened silently until there was only soft breathing to be heard.

"You drugged her?" she whispered to Mrs. Flowers.

"It was what Ma*ma* thought best. She's a strong, healthy girl. It won't harm her to sleep from now through the night. Because I'm sorry to tell you, but we have another problem right now."

Elena glanced at Stefan, saw fear dawning on his face, and demanded, "What?" Absolutely nothing was coming through their link. He'd shut it down.

Elena turned to Mrs. Flowers. *"What?"*

"I'm very worried about dear Matt."

"Matt," agreed Stefan, looking around the table as if to show that Matt wasn't there. He was trying to protect Elena from the chills racing through him.

At first Elena wasn't alarmed. "I know where he might be," she said brightly. She was remembering stories that Matt had told of being in Fell's Church while she and the others had been in the Dark Dimension. "Dr. Alpert's place. Or out with her, making the rounds of home visits."

Mrs. Flowers shook her head, her expression bleak. "I'm afraid not, Elena dear. Sophia—Dr. Alpert—called me and told me she was taking Matt's mother, your own family, and several other people with her and escaping Fell's Church entirely. And I don't blame her a bit—but Matt wasn't one of those going. She said he meant to stay and fight. That was around twelve thirty."

Elena's eyes automatically went to the kitchen clock.

Horror shot through her, flipping her stomach and reverberating out to her fingertips. The clock said 4:35—4:35 P.M.! But that *had* to be wrong. She and Stefan had only joined minds a few minutes ago. Meredith's rage hadn't lasted that long. This was impossible!

"That clock—it's not right!" She appealed to Mrs. Flowers, but heard at the same time Stefan's telepathic voice, *It's the mind-blending. I didn't want to rush. But I was lost in it too—it's not your fault, Elena!*

"It *is* my fault," Elena snapped back aloud. "I never meant to forget about my friends for the entire afternoon! And Matt—Matt would *never* scare us by keeping us waiting for his call! I should have called him! I shouldn't have been—" She looked at Stefan with unhappy eyes. The only thing burning inside her right now was the shame of failing Matt.

"I did call his mobile number," Mrs. Flowers said very gently. "Ma*ma* advised me to do so, all the way back at half past twelve. But he didn't answer. I've called every hour since. Ma*ma* won't say more than that it's time we looked into things directly."

Elena ran to Mrs. Flowers and wept on the soft cambric lacework at the old woman's neck. "You did our job for us," she said. "Thank you. But now we have to go and find him."

She whirled on Stefan. "Can you put Meredith in the

first-floor bedroom? Just take off her shoes and put her on top of the covers. Mrs. Flowers, if you're going to be alone here, we'll leave Saber and Talon to take care of you. Then we'll keep in touch by mobile. And we'll search every house in Fell's Church—but I guess we should go to the thicket first . . ."

"Wait, Elena my dear." Mrs. Flowers had her eyes shut. Elena waited, shifting impatiently from one foot to the other. Stefan was just returning from putting Meredith in the front room.

Suddenly, Mrs. Flowers smiled, eyes still shut. "Ma*ma* says she will do her utmost for you two, since you are so devoted to your friend. She says that Matt is not anywhere in Fell's Church. And she says, take the dog, Saber. The falcon will watch over Meredith while we are away." Mrs. Flowers's eyes opened. "Although we might plaster her window and door with Post-it Notes," she said, "just to make sure."

"No," Elena said flatly. "I'm sorry, but I won't leave Meredith and you on your own with only a bird for protection. We'll take you both with us, covered in amulets if you like, and then we can take both animals, too. Back in the Dark Dimension, they worked together when Bloddeuwedd was trying to kill us."

"All right," Stefan said at once, knowing Elena well enough to realize that a half-hour-long argument could ensue and Elena would never be moved an inch from her position. Mrs. Flowers must have known it too, for she rose, also immediately, and went to get ready.

Stefan carried Meredith out to her car. Elena gave a tiny whistle for Saber, who was instantly underfoot, seeming bigger than ever, and she raced him up the stairs to Matt's room. It was disappointingly clean—but Elena fished a pair of briefs from between bed and wall. She gave these to Saber to delight in, but found she couldn't stand still. Finally, she ran up to Stefan's room, snatched her diary from under the mattress, and began scribbling.

Dear Diary,

I don't know what to do. Matt has disappeared. Damon has taken Bonnie to the Dark Dimension—but is he taking care *of her?*

There's no way to know. We don't have any way to open a Gate ourselves and go after them. I'm afraid Stefan will kill Damon, and if something—anything—has happened to Bonnie, I'll want to kill him too. Oh, God, what a mess!

And Meredith . . . of all people, Meredith turns out to have more secrets than all of us combined.

All Stefan and I can do is hold each other and pray. We've been fighting Shinichi so long! I feel as if the end is coming soon . . . and I'm afraid.

* * *

"Elena!" Stefan's shout came from below. "We're all ready!"

Elena quickly stuffed the diary back under the mattress. She found Saber waiting on the stairs, and followed him down, running. Mrs. Flowers had two overcoats covered in amulets.

Outside, a long whistle from Stefan was met by an answering *keeeeeeee* from above and Elena saw a small dark body circling against the white-streaked August sky. "She understands," Stefan said briefly, and took the driver's seat of the car. Elena got into the backseat behind him, and Mrs. Flowers into the front passenger seat. Since Stefan had buckled up Meredith into the middle of the backseat, this left Saber a window to put his panting head through.

"Now," Stefan said, over the purring of the engine, "where are we going, exactly?"

"Mama said *not* in Fell's Church," Mrs. Flowers repeated to Stefan. "And that means not the thicket."

"All right," Stefan said. "If he's not there, then where else?"

"Well," Elena said slowly, "it's the police, isn't it? They've caught him." Her heart felt as if it were in her stomach.

Mrs. Flowers sighed. "I suppose so. Ma*ma* should have told me that, but the atmosphere is full of strange influences."

"But the sheriff's department is in Fell's Church. What there is of it," Elena objected.

"Then," Mrs. Flowers said, "what about the police in another city close by? The ones who came looking for him before—"

"Ridgemont," Elena said heavily. "That's where those police that searched the boardinghouse were from. That's where that Mossberg guy came from, Meredith said." She looked at Meredith, who didn't even murmur. "That's where Caroline's dad has all his big-shot friends—and Tyler Smallwood's dad does too. They belong to all those no-women clubs with secret handshakes and stuff."

"And do we have anything like a plan for when we get there?" Stefan asked.

"I have a sort of Plan A," Elena admitted. "But I don't *know* that it will work—you may know better than I do."

"Tell me."

Elena told him. Stefan listened and had to stifle a laugh. "I think," he said soberly afterward, "that it just might work."

Elena immediately began to think about Plans B and C so that they wouldn't be stuck if Plan A should fail.

They had to drive through Fell's Church to get to Ridgemont. Elena saw the burnt-out houses and the blackened trees through tears. This was her town, the town which, as a spirit, she had watched over and protected. How could it have come to this?

And, worse, how could it ever possibly be put back together again?

Elena began to shiver uncontrollably.

* * *

Matt sat grimly in the jury conference room. He had explored it long ago, and had found that the windows were boarded over from the outside. He wasn't surprised, as all the windows he knew back in Fell's Church were boarded up, and besides, he had tried these boards and knew that he could break out if he cared to.

He didn't care to.

It was time to face his personal crisis. He would have faced it back before Damon had taken the three girls to the Dark Dimension, but Meredith had talked him out of it.

Matt knew that Mr. Forbes, Caroline's father, had all his cronies in the police and legal system here. And so did Mr. Smallwood, the father of the real culprit. They were unlikely to give him a fair trial. But in any kind of trial, at some point they would at least have to *listen* to him.

And what they would hear was the plain truth. They might not believe it now. But later, when Caroline's twins had as little control as werewolf babies were reputed to have over their shapes—well, then they'd think of Matt, and what he'd said.

He was doing the right thing, he assured himself. Even if, right now, his insides felt as if they were made of lead.

What's the worst they can do to me? he wondered, and was unhappy to hear the echo of Meredith's voice come back. *"They can put you in jail, Matt. Real jail; you're over eighteen. And while that may be good news for some genuine, vicious, tough old felons with homemade tattoos and biceps like tree branches, it is not going to be good news for you.*" And then after a session on the Internet, "*Matt, in Virginia, it can be for life. And the minimum is five years. Matt, please; I beg you, don't let them do this to you! Sometimes it's true that discretion is the better part of valor. They hold all the cards and we're walking blindfolded in the dark . . .*"

She had gotten surprisingly worked up about it, mixing her metaphors and all, Matt thought dejectedly. But it's not exactly as if I volunteered for this. And I bet they know those boards are pretty flimsy and if I break out, I'll be chased from here to who-knows-where. And if I stay put at least I'll get to tell the truth.

For a very long time nothing happened. Matt could tell from the sun through the cracks in the boards that it was afternoon. A man came in and offered a visit to the bathroom and a Coke. Matt accepted both, but also demanded an attorney and his phone call.

"You'll have an attorney," the man grumbled at him as Matt came out of the bathroom. "One'll be appointed for you."

"I don't want that. I want a real attorney. One that I *pick*."

The man looked disgusted. "Kid like you can't have any money. You'll take the attorney appointed to you."

"My mom has money. She'd want me to have the attorney we hire, not some kid out of law school."

"Aw," the man said, "how sweet. You want Mommy to

take care of you. And her all the way out in Clydesdale by now, I bet, with the black lady doctor."

Matt froze.

Shut back in the jury room he tried frantically to think. How did they know where his mom and Dr. Alpert had gone? He tried the sound of "*black lady doctor*" on his tongue and found it tasted bad, sort of old-time-ish and just plain bad. If the doctor had been Caucasian and male, it would've sounded silly to say ". . . *gone with the white man doctor.*" Sort of like an old Tarzan film.

A great anger was rising in Matt. And along with it a great fear. Words slithered around his mind: *surveillance* and *spying* and *conspiracy* and *cover-up*. And *outwitted.*

He guessed it was after five o'clock, after everybody who normally worked at court had left, that they took him to the interrogation room.

They were just playing, he figured, the two officers who tried to talk to him in a cramped little room with a video camera in one corner of the wall, perfectly obvious even though it was small.

They took turns, one yelling at him that he might as well confess everything, the other acting sympathetic and saying things like, "Things just got out of hand, right? We have a picture of the hickey she gave you. She was hot stuff, right?" Wink, wink. "*I* understand. But then she started to give you mixed signals . . ."

Matt reached his snapping point. "*No*, we were not on a date, *no*, she did not give me a hickey, and when I tell Mr. Forbes you called Caroline hot stuff, *winkey winkey*, he's gonna get you *fired*, mister. And I've heard of mixed signals, but I've never seen them. I can hear 'no' as well as you can, and I figure one 'no' means '*no*'!"

After that they beat him up a little bit. Matt was surprised, but considering the way he had just threatened and sassed them, not too surprised.

And then they seemed to give up on him, leaving him alone in the interrogation room, which, unlike the jury room, had no windows. Matt said over and over, for the benefit of the video camera, "I'm innocent and I'm being denied my phone call and my attorney. I'm innocent . . ."

At last they came and got him. He was hustled between the good and bad cops into a completely empty courtroom. No, not empty, he realized. In the first row were a few reporters, one or two with sketchbooks ready.

When Matt saw that, just like a real trial, and imagined the pictures they'd sketch—just like he'd seen on TV, the lead in his stomach turned into a fluttering feeling of panic.

But this was what he wanted, wasn't it, to get the story out?

He was led to an empty table. There was another table, with several well-dressed men, all with piles of papers in front of them.

But the thing that held Matt's attention at that table was Caroline. He didn't recognize her at first. She was wearing a dove gray cotton dress. Gray! With no jewelry on at all, and subtle makeup. The only color was in her hair—a brazen auburn. It looked like her old hair, not the brindled color it had been when she was starting to become a werewolf. Had she learned to control her form at last? That was bad news. Very bad.

And finally, with an air of walking on eggshells, in came the jury. They had to know how irregular this was, but they kept coming in, just twelve of them, just enough to fill the jury seats.

Matt suddenly realized that there was a judge sitting at the desk high above him. Had he been there all along? No . . .

"All rise for Justice Thomas Holloway," boomed a bailiff. Matt stood and wondered if the trial was really going to start without his lawyer. But before everyone could sit, there was a crash of opening doors, and a tall bundle of papers on legs hurried into the courtroom, became a woman in her early twenties, and dumped the papers on the table beside him. "Gwen Sawicki here—present," the young woman gasped.

Judge Holloway's neck shot out like a tortoise's, to bring her into his realm of sight. "You have been appointed on behalf of the defense?"

"If it pleases Your Honor, yes, Your Honor—all of thirty

minutes ago. I had no idea we had gone to night sessions, Your Honor."

"Don't you be pert with me!" Judge Holloway snapped. As he went on to allow the prosecution attorneys to introduce themselves, Matt pondered on the word "pert." It was another of those words, he thought, that was never used toward males. A pert man was a joke. While a pert girl or woman sounded just fine. But why?

"Call me Gwen," a voice whispered beside him, and Matt looked to see a girl with brown eyes and brown hair back in a ponytail. She wasn't exactly pretty, but she looked honest and straightforward, which made her the prettiest thing in the room.

"I'm Matt—well, obviously," Matt said.

"Is this your girl, Carolyn?" Gwen was whispering, showing a picture of the old Caroline at some dance, wearing stilts, and with tanned legs that went up and up to almost meet before a miniskirt took over, black and lacy. She had on a white blouse so tight at the bust that it hardly seemed able to contain her natural assets. Her makeup was exactly the opposite of subtle.

"Her name's Caroline and she's never been my girl, but that's her—the real her," Matt whispered. "Before Klaus came and did something to her boyfriend, Tyler Smallwood. But I have to tell you what happened when she found out she was pregnant—"

She'd gone nuts, was what had happened. No one knew

where Tyler was—dead after the final fight against Klaus, turned into a full wolf in hiding; whatever. So Caroline had tried to pin it on Matt—until Shinichi appeared and became her boyfriend.

But Shinichi and Misao were playing a cruel joke on her, pretending that Shinichi would marry her. It was after she realized that Shinichi didn't care at all that Caroline had gone totally ballistic, and had really tried to make Matt fit the gaping hole in her life. Matt did his best to explain this to Gwen so she could explain it to the jury, until the judge's voice interrupted him.

"We will dispense with opening arguments," said Judge Holloway, "since the hour is so late. Will the prosecution call its first witness?"

"Wait! Objection!" Matt shouted, ignoring Gwen's tugging at his arm and her hissing: *"You can't object to the judge's rulings!"*

"And the judge can't do this to me," Matt said, twitching his T-shirt back from between her fingers. "I haven't even had a chance to meet with my public defender yet!"

"Maybe you should have accepted a public defender earlier," replied the judge, sipping from a glass of water. He suddenly thrust his head at Matt and snapped, "Eh?"

"That's ridiculous," cried Matt. "You wouldn't give me my phone call to get a lawyer!"

"Did he ever ask for a phone call?" Judge Holloway

snapped, his eyes traveling around the room.

The two officers who had beat Matt up solemnly shook their heads. At this, the bailiff, whom Matt suddenly recognized as the guy who'd kept him in the jury room for around four hours, began wagging his head back and forth in the negative. They all three wagged, almost in unison.

"Then you forfeited that right by not asking for it," the judge snapped. It seemed to be his only way of speaking. "You can't demand it in the middle of a trial. Now, as I was saying—"

"*I object!*" Matt shouted even louder. "They're all lying! Look at your own tapes of them interrogating me. All I kept saying—"

"Counselor," the judge snarled at Gwen, "control your client or you will be held in contempt of court!"

"You have to *shut up*," Gwen hissed at Matt.

"You can't make me shut up! You can't have this trial while you're breaking all the rules!"

"*Shut your trap!*" The judge belted out the words at a surprising volume. He then added, "The next person to make a remark without my express permission shall be held in contempt of court to the tune of a night in jail and five hundred dollars."

He paused to look around to see if this had sunk in. "Now," he said. "Prosecution, call your first witness."

"We call Caroline Beulah Forbes to the stand."

Caroline's figure had changed. Her stomach was sort of upside-down-avocado-shaped now. Matt heard murmurs.

"Caroline Beula Forbes, do you swear that the testimony you shall give will be the truth, the whole truth, and nothing but the truth?"

Somewhere deep inside, Matt was shaking. He didn't know if it was mostly anger or mostly fear or an equal combination of both. But he felt like a geyser ready to blow—not necessarily because he wanted to, but because forces beyond his control were taking hold of him. Gentle Matt, Quiet Matt, Obedient Matt—he had left all those behind somewhere. Raging Matt, Rampaging Matt, that was about all he could be.

From a dim outside world, voices came filtering into his reverie. And one voice pricked and stung like a nettle.

"Do you recognize the boy you have named as your former boyfriend Matthew Jeffrey Honeycutt here in this room?"

"Yes," the prickly nettle voice said softly. "He's sitting at the defense table, in the gray T-shirt."

Matt's head flew up. He looked Caroline straight in the eye.

"You *know* that's a lie," he said. "We never went on one date together. Ever."

The judge, who had seemed to be asleep, now woke up. "Bailiff!" he snapped. "Restrain the defendant immediately."

Matt tensed. As Gwen Sawicki moaned, Matt suddenly found himself being held while duct tape was wrapped round and round his mouth.

He fought. He tried to get up. So they duct-taped him around his waist to the chair. As they finally left him alone, the judge said, "If he runs off with that chair, you will pay it out of your own salary, *Miz* Sawicki."

Matt could feel Gwen Sawicki trembling beside him. Not with fear. He could recognize the about-to-explode expression and realized that she was going to be next. And then the judge would hold her in contempt and who would speak up for him?

He met her eyes and shook his head firmly at her. But he also shook his head at every lie Caroline came up with.

"We had to keep it a secret, our relationship," Caroline was saying demurely, straightening the gray dress. "Because Tyler Smallwood, my previous boyfriend, might have found out. Then he would have—I mean, I didn't want any trouble between them."

Yeah, Matt thought bitterly: you'd better walk carefully—because Tyler's dad probably has as many good friends in here as yours does. More. Matt tuned out until he heard the prosecutor say, "And did anything unusual happen on the night in question?"

"Well, we went out together in his car. We went over near the boardinghouse . . . no one would see us there . . .

Yes, I—I'm afraid I did give him a . . . a love-bite. But after that I wanted to leave, but he didn't stop. I had to try to fight him off. I scratched him with my nails—"

"The prosecution offers Peoples' Exhibit 2—a picture of the deep fingernail scores on the defendant's arm—"

Gwen's eyes, meeting Matt's, looked dull. Beaten. She showed Matt a picture of what he remembered: the deep marks made by the huge malach's teeth when he had pulled his arm out of its mouth. "The defense will stipulate . . ."

"So admitted."

"But no matter how I screamed and fought . . . well, he was too strong, and I—I couldn't—" Caroline tossed her head in agony of remembered shame. Tears flooded from her eyes.

"Your Honor, perhaps the defendant needs a break to freshen her makeup," Gwen suggested bitterly.

"Young lady, you are getting on my *nerves*. The prosecution can care for its own clients—I mean witnesses—"

"Your witness . . ."—from the prosecution.

Matt had scribbled as much of the real story as he could onto a blank sheet of paper while Caroline's theatrics had gone on. Gwen was now reading this.

"So," she said, "your ex, Tyler Smallwood, is not and has never been a"—she swallowed—"a werewolf."

Through her tears of shame Caroline laughed lightly. "Of course not. Werewolves aren't real."

"Like vampires."

"Vampires aren't real either, if that's what you mean. How *could* they be?" Caroline was looking into every shadow of the room as she said this.

Gwen was doing a good job, Matt realized. Caroline's demure patina was beginning to chip.

"And people never come back from the dead—in these modern times, I mean," Gwen said.

"Well, as to that"—malice had crept into Caroline's voice—"if you just go to the boardinghouse in Fell's Church, you can see that there's a girl called Elena Gilbert, who was *supposed* to have drowned last year. On Founder's Day, after the parade. She was Miss Fell's Church, of course."

There was a murmur among the reporters. Supernatural stuff sold better than anything else, especially if a pretty girl was involved. Matt could see a smirk making the rounds.

"Order! Miz Sawicki, you will keep to the facts in this case!"

"Yes, Your Honor." Gwen looked thwarted. "Okay, Caroline, let's go back to the day of the alleged assault. After the events you have narrated, did you call the police at once?"

"I was . . . too ashamed. But then I realized I might be pregnant or have some horrid disease, and I knew I had to tell."

"But that horrid disease wasn't lycanthropy—being a

werewolf, right? Because that couldn't be true."

Gwen looked anxiously down at Matt and Matt looked bleakly up at her. He'd hoped that if Caroline were forced to keep talking about werewolves she would eventually start to twitch. But she seemed to have complete control over herself now.

The judge seemed furious. "Young lady, I won't have my court made a joke with any more supernatural nonsense!"

Matt stared at the ceiling. He was going to jail. For a long time. For something he hadn't done. For something he would never do. And besides, now, there might be reporters going over to the boardinghouse to bother Elena and Stefan. Damn! Caroline had managed to get that in despite the blood oath she'd made never to give their secret away. Damon had signed that oath as well. For a moment Matt wished that Damon were back and right here, to take revenge on her. Matt didn't care how many times he got called "Mutt" if Damon would just appear. But Damon didn't.

Matt realized that the duct tape around his middle was low enough that he could slam his head against the defense table. He did this, making a small boom.

"If your client wishes to be completely immobilized, Miz Sawicki, it can be—"

But then they all heard it. Like an echo, but delayed. And much louder than the sound of a head striking a table.

BOOM!

And again.

BOOM!

And then the distant, disturbing sound of doors slamming open as if they had been hit by a battering ram.

At this point the people in the courtroom still could have scattered. But where was there to go?

BOOM! Another, closer door slamming open.

"Order! Order in the courtroom!"

Footsteps sounded down the wooden floor of the corridor.

"Order! Order!"

But no one, not even a judge, could stop this many people from muttering. And late in the evening, in a locked courthouse, after all that talk of vampires and werewolves . . .

Footsteps coming closer. A door, quite near, crashing and creaking.

A ripple of . . . something . . . went through the courtroom. Caroline gasped, clutching at her bulging stomach.

"Bar those doors! Bailiff! Lock them!"

"Bar them how, Your Honor? And they only lock from the outside!"

Whatever it was, it was very close—

The doors to the courtroom opened, creaking. Matt put a calming hand on Gwen's wrist, twisting his neck to see behind him.

Standing in the doorway was Saber, looking, as always,

as big as a small pony. Mrs. Flowers walked beside him; Stefan and Elena drew up the rear.

Heavy clicking footsteps as Saber, alone, went up to Caroline, who was gasping and quivering.

Utter silence as everyone took in the sight of the giant beast, his coat ebony black, his eyes dark and moist as he took a leisurely look around the courtroom.

Then, deep in his chest, Saber went *hmmf.*

Around Matt people were gasping and writhing, as if they itched all over. He stared and saw Gwen staring along with him as the gasping became a panting.

Finally Saber tilted his nose to the ceiling and *howled.*

What happened after that wasn't pretty from Matt's point of view. Not seeing Caroline's nose and mouth jut out to make a muzzle. Not seeing her eyes recede into small, deep, fur-lined holes.

And her hands, fingers shrinking into helplessly waving paws, widespread, with black claws. That wasn't pretty.

But the animal at the end was beautiful. Matt didn't know if she'd absorbed her gray dress or shucked it off or what. He did know that a handsome gray wolf leaped from the defendant's chair to lick up at Saber's chops, rolling all the way on the floor to frolic around the huge animal, who was so obviously the alpha wolf.

Saber made another deep *hmmf* sound. The wolf that had been Caroline rubbed her snout lovingly against his neck.

And it was happening in other places in the room. Both of the prosecutors, three of the jurors . . . the judge himself . . .

They were all changing, not to attack, but to forge their social bonds with this huge wolf, an alpha if ever there was one.

"We talked to him all the way," Elena explained in between cursing the duct tape in Matt's hair. "About not being aggressive and snapping off heads—Damon told me he did that once."

"We didn't want a bunch of murders," Stefan agreed. "And we knew no animal would be as big as he was. So we concentrated on bringing out all the wolf in him we could—wait, Elena—I've got the tape on this side. Sorry about this, Matt."

A sting as tape ripped free—and Matt put a hand to his mouth. Mrs. Flowers was snipping the duct tape that held him to the chair. Suddenly he was entirely free and he felt like shouting. He hugged Stefan, Elena, and Mrs. Flowers, saying, "*Thank you!*"

Gwen, unfortunately, was being sick in a trash can. Actually, Matt thought, she was lucky in having secured one. A juror was being sick over the railing.

"This is Ms. Sawicki," Matt said proudly. "She came in after the trial had begun, and did a really good job for me."

"He said 'Elena,'" Gwen whispered when she could speak. She was staring at a small wolf, with patches of thinning hair, that came limping down from the judge's chair to cavort around Saber, who was accepting all such gestures with dignity.

"I'm Elena," said Elena, in between giving Matt mighty hugs.

"The one who's . . . supposed to be dead?"

Elena took a moment out to hug Gwen. "Do I feel dead?"

"I—I don't know. No. But—"

"But I have a pretty little headstone in the Fell's Church cemetery," Elena assured her—then suddenly, with a change in countenance, "Did Caroline tell you that?"

"She told the whole room that. Especially the reporters."

Stefan looked at Matt and smiled wryly. "You may just live to have your revenge on Caroline."

"I don't want revenge anymore. I just want to go home. I mean—" He looked at Mrs. Flowers in consternation.

"If you can think of my house as 'home' while your dear mother is away, I am very happy," said Mrs. Flowers.

"Thank you," Matt said quietly. "I really mean that. But Stefan . . . what are the reporters going to write?"

"If they're smart, they won't write anything at all."

23

In the car, Matt sat by the sleeping Meredith with Saber crammed in at their feet, listening in shock and horror as they recounted Meredith's story. When they were done, he was able to speak about his own experiences.

"I'm going to have nightmares all my life about Cole Reece," he admitted. "And even though I slapped an amulet on him, and he cried, Dr. Alpert said he was still infected. How can we fight something this far out of control?"

Elena knew he was looking at her. She dug her nails into her palms. "It isn't that I haven't tried to use *Wings of Purification* over the town. I've tried so hard that I feel as if I'll burst. But it's no good. I can't control any Wings Powers at all! I think—after what I've learned about

Meredith—that I may need training. But how do I get it? Where? From who?"

There was a long silence in the car. At last Matt said, "We're all in the dark. Look at that courtroom! How can they have so many werewolves in one town?"

"Wolves are sociable," Stefan said quietly. "It looks as if there is a whole community of werewolves in Ridgemont. Seeded among the various Bear and Moose and Lions Clubs of course. For spying on the only creatures they're scared of: humans."

At the boardinghouse Stefan carried Meredith to the first-floor bedroom and Elena pulled the covers over her. Then she went to the kitchen, where the conversation was continuing.

"What about those werewolves' families? Their wives?" she demanded as she rubbed Matt's shoulders where she knew the muscles must hurt fiercely from being handcuffed behind his back. Her soft fingers soothed bruises, but her hands were strong, and she kept kneading and kneading until her own shoulder muscles began to swear at her . . . and beyond.

Stefan stopped her. "Move over, love, I've got evil vampire magic. This is necessary medical treatment," he added sternly to Matt. "So you have to take it no matter how much it hurts." Elena could still feel him, if faintly, through their connection and she saw how he anesthetized

Matt's mind and then dug into the knotted shoulders as if he was kneading stiff dough, meanwhile reaching out with his Powers of healing.

Mrs. Flowers came by just then with mugs of hot, sweet cinnamon tea. Matt drained his mug and his head fell back slightly. His eyes were shut, his lips parted. Elena *felt* a huge wave of pain and tension flood away from him. And then she hugged both of her boys and cried.

"They picked me up on my own driveway," Matt admitted as Elena sniffled. "And they did it by the book, but they wouldn't even look at the—the *chaos* all around them."

Mrs. Flowers approached again, looking serious. "Dear Matt, you've had a terrible day. What you need is a long rest." She glanced at Stefan, as if to see how this would impact him, with so few blood donors. Stefan smiled reassuringly at her. Matt, still being kneaded pliant, had just nodded. After that his color started coming back and a little smile curved his lips.

"There's m'main man," he said, when Saber butted his way through traffic to pant directly in Matt's face. "Buddy, I love your dog breath," he declared. "You saved me. Can he have a treat, Mrs. Flowers?" he asked, turning slightly unfocused blue eyes on her.

"I know just what he'd like. I have half a roast left in the refrigerator that just needs to be heated a bit." She punched buttons and in a short while, said, "Matt, would you like to do the honors? Remember to take the bone out—he might choke on it."

Matt took the large pot roast, which, heated, smelled so good it made him aware that he was starving. He felt his morals collapse. "Mrs. Flowers, do you think I could make a sandwich before I give it to him?"

"Oh, you poor dear boy!" she cried. "And I never even thought—of course they wouldn't give you lunch or dinner."

Mrs. Flowers got bread and Matt was happy enough with that, bread and meat, the simplest sandwich imaginable—and so good it curled his toes.

Elena wept just a little more. So easy to make two creatures happy with one simple thing. More than two—they were all happy to see Matt safe and to watch Saber get his proper reward.

The enormous dog had followed every movement of that roast with his eyes, tail swishing back and forth on the floor. But when Matt, still chomping, offered him the large piece of meat that was left, Saber just cocked his head to one side, staring at it as if to say, "You have to be joking."

"Yes, it's for you. Go on and take it now," Mrs. Flowers said firmly. Finally, Saber opened his enormous mouth to take hold of the end of the roast, tail twirling like a helicopter blade. His body language was so clear that Matt laughed out loud.

"This once on the floor with us," Mrs. Flowers added magnificently, spreading a large rug over the kitchen floorboards.

Saber's joy was only surpassed by his good manners. He put the roast on the rug and then trotted up to each of the humans to push a wet nose into hand or waist or under a chin, and then he trotted back and attacked his prize.

"I wonder if he misses Sage?" Elena murmured.

"*I* miss Sage," Matt said indistinctly. "We need all the magic help we can get."

Meanwhile Mrs. Flowers was hurrying around the kitchen making ham and cheese sandwiches and bagging them like school lunches. "Anybody who wakes up tonight hungry must have *something* to eat," she said. "Ham and cheese, chicken salad, some nice crisp carrots, and a big hunk of apple pie." Elena went to help her. She didn't know why, but she wanted to cry some more. Mrs. Flowers patted her. "We are all feeling—er, *strung out*," she announced gravely. "Anyone who doesn't feel like going right to sleep is probably running on too much adrenaline. My sleeping aid will help with that. And I think we can trust our animal friends and the wards on the roof to keep us safe tonight."

Matt was practically asleep on his feet now. "Mrs.

Flowers—someday I'll repay you . . . but for now, I can't keep my eyes open."

"In other words, bedtime, kiddies," Stefan said. He closed Matt's fingers firmly around a packed lunch, then steered him toward the stairs. Elena gathered several more lunches, kissed Mrs. Flowers twice, and went up to Stefan's room.

She had the attic bed straightened and was opening a plastic bag when Stefan came in from putting Matt to bed.

"Is he okay?" she said anxiously. "I mean, will he be okay tomorrow?"

"He'll be okay in his body. I got most of the damage healed."

"And in his *mind*?"

"It's a tough thing. He just ran smack into Real Life. Arrested, knowing they might lynch him, not knowing if anybody would be able to figure out what had happened to him. He thought that even if we tracked him it would come down to a fight, which would have been hard to win—with so few of us, and not much magic left."

"But Saber fixed 'em," Elena said.

She looked thoughtfully at the sandwiches she'd laid out on the bed. "Stefan, do you want chicken salad or ham?" she asked.

There was a silence. But it was moments before Elena looked up at him in astonishment. "Oh, Stefan—I—I actually *forgot.* I just—today has been so strange—*I forgot*—"

"I'm flattered," Stefan said. "And you're sleepy. Whatever Mrs. Flowers puts in her tea—"

"I think the government would be interested in it," Elena offered. "For spies and things. But for now . . ." She held her arms out, head bent back, neck exposed.

"No, love. I remember this afternoon, if you don't. And I swore I was going to start hunting, and I am," Stefan said firmly.

"You're going to leave me?" Elena said, startled out of her warm satisfaction. They stared at each other.

"*Don't* leave," Elena said, combing her hair away from her neck. "I had it all planned out, how you'll drink, and how we'll sleep holding each other. *Please* don't leave, Stefan."

She knew how hard he found it to leave her. Even if she *was* grimy and worn out, even if she *was* wearing grungy jeans and had dirt under her fingernails. She was endlessly beautiful and endlessly powerful and mysterious to him. He longed for her. Elena could feel it through their bond, which was beginning to hum, beginning to warm up, beginning to draw him in close.

"But, Elena," he said. He was trying to be sensible! Didn't he know she didn't want sensible at this particular moment?

"Right here." Elena tapped the soft spot on her neck.

Their bond was singing like an electric power line now. But Stefan was stubborn. "You need to eat, yourself. You have to keep your strength up."

Elena immediately picked up a chicken salad sandwich and bit into it. Mmm . . . yummy. Really good. She would have to pick Mrs. Flowers a wildflower bouquet. They were all so well taken care of here. She had to think of more ways to help.

Stefan was watching her eat. It made him hungry, but that was because he was used to being fed round the clock, and not used to exercise. Elena could hear everything through their connection and she heard him thinking that he was glad to see Elena renewing herself. That he had learned discipline now; that it wouldn't do him any harm to go to bed one night *feeling* hungry. He would hold his sleepy adorable Elena all night.

No! Elena was horrified. Since he'd been imprisoned in the Dark Dimension, anything that hinted at Stefan going without filled her with appalling terror. Suddenly she had trouble swallowing the bite she'd taken.

"Right here, right here . . . please?" she begged him. She didn't want to have to seduce him into it, but she would if he forced her to. She would wash her hands into pristine cleanliness, and change into a long, clinging nightgown, and stroke his stubborn canines in between kisses, and touch them with her tongue tip gently, just at the base where they wouldn't cut her as they responded and grew. And by then he would be dizzy, he would be out of control, he would be hers completely.

All right, all right! Stefan thought to her. *Mercy!*

"I don't want to give you mercy. I don't want you to let me go," she said, holding her arms out to him, and heard her own voice soft and tender and yearning. "I want you to hold me and keep me forever, and I want to hold you and keep you forever."

Stefan's face had changed. He looked at her with the look he'd worn in prison when she had come to visit him in an outfit—very unlike the grubby one she wore now—and he'd said, bewildered, "All this . . . it's for me?"

There had been razor wire between them then. Now there was nothing to separate them and Elena could see how much Stefan wanted to come to her. She reached a little farther and then Stefan came into the circle of her arms and held her tightly but with infinite care not to use enough strength to hurt her. When he relaxed and leaned his forehead against hers, Elena realized that she would never be tired or sad or frightened without being able to think of this feeling and that it would uphold her for the rest of her life.

At last they sank down together on the sheets, comforting each other in equal measure; exchanging sweet, warm kisses. With each kiss, Elena felt the outside world and all its horrors drift farther and farther away. How could anything be wrong when she herself felt that heaven was near? Matt and Meredith, Damon and Bonnie would surely all be safe and happy too. Meanwhile, every kiss brought her closer to paradise, and she knew Stefan felt the same way. They were so happy together that Elena knew that soon the entire universe would echo with their own joy, which overflowed like pure light and transformed everything it touched.

Bonnie woke and realized she had only been unconscious for a few minutes. She began to shiver, and once she started she couldn't seem to stop. She felt a wave of heat envelop her, and she knew that Damon was trying to warm her, but still the trembling wouldn't go away.

"What's wrong?" Damon asked, and his voice was different from usual.

"I don't know," Bonnie said. She didn't. "Maybe it's because they kept starting to throw me out the window. I wasn't going to scream about that," she added hastily, in case he assumed she would. "But then when they talked about torturing me—"

She felt a sort of spasm go through Damon. He was holding her too hard. "Torturing you! They threatened you with that?"

"Yes, because, you know, Misao's star ball was gone. They knew that it had been poured out; I didn't tell them that. But I had to tell them that it was my fault that the last half got poured out, and then they got mad at me. Oh! Damon, you're hurting me!"

"So it was *your* fault it got poured out, was it?"

"Well, I figure it was. You couldn't have done it if I hadn't gotten drunk, and—wh-what's wrong, Damon? Are you mad too?" He really was holding her so that she really couldn't breathe.

Slowly, she felt his arms loosen a little. "A word of advice, little redbird. When people are threatening to torture and kill you, it might be more—expedient—to tell them that it's someone else's fault. Especially if that happens to be the truth."

"I know that!" Bonnie said indignantly. "But they were going to kill me anyway. If I'd told about *you*, they'd've hurt *you*, too."

Damon pulled her roughly back now, so that she had to look him in the face. Bonnie could also feel the delicate touch of a telepathic mind probe. She didn't resist; she was too busy wondering why he had plum-colored shadows under his eyes. Then he shook her a little, and she stopped wondering.

"Don't you understand even the basics of self-preservation?" he said, and she thought he looked angry again. He was certainly different from any other time that she'd seen him—except once, she thought, and that was when Elena had been "Disciplined" for saving Lady Ulma's life, back when Ulma had been a slave. He'd had the same expression then, so menacing that even Meredith had been frightened of him, and yet so filled with guilt that Bonnie had longed to comfort him.

But there had to be some other reason, Bonnie's mind told her. Because you're not Elena, and he's never going to treat you the way he treats Elena. A vision of the brown room rose before her, and she felt certain that he would never have put Elena there. Elena wouldn't have let him, for one thing.

"Do I have to go back?" she asked, realizing that she was being petty and silly and that the brown room had seemed like a haven just a little while ago.

"Go back?" Damon said, a little too quickly. She had the feeling that he'd seen the brown room too, now, through her eyes. "Why? The landlady gave me everything in the room. So I have your real clothes and a bunch of star balls down there, in case you weren't through with one. But why would you think you might have to go back?"

"Well, I know you were looking for a lady of quality, and I'm not one," Bonnie said simply.

"That was just so I could change back into a vampire," Damon said. "And what do you think is holding you up in the air right now?" But this time Bonnie knew somehow that the sensations from the "Never Ever" star balls were still in her mind and that Damon was seeing them too. He was a vampire again. And the contents of these star balls were so abominable that Damon's stony exterior finally cracked. Bonnie could almost guess what he thought of them, and of her, left to shiver under her one blanket every night.

And then, to her total astonishment, Damon, the ever-composed, brand-new vampire blurted, "I'm sorry. I didn't think about how that place would be for you. Is there anything that will make you feel better?"

Bonnie blinked. She wondered, seriously, if she were dreaming. Damon didn't apologize. Damon *famously* didn't apologize, or explain, or speak so nicely to people, unless he wanted something from them. But one thing seemed real. She didn't have to sleep in the brown room anymore.

This was so exciting that she flushed a little, and dared say, "Could we go down to the ground? Slowly? Because the truth is that I'm just terrified of heights."

Damon blinked, but said, "Yes, I think I can manage that. Is there anything else you'd like?"

"Well—there are a couple of girls who'd be donors—happily—if—well—if there's any money left—if you could save them . . ."

Damon said a little sharply, "Of course there's some

money left. I even wrung your share back out of that hag of a landlady."

"Well, then, there's that secret that I told you, but I don't know if you remember."

"How soon do you think you'll feel well enough to start?" asked Damon.

24

Stefan woke early. He spent the time from dawn until breakfast just watching Elena, who even in sleep had an inner glow like a golden flame through a faintly rose-colored candle.

At breakfast, everyone was more or less still wrapped up in thoughts of the day before. Meredith showed Matt the picture of her brother, Cristian, the vampire. Matt briefly told Meredith about the inner workings of the Ridgemont court system and painted her a picture of Caroline as werewolf. It was clear that both of them felt safer at the boardinghouse than anywhere else.

And Elena, who had woken up with Stefan's mind all around her, embracing her, and her own mind still full of light, was completely at a loss for a Plan A or any other letter. She had to be told gently by the others that only one thing made sense.

"Stefan," Matt said, draining a mug of Mrs. Flowers's pitch-black coffee. "He's the only one who might be able to use his mind instead of Post-it Notes on the kids."

And, "Stefan," said Meredith. "He's the only one Shinichi might be afraid of."

"I'm no use at all," Elena said sadly. She had no appetite. She had gotten dressed with a feeling of love and compassion toward all humankind and a desire to help protect her hometown, but as everyone pointed out, she was probably going to have to spend the day in the root cellar. Reporters might come to call.

They're right, Stefan sent to Elena. *I'm the only logical person to find out what's really going on in Fell's Church.*

He actually went while the rest of them were finishing breakfast. Only Elena knew why; only she could feel him at the limits of her telepathic range.

Stefan was hunting. He drove into the New Wood, got out, and finally startled a rabbit out of the brush. He Influenced it to rest and not be frightened. Surreptitiously, in this thin woodland without cover, he took a little blood from it . . . and *choked.*

It tasted like some kind of hideous liquid flavored with rodent. Was a rabbit a rodent? He had been lucky enough to find a rat one day in his prison cell and it had tasted vaguely like this.

But now, for days, he had been drinking human blood. Not just that, but the rich, potent blood of strong, adventurous, and in several cases paranormally talented individuals—the crème de la crème. How could he have gotten used to it so quickly?

It shamed him now, to think of what he'd taken. Elena's blood, of course, was enough to drive any vampire wild. And Meredith, whose blood had the deep crimson taste of some primordial ocean, and Bonnie, who tasted like a telepath's dessert. And finally Matt, the All-American red-blooded boy.

They'd fed him and fed him by the hour, far past what he needed to survive. They'd fed him until he'd begun to heal, and seeing that he was healing, they'd fed him more. And it had gone on and on, ending with Elena last night—Elena, whose hair was taking on a silvery cast and whose blue eyes seemed almost radiant. Back in the Dark Dimension, Damon hadn't exercised any restraint at all. Elena hadn't exercised any on her own behalf.

That silvery cast . . . Stefan's stomach clenched when he thought about it, about the last time he'd seen her hair that way. She'd been dead then. On her feet, but dead just the same.

Stefan let the rabbit scamper away. He was taking another oath. He must *not* make Elena into a vampire again. That meant no significant blood exchange between the two of them for at least a week—either giving or taking might tip her over the edge.

He must once again adjust to the taste of animal blood.

Stefan shut his eyes briefly, remembering the horror of the first time. The cramps. The shakes. The agony that seemed to tell his entire body that it wasn't getting fed. The feeling that his veins might explode into flame at any moment, and the pain in his jaws.

He stood up. He was lucky to be alive. Luckier than he ever could have dreamed he would be in having Elena beside him. He would work through the readjustment without bothering her by telling her, he decided.

Just two hours later Stefan was back at the boardinghouse, limping slightly. Matt, who met him at the heavy front door, noticed the limp. "You okay? You'd better get in and ice it."

"Just a cramp," Stefan said briefly. "I'm not used to exercise. Didn't get any back there in—you know." He looked away, flushing. So did Matt, hot and cold and furious at the people who had put Stefan in this condition. Vampires were pretty resilient, but he had the feeling—no, he *knew*—that Stefan had almost died in his prison cell. One day under lock and key had convinced Matt that *he* never wanted to be imprisoned again.

He followed Stefan to the kitchen where Elena,

Meredith, and Mrs. Flowers were—what else?—drinking mugs of tea.

And Matt felt a twinge when Elena instantly noticed the limp and got up and went to Stefan, and Stefan held her tightly, running reassuring fingers through her hair. Matt couldn't help but wonder, though—was that glorious golden hair turning lighter? More like the silvery gold it had been when Elena had first gone with Stefan and was on her way to turning into a vampire? Stefan certainly seemed to be inspecting it closely, turning each handful as he raked his fingers through it.

"Any luck?" Elena asked him, tension in her voice.

Wearily, Stefan shook his head. "I went up streets and down streets and wherever I found a—a young girl who was contorted, or whirling round and round, or doing any other of the things the papers mentioned, I tried to Influence them. Well, maybe I shouldn't have bothered with the whirling girls. I couldn't catch their eyes. But the final count is zero for eleven."

Elena turned toward Meredith in agitation. "What do we do?"

Mrs. Flowers busily began rummaging through bundles of herbs that hung above her stove. "You need a nice cup of tea."

"And a rest," Meredith said, patting him lightly on the hand. "Can I get you anything?"

"Well—I've got a new idea—scrying. But I need Misao's star ball to see if it will work. Don't worry," he added, "I won't use any of the Power in it; I just need to look at the surface."

"I'll bring it," Elena offered, getting up promptly from where she was sitting on his lap. Matt started slightly and looked at Mrs. Flowers as Elena went to the door of the root cellar and pushed. Nothing moved and Mrs. Flowers simply watched benignly. It was Stefan who rose to help her, still limping. Then Matt and Meredith got up, Meredith asking, "Mrs. Flowers, are you *sure* we should keep the star ball in that same safe?"

"Ma*ma* says we're doing the right thing," Mrs. Flowers answered serenely.

After that things happened very fast.

As if they'd rehearsed it, Meredith pressed the exact place to open the root cellar door. Elena fell to her hands and knees. Faster than even he had imagined he could go, Matt went barreling toward Stefan with one shoulder down. Mrs. Flowers was frantically pulling great swaths of dried herbs down from where they hung above the kitchen table.

And then Matt was hitting Stefan with all the power in his body and Stefan was stumbling over Elena, his head going down and down and meeting no resistance on the way. Meredith was coming at him sideways and helping him do a complete forward flip in the air. As soon as the flip took him out of the doorway and he was cartwheeling down the stairs, Elena got up and shut the door and Meredith leaned against it, as Matt shouted, *"How do you keep in a kitsune?"*

"These might help," gasped Mrs. Flowers, stuffing odiferous herbs into the crack under the door.

"And—iron!" cried Elena, and she and Meredith and Matt all ran to the den where there was an enormous, tripartite iron fire screen. Somehow they bundled it back to the kitchen and set it upright against the root cellar door. Just then the first crash came from the inside against it, but the iron was heavy and the second crash against the door was weaker.

"What are you doing? Have you all gone crazy?" Stefan shouted plaintively, but as the entire group began to cover the door in Post-it Note amulets, he cursed instead and became pure Shinichi. *"You'll be sorry, damn you! Misao's not right. She cries and cries. You'll make it up to her with your blood, but not before I introduce you to some special friends of mine. The kind who know how to cause real pain!"*

Elena lifted her head, as if hearing something. Matt watched her frown. Then she called to Shinichi, "Don't even try to probe for Damon. He's gone. And if you try to track him I'll fry your brains."

Sullen silence greeted her from the root cellar.

"My goodness gracious, what next?" murmured Mrs. Flowers.

Elena simply nodded for the others to follow her, and they went all the way to the very top of the house—Stefan's room—and spoke in whispers.

"How did *you* know?"

"Did you use telepathy?"

"*I* didn't know at first," Matt admitted, "but Elena was acting as if the star ball was in the root cellar. Stefan knows it's not there. I guess," he added with a guilty start, "that I invited him in."

"I knew as soon as he started *groping* my hair," Elena said with a shudder. "Stefan and D—I mean, *Stefan* knows I only like it touched lightly, and at the ends. Not *mauled* like that. Remember all Shinichi's little songs about golden hair? He's a nutcase. Anyway, I could tell from the feel of his mind."

Matt felt ashamed. All his wondering about Elena maybe changing into a vampire . . . and this was the answer, he thought.

"I noticed his lapis ring," Meredith said. "I saw him with it on his right hand as he went out earlier. When he came back he had it on his left hand."

There was a brief pause as they all stared at her. She shrugged. "It was part of my training, noticing little things."

"Good point," Matt said at last. "Good point. He

wouldn't be able to change it in sunlight."

"How did *you* know, Mrs. Flowers?" Elena asked. "Or was it just the way *we* were behaving?"

"Goodness, no, you're all very good little actors. But as soon as he stepped over the threshold Ma*ma* fairly shrieked at me: 'What are you doing, letting a kitsune into your house?' So then I knew what we were in for."

"We beat him!" Elena said, beaming. "We actually caught Shinichi off guard! I can hardly believe it."

"Believe it," Meredith said with a wry smile. "He was off guard for a *moment.* He'll be thinking up revenge right now."

Something else was worrying Matt. He turned to Elena. "I thought that you said that both you and Shinichi had keys that could take you anywhere, anytime. So why couldn't he have just said, 'Take me inside the boarding-house where the star ball is'?"

"Those were different keys from the Twin Fox key," Elena said, her brows drawn together. "They're, like, the Master Keys and Shinichi and Misao still have them both. I don't know why he didn't use his. Although it would have given him away the moment he was inside."

"Not if he went inside the root cellar, and stayed there the whole time," Meredith said. "And maybe a Master Key can override the 'not invited inside' rule."

Mrs. Flowers said, "But Ma*ma* still would have told me.

Also there are no keyholes in the root cellar. At all."

"'No keyholes' wouldn't matter, I don't *think*," Elena answered. "I think he just wanted to show how clever he was, and how he could fool us into *giving* him Misao's star ball."

Before anyone else could say a word, Meredith held out her palm, with a shining key on it. The key was golden with diamonds inset and had a very familiar outline.

"That's one of the Master Keys!" cried Elena. "It's what we thought the Twin Fox key would look like!"

"It sort of came out of his jeans pocket when he did that flip," Meredith said innocently.

"When you were flipping him over me, you mean," said Elena. "I suppose you picked his pocket too."

"So, right *now*, Shinichi doesn't have a key to escape with!" Matt said excitedly.

"No key to make keyholes," Elena agreed, dimpling.

"He can have fun changing into a mole and burrowing out of the root cellar," Meredith said coolly. "That's if he's got his transforming gear or whatever with him." She added, with a troubled change in her voice, "I wonder . . . if we should have Matt tell one other person where he's actually hidden the star ball. Just . . . well, just in case."

Matt saw knitted brows all around him. But suddenly the realization hit him that he *had* to tell someone that he'd hidden the star ball in his closet. The group—including

Stefan—had picked him to hide it because he had so stubbornly resisted when Shinichi was using Damon's body as a puppet to torture him a month ago. Matt had proved then that he would die in hideous pain rather than endanger his friends. But if Matt were to die *now*, Misao's star ball might be lost to the group forever. And only Matt knew how close he had come today to tumbling down the stairs along with Shinichi.

Far below they all heard a shout. "Hello! Is anybody home? Elena!"

"That's my Stefan," Elena said and then, without a shred of dignity, she ran to launch herself from the foyer into his arms. He looked startled, but managed to break her fall before they both went down on the porch.

"What's been going on?" he said, his body vibrating infinitesimally, as with the urge to fight. "The whole house smells like kitsune!"

"It's all right," Elena said. "Come and see." She led him upstairs to his room. "We've got him in the root cellar," she added.

Stefan looked confused. "You've got who in the root cellar?"

"With iron against the door," Matt said triumphantly. "And herbs and amulets all over it. And, anyway, Meredith got his *key*."

"His *key*? You're talking about—Shinichi?" Stefan

turned on Meredith, green eyes wide. "While I've been gone?"

"It was mostly an accident. I sort of stuck my hand in his pocket when he was upside down and off balance. And I lucked out and got the Master Key—unless this is an ordinary house key."

Stefan stared at it. "It's the real thing. Elena knows that. Meredith, you're incredible!"

"Yes, it's the right one," Elena confirmed. "I remember the shape—pretty elaborate, yes?" She took it from Meredith's hand.

"What are you going to—"

"Might as well test it," Elena said with a mischievous smile. She walked to the door of the room, shut it, said, "The den downstairs," inserted the winged key in the lock, and opened the door, stepping through and shutting the door behind her. Before anyone could speak, she was back, with the poker from the den held aloft in triumph.

"It works!" Stefan cried.

"That's amazing," Matt said.

Stefan looked almost feverish. "But don't you realize what it means? It means we can *use* this key. We can go anywhere we like without using Power. Even to the Dark Dimension! But first—while he's still here—we ought to *do* something about Shinichi."

"You're in no condition to do that now, dear Stefan,"

Mrs. Flowers said, shaking her head. "I'm sorry, but the truth is that we have been very, very lucky. That wicked kitsune was off guard back then. He won't be now."

"I still have to try," Stefan said quietly. "Every one of you has been tormented or had to fight—whether with your fists or your minds," he added, bowing slightly to Mrs. Flowers. "I've suffered but I've never had a chance to *fight* him. I *have* to try."

Matt said, just as quietly, "I'll go with you."

Elena added, "We can all fight together. Right, Meredith?"

Meredith nodded slowly, taking Stefan's poker from *his* fireplace. "Yes. It may be a low blow, but—together."

"I say it's a higher blow than letting him live and go on hurting people. Anyway, we'll take care of it . . . together," Elena said firmly. "Right *now*!"

Matt started to get up, but his motion was frozen in midair as he stared in horror. Simultaneously, with the grace of hunting lionesses or ballet dancers the two girls closed in on Stefan, and simultaneously they swung their separate pokers; Elena hitting him in the head and Meredith hitting him squarely in the groin. Stefan reeled away from the blow to the head, but simply said, "Ow!" when Meredith hit him. Matt knocked Elena out of the way and then, turning as precisely as if he were on the football field, got Meredith out of "Stefan's" way too.

But this imposter had obviously decided not to fight back. Stefan's form melted. Misao, green leaves woven into her scarlet-tipped black hair, stood before them. To Matt's shock, her face was pinched and pale. She was obviously very ill, although still defiant. But there was no mockery in her voice tonight.

"What have you done with my star ball? And my *brother*?" she demanded feebly.

"Your brother's safely locked up," Matt said, hardly knowing what he was telling her. Despite all the crimes Misao had committed he couldn't help feeling sorry for her. She was clearly desperate and ill.

"I *know* that. I was going to *say* my brother will kill you all—not as a game, but in *anger*." Now Misao looked wretched and frightened. "You've never seen him *really* angry."

"You've never seen Stefan angry either," Elena said. "At least not when he had all his Power."

Misao just shook her head. A dried leaf floated from her hair. "You don't understand!"

"I doubt we understand anything. Meredith, have we searched this girl?"

"No, but surely she wouldn't have brought the other one—"

Elena said crisply, "Matt, take a book and read it. I'll tell you when we're done."

Matt was reluctant to turn his back on a kitsune, even a sick one. But when even Mrs. Flowers nodded gently he obeyed. Still, back turned or not, he could hear noises. And the noises suggested that Misao was being held tightly and searched thoroughly. At first the sounds were all negative murmurs.

"Huh-uh . . . huh-uh . . . huh-uh . . . huh-*oops*!" There was a rattle of metal on wood.

Matt only turned when Elena said, "Okay, you can look. It was in her front pocket." She added to Misao, who was looking as if she might faint, "We didn't *want* to have to hold you and search you. But this key—where in *heaven's* name did you get keys like this, anyway?"

A pink spot showed on Misao's cheeks. "Heaven is right. They're the only two left of the Master Keys—and they belong to Shinichi and me. *I* figured out how to steal them from the Celestial Court. That was . . . a long time ago."

At that moment they heard a car on the road—Stefan's Porsche. In the dead silence that followed, they could also see the car through Stefan's window as it swung into the driveway.

"No one goes down," Elena said tersely. "No one invites him in."

Meredith shot her a keen glance. "Shinichi could have tunneled out like a mole by now. And he's *already* been invited in."

"My fault for not warning you all—but anyway, if it is Shinichi and he's done anything to hurt Stefan he's going to see me when *I'm* angry. The words *Wings of Destruction* just popped into my head and something inside me wants to say them."

There was a chill in the room.

No one met Stefan, but in a moment they could all hear running footsteps. Stefan appeared at his door, burst through, and found himself confronted with a row of people all looking at him suspiciously.

"What the *hell* is going on?" he demanded, staring at Misao, who was being held up between Meredith and Matt. "Misao—"

Elena took two steps toward him—and wound herself around him, drawing him into a deep kiss. For a moment he resisted, but then, bit by bit, his opposition collapsed despite the roomful of observers.

When Elena finally let go, she just leaned against Stefan, breathing hard. The others were all crimson with embarrassment. Stefan, flushed as he was, held her tightly.

"I'm sorry," Elena whispered. "But you've already 'come home' twice. First, it was Shinichi and we locked him in the root cellar. Then it was *her*." She pointed, without looking, toward the cowering Misao. "I didn't know how to make sure that Shinichi hadn't escaped somehow—"

"And you're sure now?"

"Oh, yes. I recognize you. You're always ready to let me in."

Matt realized that she was shaking and quickly stood up so she could sit, for at least a minute or two, in peace.

The peace lasted less than a minute.

"I want my star ball!" Misao cried. "I need to put Power in it or I'll go on weakening—and then you'll have murdered me."

"Go on weakening? Is the liquid evaporating out of the star ball or something?" Meredith asked. Matt was thinking about what he'd seen on his home block before the Ridgemont sheriffs had got him.

"You've gathered Power to put in it?" he asked mildly. "Power from yesterday, maybe?"

"Power from ever since you took it. But it isn't joined with . . . me. With my star ball. It's mine, but not *yet*."

"Like maybe some Power from making Cole Reece eat his guinea pig while it was alive? From making kids burn down their own houses?" Matt's voice was gravelly.

"What does it matter?" Misao retorted sullenly. "It's mine. They were my ideas, not yours. You can't keep me away—"

"Meredith, keep *me* away from *her*. I've known that kid Cole since he was born. I'll always have nightmares . . ."

Misao perked up like a wilting plant getting water. "Have nightmares, have nightmares," she whispered.

There was a silence. Then Meredith said, carefully and expressionlessly, as if she were thinking of the stave, "You're a nasty little thing, aren't you? Is that your food? Bad memories, nightmares, fear of the future?"

Misao was plainly stumped. She couldn't see the catch. It was like asking a regular hungry teenager "How about some pizza and a Coke? Is that what you want?" Misao couldn't even see that her appetites were wrong, so she couldn't lie.

"You were right before," Stefan said forcefully. "We have your star ball. The only way to make us give it back would be to do something for us. We're supposed to be able to control *you* anyway because we have it—"

"Old-ways thinking. Obsolete," Misao growled.

There was a dead silence. Matt felt his stomach plummet.

They had been betting on "old-ways thinking" all along. To get Shinichi's star ball by making Misao tell them where it was. Their ultimate goal had been to control Shinichi using *his* star ball.

"You don't understand," Misao said, pitifully and yet angrily at the same time. "My brother will help me fill my star ball again. But what we did in this town—it was an *order*, not just for fun."

"Could'a fooled me," Elena murmured, but Stefan's head jerked up and he said, "An *order*? From *who*?"

“*I . . . don’t . . . know!*” Misao screamed. “Shinichi gets the orders. Then he tells me what to do. But whoever it is should be happy by now. The town is almost destroyed. He ought to give me some *help* here!” She glared at the group, and they stared back.

Without knowing that he was going to say it, Matt said, “Let’s put her in the root cellar with Shinichi. I’ve got this feeling that we might all be sleeping in the storage room tonight.”

"Sleeping in the storage room with every wall covered in Post-it Note amulets," added Meredith grimly. "If we have enough. I got another packet, but it doesn't go very far when you're trying to cover a room."

"Okay," Elena said. "Who's got Shinichi's key?"

Matt raised his hand. "In my—"

"Don't tell me!" exclaimed Elena. "I've got hers. *We can't lose them.* Stefan and I are one team; you guys are the other."

They half-led and half-supported Misao out of Stefan's room and down the stairs. Misao didn't try to run away from them, to struggle, or to speak to them. This only made Matt more suspicious of her. He saw Stefan and Elena glance toward each other and knew they were feeling the same way.

But what else was there to do with her? There was no other way, humanely, or even inhumanely, to restrain her for days. They had her star ball, and according to books that was supposed to allow them to control her, but she was right, it seemed to be an obsolete notion, because it didn't work. They'd tried with Stefan and Meredith holding her tightly, while Matt got the star ball from where he'd been keeping it in a shoebox on the upper shelf above the clothes in his closet.

He and Elena had tried to get Misao to do things while holding the almost empty sphere: to make Misao tell where her brother's star ball was, and so on. But it simply didn't work.

"Maybe when there's so little Power in it, it doesn't apply," Elena said finally. But that was small comfort at best.

As they took Misao to the kitchen, Matt thought that it had been a stupid plan of the kitsune: imitating Stefan twice. Doing it the second time, when the humans were on guard, that was *stupid.* Misao didn't seem as stupid as that.

Matt had a bad feeling.

Elena had a very bad feeling about what they were doing. As she looked around at the faces of the others, she saw that they did too. But nobody had come up with a better plan. They couldn't kill Misao. They weren't murderers who could kill a sickly, passive girl in cold blood.

She figured that Shinichi must have very keen hearing, and had already heard them walking on the creaking kitchen floorboards. And she had to assume that he knew—by mindbond, or just logic, or whatever—that Misao was right above him. There was nothing to lose by shouting, through the closed door, "Shinichi, we've got your sister here! If you want her back you'll stay quiet and not make us throw her down the stairs."

There was silence from the root cellar. Elena chose to think of it as submissive silence. At least Shinichi wasn't yelling threats.

"Okay," Elena whispered. She'd taken a position directly behind Misao. "When I count to three, we push as hard as we can."

"Wait!" Matt said in a miserable whisper-shout. "You said we *wouldn't* throw her down the stairs."

"Life isn't fair," Elena said grimly. "You think he doesn't have some surprise for us?"

"But—"

"Leave it, Matt," said Meredith quietly. She had the stave ready in her left hand and with her right was ready to push on the panel for opening the door. "Everybody ready?"

Everyone nodded. Elena felt sorry for Matt and Stefan, who were the most honest and sensitive of all of them.

"One," she whispered softly, "two, *three*."

On three Meredith hit the concealed wall switch. And then things began to happen in very slow motion.

By "two" Elena had already begun to shove Misao toward the door. On "three" the others joined her.

But the door seemed to take forever to open. And before the ending of forever, everything went wrong.

The greenery around Misao's head spread twigs in all directions. One strand shot out and snagged Elena around the wrist. She heard a yell of outrage from Matt and knew that another strand had gotten him.

"*Push!*" Meredith shouted and then Elena saw the stave coming at her. Meredith whisked with the stave through the greenery connected to Misao. The vine that had been cutting into Elena's wrist fell to the floor.

Any remaining misgivings about throwing Misao down the stairs vanished. Elena joined in the crowd trying to push her through the opening. But there was something wrong in the basement. For one thing, they were shoving Misao into pitch-darkness . . . and movement.

The basement was full of—something. Some *things*.

Elena looked down at her ankle and was horrified to see a gigantic maggot that seemed to have crawled out of the root cellar. Or at least a maggot was the first thing she could think of to compare it to—maybe it was a headless slug. It was translucent and black and about a foot long, but far too fat for her to have put a hand around it. It seemed to have two ways of moving, one by the familiar hunch-and-straighten method and the other by simply sticking to other maggots, which were exploding up over Elena's head like a hideous fountain.

Elena looked up and wished she hadn't.

There was a cobra waving over them, out of the root cellar and into the kitchen. It was a cobra made of black translucent maggots stuck together, and every so often one would fall off and land among the group and there would be a cry.

If Bonnie had been with them, she would have screamed until the wineglasses in the cupboards shattered, Elena thought wildly. Meredith was trying to attack the cobra with the stave and reach into her jeans pocket for Post-it Notes at the same time.

"I'll get the notes," Elena gasped, and wriggled her hand into Meredith's pocket. Her fingers closed on a small sheaf of cards and she tugged it out triumphantly.

Just then the first glistening fat maggot fell on her bare skin. She wanted to scream with pain as its little feet or teeth or suckers—whatever kept it attached to her—burned and stung. She pulled a thin card from the sheaf, which was not a Post-it Note but the same amulet on a small rather flimsy note card, and slapped it on the maggot-like thing.

Nothing happened.

Meredith was thrusting the stave into the middle of the

cobra now. Elena saw another of the creatures fall almost onto her upturned face and managed to turn away so that it hit her collar instead. She tried another card from the sheaf and when it just floated away—the maggots *looked* gooey but weren't—she gave a primal scream and ripped with both hands at the ugly things attached to her. They gave way, leaving her skin covered with red marks and her T-shirt torn at the shoulder.

"The amulets aren't working," she yelled to Meredith.

Meredith was actually standing under the swaying, hooded head of the maggot-cobra, stabbing and stabbing as if to reach the center. Her voice was muffled. "Not enough amulets anyway! Too many of these grubs. You'd better run."

An instant later Stefan shouted, "Everybody get away from here! There's something solid in there!"

"That's what I'm trying to get!" Meredith shouted back.

Frantically, Matt yelled, "Where's Misao?"

The last time Elena had seen her she had been diving into the writhing mass of segmented darkness. "Gone," she shouted back. "Where's Mrs. Flowers?"

"In the kitchen," said a voice behind her. Elena glanced back and saw the old woman pulling down herbs with both hands.

"Okay," Stefan shouted. "Everybody, take a few steps

back. I'm going to hit it with Power. Do it—now!"

His voice was like a whiplash. Everyone stepped back, even Meredith who had been probing the snake with her stave.

Stefan curled his hand around nothingness, around air, and it turned to sparkling, swirling bright energy. He threw it point-blank into the cobra made of maggots.

There was an explosion, and then suddenly it was raining maggots. Elena had her teeth locked so as to keep herself from screaming. The oval translucent bodies of the maggots broke open on the kitchen floor like overripe plums, or else bounced. When Elena dared look up again she saw a black stain on the ceiling.

Beneath it, smiling, was Shinichi.

Meredith, lightning quick, tried to put the stave through him. But Shinichi was faster, leaning out of her way, and out of the next thrust, and the next.

"You humans," he said. "All the same. All stupid. When Midnight finally comes you'll see how stupid you were." He said "Midnight" as if he were saying "the Apocalypse."

"We were smart enough to discover that you weren't Stefan," Matt said from behind Shinichi.

Shinichi rolled his eyes. "And to put me into a little room roofed with *wood*. You can't even remember that kitsune control all plants and trees? The walls are all full of malach grubs by now, you know. Thoroughly infested."

His eyes flickered—and he glanced backward, Elena saw, looking toward the open door of the root cellar.

Her terror soared, and at the same time Stefan shouted, "Get out of here! Out of the house! Go to somewhere safe!"

Elena and Meredith stared at each other, paralyzed. They were on different teams, but they couldn't seem to let go of each other. Then Meredith snapped out of it and turned to the back of the kitchen to help Mrs. Flowers. Matt was already there, doing the same thing.

And then Elena found herself swept off her feet and moving fast. Stefan had her and was running toward the front door. Distantly, she heard Shinichi shout, "Bring me back their bones!"

One of the maggots that Elena batted out of the way burst its skin and Elena saw something crawling out. These really were malach, she realized. Smaller editions of the one that had swallowed Matt's arm and left those long, deep scratches when he pulled it out again.

She noticed that one was stuck on Stefan's back. Reckless with fury, she grabbed it near one end and ripped it off, yanking relentlessly even though Stefan gasped in pain. When it came free she got a glimpse of what looked like dozens of small children's teeth on the bottom side. She threw it against a wall as they reached the front door.

There they almost collided with Matt, Meredith, and

Mrs. Flowers, coming through the den. Stefan wrenched the door open and when they all were through Meredith slammed it shut. A few malach—grubs and still-wet flying ones—made it out with them.

"Where's safe?" snapped Meredith. "I mean, really safe, safe for a couple of days?" Neither she nor Matt had released their grip on Mrs. Flowers and from their speed Elena guessed that she must be almost as light as a straw figure. She kept saying, "My goodness! Oh, gracious!"

"My house?" Matt suggested. "The block's bad, but it was okay the last time I saw it, and my mom's gone with Dr. Alpert."

"Okay, Matt's house—using the Master Keys. But let's do it from the storage room. I do *not* want to open this front door again, no matter what," Elena said.

When Stefan tried to pick her up she shook her head. "I'm fine. Run as fast as you can and smash any malach you see."

They made it to the storage room, but now a sound like *vipvipvip*—a sort of high-pitched buzzing that could only have been produced by the malach—was following them.

"What now?" Matt panted, helping Mrs. Flowers to sit on the bed.

Stefan hesitated. "Is your house really safe, do you think?"

"Is anywhere safe? But it's empty, or it should be."

Meanwhile, Meredith drew Elena and Mrs. Flowers

aside. To Elena's horror, Meredith was holding one of the smaller grubs, gripping it so that its underside was turned upward.

"Oh, God—" Elena protested, but Meredith said, "They look a lot like a little kid's teeth, don't they?"

Suddenly Mrs. Flowers became animated. "They do indeed! And you're saying that the femur we found in the thicket—"

"Yes. It was certainly human but maybe not chewed *by* humans. Human children," Meredith said.

"And Shinichi yelled to the malach to bring back our bones . . ." Elena said and swallowed. Then she looked at the grub again. "Meredith, get rid of that thing somehow! It's going to pop out as a flying malach."

Meredith looked around the storage room blankly.

"Okay—just drop it and I'll step on it," Elena said, holding her breath to hold in her nausea.

Meredith dropped the fat, translucent, black thing, which exploded on impact. Elena stamped on it, but the malach inside didn't crush. Instead, when she lifted her foot, it tried to skitter under the bed. The stave cut it cleanly in two.

"Guys," Elena said sharply to Matt and Stefan, "we have to go *now*. Outside are a bunch of flying malach!"

Matt turned toward her. "Like the one that—"

"Smaller, but just like the one that attacked you, I think."

"Okay, here's what we figured out," Stefan said in a way that immediately made Elena uneasy. "Somebody has to go to the Dark Dimension anyway to check on Bonnie. I guess I'm the only one to do that, since I'm a vampire. You couldn't get in—"

"Yes, we could," Meredith said. "With these keys, we could just say 'Take us to Lady Ulma's house in the Dark Dimension.' Or 'Take me to wherever Bonnie is.' Why shouldn't it work?"

Elena said, "Okay. Meredith, Matt, and Mrs. Flowers can stay here and try to figure out what 'Midnight' is. From the way Shinichi said it, it sounded *bad*. Meanwhile, Stefan and I go to the Dark Dimension and find Bonnie."

"No!" Stefan said. "I won't take you to that horrible place again."

Elena looked him straight in the eye. "You promised," she said, indifferent to the other people in the room. "You *promised*. Never to go again on a quest without me. No matter how short the time, no matter what the cause. You *promised*."

Stefan looked at her desperately. Elena knew he wanted to keep her safe—but which world was truly safe now? Both were filled with horror and danger.

"Anyway," she said with a grim smile, "I have the key."

26

"Now you know how it's done?" Elena asked Meredith. "You put the key in the keyhole and say where you want to go. Then open the door and go through. That's it."

"You three go first," Stefan added. "And quick."

"I'll turn the key," Meredith told Matt. "You take care of Mrs. Flowers."

Just then Elena thought of something that she didn't want to say aloud, only to Stefan. But she and he were physically so close, she knew he would pick it up. *Saber!* she thought to Stefan. *We can't leave him to these malach!*

We won't, she heard Stefan's voice in her head say. *I showed him the way to Matt's house, and told him to go there and take Talon and protect the people who will be coming.*

At the same time Matt was saying, "Oh, my God!

Saber! He saved my life—I can't just leave him."

"Already taken care of," Stefan reassured him and Elena patted him on the back. "He'll be at your house in a little while, and if you go somewhere else he'll track you."

Elena turned her pats into gentle pushes. "Be good!"

"Matt Honeycutt's bedroom in Fell's Church," Meredith said, thrusting the key at the door handle, and opening the door. She and Mrs. Flowers and Matt all stepped forward. The door shut.

Stefan turned to Elena. "I'm going first," he said flatly. "But I'm holding on to you. I'm not going to let you go."

"Never let me go, never let me go," Elena whispered in an imitation of Misao's "Have nightmares." Then she had a thought.

"Slave bracelets!"

"What?" Stefan said. Then, "Oh, I remember, you told me. But what are they supposed to look like?"

"Like any two bracelets, matching if possible." Elena was scrambling around the back of the room, where furniture was piled up, opening drawers, closing them. "Come on, bracelets! Come on! This house is supposed to have everything!"

"What about these things you wear in your hair?" Stefan asked. Elena looked back and he tossed her a bag of soft cotton ponytail holders.

"You're a genius! They won't even hurt my wrists.

And here are two white ones so they'll match!" Elena said happily.

They arranged themselves in front of the door, with Stefan to Elena's left so he could see what was out there before they stepped in. He also had a firm grip on Elena's left arm.

"Wherever our friend Bonnie McCullough is," Stefan said, and thrust the key into the lockless door handle, turning it. Then, after giving Elena the key, he gingerly opened the door.

Elena wasn't sure what she was expecting. A blaze of light maybe, as they traveled through dimensions. Some kind of spiraling tunnel, or shooting stars. At least a feeling of motion.

What she got was steam. It soaked through her T-shirt and dampened her hair.

And then she got noise.

"Elena! *Eleeeeeeeeeeeeeeena! You're here!*"

Elena recognized the voice but couldn't locate the screamer in the steam.

Then she saw an immense bathtub made of tiles of malachite, and a frightened-looking girl tending a charcoal fire at the bath's foot, while two other young attendants holding scrubbing brushes and pumice stones cowered against the other wall.

And in the bath was Bonnie! It was obvious that the

tub was very deep, because Bonnie wasn't able to touch bottom in the middle but she was half-leaping out of the water like a foam-covered dolphin over and over to attract attention.

"There you are," gasped Elena. She dropped to her knees on a thick, soft blue rug. Bonnie made a spectacular leap and just for a moment Elena could feel a small soapy, sudsy body in her arms.

Then Bonnie went down again and came up laughing. "And is that Stefan? It's Stefan! Stefan, *hello*! *Helloooo!*"

Stefan glanced back, as if trying to assess the suds situation. He seemed satisfied with it, turned slightly, and waved.

"Hey, Bonnie?" he asked, voice muffled by the sounds of continual splashing. "Where are we?"

"It's Lady Ulma's house! You're safe—you're all safe!" She turned a small hopeful face to Elena. "Where's Meredith?"

Elena shook her head, thinking of all the things about Meredith that Bonnie didn't know yet. Well, she decided, this wasn't the time to mention them. "She had to stay behind, to protect Fell's Church."

"Oh," Bonnie looked down, troubled. "Still bad, is it?"

"You wouldn't believe it. Really; it's—indescribable. That's where Matt and Mrs. Flowers and Meredith are. I'm sorry."

"No, I'm just so glad to see you! Oh my God, but you're

hurt." She was looking at the small tooth wounds on Elena's arm, and the blood on her torn T-shirt. "I'll get out and—hey, no, *you* get *in*! There's plenty of room; plenty of hot water, and . . . *plenty of clothes*! Lady Ulma even designed some for us, for 'when we came back'!"

Elena, smiling reassuringly at the bath girls, was already stripping as fast as she could. The tub, which was big enough for six to swim in, looked too luxurious to miss and, she reasoned, it made sense to be clean when you greeted your hostess.

"Go have fun," she shouted to Stefan. "Is Damon here?" she added in a whispered aside to Bonnie, who nodded. "Damon's here, too," Elena caroled. "If you find Lady Ulma, tell her Elena's coming, but she's getting washed up first." She didn't actually dive into the pearl pink steaming water, but she got onto the second step down and let herself slide from there.

Instantly, she was immersed in delicious heat that seeped straight into her body, pulling some magic string that relaxed all her muscles at once. Perfumes suffused the air. She flung her wet hair back and saw Bonnie laughing at her.

"So you got out of your hole and you've been here wallowing in luxury while we've been worried sick?" Elena couldn't help but hear the way her voice went up at the end, making it a question.

"No, I got picked up by some people, and—" Bonnie

broke off. "Well . . . the first few days were tough, but never mind. Thank God we got to Lady Ulma's in the end. Want a bath brush? Some soap that smells just like roses?"

Elena was looking at Bonnie with slightly narrowed eyes. She knew that Bonnie would do just about anything for Damon. That included covering up for him. Delicately, all the while enjoying the brushes and unguents and many kinds of soaps laid out on a shelf for easy reach, she began an inquisition.

Stefan got out of the steamy room before he was soaking wet. Bonnie was safe and Elena was happy. He found he had stepped into another room, in which were a number of couches made of some soft spongy material. For drying? Massage? Who knew?

The next room he entered had gas lanterns that were turned high enough to rival electrical light. Here were three more couches—he had no idea what for—a full-length silvered-glass mirror, and smaller mirrors in front of chairs. Obviously a place for makeup and beautifying.

This last room opened onto a hallway. Stefan stepped out and hesitated, spreading delicate tendrils of Power in different directions, hoping to find Damon before Damon noticed his presence in the estate. The Master Key had proved that it could overcome the fact that he hadn't been invited here. That meant that maybe he could . . .

At that moment he got a hit, and withdrew his probe immediately, startled. He stared down the long corridor. He could actually see Damon, pacing in the room at the end, talking to someone Stefan couldn't see behind the door.

Stefan crept very quietly down the hallway, stalking. He made it to the door without his brother even noticing, and there he saw that the person Damon was talking to was a woman wearing what looked like buckskin breeches and shirt, who had weathered skin, and a general aura of being more at home outside civilization than inside it. Damon was saying, "Make sure there are enough warm clothes for the girl. She's not exactly hardy, you know—"

"Then where are you taking her—and why?" Stefan asked, leaning against the doorjamb.

He had the good fortune to once—just this once—take Damon unaware. His brother glanced up, and then jerked like a startled cat. It was priceless to watch Damon scrambling for a mask until he decided on the façade of absent amiability. Stefan guessed that no one had ever put so much effort into walking over to a desk chair, sitting down, and *forcing* himself to lounge.

"Well, well! Little brother! You dropped in for a visit! How . . . nice. What a pity, though, that I'm practically running out the door on a journey, and there's no room for you."

At this point the weather-beaten woman who had been taking notes—and who had risen when Stefan entered the room—spoke up. "Oh, no, my lord. The thurgs won't mind the extra weight of this gentleman. They probably won't notice it. If his baggage can be ready by tomorrow you can start out in the early morning just as you planned."

Damon gave her his best "shut up or die" glare. She shut up. Through clenched teeth, Damon managed to say, "This is Pelat. She's the coordinator of our little expedition. Hello, Pelat. Good-bye, Pelat. You may go."

"As you wish, my lord."

Pelat bowed and left.

"Aren't you taking this 'my lord' thing a bit too seriously?" Stefan asked. "And *what* is that costume you're wearing?"

"It's the uniform of the captain of the guard of Madame le Princess Jessalyn D'Aubigne," Damon said coldly.

"You got a *job*?"

"It was a *position*." Damon bared his teeth. "And it's none of your business."

"Got your canines back, too, I see."

"And that's none of your business either. But if you *want* me to knock you out and trample over your undead body, I'll be delighted to oblige."

Something was wrong, Stefan thought. Damon should be through the taunting phase and be actually trampling on him by now. It only made sense if . . .

"I've already spoken to Bonnie," he said. And so he had, to ask where he was. But to a guilty mind, apparent foreknowledge often worked wonders.

And Damon hastily said exactly what Stefan hoped he wouldn't. "I can explain!"

"Oh, God," Stefan said.

"If she'd just done as I told her—"

"While you were off becoming a princess's captain of the guard? And she was—where?"

"She was safe, at least! But, no, she had to go out into the street and then to that shop—"

"Shocking! She actually walked in the street?"

Damon ground his teeth. "You don't know how it is around here—or how the slave trade works. Every day—"

Stefan slammed both hands on the desk, now truly angry. "She was picked up by *slavers*? While you were sleazing around with a *princess*?"

"Princess Jessalyn does not sleaze," Damon replied icily. "Nor do I. And anyway it all turned out to be a good thing because now we know where the Seven Kitsune Treasures are."

"What treasures? And who cares about treasures when there's a town being destroyed by kitsune?"

Damon opened his mouth, shut it, then looked narrowly at Stefan. "You said that you'd talked to Bonnie about all this."

"I *did* talk to Bonnie," Stefan said flatly. "I said hello."

Damon's dark eyes flared. For a moment Stefan thought he was going to snarl or start a fight. But then, through clenched teeth, he said, "It's all for the damned town, don't you see that? Those treasures include the largest star ball ever to be filled with Power. And that Power may be enough to save Fell's Church. At least to stop its total annihilation. Maybe to even clear out every malach that exists and destroy Shinichi and Misao with a single blow. Is that noble enough for you, little brother? Is it reason enough?"

"But taking Bonnie—"

"You stay with her here if you like! Spend your lives here! I might mention that without her I would never have been able to set up an expedition, and that she's determined to go. Besides, we're not coming back this way. There has to be an easier route from the Gatehouse to Earth. We wouldn't survive coming back, so you'd better hope like hell that there *is* one."

Stefan was surprised. He had never heard his brother speak with such passion about anything that involved humans. He was about to reply, when behind him there came a scream of pure, unadulterated rage. It was frightening—and worrying, too, because Stefan would recognize that voice anywhere, anytime. It was Elena's.

27

Stefan whirled around and saw Bonnie, with only a towel wrapped around her, trying to physically restrain Elena, who was similarly clad. Elena's hair was wet and uncombed. Something had caused her to leap out of the bathing pool and run directly into the corridor.

Stefan was surprised by Damon's reaction. Was that a spark of alarm in the endlessly dark eyes that had remained impassive watching a thousand disasters, calamities, cruelties?

No, it couldn't be. But it certainly looked like one.

Elena was getting closer. Her voice rang out clearly through the hallway, which was spacious enough to give it a slight echo. "Damon! *I see you!* You wait right there—*I'm coming to kill you!*"

This time the flicker was unmistakable. Damon glanced at the window, which was partly open.

Meanwhile Bonnie had lost the fight and Elena was running like a gazelle toward the office. Her eyes, however, were definitely not doe-like. Stefan saw them glitter dangerously as Elena herself eluded him—mainly because he didn't dare grab her by the towel, and every other part of her was slippery. Elena was now facing Damon, who had risen from his chair.

"How *could* you?" she cried. "*Using* Bonnie like that—Influencing her, drugging her—all to get at what didn't belong to you! Using almost all the Power that was left in Misao's star ball—what did you think Shinichi would do when you did that? He came after *us*, that's what he did—and who knows if the boardinghouse is still standing?"

Damon opened his mouth, but Elena wasn't finished.

"And then to bring Bonnie to the Dark Dimension with you—I don't care if you didn't want to waste opening the Gate or not. You *knew* you shouldn't be taking her here."

Damon was angry now. "I—"

But Elena cut him off without even hesitating. "Then once you drag her here you abandon her. You leave her terrified, alone, in a room where she's not even allowed to look out of the window, with a collection of star balls that you don't even bother to examine—but which are completely unsuitable and give her nightmares! You—"

"If the little dolt had just had the sense to wait quietly—"

"What? *What did you say?*"

"I *said*, if the little dolt had just had the sense—"

Stefan, who was already on the move, shut his eyes briefly. He opened them again in time to see the slap and to feel Elena putting all her Power into it. It snapped Damon's head around.

What astonished him—even though he positioned himself precisely in case of it—was to see Damon's hand flash up as quick as a cobra's strike. There was no follow-through, but Stefan had already picked Elena up bodily and pulled her back out of range.

"Let go!" Elena cried, struggling to get out of Stefan's arms, or at least get her feet on the ground. "I'm going to *kill* him!"

The next astonishing thing—discontinuing the raw fury that Stefan could feel coursing through Elena's aura—was that Elena was actually winning the struggle, despite the fact that he was orders of magnitude stronger than she was. Part of it had to do with the towel, which was threatening to drop at any moment. The other part was that Elena had acquired a unique style of fighting stronger opponents—at least those with any conscience. She deliberately threw herself against any point at which it would hurt her to restrain her, and she didn't give up. Eventually he was going to have to choose between injuring her and letting her go.

At that moment, however, Elena stopped moving. She froze, head turned as she looked behind him.

Stefan glanced backward too, and felt an electrical shock shoot through him.

Bonnie was standing directly behind them, looking at Damon, her lips parted in anguish, tears in her wide brown eyes and streaming down her cheeks.

Instantly, even before he could register Elena's pleading glance, Stefan released her. He understood: Her mood and the dynamics of this situation had just been turned upside down.

Elena adjusted her towel and turned to Bonnie, but by then Bonnie was running away down the corridor. Elena's longer strides allowed her to reach Bonnie in a moment and she caught the smaller girl and held her, not so much by force as by sisterly magnetism. "Don't worry about that *snake*," Elena's voice came back to them clearly, as it was obviously meant to. "He's a—" And here Elena indulged in some very creative cursing.

Stefan could hear all of it distinctly and noticed that it broke off into tiny hushing sounds just as Elena turned into the door of the bathing salon.

Stefan glanced sideways at Damon. He didn't mind fighting his brother in the least right now; he was full of rage himself on behalf of Bonnie. But Damon ignored him as if he were part of the wallpaper, staring at nothing with an expression of icy fury.

At that moment Stefan heard a faint sound from the farthest end of the corridor, which was quite a distance away. But his vampire senses informed him that surely the person in front was a woman of consequence, probably their hostess. He stepped forward so that at least she could be greeted by someone who was wearing clothing.

However, at the last moment, Elena and Bonnie appeared in front of him, clad in dresses—gowns, rather—that were both casual and works of genius. Elena's was an informal robe of deep lapis blue, with her hair drying into a soft golden mass around her shoulders. Bonnie was wearing something shorter and lighter: pale violet, shot with threads of silver in no particular pattern. Both outfits, Stefan grasped suddenly, would look as good in the interminable sunlight as in a closed room with no windows and gas lamps.

He remembered the stories Elena had told about Lady Ulma designing gowns for her, and he realized that whatever else his hostess might be, she was truly a genius couturier.

And then Elena was running, dainty gold sandals flying, and Bonnie's silver slippers were following and Stefan began to run too, fearing some unknown danger. They all arrived at the far end of the hallway at the same time, and

Stefan saw that the woman standing there was dressed even more splendidly than the girls. She was wearing a deep red raw silk gown with a heavy diamond-and-ruby necklace and ring—but no bracelets.

The next minute the girls were both curtseying, deep, graceful curtseys. Stefan made his best bow.

Lady Ulma held out both hands to Elena, who seemed to be almost frantic over something that Stefan didn't understand. Elena took the extended hands, breathing quickly and shallowly. "Lady Ulma—you're so thin—"

Just then the babbling of a baby could be heard. Elena's face lit up and she smiled at Lady Ulma, letting out a quick breath. A young servant—even younger-looking than Bonnie—gently put a tiny bundle made of lace and sheerest lawn into Lady Ulma's arms. Both Elena and Bonnie blinked away tears, all the while beaming at the child and making little nonsense noises. Stefan could understand that—they'd known the Lady since she was a whip-torn slave, trying not to miscarry.

"But *how*—?" Elena began spluttering. "We saw you only a few days ago, but this baby is months old—"

"A few days? Is that how long it seems to you?" asked Lady Ulma. "To us, it has been many months. But the magic still works, Elena! Your magic remained! It was an easy delivery—easy! And then Dr. Meggar says that you saved me before she suffered injury from the abuse I went through. She is trying to speak already! It is you, Elena, it is your magic!"

At this the Lady made a movement as if to kneel at Elena's feet. She got no farther than a few inches, though, because Elena caught her hands, crying, "Lady Ulma, *no*!" while Stefan, at his best speed, slipped beside the girl servant and caught the Lady by her elbows, supporting her weight.

"And I'm not magic," Elena added. "Stefan, tell her that I'm not magic."

Obediently, Stefan leaned toward the ear of the tall woman. "Elena is the most magic I've ever encountered," he stage-whispered. "She has Powers that I can't even understand."

"*Ahh!*" Elena made a wordless exclamation of frustration.

"Do you know what I'm naming her?" the Lady continued. Her face, if not conventionally beautiful, was striking, with an aristocratic combination of Roman nose and high cheekbones.

"No." Elena smiled—and then "No!" Elena cried. "Please! Don't condemn her to a life of expectations and terror. *Don't* tempt anyone to hurt her while she's still a child. Oh, Lady Ulma!"

"But my dear savior . . ."

Then Elena began to manage things. Once she took

a situation in hand there was no way not to go with the flow of it. "Lady Ulma," she said clearly, "forgive me for interfering in your affairs. But Bonnie has told me—" She stopped, hesitated.

"Of the troubles of strong and hopeful young girls, for the most part poor or enslaved, who have taken on the names of the three bravest young women who ever graced our world," Lady Ulma finished for her.

"Something like that," Elena said, flushing.

"Nobody's calling themselves Damon," put in the young nurse cheerfully and with the utmost goodwill. "Neither boys *nor* girls."

Stefan could have kissed her.

"Oh, Lakshmi!" Elena hugged the coltish-looking teenager. "I didn't even *see* you properly. Let me look at you." She held the girl at arm's length. "Do you know, you've grown at least an inch since I last saw you?"

Lakshmi beamed.

Elena turned back to Lady Ulma. "Yes, I am afraid for the child. Why not call her Ulma?"

The patrician lady half shut her eyes. "Because, my dear Elena, Helena, Aliena, Alliana, Laynie, Ella—I would not wish 'Ulma' on anyone, much less my lovely daughter."

"Why not call her Adara?" Lakshmi put in suddenly. "I always thought that was pretty, since I was a kid."

There was a silence—almost a stunned silence. Then Elena said, "Adara—it's a *lovely* name."

"And not at all dangerous," Bonnie said.

Stefan said, "It wouldn't stop her from starting a revolution if she wanted to."

There was a pause. Everyone looked at Damon, who was looking out the window expressionlessly. Everyone waited.

He finally turned. "Oh, excellent," he said blankly, clearly having no idea—and less interest—in what they were talking about.

"Oh come on, Damon." Bonnie's eyes were still swollen, but she spoke brightly. "Make it unanimous! That way Lady Ulma will be sure." Good God, Stefan thought, she must be the most forgiving girl in the universe.

"Certainly, then," Damon said indifferently.

"Forgive us," Elena said tightly to the room in general. "We've *all* been going through a bit of a hard time."

That gave Lady Ulma her cue. "Of course you have," she said, smiling the smile of one who has known bitter suffering. "Bonnie has told us of the destruction of your town. I am deeply sorry. What you need now is food and rest. I'll have someone conduct you to your rooms."

"I should have introduced Stefan at the start, but I was so worried I forgot to," Elena said. "Stefan, this is Lady Ulma, who was so good to us before. Lady Ulma—well, you know who this is." She went on tiptoe to kiss Stefan lingeringly. Lingeringly enough that Stefan had to gently detach her and put her down. He was almost frightened at this display of bad manners. Elena was *really* angry at Damon. And if she didn't forgive him, the scenes would only continue to escalate—and if he was right, Elena was truly getting closer to being able to cast *Wings of Destruction*.

He didn't even consider asking Damon to forgive anyone.

After the girls had whispered raptures over the baby again, they were conducted to opulent bed chambers, each furnished in excellent taste, down to the smallest decoration. As usual, though, they all congregated in one room, which happened to be Stefan's.

There was more than enough space on the bed for the three of them to sit or flop. Damon wasn't present but Stefan would bet his undead life that he was listening in.

"All right," Elena said briskly, and went into storytelling mode. She explained to Bonnie everything that had happened through their taking the Master Keys from Shinichi and Misao, to their flight to Lady Ulma's bathing chamber.

"To have so much Power suddenly torn away from you in an instant . . ." Bonnie had her head down, and it wasn't hard to guess who she was thinking about. She looked up. "Please, Elena. Don't be so angry at Damon. I know he's done some bad things—but he's been so unhappy . . ."

"That's no excuse," Elena began. "And, frankly, I'm—"

Don't, Elena! Don't tell her that you're ashamed of her for putting up with it! She's already ashamed of herself!

"I'm surprised at him," Elena said with only the smallest hesitation. "I know for a fact that he cares for you. He even has a pet name for you: his little redbird."

Bonnie sniffed. "You always say that pet names are stupid."

"Well, but I meant names like—oh—if he called you 'Bonbon' or something."

Bonnie's head came up. "Even that would be okay for the baby," she said, with a sudden smile, like a rainbow after a storm.

"Oh, yes, isn't she adorable? I never saw such a happy baby. Margaret used to just look at you with big eyes. Adara—if she *is* Adara—should have such a happy life . . ."

Stefan settled back against the headboard. Elena had the situation in hand.

Now he could worry about where Damon was going. After a moment he tuned back in, to find Bonnie talking about treasure.

"And they kept asking me and asking me and I couldn't figure out why since the star ball with the story on it was right there. Only the story is gone now—Damon checked. Shinichi was going to throw me out the window, and that was when Damon rescued me, and the Guardians asked me about the story too."

"Strange," Stefan said, sitting up alertly. "Bonnie, tell me how you first felt this story; where you were and all."

Bonnie said, "Well, first I saw a story about a little girl named Marit going to buy a sugarplum—that was why I tried to do the same thing the next day. And then I went to bed, but I couldn't sleep. So then I picked up the star ball again and it showed me the story about the kitsune treasures. The stories are shown in order, so it *had* to be the one right after the sweetshop story. And then suddenly I was out of my body, and I was flying with Elena right over Alaric's car."

"Did you do anything in between experiencing the story and going to bed?" Stefan asked.

Bonnie thought; her rosebud mouth pursed. "I suppose I turned down the gas lamp. Every night I would turn the lamp way down so that it was only a flicker."

"And did you turn it back up again when you couldn't sleep and reached for the star ball again?"

"Um . . . no. But they're not books! You don't have to see to experience a story."

"That wasn't what I meant. How did you find the star ball in that dim room? Was it the only star ball on the floor near you?"

Bonnie's brows came together. "Well . . . no. There were twenty-six. Two others were hideous; I'd kicked those into a corner. Twenty-five were soap operas—so boring. It's not as if I had shelves or anywhere else to put them—"

"Bonnie, do you want to know what *I* think happened?"

Bonnie blinked and nodded.

"I think that you read a children's story and then you went to bed. And you actually fell asleep very quickly, even though you dreamed you were awake. Then you dreamed a premonition—"

Bonnie groaned. "Another one of those? But there wasn't even anyone to tell it to then!"

"Exactly. But you wanted to tell it to someone, and that longing brought you—your spirit—to where Elena was. But Elena was so worried about getting word across to Alaric that *she* was having an out-of-body experience. She'd been asleep too, I'm sure of it." Stefan looked at Elena. "What do you think of that?"

Elena was nodding slowly. "It would work with what happened to me. At first I was alone out of my body, but then I saw Bonnie beside me."

Bonnie bit her lip. "Well . . . the first thing *I* saw was Elena and we were both flying. I was a little behind her. But Stefan, why do you think I fell asleep and dreamed a whole story? Why can't my version just be true?"

"Because I think the first thing you'd have done would be to turn the light on—if you really were lying there awake. Otherwise, you might well have picked up a soap opera—so boring!"

Bonnie's forehead smoothed at last. "That would explain why nobody believed me even when I told them exactly where the story was! But why didn't I tell Elena about the treasure?"

"I don't know. But sometimes when you wake up—and I think you did wake up to have the out-of-body experience—you forget the dream if something interesting is going on. But then you might remember it later if something reminds you of it."

Bonnie stared into a middle distance, thinking. Stefan was silent, knowing that only she could unravel the riddle for herself.

At last Bonnie nodded. "It could be that way! I woke up and the first thing I thought of was the sweetshop. And after that I never gave another thought to the treasure dream until somebody asked for stories. And it just popped into my head."

Elena pushed the deep blue-green velvet coverlet one way to make it green, then the other way to smooth it into blueness.

"I was going to forbid Bonnie to go on the expedition," she said: this slave who didn't have a gem on her body except Stefan's pendant which hung from a fine chain around her neck, and was still in the simplest kind of after-bath robe. "But if it's something we *have* to do, I'd better talk to Lady Ulma. It sounds as if time is precious."

"Remember—time runs differently here than back on Earth. But we're supposed to leave in the morning," Bonnie said.

"Then I definitely need to talk to her—right now."

Bonnie jumped up, excited. "I'll help!"

"Wait." Stefan put a gentle hand on Bonnie's arm. "I have to say this. I think you're a miracle, Bonnie!" Stefan knew his eyes must be shining in a way that showed he could hardly rein in his excitement. In spite of the danger—in spite of the Guardians—in spite of everything . . . the largest star ball—full of Power!

He gave Bonnie a sudden impetuous hug, sweeping her off the bed and whirling her before putting her down again. "You and your precognitions!"

"Oooh. . ." Bonnie said dizzily, gazing up at him. "Damon was excited, too, when I told him about the Gateway of the Seven Treasures."

"You know why, Bonnie? It's because *everybody* has heard about those seven treasures—but *no one* had any idea where they are . . . until you dreamed it. You do know exactly where they are?"

"Yes, if the precognition was true." Bonnie was flushed with pleasure. "And you agree that that giant star ball will save Fell's Church?"

"I'd bet my life on it!"

"Woo-hoo!" cried Bonnie, pumping a fist. "Let's go!"

"So you see," Elena was saying, "it'll mean twice as much of everything. I don't see how we can start tomorrow."

"Now, now, Elena. As we discovered, oh, eleven

months ago when you left, any job can be done quickly if we summon enough hands. I am now the regular employer of all those women we used to call in to make your ball gowns." As Lady Ulma spoke she quickly and gracefully took Elena's measurements—why do only one thing when you can do two at once? She glanced at her measuring tape. "Still exactly the same as when I last saw you. You must lead a very healthy life, Elena."

Elena laughed. "Remember, for us it's only been a few days."

"Oh, yes." Lady Ulma laughed, too, and Lakshmi, who was seated on a stool amusing the baby, made what Elena knew was one last appeal.

"I could go with you," she said earnestly, looking at Elena. "I can do all sorts of helpful things. And I'm tough—"

"Lakshmi," Lady Ulma said gently, but in a voice that wore the hat of authority. "We're already doubling the size of the wardrobe needed to accommodate Elena and Stefan. You wouldn't want to take Elena's place, would you?"

"Oh, no, no," the young girl said hastily. "Oh, well," she said, "I'll take such good care of little Adara that she's no bother to you while you supervise Elena's and Stefan's clothes."

"Thank you, Lakshmi," Elena said from her heart, noting that Adara now seemed to be the baby's official name.

"Well, we can't let out any of Bonnie's things to fit you, but we can call in reinforcements and have a full set of garments ready for you and Stefan by the morning. It's just a matter of leather and fur to keep you warm. We use the pelts of the animals up north."

"They're not nice, cuddly baby animals, either," Bonnie said. "They're vicious nasty things that are used for training, or they might come up from the dimension below and attack all the people on the northern fringes here. And when they finally get killed, the bounty hunters sell the leather and fur to Lady Ulma."

"Oh, well . . . good," Elena said, deciding not to make an animal rights speech just now. The truth was that she was still very shaken by her actions—her reactions—toward Damon. Why had she acted that way? Was it just to let off pressure? She still felt as if she could smack him a good one for taking poor Bonnie away, and then leaving her alone. And . . . and . . . for taking poor Bonnie—*and not taking her*!

Damon must hate her now, she thought, and suddenly the world developed a sickening, out-of-control motion, as if she were trying to balance on a seesaw. And Stefan—what else could he think but that she was a woman scorned, the kind that Hell had no fury like? How could he be so kind, so caring, when anyone in their right mind would know she'd gone mad with jealousy?

Bonnie didn't understand either. Bonnie was a child, not a woman. Although, although, she'd grown somehow—in goodness, in understanding. She was willfully blind, like Stefan. But—didn't that take maturity?

Could Bonnie be more of a woman than she, Elena, was?

"I'll have a private supper sent up to your rooms," Lady Ulma was saying, as she quickly and deftly used the measuring tape on Stefan. "You get a good night's sleep; the thurgs—and your wardrobes—will be waiting tomorrow." She beamed at all of them.

"Could I have—I mean, is there any Black Magic at all?" Elena stumbled. "The excitement . . . I'm going to sleep in my room alone. I want to get a good night's rest. We're going on a quest, you know?" All the truth. All a lie.

"Of course, I'll have a bottle sent to—" Lady Ulma hesitated and then quickly recovered. "To your room, but why don't we all have a nightcap now? It looks just the same outside," she added to Stefan, the newcomer, "but it's really rather late."

Elena drank her first glass in one draft. The attendant had to refill it immediately. And again a moment later. After that her nerves seemed to relax a bit. But the seesaw feeling never entirely left, and though she slept alone in her room, Damon didn't visit to quarrel with her, mock her, or kill her—and certainly not to kiss.

* * *

Thurgs, Elena discovered, were something like two elephants stitched together. Each had two side-by-side trunks and four wicked-looking tusks. Each also had a high, wide, long ridged tail, like a reptile. Their small yellow eyes were placed all around their domelike heads, so that they could see 360 degrees around, looking for predators. Predators that could take down a thurg!

Elena imagined a sort of saber-toothed cat, enormous, with a milk-white pelt big enough to line several garments of hers and Stefan's. She was pleased with her new outfits. Each one was essentially a tunic and breeches, soft, pliable, rain-shedding leather on the outside; and warm, luxurious fur on the inside. But they wouldn't be genuine Lady Ulma creations if that was all there were to them. The inner bodysuit of white fur was reversible and removable so you could change depending on the weather. There were triple-thick wind-around collars, which trailed behind or could be turned into scarves that wrapped a face up to the eyes. The white pelts spilled out of the leather at the wrists to make mittens you couldn't lose. The guys had straight leather tunics that just met at the breeches, and fastened with buttons. The girls' tunics were longer and flared out a bit. They were neatly fringed, but not stained or dyed except for Damon's, which, of course, were black with sable fur.

One thurg would carry the travelers and their baggage. A second, larger and wilder looking, would carry heating stones to help cook human food and all the food (it looked like red hay) that the two thurgs would eat on the way to the Nether World.

Pelat showed them how to move the giant creatures, with the lightest of taps of a very long stick, which could scratch a thurg behind its hippo-like ears or give it a ferocious tap at that sensitive spot, signaling it to hasten forward.

"Is it safe, having Biratz carry all the thurg food? I thought you said she was unpredictable," Bonnie asked Pelat.

"Now, miss, I wouldn't give her to you if she wasn't safe. She'll be roped to Dazar so all she has to do is follow," Pelat replied.

"We ride these?" Stefan said, craning his neck to get a look at the small, enclosed palanquin on top of the very large animal.

"We have to," Damon said flatly. "We can hardly walk all the way. We're not allowed to use magic like that fancy Master Key you used to get here. No magic but telepathy works up at the very top of the Dark Dimension. These dimensions are flat like plates, and according to Bonnie, there's a fracture, just at the far north of this one—not too far from here, in other words. The crack is small by dimensional standards, but big enough for us to get through. If we want to reach the Gatehouse of the Seven Treasures we start on thurgs."

Stefan shrugged. "All right. We're doing it your way."

Pelat was putting a ladder up. Lady Ulma, Bonnie, and Elena were weeping and laughing over the baby together.

They were still laughing as they left on their way.

The first week or so was boring. They sat in the palanquin on the back of the thurg named Dazar, with a compass from Elena's backpack dangling from the roof. They generally kept all the sides of the palanquin's curtains rolled up, except the one facing west, where the bloated, bloody red sun—too bright to look at in the higher, cleaner air outside the city—constantly loomed on the horizon. The view all around them was dreadfully monotonous—mind-bendingly so, with few trees and many miles of dried brown grassy hills. Nothing interesting to a non-hunter ever showed up. The only thing that changed was as they traveled farther north, it got colder.

It was difficult for all of them, living in such close quarters. Damon and Elena had reached an equilibrium—or at least a pretense—of ignoring each other, something Elena would never have imagined could be possible. Damon made it easier by working on a different sleep cycle than the others—which helped to guard them as the thurgs trudged onward, day and night. If he was awake when Elena was, he would ride outside the palanquin, on the thurg's enormous neck. They both had such stiff necks, Elena thought. Neither of them wanted to be the first to bend.

Meanwhile those inside the palanquin began to play little games, like picking the long dried grasses from the side of the road and trying to weave them into dolls, fly whisks, hats, whips. Stefan proved to be the one who made the tightest weave, and he made fly whisks and broad fans for each of them.

They also played various card games, using stiff little place cards (had Lady Ulma thought they might give a dinner party on the way?) as playing cards, after carefully marking them with the four suits. And of course, the vampires hunted. Sometimes this took quite a long time, since game was scarce. The Black Magic Lady Ulma had stocked helped them stretch the time between hunts.

When Damon visited the palanquin, it was as if he were crashing a private party and thumbing his nose at the hosts.

Finally Elena couldn't stand it any longer, and had Stefan float her up the side of the thurg (looking down or climbing up were definitely not options) while flying magic still worked. She sat down on the saddle beside

Damon and gathered her courage.

"Damon, I know you have a right to be angry with me. But don't take it out on the others. Especially Bonnie."

"Another lecture?" Damon asked, giving her a look that would freeze a flame.

"No, just a—a request." She couldn't bring herself to say "a plea."

When he didn't answer and the silence became unbearable, she said, "Damon, for us—we're not going on a quest for treasure out of greed or adventure or any normal reason. We're going because we need to save our town."

"From Midnight," a voice just behind her said. "From the Last Midnight."

Elena whirled to stare. She expected to see Stefan holding Bonnie clasped to him hard. But it was only Bonnie at her head level, hanging on to the thurg ladder.

Elena forgot she was afraid of heights. She stood up on the swaying thurg, ready to climb down on the sun side if there wasn't enough room for Bonnie to sit down fast in the driver's saddle.

But Bonnie had the slimmest hips in town and there was just room for all three of them.

"The Last Midnight is coming," Bonnie repeated. Elena knew that monotonous voice, knew the chalk-white cheeks, the blank eyes. Bonnie was in trance—and moving. It must be urgent.

"Damon," Elena whispered. "If I speak to her, she'll break trance. Can you ask her telepathically what she means?"

A moment later she heard Damon's projection. *What is the Last Midnight? What's going to happen then?*

"That's when it starts. And it's over in less than an hour. So . . . no more midnights."

I beg your pardon? No more midnights?

"Not in Fell's Church. No one left to see them."

And when is this going to happen?

"Tonight. The children are finally ready."

The children?

Bonnie simply nodded, her eyes far away.

Something's going to happen to all the children?

Bonnie's eyelids drooped to half mast. She didn't seem to hear the question.

Elena needed to hold on to something. And suddenly she was. Damon had reached across Bonnie's lap and taken her hand.

Bonnie, are the children going to do *something at midnight?* he asked.

Bonnie's eyes filled and she bowed her head.

"We've got to go back. We have to go to Fell's Church," Elena said, and scarcely knowing what she was doing, unclasped Damon's hand and climbed down the ladder. The bloated red sun looked different—smaller. She tugged at the curtain and almost bumped heads with Stefan as he rolled it up to let her in.

"Stefan, Bonnie's in trance and she said—"

"I know. I was eavesdropping. I couldn't even catch her on the way up. She jumped onto the ladder and climbed like a squirrel. What do you think she means?"

"You remember in the out-of-body experience she and I had? A little spying on Alaric? That's what's going to happen in Fell's Church. All the children, all at once, just at midnight—that's why we have to get back—"

"Easy. Easy, love. Remember what Lady Ulma said? Nearly a year here came out to be only days in our world."

Elena hesitated. It was true; she couldn't deny it. Still, she felt so cold . . .

Physically cold, she realized suddenly, as a blast of frigid air swirled around her, cutting through her leather like a machete.

"We need our inner furs," Elena gasped. "We must be getting near the fracture."

They yanked down the palanquin covers and secured them and then hastily rummaged through the neat cabinet that was set on the rump of the thurg.

The furs were so sleek that Elena could fit two under her leather easily.

They were disturbed by Damon coming inside with Bonnie in his arms.

"She stopped talking," he said, and added, "Whenever you're warm enough, I suggest that you come out."

Elena laid Bonnie down on one of the two benches inside the palanquin and piled blanket after blanket over her, tucking them in around her. Then Elena made herself climb back up.

For a moment she felt blinded. Not by the surly red sun—they had left that behind some mountains, which it turned a pink sapphire color—but by a world of white. Seemingly endless, flat, featureless whiteness stretched out before her until a bank of fog obscured whatever was behind it.

"According to legend, we should be headed toward the Silver Lake of Death," Damon's voice said from behind Elena. And, oddly, throughout all this chill, his voice was warm—almost friendly. "Also known as Lake Mirror. But I can't change into a crow to scout ahead. Something's hindering me. And that fog in front of us is impenetrable to psychic probing."

Elena instinctively glanced around her. Stefan was still inside the palanquin, obviously still tending to Bonnie.

"You're looking for the lake? What's it like? I mean, I can guess why it might be called Silver and Lake Mirror," she said. "But what's the Death bit?"

"Water dragons. At least that's what people say—but who has been there to bring back the story?" Damon looked at her.

He took care of Bonnie while she was in trance, Elena thought. And he's talking to me at last.

"Water . . . dragons?" she asked him and she made her voice friendly, too. As if they'd just met. They were starting over.

"I've always suspected kronosaurus, myself," Damon said. He was right behind her now; she could feel him blocking the icy wind—no, more than that. He was generating an envelope of heat for her to stand in. Elena's shivering stopped. She felt for the first time that she could unwrap her arms from clutching herself.

Then she felt a pair of strong arms folding around her, and the heat abruptly got quite intense. Damon was standing behind her, holding her, and all at once she was very warm indeed.

"Damon," she began, not very steadily, "we can't just—"

"There's a rock outcropping over there. No one could see us," the vampire behind her offered—to Elena's absolute shock. A week of not speaking at all—and now *this*.

"Damon, the guy in the palanquin just below us is my—"

"Prince? Don't you need a knight, then?" Damon breathed this directly into her ear. Elena stood like a statue. But what he said next rocked her entire universe. "You like the story of Camelot, don't you? Only here *you're* the queen, princess. You married your not-quite-fairy-tale prince, but along came a knight who knew even more of your secrets, and he called to you . . ."

"He forced me," Elena said, turning to meet Damon's dark eyes straight on, even as her brain screamed for her to let it go. "He didn't wait for me to hear his call. He just . . . took what he wanted. Like the slavers do. I didn't know how to fight—then."

"Oh, no. You fought and fought. I've never seen a human fight so hard. But even when you fought, you felt the call of my heart to yours. Try to deny that."

"Damon—why now—all of a sudden . . .?"

Damon made a move as if to turn away, then turned back. "Because by tomorrow we may be dead," he said flatly. "I wanted you to know how I felt about you before I died—or you did."

"But you haven't told me a word about how *you* feel about *me*. Only about what you think *I* feel about *you*. And I'm sorry that I slapped you the first day I was here, but—"

"You were magnificent," Damon said outrageously. "Forget it now. As for how I feel—maybe I'll get a chance to really show it to you someday."

Something sparked inside Elena—they were back to fencing with words, as they had been when they'd first met. "Someday? Sounds convenient. And why not now?"

"Do you mean that?"

"Do I habitually say things I don't mean?"

She was waiting for some kind of apology, some words spoken as simply and sincerely as she had been speaking to him. Instead, with the utmost gentleness, and without glancing around to see if anyone was watching them, Damon cupped Elena's scarf-bound cheeks with his bare hands, pulled the scarf just below her lips with his thumbs, and kissed her softly. Softly—but not briefly, and something in Elena kept whispering to her that *of course* she had heard his call from the moment she first saw him, first felt his aura call to her. She hadn't known that it was an aura then; she hadn't believed in auras. She hadn't believed in vampires. She'd been an ignorant little idiot . . .

Stefan! A voice like crystal sounded off two notes in her brain, and suddenly she was able to step back from Damon's embrace and look at the palanquin again. No sign of motion there.

"I have to go back," she told Damon brusquely. "I have to know what's going on with Bonnie."

"You mean to see what's going on with Stefan," he said. "You needn't worry. He's fast asleep, and so is our little girl."

Elena tensed. "You Influenced them? Without seeing them?" It was a wild guess, but one side of Damon's mouth crooked up, as if congratulating her. "How *dare* you?" she said.

"To be honest, I don't know how I dare." Damon leaned in close again, but Elena turned her cheek, thinking, *Stefan!*

He can't hear you. He's dreaming about you.

Elena was surprised at her own reaction to that. Damon had caught and held her eyes again. Something inside her melted in the intensity of his steady black gaze.

"I'm not Influencing you; I give you my word"—in a whisper. "But you can't deny what happened between us the last time we were in this dimension." His breath was on her lips now—and Elena didn't turn aside. She trembled.

"Please, Damon. Show some respect. I'm—*oh, God! God!*"

"Elena? *Elena! Elena! What's wrong?*"

Hurts—that was all Elena could think. A terrible agony had lanced through her chest on the left side. As if she'd been stabbed through the heart. She stifled a scream.

Elena, talk to me! If you can't send your thoughts, speak!

Through numb lips, Elena said, "Pain—heart attack—"

"You're too young and healthy for that. Let me check." Damon was unfastening her top. Elena let him. She could do nothing for herself, except gasp, *"Oh God! It hurts!"*

Damon's warm hand was inside her leather and furs. His hand came to rest slightly to the left of center, with only her camisole between his probing fingers and her flesh. *Elena, I'm going to take the pain away now. Trust me.*

Even as he spoke, the stabbing anguish drained. Damon's eyes narrowed, and Elena knew he'd taken the pain into himself, to analyze it.

"It's not a heart attack," he said a moment later. "I'm as sure as I can be. It's more as if—well, as if you'd been staked. But that's silly. Hmm . . . it's gone now."

For Elena it had been gone since he'd taken it, protecting her. "Thank you," she breathed, suddenly realizing that she had been clinging to him, in utter terror that she was dying. Or that he was.

He gave her a rare, full, genuine smile. "We're both fine. It must have been a cramp." His gaze had dropped to her lips. "Do I deserve a kiss?"

"I . . ." He had comforted her; he had taken the terrible pain away. How could she sanely say no? "Just one," she whispered.

A hand under her chin. Her eyelids wanted to melt closed, but she widened her eyes and wouldn't let them.

As his lips touched hers, his arm around her . . . changed somehow. It was no longer trying to restrain her. It seemed to be wanting to comfort her. And when his other hand stroked her hair softly at the very ends, crushing the waves gently, and just as gently smoothing them out, Elena felt a rush of shivering warmth.

Damon wasn't deliberately trying to batter her with the strength of his aura, which at the moment was filled with nothing but his feelings for her. The simple fact, though, was that although he was a new-made vampire, he was exceptionally strong and he knew all the tricks of an experienced one. Elena felt as if she had stepped into clear calm water, only to find herself caught in a fierce undertow that there was no resisting; no bargaining with; and certainly no possibility of reaching by reason. She had no choice but to surrender to it and hope that it was taking her, eventually, to a place she could breathe and live. Otherwise, she would drown . . . but even that possibility didn't seem so dire, now that she could see the tide was made of a chain of little moments strung like pearls. In each one of them was a tiny sparkle of admiration that Damon had for her: pearls for her courage, for her intelligence, for her beauty. It seemed that there was no slightest motion she had made, no briefest word that she had said, that he had not noticed and locked in his heart as a treasure.

But we were fighting then, Elena thought to him, seeing in the undertow a sparkling moment when she had cursed him.

Yes—I said you were magnificent when you were angry. Like a goddess come to put the world to rights.

I do want to put the world to rights. No, two worlds: the Dark Dimension and my home. But I'm no goddess.

Suddenly she felt that keenly. She was a schoolgirl who hadn't even finished high school—and it was in part because of the person who was kissing her wildly now.

Oh, think of what you're learning on this trip! Things that no one else in the universe knows, Damon said in her mind. *Now pay attention to what you're doing!*

Elena paid attention, not because Damon wanted her to, but because she couldn't help it. Her eyes drifted shut. She realized that the way to calm this maelstrom was to become part of it, neither giving in nor forcing Damon to, but by meeting the passion in the undertow with what was inside her own heart.

As soon as she did, the undertow became wind, and she was flying and not drowning. No, it was better than flying, better than dancing, it was what her heart always yearned for. A high still place where nothing could ever harm them or disturb them.

And then, when she was most vulnerable, the pain came again, drilling through her chest, a little to the left. This time Damon was so mindlocked with her that he felt it from the beginning. And she could hear clearly a phrase in Damon's mind: *staking is just as effective on humans as it is on vampires,* and his sudden fear that this was a precognition.

In the swaying little room, Stefan was asleep holding Bonnie by his side, with the sparkling of Power engulfing them both. Elena, who had a good grip on the palanquin's ladder, vaulted the rest of the way inside. She put a hand on Stefan's shoulder and he woke.

"What is this? Is something wrong with her?" she asked, with a third question: "Do you know?" buzzing around in her head.

But when Stefan lifted his green eyes to her, they were simply worried. Clearly he was not invading her thoughts. He was focused entirely on Bonnie. Thank God, he's such a gentleman, Elena thought for the thousandth time.

"I'm trying to get her warm," Stefan said. "After she came out of trance, she was shivering. Then she stopped shivering, but when I took her hand, it was colder than ever. Now I've put an envelope of heat around her. I guess I dozed off for a little while after that." He added, "Did you find anything?"

I found Damon's lips, Elena thought wildly, but she forced herself to blank out the memory. "We're looking for Lake Silver Death Mirror," she said. "But all I could see was white. The snow and the fog seem to go on forever."

Stefan nodded. Then he carefully went through the motions of plucking apart two layers of air and slid in a hand to touch Bonnie's cheek. "She's warming up," he said, and smiled.

It took a long while before Stefan was satisfied that Bonnie was warm. When he did, he gently unwrapped her from the heated air that had formed the "envelope" and lay her on one bench, coming to sit with Elena on the other.

Eventually Bonnie sighed, blinked, and opened her eyes.

"I had a nap," she said, obviously aware that she had lost time.

"Not exactly," Elena said, keeping her voice gentle and reassuring. Let's see, how did Meredith do this? "You went into trance, Bonnie. Do you remember anything about it?"

Bonnie said, "About the treasure?"

"About what the treasure is for," Stefan said quietly.

"No . . . No . . ."

"You said that this was the Last Midnight," Elena said. As far as she could remember, Meredith was pretty direct. "But we think you were talking about back at home," she added hastily, seeing terror leap in Bonnie's eyes.

"The Last Midnight—and no morning afterward," Bonnie said. "I think—I heard someone saying those words. But no more."

She was as skittish as a wild colt. Elena reminded her about time running differently between the two worlds but it didn't seem to comfort her. Finally, Elena just sat by her and held her.

Her head was spinning with thoughts of Damon. He'd forgiven her. That was good, even though he'd taken his own time about it. But the real message was that he was willing to *share* her. Or at least willing to *say* he would to get in her good graces. If she knew him at all, if she ever agreed—oh, God, he might *murder*

Stefan. Again. After all, that was what he had done when Katherine had had the same sentiment.

Elena could never think of him without longing. She could never think of him without thinking of Stefan. She had no idea what to do.

She was in trouble.

"Oi!" Damon shouted from outside the palanquin. "Is anybody else looking at this?"

Elena was. Both Stefan and Bonnie had their eyes shut; Bonnie was wrapped in blankets and cuddled against Elena. They had rolled down all the curtains of the palanquin except one.

But Elena had watched through the single window, and had seen how tendrils of fog had begun drifting by, first just filmy tatters of mist, but then longer, fuller veils, and finally blankets, engulfing them whole. It seemed to her that they were being deliberately cut off from even the perilous Dark Dimension, that they were passing a border into a place they weren't meant to know about, much less enter.

"How do we know we're going in the right direction?"

Elena shouted to Damon after Stefan and Bonnie woke. She was glad to be able to talk again.

"The thurgs know," Damon called back. "You set them on a line and they walk that line until somebody stops them, or—"

"Or what?" Elena yelled out of the opening.

"Until we get to a place like this."

This was obviously bait, and neither Stefan nor Elena could resist taking it—especially when the thurg they were riding stopped.

"Stay here," Elena said to Bonnie. She pushed a curtain out of the way and found herself looking too far down at white ground. God, these thurgs were big. The next moment, though, Stefan was on the ground holding up his arms.

"Jump!"

"Can't you come up and float me?"

"Sorry. Something about this place inhibits Power."

Elena didn't give herself time to think. She launched into the air and Stefan caught her neatly. Spontaneously, she clung to him, and felt the familiar comfort of his embrace.

Then he said, "Come look at this."

They had reached a place where the land ended and the mist divided, like curtains being held to either side. Directly in front of them was a frozen lake. A silvery frozen lake, almost perfectly round in shape.

"Lake Mirror?" Damon said, cocking his head to one side.

"I always thought that was a fairy tale," Stefan said.

"Welcome to Bonnie's storybook."

Lake Mirror formed a vast body of water in front of them, frozen right into the ice sheet below her feet, or so it seemed. It did look like a mirror—a purse mirror after you'd breathed softly on it.

"But the thurgs?" Elena said—or rather whispered. She couldn't help whispering. The silent lake pressed on her, as did the lack of any kind of natural sound: There were no birds singing, no rustling in the bushes—no bushes! No trees! Instead, just the mist surrounding the frozen water.

"The thurgs," Elena repeated in a slightly louder voice. "They can't possibly walk on that!"

"Depends on how thick the lake ice is," Damon said, flashing his old 250-kilowatt smile at her. "If it's thick enough, it'll be just like walking on land for them."

"And if it isn't?"

"Hmm . . . Do thurgs float?"

Elena gave him an exasperated glance and looked at Stefan. "What do you think?"

"I don't know," he said doubtfully. "They're very large animals. Let's ask Bonnie about the kids in the fairy tale."

Bonnie, still wrapped in fur blankets that began

collecting chunks of ice as they dragged on the ground, looked at the lake grimly. "The story didn't go into detail," she said. "It just said that they went down, down, down, and that they had to pass tests of their courage and—and—wittiness—before they got there."

"Fortunately," Damon said, smiling, "I have large enough amounts of both to make up for my brother's entire lack of either—"

"Stop it, Damon!" Elena burst out. The moment she'd seen the smile, she'd turned to Stefan, pulled him down to her height, and begun kissing him. She knew what Damon would see when he turned back toward them—her and Stefan locked in an embrace, Stefan hardly aware of anything being said. At least they could still touch with their minds. And it was intriguing, Elena thought, Stefan's warm mouth when everything else in the world was cold. She looked quickly at Bonnie, to make sure she hadn't upset her, but Bonnie was looking quite cheerful.

The farther I seem to drive Damon away, the happier she is, Elena thought. Oh, God . . . this *is* a problem.

Stefan spoke up quietly. "Bonnie, what it comes down to is that it has to be your choice. Don't try to use courage or wit or anything except your inner feelings. Where do we go?"

Bonnie glanced back at the thurgs, then looked at the lake.

"That way," she said, without hesitation, and she pointed straight across the lake.

"We'd better carry some of the cooking stones and fuel and backpacks with iron rations in them," Stefan said. "That way, if the worst happens, we'll still have basic supplies."

"Besides," said Elena, "it'll lighten that thurg's load—if only by a little."

It seemed a crime to put a backpack on Bonnie, but she insisted. Finally, Elena arranged one filled entirely with the warm, curiously light fur clothes. Everyone else was carrying furs, food, and poop—the dried animal dung that would from now on be their only fuel.

It was difficult from the first. Elena had only had a couple of experiences with ice that she had reason to be wary of—but one of those had almost been disastrous for Matt. She was ready to jump and whirl at any crack—any sound that the ice was breaking. But there were no cracks; no water flowing up to slosh onto her boots.

The thurgs were the ones who seemed actually built for walking on frozen water. Their feet were pneumatic, and could spread out to almost half again their original size, avoiding putting too much pressure on any one section of ice.

Crossing the lake was slow, but Elena didn't see anything particularly deadly about it. It was simply the smoothest, slickest ice she had ever encountered. Her boots wanted to skate.

"Hey, everybody!" Bonnie *was* skating, exactly as if she were in a rink, backward and forward and sideways. "This is fun!"

"We're not here to have fun," Elena shouted back. She longed to try it herself, but was afraid to make cuts—even scuffs—in the ice. And beside that, Bonnie was expending twice as much energy as she needed to.

She was about to call out to Bonnie and tell her this, when Damon, in a voice of exasperation, made all the points she had thought of, and a few more.

"This isn't a pleasure cruise," he said shortly. "It's for the fate of your town."

"As if you care," Elena murmured, turning her back on him and touching the unhappy Bonnie's hand both to give comfort and to get them going at arm's length again. "Bonnie, do you sense anything magical about the lake?"

"No." But then Bonnie's imagination seemed to fly into high gear. "But maybe it's where the mystics from both dimensions all gathered to exchange spells. Or maybe it's where they used the ice like a real magic mirror to see faraway places and things."

"Maybe both of them," Elena said, secretly amused, but Bonnie nodded solemnly.

And that was when it came. The sound Elena had been waiting for.

Nor was it a distant booming which could be ignored or discussed. They had been walking at arm's length from one another to avoid stressing the ice, while the thurgs walked behind them, and to either side—like a flock of geese with no leaders.

This noise was a dreadfully near crack like the report of a gun. Immediately, it sounded again, like a whiplash, and then a crumbling.

It was to Elena's left, on Bonnie's side.

"Skate, Bonnie," she shouted. "Skate as fast as you can. Scream if you see land."

Bonnie didn't ask a single question. She took off like an Olympic speed skater in front of Elena, and Elena swiftly turned.

It was Biratz, the thurg Bonnie had asked Pelat about. She had one monstrous back leg in the ice, and as she struggled, more ice cracked.

Stefan! Can you hear me?

Faintly. I'm coming for you.

Yes—but only come as close as you need to Influence the thurg.

Influence the—?

Make her calm, put her out, whatever. She's ripping up the ice and it'll just make it harder to get her out!

This time there was a pause before Stefan's answer came. She knew though, by faint echoes, that he was talking telepathically with someone else. *All right, love, I'll do it. I'll take care of the thurg, too. You follow Bonnie.*

He was lying. Or, not lying, but keeping something from her. The person he'd been sending thoughts to was Damon. They were humoring her. They didn't mean to help at all.

Just at that moment she heard a shrill scream—not so far away. It was Bonnie in trouble—no! Bonnie had found land!

Elena didn't lose another second. She dumped her backpack on the ice and skated straight back to the thurg.

There it was, so huge, so pathetic, so helpless. The very thing that had kept it safe from other Godawful Hellacious monsters in the Dark Dimension—its great bulk—was now turned against it. Elena felt her chest tighten as if she were wearing a corset.

Even as she watched, though, the animal became calmer. She stopped trying to get her left hind leg out of the ice, which meant that she stopped churning up the ice around it.

Now Biratz was in a sort of crouching position, trying to keep her three dry legs from going under. The problem was that she was trying too hard, and that there was nothing to push against except breakable ice.

"Elena!" Stefan was within earshot now. "Don't get any closer!"

But even as he said it, Elena saw a Sign. Just a few feet away, lying on the ice was the tickle-prod that Pelat had used to get the thurgs going.

She picked it up as she skated by and then she saw another Sign. Reddish hay and the original covering for the hay—a giant tarpaulin—were lying behind the thurg. Together they formed a broad wide path that was neither wet nor slick.

"Elena!"

"This is going to be easy, Stefan!"

Elena pulled a pair of dry socks out of her pocket and drew them up over her boots. She fastened the tickle stick to her belt. And then she started the run of her life.

Her boots were fur with something like felt underneath and with the socks to aid them, they caught on the tarpaulin and propelled her forward. She leaned into it, vaguely wishing Meredith were here, so she could do this instead, but all the time getting closer. And then she saw her mark: the end of the tarp and beyond it floating chunks of ice.

But the thurg looked climbable. Very low in back, like a dinosaur halfway into a tar pit, but then rising up along the curved backbone. If she could just somehow land there . . .

Two steps till jump-off. One step till jump-off.

JUMP!

Elena pushed off with her right foot, flew through the air for an endless time, and—hit the water.

Instantly, she was soaked from head to foot and the shock of the icy water was unbelievable. It caught hold of her like some monster with a handful of jagged ice shards. It blinded her with her own hair, it squeezed all the sound out of the universe.

Somehow, clawing at her face, she freed her mouth and eyes from hair. She realized that she was only slightly below the surface of the water, and that was all she needed to *push* upward until her mouth broke the surface and she could suck in a lungful of delicious air, after which she had a coughing fit.

First time up, she thought, remembering the old superstition that a drowning person will rise three times and then sink forever.

But the strange thing was that she wasn't sinking. There was a dull pain in her thigh but she wasn't going under.

Slowly, slowly, she realized what had happened. She had missed the back of the thurg, but landed on its thick reptilian tail. One of the serrated fins had gashed her, but she was stable.

So . . . now . . . all I have to do is climb the thurg, she puzzled out slowly. Everything seemed slow because there were icebergs bobbing around her shoulders.

She put up a fur-lined gloved hand and reached for the next fin up. The water, while making her soaking clothes heavier, supported some of her weight. She managed to pull herself up to the next fin. And the next. And then here was the rump, and she had to be careful—no more footholds. Instead she grabbed for handholds and found something with her left hand. A broken strap from the hay carrier.

Not a good idea—in retrospect.

For a few minutes that qualified as among the worst in her life she was showered with hay, pounded with rocks, and smothered in the dust of old dung.

When it was finally over she looked around, sneezing and coughing, to find that she was still on the thurg. The tickle stick had been broken but enough remained for her to use. Stefan was frantically asking, both aloud and by telepathy, if she was all right. Bonnie was skating back and forth like a Tinker Bell guide, and Damon was cursing at Bonnie to get back to land and stay there.

Meanwhile Elena was inching up the rump of the thurg. She made it through the crushed supply basket. She finally reached the thurg's summit, and she settled just behind the domed head, in the seat where a driver would sit.

And then she tickled the thurg behind the ears.

"Elena!" Stefan shouted, and then *Elena, what are you trying to do?*

"I don't know!" she shouted back. "Trying to save the thurg!"

"You *can't*," Damon interrupted Stefan's answer in a voice as cold and still as the place they were in.

"She can make it!" Elena said fiercely—precisely because she herself was having doubts about whether the animal could. "You could help by pulling on her bridle."

"There's no point," Damon shouted, and turned about-face, walking quickly into the mist.

"I'll give it a try. Throw it out in front of her," Stefan said.

Elena threw the knotted bridle as hard as she could. Stefan had to run almost to the edge of the ice to grab it before it fell in. Then he held it aloft triumphantly. "Got it!"

"Okay, pull! Give her a direction to start in."

"Will do!"

Elena tapped Biratz again behind her right ear. There was a faint rumble from the animal and then nothing. Elena could see Stefan straining at the bridle.

"*Come on*," Elena said, and slapped sharply with the stick.

The thurg lifted up a giant foot, placed it farther on the ice, and struggled. As soon as she did, Elena smacked hard behind the left ear.

This was the crucial moment. If Elena could keep

Biratz from crushing all the ice between her back legs, they might have a chance.

The thurg tentatively lifted her left hind leg and stretched it until it made contact with the ice.

"Good, Biratz! *Now!*" Elena shouted. Now if Biratz would only surge forward . . .

There was a great upheaval underneath her. For several minutes Elena thought that perhaps Biratz had broken through the ice with all four legs. Then the thrashing changed to a rocking motion and suddenly, dizzyingly Elena knew that they had won.

"Easy, now, easy," she called to the animal, giving her a gentle tickle with the stick. And slowly, ponderously, Biratz moved forward. Her domed head drooped farther and farther as she went, and she foundered at the edge of a bank of mist, breaking the ice again. But there she only sank a few inches before meeting mud.

A few more steps and they were on solid ground. Elena had to suck in her breath to stifle a scream as the thurg's domelike head slumped, giving her a short and scary ride to where the tusks re-curved on themselves. Somehow she slid right between them and had to hastily scramble off Biratz's trunks.

"It was pointless, you know, doing that," Damon said from somewhere in the mist beside her. "Risking your own life."

"What d-do you mean p-pointless?" Elena demanded. She wasn't frightened; she was freezing.

"The animals are going to die anyway. The next trial is one they can't manage and even if they could, this isn't a place where anything grows. Instead of a quick clean death in the water, they're going to starve, slowly."

Elena didn't answer; the only answer she could think of was, "Why didn't you tell me earlier?" She had stopped shivering, which was a good thing, because a moment ago her body had felt as if she might shake herself apart.

Clothes, she thought vaguely. That was the problem. It certainly couldn't be as cold here in the air as it had been in that water. It was her clothes that were making her so cold.

She began, with numb fingers, to take them off. First, she unfastened her leather jacket. No zippers here: buttons. That was a real problem. Her fingers felt like frozen hot dogs, and only nominally under her direction. But somehow or other she managed to undo the fastenings and the leather dropped to the ground with a muffled thump—it had taken a layer of her inner fur off with it. Ick. The smell of wet fur. Now, now she had to—

But she couldn't. She couldn't do anything because someone was holding her arms. Burning her arms. Those hands were annoying, but at least she knew who they belonged to. They were firm and very gentle but very strong. All that added up to Stefan.

Slowly, she raised her dripping head to ask Stefan to stop burning her arms.

But she couldn't. Because on Stefan's body there was Damon's head. Now that was *funny*. She'd seen a lot of things that vampires could do, but not this swapping heads business.

"Stefan-Damon—please stop," she gasped between hysterical whoops of laughter. "It hurts. It's too hot!"

"Hot? You're frozen, you mean." The deft, searing hands were rubbing up and down her arms, pushing back her head to rub her cheeks. She let it happen, because it seemed to be only sense that if it was Damon's head, they were Stefan's hands. "You're cold but you're not shivering?" a grim Damon-voice said from somewhere.

"Yes, so you see I must be warming up." Elena didn't feel very warmed up. She realized that she still had on a longer fur garment, one that reached to her knees under her leather breeches. She fumbled with her belt.

"You're not warming up. You're going into the next stage of hypothermia. And if you don't get dry and warm right *now*, you're going to die." Not roughly, he tilted her chin up to look into her eyes. "You're delirious now—can you understand me, Elena? We need to *really* get you warm."

Warm was a concept as vague and faraway as life before she had met Stefan. But delirious she understood. That was not a good thing. What to do about it except laugh?

"All right. Elena, just wait for a moment. Let me find—" In a moment he was back. Not quick enough to stop her from unwrapping the fur down to her waist, but back before she could get her camisole off.

"Here." He stripped off the damp fur and wrapped a warm, dry one around her, over her camisole.

After a moment or two she began to shiver.

"That's my girl," Damon's voice said. It went on: "Don't fight me, Elena. I'm trying to save your life. That's all. I'm not going to try to do anything else. I give you my word."

Elena was bewildered. Why should she think that Damon—this must be Damon, she decided—would want to hurt her?

Although he could be a bastard sometimes . . .

And he was taking off her clothes.

No. *That* shouldn't be happening. Definitely not. Especially since Stefan must be somewhere around.

But by now Elena was shivering too hard to talk.

And now that she was in her underwear, he was making her lie down on furs, tucking other furs around her. Elena didn't understand anything that was happening, but it was all starting not to matter. She was floating somewhere outside herself, watching without much interest.

Then another body was slipping in under the furs. She snapped back from the place she had been floating. Very briefly she got a look at a bare chest. And then a warm, compact body slid into the makeshift sleeping bag with her. Warm, hard arms went around her, keeping her in contact all over her body.

Through the mist she vaguely heard Stefan's voice.

"*What the hell are you doing?*"

30

"Strip to your underwear and get in on the other side," Damon said. His voice was neither angry nor fatuous. He added shortly, "Elena is dying."

The last three words seemed to affect Stefan particularly, although Elena couldn't parse them. Stefan wasn't moving, just breathing hard, his eyes wide. "Bonnie and I have been gathering hay and fuel and we're all right."

"You've been exercising—moving about—wearing clothes that kept you warm. She's been dunked in ice water and sitting still—high up in the wind. I got the other thurg to break off wood from the dead trees around here and try it on the fire. Now get the hell in, Stefan, and give her some body warmth, or I'm going to make her a vampire."

"Nnn," Elena tried to say, but Stefan didn't seem to understand.

Damon, however, said, "Don't worry. He's going to warm you up from the other side. You won't have to become a vampire just yet. For God's sake," he added suddenly, explosively, "some prince you picked!"

Stefan's voice was quiet and tense. "You tried putting her in a thermal envelope?"

"Of course I tried, you idiot! *No* magic works beyond the Mirror except telepathy."

Elena had no sense of time going by, but suddenly there was a familiar body pressed against hers from the other side.

And somewhere directly in her mind: *Elena? Elena? You're all right, aren't you, Elena? I don't care whether you're playing a joke on me. But you're* really *all right, aren't you? Just tell me that, love.*

Elena wasn't able to answer at all.

Dimly, fragments of sound came to her ears: "Bonnie . . . on top of her and . . . pack ourselves back on either side."

And dull feelings stirred her sense of touch: a small body, almost weightless, like a thick blanket, pressing down on her. Someone sobbing, tears dripping on her neck from above. And warmth on either side.

I'm asleep with the other kittens, she thought, dozing. Maybe we'll have a nice dream.

"I wish we could know how they're doing," Meredith said, on a pause from one of her pacing bouts.

"I wish they knew how we're doing," Matt said wearily as he taped another note card amulet onto a window. And another.

"Do you know, my dears, I kept hearing a child crying last night in my dreams," Mrs. Flowers said slowly.

Meredith turned, startled. "So did I! Right out on the front porch, it sounded like. But I was too tired to get up."

"It might mean something—or nothing at all." Mrs. Flowers frowned. She was boiling tap water for tea. The electricity was sporadic. Matt and Saber had driven back to the boardinghouse earlier that day so that Matt could gather Mrs. Flowers's most important instruments—her herbs for teas, compresses, and poultices. He hadn't had the heart to tell her about the state of the boardinghouse, or what those maggot malach had done to it. He'd had to find a loose board from the garage to get from the hall to the kitchen. There was no third floor anymore and very little second.

At least he hadn't run into Shinichi.

"What I'm saying is that maybe there's some real kid out there," Meredith said.

"At night alone? Sounds like a Shinichi zombie," Matt said.

"Maybe. But maybe not. Mrs. Flowers, do you have any idea of when you hear the crying? Early in the night or late?"

"Let me think, dear. It seems to me that I hear it

whenever I wake up—and old people wake up quite frequently."

"I usually hear it toward the morning—but I usually sleep without dreaming for the first few hours and wake up early."

Mrs. Flowers turned to Matt. "What about you, Matt, dear? Do you ever hear a sound like crying?"

Matt, who deliberately overworked himself these days to try to get a solid six hours of sleep at night, said, "I've heard the wind kind of moaning and sobbing around midnight, I guess."

"It sounds as if we have an all-night ghost, my dears," Mrs. Flowers said calmly and poured them each a mug of tea.

Matt saw Meredith glance at him uneasily—but Meredith didn't know Mrs. Flowers as well as he did.

"You don't really think it's a ghost," he said now.

"No, I don't. Ma*ma* hasn't said a word about it, and then it's *your* house, Matt, dear. No gruesome murders or hideous secrets in its past, I should think. Let me see . . ." She shut her eyes and let Matt and Meredith go on with their tea. Then she opened her eyes and gave them a puzzled smile.

"Ma*ma* says 'search the house for your ghost. Then listen well to what it has to say.'"

"Okay," Matt said poker-faced. "Since it's my house,

I guess I'd better search for it. But when? Should I set an alarm?"

"I think the best way would be to arrange a watch rota," Mrs. Flowers said.

"Okay," Meredith agreed promptly. "I'll take the middle watch, from midnight to four; Matt can have the first one; and Mrs. Flowers, you can have the early-morning one, and get a nap in the afternoon if you want."

Matt felt uneasy. "Why don't we just break it up into two watches and the two of you can share one? I'll take the other."

"Because, dear Matt," Meredith said, "we don't want to be treated like 'ladies.' And don't argue"—she hefted the fighting stave—"because I'm the one with the heavy equipment."

Something was shaking the room. Shaking Matt with it. Still half-asleep, he put his hand under his pillow and pulled out the revolver. A hand grabbed it and he heard a voice.

"Matt! It's me, Meredith! *Wake up*, will you?"

Groggily, Matt reached for the lamp switch. Again, strong, slim cold fingers prevented him from doing what he wanted.

"No light," Meredith whispered. "It's very faint, but if you come with me quietly, you can hear it. The crying."

That woke Matt up the rest of the way. "Right now?"

"Right now."

Doing his best to walk quietly through the dark halls, Matt followed Meredith to the downstairs living room.

"Sh!" Meredith warned. "Listen."

Matt listened. He could hear some sobbing all right, and maybe some words, but they didn't sound all that ghostly to him. He put his ear to the wall and listened. The crying was louder.

"Do we have a flashlight?" Matt asked.

"I have two, my dears. But this is a very dangerous time of night." Mrs. Flowers was a shadow against darkness.

"Please give the flashlights to us," said Matt. "I don't think our ghost is very supernatural. What time is it, anyway?"

"About twelve forty A.M.," Meredith answered. "But why do you think it isn't supernatural?"

"Because I think it's living in our basement," Matt said. "I think it's Cole Reece. The kid who ate his guinea pig."

Ten minutes later, with the stave, two flashlights, and Saber, they had caught their ghost.

"I didn't mean anything bad," Cole sobbed, when they had lured him upstairs with promises of candy and "magic" tea that would let him sleep.

"I didn't hurt anything, honest," he choked, wolfing

down Hershey bar after Hershey bar from their emergency rations. "I'm scared that he's onto me. Because after you hit me with that sticky note, I haven't been able to hear him in my head anymore. And then you came here"—he gestured around Matt's house—"and you had amulets and I figured it would be better to stay inside them. Or it could be *my* Last Midnight too."

He was babbling. But something about the last words made Matt say, "What do you mean . . . 'your Last Midnight too'?"

Cole looked at him in terror. The rim of melted Hershey bar around his lips made Matt remember the last time he'd seen the boy.

"You know, don't you?" Cole faltered. "About the midnights? The countdown? Twelve days till the Last Midnight? Eleven days till the Last Midnight? And now . . . tonight is one day till the Last Midnight . . ." He began to sob again, even while cramming chocolate into his mouth. It was clear that he was starving.

"But what happens on the Last Midnight?" Meredith asked.

"You know, don't you? That that's the time when . . . *you* know." Maddeningly Cole seemed to think they were testing him.

Matt put his hands on Cole's shoulders, and to his horror felt bones under his fingers. The kid *really* was starving, he thought, forgiving him all the Hershey bars. His eyes met Mrs. Flowers's eyes and she immediately went to the kitchen.

But Cole wasn't answering; he was mumbling incoherently. Matt forced himself to apply pressure to those bony shoulders.

"Cole, talk louder! What's this Last Midnight about?"

"*You* know. That's when . . . all the kids . . . *you* know, they wait up and at midnight . . . they get knives or guns. *You* know. And we go into our parents' room while they're asleep and . . ." Cole broke down again, but Matt noticed he had slipped into saying "we" and "our" by the end.

Meredith spoke in her calm, steady voice. "The children are going to kill their parents, is that right?"

"He showed us where to slash or stab. Or if there's a gun—"

Matt had heard enough. "You can stay—in the basement," he said. "And here are some amulets. Put them on you if you feel like you're in danger." He gave Cole a whole packet of Post-it Notes.

"Just don't be afraid," Meredith added, as Mrs. Flowers came in with a plate of sausages and fried potatoes for Cole. At any other time the smell would have made Matt hungry.

"It's just like that island in Japan," he said. "Shinichi and Misao made it happen there, and they're going to do it again."

"I say time's running out. Actually it's already the Last Midnight day—it's nearly one thirty in the morning," Meredith said. "We have less than twenty-four hours. We should either get out of Fell's Church or do something to arrange a confrontation."

"A confrontation? Without Elena or Damon or Stefan?" Matt said. "We'll be murdered. Don't forget Sheriff Mossberg."

"He didn't have this." Meredith tossed the fighting stave into the air, caught it neatly, and put it at her side.

Matt shook his head. "Shinichi will still kill you. Or some little kid will, with the semi-automatic from Daddy's closet."

"We have to do *something*."

Matt thought. His head was pounding. Finally he said, head lowered, "When I got the herbs I got Misao's star ball, too."

"You're kidding. Shinichi *still* didn't find it?"

"No. And maybe we could do something with it."

Matt looked at Meredith, who looked at Mrs. Flowers. Mrs. Flowers said, "What about pouring out the liquid in different places in Fell's Church? Just a drop here and a drop there? We could ask the Power in it to protect the town. Maybe it would listen."

Meredith said, "That was the exact reason we wanted to get Shinichi's and Misao's star balls in the first place.

The star balls control their owners, according to legend."

Matt said, "It may be old-ways thinking, but I agree."

Meredith said, "Then let's do it *right now*."

While the other two waited, Matt got Misao's star ball. It had a very, very little liquid on the bottom.

"After the Last Midnight she plans to fill it to the top with the energy of the new lives that get taken," Meredith said.

"Well, she's not going to get a chance to do that," Matt said flatly. "When we're done we'll destroy the container."

"But we probably should hurry," Meredith added. "Let's get some weapons together: something silver, something long and heavy, like a fire iron. Shinichi's little zombies are not going to be happy—and who knows who's on his side?"

31

Elena woke up feeling stiff and cramped. But that wasn't surprising. Three other people seemed to be on top of her.

Elena? Can you hear me?

Stefan?

Yes! You're awake?

I'm all cramped . . . and hot.

A different voice interrupted. *Just give us a moment and you won't be cramped anymore.* Elena felt Damon move away. Bonnie rolled into his place.

But Stefan clung to her for a moment. *Elena, I'm sorry. I never even realized what condition you were in. Thank God for Damon. Can you forgive me?*

Despite the heat, Elena cuddled closer to him. *If you can forgive* me *for putting the whole party in danger. I did that, didn't I?*

I don't know. I don't care. All I know is that I love you.

It was several minutes before Bonnie woke up. Then she said feebly, "Hey! Whachoo doin' in my bed?"

"Getting out of it," Elena said, and tried to roll over and get up. The world was wobbly. She was wobbly—and bruised. But Stefan was never more than a few inches away, holding her, righting her when she started to fall. He helped her get dressed without making her feel like a baby. He examined her backpack, which fortunately hadn't gone into the water, and then he took out anything heavy inside. He put the heavy things in his own pack.

Elena felt much better after being given some food, and after seeing the thurgs—both of them—eating too; either stretching their great double trunks up to break off pieces of wood from the barren trees, or scooping away snow to find dry grass underneath. They clearly were not going to die after all.

Elena knew everyone was watching her to gauge whether or not she was up to any more that day. She hurried to finish drinking the tea heated over a dung fire, trying to conceal the fact that her hands shook. After forcing some jerky down, she said in her most cheerful voice, "So what next?"

How do you feel? Stefan asked her.

"Little sore, but I'll be fine. I guess everyone expects me to have pneumonia, but I don't even have any cough."

Damon, after one heavy-lidded glance at Stefan, took both her hands and stared at her. She couldn't—she didn't dare—meet his eyes, so she focused on Stefan, who was looking at her comfortingly.

At last Damon dropped Elena's hands abruptly. "I went in as far as I could. You should know how far that is," he added to Stefan. "She's sound, her nose is wet, and her coat is shiny."

Stefan looked as if he were going to smack him one, but Elena took his hand soothingly. "I'm healthy," she said. "So that's two votes for me going on to save Fell's Church."

"I've always believed in you," Stefan said. "If you think you can go on, you can go on."

Bonnie sniffled. "Just don't take any more chances, okay?" she said. "You scared me."

"I'm really sorry," Elena said gently, feeling the void of Meredith's absence. Meredith would be a great help to both of them now. "So, shall we continue? And where are we heading? I'm all turned around."

Damon stood. "I think we just keep in a straight line. The path is narrow after this—and who knows what the next trial is?"

The path was narrow—and misty. Just as before, it started in filmy veils and ended up blinding them. Elena let Stefan, with his catlike reflexes, go first, and she held on to his pack. Behind her, Bonnie clung like a burr. Just when Elena thought she was going to scream if she had to keep traveling through the white blanket any farther, it cleared.

They were near the top of some mountain.

Elena took off after Bonnie, who had hurried ahead at the sight of transparent air. She was just fast enough to grab on to Bonnie's pack and pull her backward as she reached the place where the land stopped.

"No *way*!" Bonnie cried, setting up a clamoring echo from below. "There is *no way* I'm going across *that*!"

That was a chasm with a very thin bridge spanning it.

The chasm was frosty white on either side at the top, but when Elena gripped the bridge's ice-cold metal poles and leaned a little forward she could see glacial blues and greens at the very bottom. A chill wind hit her face.

The gap between this bit of the world and the next bit directly in front of them was about a hundred yards long.

Elena looked from the shadowy depths to the slender bridge, which was made of wooden slats and just wide enough for one person to walk on. It was supported here and there by ropes which ran to the sides of the chasm and were sunk with metal posts into barren, icy rock.

It also swooped magnificently down and then back up again. Even looking at it gave the eye a sort of mini–thrill ride. The only problem was that it didn't include a safety belt, a seat, two handrails, and a uniformed guide saying,

"Hands and feet must be kept inside the attraction at all times!" It did have a single, thin, creeper-woven rope to hold on to on the left.

"Look," Stefan was saying, as quietly and intently as Elena had ever heard him speak, "we can hold onto each other. We can go go one by one, very slowly—"

"NOOO!" Bonnie put into that one word a psychic shriek that almost defeaned Elena. *"No, no, no, no, NO! You don't understand! I can't DO IT!"* She flung her backpack down.

Then she began laughing and crying at the same time in a full-blown attack of hysterics. Elena had an impulse to dash water in her face. She had a stronger impulse to throw herself down beside Bonnie and shriek, "And neither can I! It's insane!" But what good would that do?

A few minutes later Damon was talking quietly to Bonnie, unaffected by the outburst. Stefan was pacing in circles. Elena was trying to think of Plan A, while a little voice chanted inside her head, *You can't do it, you can't do it, you can't do it, either.*

This was all just a phobia. They could probably train Bonnie out of it—if, say, they had a year or two.

Stefan, on one of his circular trips near her, said, "And how are *you* about heights, love?"

Elena decided to put a brave face on it. "I don't know. I think I can do it."

Stefan looked pleased. "To save your hometown."

"Yes . . . but it's too bad nothing works here. I could try to use my Wings for flying, but I can't control them—"

And that kind of magic is simply not available here, Stefan's voice said in her mind.

But telepathy is. You can hear me, too, can't you?

They thought of the answer simultaneously, and Elena saw the light of the idea breaking on Stefan's face even as she began to speak.

"*Influence* Bonnie! Make her think she's a tightrope walker—a performer since she was a toddler. But don't make her too playful so she doesn't bounce the rest of us off!"

With that light in his face, Stefan looked . . . too good. He seized both Elena's hands, whirled her around once as if she weighed nothing, picked her up, and kissed her.

And kissed her.

And kissed her until Elena felt her soul dripping off her fingertips.

They shouldn't have done it in front of Damon. But Elena's euphoria was clouding her judgment, and she couldn't control herself.

Neither of them had been trying for a deep mind probe. But telepathy was all they had left, and it was warm and wonderful and it left them for an instant in the circle of each other's arms, laughing, panting—with electricity flashing between them. Elena's whole body felt as if she'd just gotten a sizable jolt.

Then she pulled herself out of his arms, but it was too late. Their shared gaze had gone on much too long, and Elena felt her heart pounding in fear. She could feel Damon's eyes on her. She barely managed to whisper, "Will you tell them?"

"Yes," Stefan said softly. "I'll tell them." But he didn't move until she actually turned her back on Bonnie and Damon.

After that she peeked over her shoulder and listened.

Stefan sat down by the sobbing girl and said, "Bonnie, can you look at me? That's all I want. I promise you, you don't have to go across that bridge if you don't want to. You don't even have to stop crying, but try to look me in the eye. Can you do that? Good. Now . . ." His voice and even his face changed subtly, becoming more forceful—mesmerizing. "You're not afraid of heights at all, are you? You're an acrobat who could walk a tightrope across the Grand Canyon and never turn a hair. You're the very best of all your family, the flying McCulloughs, and *they're* the best in the world. And right now, you're going to choose whether to cross over that wooden bridge. If so, you'll lead us. You'll be our leader."

Slowly, while listening to Stefan, Bonnie's face had changed. With swollen eyes fixed on Stefan's, she seemed to be listening intently to something in her own head. And finally, as Stefan said the last sentence, she jumped up and looked at the bridge.

"Okay, let's go!" she cried, picking up her backpack, while Elena sat staring after her.

"Can you make it?" Stefan asked, looking at Elena. "We'll let her go first—there's really no way she can fall off. I'll go after her. Elena can come after me and hold on to my belt, and I'm counting on you, Damon, to hold on to *her.* Especially if she starts to faint."

"I'll hold her," Damon said quietly. Elena wanted to ask Stefan to Influence her, too, but everything was happening so fast. Bonnie was already on the bridge, only pausing when called back by Stefan. Stefan was looking behind him at Elena, saying, "Can you get a good grip?" Damon was behind Elena, putting a strong hand on her shoulder, and saying, "Look straight ahead, not down. Don't worry about fainting; I'll catch you."

But it was such a frail wooden bridge, and Elena found that she was always looking down and her stomach floated up outside her body and above her head. She had a death-grip on Stefan's belt with one hand, and on the woven creeper with the other.

They came to a place where a slat had detached and the slats on either side looked as if they might go at any moment.

"Careful with these!" Bonnie said, laughing and leaping over all three.

Stefan stepped over the first chancy slat, over the missing one, and put his foot on the next.

Crack!

Elena didn't scream—she was beyond screaming. She couldn't look. The sound had shut her eyes.

And she couldn't move. Not a finger. Certainly not a foot.

She felt Damon's arms around her waist. Both of them. She wanted to let him support her weight as he had many times before.

But Damon was whispering to her, words like spells that allowed her legs to stop shaking and cramping and even let her stop breathing so fast that she might faint. And then he was lifting her and Stefan's arms were going around her and for a moment they were both holding her firmly. Then Stefan took her weight and gently put her feet down on firm slats.

Elena wanted to cling to him like a koala, but she knew that she mustn't. She would make them both fall. So somewhere, from inner depths she didn't know she had, she found the courage to take her own weight on her feet and fumbled for the creeper.

Then she lifted her head and whispered as loudly as she could, "Go on. We need to give Damon room."

"Yes," Stefan whispered back. But he kissed her on the forehead, a quick protective kiss, before he turned and stepped toward the impatient Bonnie.

Behind her, Elena heard—and felt—Damon jumping catlike over the gap.

Elena raised her eyes to stare at the back of Stefan's head again. She couldn't compass all the emotions she was feeling at that moment: love, terror, awe, excitement—and, of course, gratitude, all at once.

She didn't dare turn her head to look at Damon behind her, but she felt exactly the same things for *him*.

"A few more steps," he kept saying. "A few more steps."

A brief eternity later, they were on solid ground, facing a medium-sized cavern, and Elena fell to her knees. She was sick and faint, but she tried to thank Damon as he passed by her on the snowy mountain trail.

"You were in my way," he said shortly and as coldly as the wind. "If you had fallen you might have upset the entire bridge. And I don't happen to feel like dying today."

"What are you saying to her? What did you just say?" Stefan, who had been out of earshot, came hurrying back. "What did he say to you?"

Damon, examining his palm for creeper thorns, said without looking up, "I told her the truth, that's all. So far she's zero for two on this quest. Let's hope that as long as you make it through they let you in the Gatehouse, because if they're grading on performance we've flunked. Or should I say, one of us has flunked?"

"Shut up or I'll shut you up," Stefan said in a different voice than Elena had ever heard him use before. She stared. It was as if he'd grown ten years in one second. "Don't you *ever* talk to her or about her that way again, Damon!"

Damon stared at him for a moment, pupils contracted. Then he said, "Whatever," and strolled away.

Stefan bent down to hold Elena until her shaking stopped.

And that's that, Elena thought. An ice-cold rage gripped her. Damon had no respect for her at all; he had none for anyone but himself. She couldn't protect Bonnie from Bonnie's own feelings—or stop him from insulting her. She couldn't stop Bonnie for forgiving. But she, Elena, was done with Damon. This last insult was the end.

The fog came in again as they walked through the cavern.

"Damon doesn't mean to be such a—a bastard," Bonnie said explosively. "He's just—so often he feels like it's the three of us against him—and—and—"

"Well, who started that? Even back riding the thurgs," Stefan said.

"I know, but there's something else," Bonnie said humbly. "Since it's only snow and rock and ice—he's—I don't know. He's all tight. Something's wrong."

"He's hungry," Elena said, stricken by a sudden realization. Since the thurgs there had been nothing for the two vampires to hunt. They couldn't exist, like foxes, on insects and mice. Of course Lady Ulma had provided plenty of Black Magic for them, the only thing that even resembled a substitute for blood. But their supply was dwindling, and of course, they had to think of the trip back, as well.

Suddenly Elena knew what would do her good.

"Stefan," she murmured, pulling him into a nook in the craggy stone of the cave entrance. She pushed off her hood and unrolled her scarf enough to expose one side of her neck. "Don't make me say 'please' too many times," she whispered to him. "I can't wait that long."

Stefan looked into her eyes, saw that she was serious—and determined—and kissed one of her mittened hands.

"It's been long enough now, I think—no, I'm sure, or I would never even attempt this," he whispered. Elena tipped her head back. Stefan stood between her and the wind and she was almost warm. She felt the little initial pain and then Stefan was drinking and their minds slid together like two raindrops on a glass window.

He took very little blood. Just enough to make the difference in his eyes between still green pools and sparkling, effervescent streams.

But then his gaze went still again. "Damon . . ." he said, and paused awkwardly.

What could Elena say? I just severed all ties with him? They were supposed to help one another along these trials; to show their wit and courage. If she refused, would she fail again?

"Send him quick then," she said. "Before I change my mind."

Five minutes later Elena was again tucked into the little nook, while Damon turned her head back and forth with dispassionate precision, then suddenly darted forward and sank his fangs into a prominent vein. Elena felt her eyes go wide.

A bite that hurt this much—well, she hadn't experienced it since the days when she had been stupid and unprepared and had fought with all her strength to get free.

As for Damon's mind—there was a steel wall. Since she had to do this, she had been hoping to see the little boy who lived in Damon's inmost soul, the one who was the unwilling Watch-Keeper over all of his secrets, but she couldn't even thaw the steel a little.

After a minute or two, Stefan pulled Damon off of her—not gently. Damon came away sullenly, wiping his mouth.

"Are you okay?" Bonnie asked in a worried whisper, as Elena rummaged through Lady Ulma's medicine box for a piece of gauze to staunch the unhealed wounds in her neck.

"I've been better," Elena said briefly, as she wrapped up her scarf again.

Bonnie sighed. "Meredith is the one who really belongs here," she said.

"Yes, but Meredith really belongs in Fell's Church, too. I only hope they can hold on long enough for us to come back."

"I only hope that we can come back with something that will help them," Bonnie whispered.

Meredith and Matt spent the time from 2:00 A.M. to dawn pouring infinitesimal drops from Misao's star ball onto the streets of the town, and asking the Power to—somehow—help them in the fight against Shinichi. This brisk movement from place to place had also netted a surprising bonus: kids. Not crazy kids. Normal ones, terrified of their brothers and sisters or of their parents, not daring to go home because of the awful things they had seen there. Meredith and Matt had crammed them into Matt's mother's second-hand SUV and brought them to Matt's house.

In the end, they had more than thirty kids, from ages five to sixteen, all too frightened to play, or talk, or even to ask for anything. But they'd eaten everything Mrs. Flowers could find that wasn't spoiled in Matt's refrigerator and pantry, and from the pantries of the deserted houses on either side of the Honeycutts'.

Matt, watching a ten-year-old girl cramming plain white bread into her mouth with wolfish hunger, tears running down her grimy face as she chewed and swallowed, said quietly to Meredith, "Think we've got any ringers in here?"

"I'd bet my life on it," she replied just as quietly. "But what are we going to do? Cole doesn't know anything helpful. We'll just have to pray that the un-possessed kids will be able to help us when Shinichi's ringers attack."

"I think the best option when confronted by possessed kids who may have weapons is to run."

Meredith nodded absently, but Matt noticed she took the stave everywhere with her now. "I've devised a little test for them. I'm going to smack every one with a Post-It, and see what happens. Kids who've done things they regret may get hysterical, kids who're already just terrified may get some comfort, and the ringers will either attack or run."

"This I have to see."

Meredith's test lured out only two ringers in the whole mob, a thirteen-year-old boy and a fifteen-year-old girl. Each of them screamed and darted through the house, shrieking wildly. Matt couldn't stop them. When it was all over and the older kids were comforting the younger ones, Matt and Meredith finished boarding up the windows and pasting amulets between the boards. They spent the evening scouting for food, questioning the kids about Shinichi and the Last Midnight, and helping Mrs. Flowers treat injuries. They tried to keep one person on guard at all times, but since they had been up and moving since 1:30 A.M., they were all very tired.

At a quarter to eleven Meredith came to Matt, who was cleaning the scratches of a yellow-haired eight-year-old. "Okay," she said quietly, "I'm going to take my car and get the new amulets Mrs. Saitou said she'd have done by now.

Do you mind if I take Saber?"

Matt shook his head. "No, I'll do it. I know the Saitous better, anyway."

Meredith gave what, in a less refined person, might have been called a snort. "I know them well enough to say, excuse me, Inari-Obaasan; excuse me, Orime-san; we're the troublemakers who keep asking for huge amounts of anti-evil amulets, but you don't mind that, do you?"

Matt smiled faintly, let the eight-year-old go, and said, "Well, they might mind it less if you got their names straight. 'Obaasan' means 'grandma,' right?"

"Yes, of course."

"And 'san' is just a thingy you put at the end of a name to be polite."

Meredith nodded, adding, "And 'a thingy at the end' is called an 'honorific suffix.' "

"Yeah, yeah, but for all your big words you've got their names wrong. It's Orime-grandma and Orime-Isobel's-mother. So Orime-Obaasan and Orime-san, too."

Meredith sighed. "Look, Matt, *Bonnie and I* met them first. Grandma introduced *herself* as Inari. Now I know she's a little wacky, but she would certainly know her own name, right?"

"And she introduced herself to *me* and said not just that she was named Orime, but that her daughter was named after her. Talk your way out of *that* one."

"Matt, shall I get my notebook? It's in the boarding-house den—"

Matt gave a short sharp laugh—almost a sob. He looked to make sure Mrs. Flowers wasn't around and then hissed, "It's somewhere down at the center of the earth, maybe. There *is* no den anymore."

For a moment Meredith looked simply shocked, but then she frowned. Matt glared darkly. It didn't help to think that they were the two most unlikely of their group to quarrel. Here they were, and Matt could practically see the sparks flying. "All right," Meredith said finally, "I'll just go over there and ask for Orime-Obaasan, and then tell them it was all your fault when they laugh."

Matt shook his head. "Nobody's going to laugh, because you're going to get it right that way."

"Look, Matt," Meredith said, "I've been reading so much on the Internet that I even *know* the name Inari. I've come across it somewhere. And I'm sure I would have made . . . made the connection . . ." Her voice trailed off. When Matt turned his eyes down from the ceiling, he started. Meredith's face was white and she was breathing quickly.

"Inari . . ." she whispered. "I do know that name, but . . ." Suddenly she grabbed Matt's wrist so hard that it hurt. "Matt, is your computer absolutely dead?"

"It went when the electricity went. By now even the generator is gone."

"But you have a mobile that connects to the Internet, right?"

The urgency in her voice made Matt, in turn, take her seriously. "Sure," he said. "But the battery's been kaput for at least a day. Without electricity I can't recharge it. And my mom took hers. She can't live without it. Stefan and Elena must've left their stuff at the boardinghouse—" He shook his head at Meredith's hopeful expression and whispered, "Or, should I say, where the boardinghouse used to be."

"But we have to find a mobile or computer that works! We *have* to! I need it to work for just a minute!" Meredith said frantically, breaking away from him and beginning to pace as if trying to beat some world record.

Matt was staring at her in bewilderment. "But why?"

"Because we *have to.* I *need* it, even just for a minute!"

Matt could only gaze at her, perplexed. Finally he said, "I guess we can ask the kids."

"The kids! One of them has got to have a live mobile! Come on, Matt, we have to talk to them *right now.*" She stopped and said, rather huskily, "I pray that you're right and I'm wrong."

"Huh?" Matt had no idea what was going on.

"I said I pray that I'm wrong! You pray, too, Matt—*please*!"

Elena was waiting for the fog to disperse. It had come in as always, bit by bit, and now she was wondering if it would ever leave, or if it were actually another trial itself. Therefore, when she suddenly realized she could see Stefan's shirt in front of her, she felt her heart bound for joy. She hadn't messed anything up lately.

"I can see it!" Stefan said, pulling her up beside him. And then, "Voilà . . ."—but in a whisper.

"What, what?" cried Bonnie, bounding forward. And then she stopped too.

Damon didn't bound. He strolled. But Elena was turning toward Bonnie at the time, and she saw his face as he saw it.

In front of them was a sort of small castle, or large

gateway with spires that pierced the low clouds that hung above it. There was some kind of writing over the huge cathedral-like black doors in front, but Elena had never seen anything like the squiggles of whatever foreign language it was.

On either side of the building, there were black walls that were nearly as tall as the spires. Elena looked left and right and realized that they disappeared only off at the vanishing point. And without magic, it would be impossible to fly over them.

What the boy and girl in the story had discovered only by following the walls for days, they had simply walked straight into.

"It's the Gatehouse of the Seven Treasures, isn't it, Bonnie? Isn't it? Look!" Elena shouted.

Bonnie was already looking, both hands pressed against her heart, and for once without a word to say. As Elena watched, the diminutive girl fell to her knees in the light, powdery snow. But Stefan answered. He picked up Bonnie and Elena at the same time and whirled them both. "It is!" he said, just as Elena was saying *"It is!"* and Bonnie, the expert, gasping, "Oh, it really, *really* is!" with tears freezing on her cheeks.

Stefan put his lips to Elena's ear. "And you know what that means, don't you? If that is the Gatehouse of the Seven Treasures, you know where we are standing now?"

Elena tried to ignore the warm, tingling sensation that shot up from the soles of her feet at the feeling of Stefan's breath on her ear. She tried to focus on his question.

"Look up," Stefan suggested.

Elena did—and gasped.

Above them, instead of a fog bank or incessant crimson light from a sun that never stopped setting, were three moons. One was enormous, covering perhaps a sixth of the sky, shining in swirls of white and blue, hazy at the edges. Just in front of it was a beautiful silvery moon at least three quarters as big as it was.

Last, there was a tiny moon in high orbit, white as a diamond, that seemed to be deliberately keeping its distance from the other two. All of them were half full and shone down with gentle, soothing light on the unbroken snow around Elena.

"We're in the Nether World," Elena said, shaken.

"Oh . . . it's just like in the story," Bonnie gasped. "Exactly like. Even the writing! Even the amount of snow!"

"*Exactly* like the story?" Stefan asked. "Even to the phase of the moons? How full they are?"

"Just exactly the same."

Stefan nodded. "I thought they would be. That story was a precognition, given to you with the purpose of helping us find the largest star ball ever made."

"Well, let's go inside!" cried Bonnie. "We're wasting time!"

"Okay—but everyone on your guard. We don't want anything to go wrong now," Stefan said.

They went into the Gatehouse of the Seven Treasures in this order: Bonnie, who found that the great black doors swung open at a touch, but that she could see nothing, coming in from bright sunlight; Stefan and Elena, hand in hand; and Damon, who waited outside for a long time in the hopes, Elena thought, of being deemed "a different party."

Meanwhile the others were having the most pleasant shock since they'd taken the Master Keys from the kitsune.

"Sage—Sage!" Bonnie shrilled as soon as her eyes adjusted. "Oh, look, Elena, it's Sage! Sage, how are you? What're you doing here? Oh, it's just so good to *see* you!"

Elena blinked twice, and the dim interior of the octagonal room came into focus. She went around the only piece of furniture in the room, the large desk in the middle. "Sage, do you know how long it seems? Did you know that Bonnie almost got sold for a slave at a public auction? Did you know about her dream?"

Sage looked as he always had to Elena's eyes. The bronzed, terminally fit body, like a model of a Titan, the bare chest and bare feet, the black Levi's, the long spiraling tangles of bronze hair, and the strange bronze eyes that could cut steel, or be as gentle as a pet lamb.

"*Mes deux petits chatons*," Sage was saying. "My two little kittens, you have astounded me. I have been following your adventures. The Gatekeeper is not provided with much entertainment and is not allowed to leave this fortress, but you were most brave and amusing. *Je vous félicite*." He kissed first Elena's hand and then Bonnie's, then embraced Stefan with the Latin two-cheeked kiss. Then he resumed his seat.

Bonnie was climbing Sage as if she were a real kitten. "Did you take Misao's star ball full of Power?" she demanded, kneeling on his thigh. "Did you take half of it, I mean? To get back here?"

"*Mais oui*, I did. But I also left Madame Flowers a little—"

"Do you know that Damon used the other half to open the Gate again? And that I fell in too, even though he didn't want me? And that because of that I almost got sold as a slave? And that Stefan and Elena had to come after me, to make sure I was okay? And that on the way here Elena almost fell off the bridge, and we're not sure if the thurgs are going to make it? And do you know that in Fell's Church the Last Midnight is coming, and we don't know—"

Stefan and Elena exchanged a long, meaningful glance and then Stefan said, "Bonnie, we have to ask Sage the most important question." He looked at Sage. "Is it possible for us to save Fell's Church? Do we have enough time?"

"*Eh bien.* As far as I can tell from the chronological vortex, you have enough time and a little to spare. Enough for a glass of Black Magic to see you off. But after that, no dawdling!"

Elena felt like a crumpled piece of paper that had been straightened and smoothed. She took a long breath. They could do it. That allowed her to remember civilized behavior. "Sage, how did you get stuck way out here? Or were you waiting for us?"

"*Hélas*, no—I am assigned here as punishment. I got an Imperial Summons that I could not ignore, *mes amis*." He sighed and added, "I am just Out of Favor again. So now I am the ambassador to the Nether World, as you see." He waved a languid hand around the room. "*Bienvenue.*"

Elena had a sense of time ticking away, of precious minutes being lost. But maybe Sage himself would do something for Fell's Church. "You really have to stay in here?"

"But assuredly, until *mon père*—my *father*"—Sage said the word savagely and resentfully—"relents and I am allowed to return to the Infernal Court, or, much better, to go my ways without *ever* returning. At least until someone takes the pity on me and kills me." He looked inquiringly around the group, then sighed, and said, "Saber and Talon, they are well?"

"They were when we left," Elena said, itching to get on with their real business here.

"Bien," Sage said, looking at her kindly, "but we should have your entire group in here for the viewing, no?"

Elena glanced at the doors and then again at Stefan, but Sage was already calling—both with voice and telepathy—*"Damon,* mon poussinet, *do you not want to come in with your comrades?"*

There was a long pause, and then the doors opened and a very sullen Damon stepped in. He wouldn't reply to Sage's friendly, *"Bienvenue,"* instead saying, "I didn't come here to socialize. I want to see the treasures in time to save Fell's Church. I haven't forgotten about the damned hick town, even if everyone else has."

"Alors maintenant," Sage said, looking wounded. "You have all passed the tests in your way and may look upon the treasures. You may even use magic again, although I am not sure that it will help you. It all depends upon which treasure you seek. *Félicitations!"*

Everyone but Damon made some gesture of embarrassment.

"Now," Sage continued, "I must show each gate to you before you can pick. I will try to be quick, but be cautious, *s'il vous plaît.* Once you choose a treasure, that is the only door that will open again for any of you."

Elena found herself clutching at Stefan's hand—which

was already reaching for hers—as one by one the doors shone with a faint, silvery light.

"Behind you," said Sage, "is the very gate you entered to get into this room, yes? But next to it, ah . . ." A door brightened to show an impossible cavern. Impossible because of the gems lying on the ground or sticking out of the cave walls. Rubies, diamonds, emeralds, amethysts . . . each one as big as Elena's fist, lying thick in great piles for the taking.

"It's beautiful, but . . . no, of course!" she said firmly, and reached out to put a hand on Bonnie's shoulder.

The next door lit up, brightened, then brightened more so that it seemed to disappear. "And here," Sage sighed, "is the famous kitsune paradise."

Elena could feel her eyes widen. It was a sunny day in the most beautiful park she had ever seen. In the background a little waterfall spilled into a creek, which ran down a green hill, while directly in front of her was a stone bench, just the size for two, underneath a tree that looked like a cherry in full bloom.

Blossoms were flying in a breeze that rustled other cherry and peach trees nearby—causing a rain of dawn-colored petals. Although Elena had only seen the place for a moment, it already seemed familiar to her. She could just walk into it . . .

"No, Stefan!" She had to touch his arm. He had been

walking right into the garden.

"What?" he said, shaking his head like someone in a dream. "I don't know what happened. It just seemed as if I were going to an old, old home . . ." His voice broke off. "Sage, go on, please!"

The next door was already lighting, showing a scene with rack after rack of Clarion Loess Black Magic wine. In the distance, Elena could make out a vineyard with lush grapes hanging heavily, fruit that would never see the light of the sun until it was made into a famous liquid.

Everyone was already sipping at their glasses of Black Magic, so it was easy to say "no" even to the luscious grapes.

As the next door brightened Elena heard herself gasp. It was brilliant midday. Growing in a field as far as she could see were tall bushes thick with long-stemmed roses—the blossoms of which were a velvety-looking black.

Startled, she saw that everyone was looking at Damon, who had taken a step toward the roses as if involuntarily. Stefan put an arm out, barring his way.

"I didn't look very closely," Damon said, "but I think these are the same as the one I . . . destroyed."

Elena turned to Sage. "They're the same, aren't they?"

"But yes," Sage said, looking unhappy. "These are all Midnight roses, *noir pur*—the sort in the white kitsune's bouquet. But these are all *blanks*. The kitsune are the only ones who can put spells on them—like the removal of the curse of a vampire."

There was a general sigh of disappointment among his listeners, but Damon just looked more sullen. Elena was about to speak up, to say that Stefan shouldn't be put through this, when she tuned in to Sage's words and the next gate, and felt a surge of simple, selfish longing herself.

"I suppose you would call it '*La Fontaine* of Eternal Youth and Life,'" Sage said. Elena could see an ornate fountain playing, the effervescent spray at the top making a rainbow. Small butterflies of all colors flew around it, alighting on the leaves of the bower that cradled it in greenery.

Meredith, with her cool head and straightforward logic wasn't there, so Elena dug her nails into her palms and cried "No! Next one!" as quickly and forcefully as she could.

Sage was speaking again. She made herself listen. "The Royal Radhika Flower, which legends say was stolen from the Celestial Court many millennia ago. It changes shape."

A simple enough thing to say . . . but actually to *see* it . . .

Elena watched in astonishment as a dozen or so thick, twining stems, topped by gorgeous white calla lily blossoms, trembled slightly. The next instant she was looking at a cluster of violets with velvet leaves and a drop of dew shining on a petal. A moment later, the stems were topped with radiant mauve snapdragons—with the dewdrop still in place. Before she could remember not to reach out and touch them, the snapdragons had become deep, fully open red roses. When the roses became some exotic golden flower that Elena had never seen, she had to turn her back.

She found herself bumping into a hard, masculine, bare chest while forcing herself to think realistically. Midnight was coming—and not in the form of a rose. Fell's Church needed all the help it could get and here she was staring at flowers.

Abruptly, Sage swung her off her feet and said, "What a temptation, especially for a lover of *la beauté* like you, *belle madame*. What a foolish rule to keep you from taking just a bud! But there is something even higher and more pure than beauty, Elena. You, you are named for it. In old Greek, Elena means 'light'! The darkness is coming fast—the Last, Everlasting Midnight! Beauty will not hold it back; it is a bagatelle, a trinket, useless in times of disaster. But *light*, Elena, *light* will conquer the darkness! I believe this as I believe in your courage, your honesty, and your gentle, loving heart."

With that, he kissed her on the forehead and set her down.

Elena was dazed. Of all the things she knew, she knew best that she could not defeat the darkness that was coming—not alone.

"But you're not alone," Stefan whispered, and she

realized that he was right beside her, and that she must be wide open, projecting her thoughts as clearly as if she were speaking.

"We're all here with you," Bonnie said in a voice twice her size. "We're not afraid of the dark."

There was a pause while everyone tried not to look at Damon. At last he said, "Somehow I got talked into this insanity—I'm still wondering how it happened. But I've come this far and I'm not going to turn around now."

Sage turned toward the final door and it brightened. Not by much, however. It looked like the shady underside of a very large tree. What was odd, though, was that there was nothing at all growing under it. No ferns or bushes or seedlings, not even the normally ever-present creepers and weeds. There were a few dead leaves on the ground, but otherwise it was just dirt.

Sage said, "A planet with only one corporeal form of life upon it. The Great Tree that covers an entire world. The crown covers all but the natural freshwater lakes it needs to survive."

Elena looked into the heart of the twilit world. "We've come so far, and maybe together—maybe we can find the star ball that will save our town."

"This is the door you pick?" asked Sage.

Elena looked at the rest of the group. They all seemed to be waiting for her confirmation. "Yes—and right now.

We have to hurry." She made a motion as if to put her cup down and it disappeared. She smiled thanks at Sage.

"Strictly speaking, I shouldn't give you any help," he said. "But if you have a compass . . ."

Elena had one. It was always dangling from her backpack because she was always trying to read it.

Sage took the compass in his hand and lightly traced a line on it. He gave the compass back to Elena and she found that the needle no longer pointed to the north, but at an angle northeast. "Follow the arrow," he said. "It will take you to the trunk of the Great Tree. If I had to guess at where to find the largest star ball, I would go this way. But be wary! Others have tried this path. Their bodies have nourished the Great Tree—as fertilizer."

Elena scarcely heard the words. She had been terrified at the thought of searching an entire planet for a star ball. Of course, it might be a very small world, like . . . like . . .

Like the little diamond moon you saw over the Nether World?

The voice in Elena's mind was both familiar and not. She glanced at Sage, who smiled. Then she looked around the room. Everyone seemed to be waiting for her to take the first step.

She took it.

34

"You've been fed and taken care of as best as we can manage," Meredith said, looking at all the taut, frightened *young* faces turned toward her in the basement. "And now there's just one thing I want to ask of you in return." She made an effort and steadied her voice. "I want to know if anybody knows of a mobile phone that connects to the Internet, or a computer that is still working. Please, *please*—if you even *think* you know where one might be, tell me."

The tension was like a thick rubber cord, dragging Meredith toward each of the pale, strained faces, dragging them to her.

It was just as well that Meredith was essentially well-balanced. About twelve hands went up immediately, and their lone five-year-old whispered, "My mommy has one. And my daddy."

There was a pause before Meredith could say, "Does anybody know this kid?" and an older girl spoke up before she could.

"She just means they had them before the Burning Man."

"Is the Burning Man called Shinichi?" Meredith asked.

"'Course. Sometimes he would make the red parts of his hair burn up way over his head."

Meredith filed that little fact away under *Things I do not want to see, honest, cross my heart, ever.*

Then she shook herself free from the image.

"You guys and girls, please, *please* think. I only need one, one mobile phone with Internet access that still has power *right now.* One laptop or computer that is still working *now*, maybe because of a generator still making electricity. Just one family with a home generator still working. Anybody?"

The hands were down now. A boy she thought she recognized as being one of the Loring siblings, maybe age ten or eleven, said, "The Burning Man told us that mobile phones and computers were bad. That was why my brother got in a fistfight with my dad. He threw all the mobiles at home in the toilet."

"Okay. Okay, thanks. But anybody who's seen a working mobile or computer? Or a home generator—"

"Why, yes, my dear, I've got one." The voice came from the top of the stairs. Mrs. Flowers was standing there, dressed in a fresh sweat suit. Strangely, she had her voluminous purse in her hand.

"You had—have a generator?" Meredith asked, her heart sinking. What a waste! And if disaster came all because she, Meredith, hadn't finished reading over her own research! The minutes were ticking away, and if everyone in Fell's Church died, it would be her fault. *Her* fault. She didn't think she could live with that.

Meredith had tried, all her life, to reach the state of calm, concentration, and balance that was the other side of the coin from the fighting skills her various disciplines had taught her. And she had become good at it, a good observer, a good daughter, even a good student for all that she was in Elena's fast-paced, high-flying clique. The four of them: Elena, Meredith, Caroline, and Bonnie had fit together like four pieces of a puzzle, and Meredith still sometimes missed the old days and their daring, dominating pseudo-sophisticated capers that never really hurt anyone—except the silly boys who had milled around them like ants at a picnic.

But now, looking at herself, she was puzzled. Who was she? A Hispanic girl named for her mother's Welsh best friend in college. A hunter-slayer of vampires who had kitten canines, a vampire twin, and whose group of friends included Stefan, a vampire; Elena, an ex-vampire—and possibly another vampire, although she was extremely hesitant to call Damon a "friend."

What did that all add up to?

A girl trying to do her best to keep her balance and concentration, in a world that had gone insane. A girl still reeling from what she'd learned about her own family, and now tottering from the need to confirm a dreadful suspicion.

Stop thinking. *Stop!* You have to tell Mrs. Flowers that her boardinghouse has been destroyed.

"Mrs. Flowers—about the boardinghouse—I have to talk to you . . ."

"Why don't you use my BlackBerry first?" Mrs. Flowers came down the basement stairs carefully, watching her feet, and then the children parted before her like waves on the Red Sea.

"Your . . . ?" Meredith stared, choked up. Mrs. Flowers had opened her enormous purse and was now proffering a rather thick all-black object to her.

"It still has power," the old lady explained as Meredith took the thing in two shaking hands, as if receiving a holy object. "I just turned it on and it was working. And now I'm on the Internet!"—proudly.

Meredith's world had been swallowed up by the small, grayish, antiquated screen. She was so amazed and excited at seeing this that she almost forgot why she needed it. But her body knew. Her fingers clutched; her thumbs danced over the mini-keyboard. She went to her favorite search page and entered the word "Orime." She got pages of hits—most in Japanese. Then feeling a trembling in her knees, she typed in "Inari."

6,530,298 results.

She went to the very first hit and saw a web page with a definition. Key words seemed to rush out at her like vultures.

> Inari is the Japanese Shinto deity of rice . . . and . . . foxes. At the entrance to an Inari shrine are . . . statues of two kitsune . . . one male and one female . . . each with a key or jewel carried in mouth or paw . . . These fox-spirits are the servants and messengers of Inari. They carry out Inari's orders. . . .

There was also a picture of a pair of kitsune statues, in their fox forms. Each had a front paw resting on a star ball.

Three years ago, Meredith had fractured her leg when she was on a skiing trip with her cousins in the Blue Ridge Mountains. She had run straight into a small tree. No martial arts skills could save her at the last minute; she knew she was skiing off the groomed areas, where she could run into anything: powder, crud, or iced-over ruts. And, of course, trees. Lots of trees. She was an advanced skier, but she had been going too fast, looking in the wrong direction, and the next thing she knew, she was skiing into the tree instead of around it.

Now she had the same sensation of waking up after a head-on into wood. The shock, the dizziness and nausea that were, initially, worse than the pain. Meredith could take pain. But the pounding in her head, the sickening awareness that she had made a *big* mistake and that she was going to have to pay for it were unbearable. Plus there was a curious horror about the knowledge that her own legs wouldn't hold her up. Even the same useless questions ran through her subconscious, like: How could I be so stupid? Is this possibly a dream? and, Please, God, can I hit the Undo button?

Meredith suddenly realized that she was being supported on either side by Mrs. Flowers and their sixteen-year-old, Ava Wakefield. The mobile was on the cement floor of the basement. She must have actually started to black out. Several of the younger kids were screaming Matt's name.

"No—I—I can stand up alone . . ." All she wanted in the world was to go into the darkness and get away from this horror. She wanted to let her legs go slack and her mind go blank, to flee . . .

But she couldn't run away. She had taken the stave; she had taken the Duty from her grandfather. Anything supernatural that was out to harm Fell's Church on her watch was her problem. And the problem was that her watch never ended.

Matt came clattering down the stairs, carrying their seven-year-old, Hailey, who continually shook with petit mal seizures.

"Meredith!" She could hear the incredulity in his voice. "What is it? What did you find, for God's sake?"

"Come . . . look." Meredith was remembering detail after detail that should have set off warning bells in her mind. Matt was somehow already beside her, even as she remembered Bonnie's very first description of Isobel Saitou.

"The quiet type. Hard to get to know. Shy. And . . . nice."

And that first visit to the Saitou house. The horror that quiet, shy, nice Isobel Saitou had become: the Goddess of Piercing, blood and pus oozing from every hole. And when they had tried to carry dinner to her old, old grandmother, Meredith had noticed absently that Isobel's room was right under the doll-like old lady's. After seeing Isobel pierced and clearly unbalanced, Meredith had assumed that any evil influence must be trying to travel up, and had worried in the back of her mind about the poor, old, doll-sized grandmother. But the evil could just as easily have traveled *down*. Maybe Jim Bryce hadn't given Isobel the malach madness after all. Maybe *she* had given it to *him*, and *he* had given it to Caroline and to his sister.

And that children's game! The cruel, cruel song that Obaasan—that *Inari*-Obaasan had crooned. *"Fox and turtle had a race . . ."* And her words: *"There's a kitsune involved in this somewhere."* She'd been laughing at them, amusing herself! Come to that, it was from Inari-Obaasan that Meredith had first heard the word "kitsune."

And one more additional cruelty, that Meredith had only been able to excuse before by assuming Obaasan had very poor sight. That night, Meredith had had her back to the door and so had Bonnie—they had both been concentrating on "poor decrepit old Grandma." But Obaasan had been facing the door, and she was the only one who could have seen—must have seen—Isobel sneaking up behind Bonnie. And then, just as the cruel game song told Bonnie to look behind her . . . Isobel had been crouching there, ready to lick Bonnie's forehead with a forked pink tongue . . .

"Why?" Meredith could hear her own voice saying. "Why was I so stupid? How could I not have seen from the beginning?"

Matt had retrieved the BlackBerry and read the web page. Then he just stood, fixed, his blue eyes wide. "You were right," he said, after a long moment.

"I want so much to be wrong . . ."

"Meredith—Shinichi and Misao are Inari's *servants* . . . If that old lady is Inari we've been running around like crazy after the wrong people, the hired muscle . . ."

"The damn note cards," Meredith choked out. "The ones done by Obaasan. They're useless, flawed. All those bullets she blessed should have been no good—but maybe she *did* bless them—as a game. Isobel even came to me and changed all the characters the old lady had done for the jars to hold Shinichi and Misao. She said that Obaasan was almost blind. She left a tear on my car seat. I couldn't understand why she should be crying."

"I still can't. She's the granddaughter—probably the third generation of a monster!" Matt exploded. "Why should she cry? And why do the Post-it Notes work?"

"Because they're done by Isobel's mother," Mrs. Flowers said quietly. "Dear Matt, I truly doubt that the old woman is related to the Saitous at all. As a deity—or even a powerful magic-user named after a deity—and undoubtedly a kitsune herself, she surely just moved in with them and used them. Isobel's mother and Isobel had no choice but to carry on the charade for fear of what she'd do to them if they didn't."

"But Mrs. Flowers, when Tyrone and I pulled that leg bone out of the thicket, didn't you say that the Saitou women made such excellent amulets? And didn't you say that we could get the Saitou women to help translate the words on the clay jars when Alaric sent the pictures of them from that Japanese Island?"

As for my belief in the Saitou women, well, I'll have to quibble a little here," Mrs. Flowers said. "I couldn't know that this Obaasan was evil, and there are still two of them who are gentle and good, and who have helped us tremendously—and at great risk to themselves."

Meredith could taste the bitterness of bile in her mouth. "Isobel could have *saved* us. She could have said 'My fake grandmother is really a demon.' "

"Oh, my dear Meredith, the young are so unforgiving. This Inari was probably installed in her house when she was a child. All she knows at first is that the old woman is a tyrant, with a god's name. Then perhaps some demonstration of power—what happened to Orime's husband, I wonder, to make him go back to Japan—if indeed he went there? He may well be dead. And then Isobel is growing up: shy, quiet, introverted—frightened. This is not Japan; there are no other priestesses here to confide in. And you saw the consequences when Isobel reached out to someone outside of the family—to her boyfriend, Jim Bryce."

"And to us—well, to you and Bonnie," Matt said to Meredith. "She sicced Caroline on you."

Scarcely knowing what they were doing, they were talking faster and faster.

"We have to go there right now," said Meredith. "Shinichi and Misao may be the ones bringing on the Last Midnight, but it's Inari who gives the orders. And who knows? She may dole out the punishments as well. We don't know how big *her* star ball is."

"Or *where*," said the old woman.

"Mrs. Flowers," Matt said hastily, "you'd better stay here with the kids. Ava, here, is reliable, and where's Jacob Lagherty?"

"Here," said a boy who looked older than fifteen. He was as tall as Matt was, but gangly.

"Okay. Ava, Jake, you're in charge under Mrs. Flowers. We'll leave Saber with you too." The dog was a big hit among the kids, on his best behavior, even when the younger ones chewed his tail. "You two just listen to Mrs. Flowers, and—"

"Matt, dear, I won't be here. But the animals will surely help to protect them."

Matt stared at her. Meredith knew what he was thinking. Was Mrs. Flowers, so reliable up until now, going somewhere to hide alone? Was she abandoning them?

"And I'll need one of you to drive me to the Saitou house—quickly!—but the other can stay and protect the children as well."

Meredith was both relieved and worried, and clearly Matt was too.

"Mrs. Flowers, this is going to be a *battle*. You could get hurt or be taken hostage so easily—"

"Dear Matt, this is *my* battle. My family has lived in

Fell's Church for generations, all the way back to the pioneering times. I believe this is the battle for which I was born. Certainly the last of my old age."

Meredith stared. In the dim light of the basement, Mrs. Flowers seemed suddenly different somehow. Her voice was changing. Even her small body seemed to be changing, steadying, standing tall.

"But *how* will you fight?" Matt asked, sounding dazed.

"With this. That nice young man, Sage, left it for me with a note apologizing for using Misao's star ball. I used to be quite good with these when I was young." From her capacious purse, Mrs. Flowers pulled out something pale and long and thin as it unwound and Mrs. Flowers whirled it and snapped it with a loud crack at the empty half of the basement. It hit a Ping-Pong ball, curled around it, and brought it back to Mrs. Flowers's open hand.

A bullwhip. Made of some silvery material. Undoubtedly magical. Even Matt looked scared of it.

"Why don't Ava and Jake teach the children to play Ping-Pong while we're gone—and we really *must* go, my dears. There's not a minute to waste. A terrible tragedy is coming, Ma*ma* says."

Meredith had been watching—feeling as dazed as Matt looked. But now she said, "*I* have a weapon too." She picked up the stave and said, "I'm fighting, Matt. Ava, the children are yours to care for."

"And mine," Jacob said, and immediately proved his usefulness by adding, "Isn't that an axe hanging back there near the furnace?"

Matt ran and snatched it up. Meredith could see from his expression what he was thinking: Yes! One heavy axe, a tiny bit rusty, but still plenty sharp enough. Now if the kitsune sent plants or wood against them, *he* was armed.

Mrs. Flowers was already going up the basement stairs. Meredith and Matt exchanged one quick glance and then they were running to catch up with her.

"You drive your mom's SUV. I'll sit in back. I'm still a little bit . . . well, dizzy, I guess." Meredith didn't like to admit to a personal weakness, but better that than crashing the vehicle.

Matt nodded and was good enough not to comment on why she felt so dizzy. She still couldn't believe her own stupidity.

Mrs. Flowers said only one thing. "Matt, dear, break traffic laws."

Elena felt as if she had been doing nothing in all her life except walk under a shady canopy of high branches. It wasn't cold here, but it was cool. It wasn't dark, but it was dim. Instead of the constant crimson sunlight from the bloated red sun in the first Dark Dimension, they were walking in a constant dusk. It was unnerving, always looking up for the sky and never seeing the moon—or moons—or the planet—that might well be up there. Rather than sky, there was nothing but tangled tree branches, clearly heavy and so intricately entwined as to take up every bit of space above.

Was she crazy, thinking that maybe they were on that moon, the diamond bright tiny moon that you could see from the outside of the Nether World Gatehouse? Was it too tiny to have an atmosphere? Too small for proper gravity? She had noticed that she felt lighter here and that even Bonnie's steps seemed quite long. Could she . . .? She tensed her legs, let go of Stefan's hand, and *jumped.*

It was a long jump, but it hadn't taken her anywhere near the canopy of woven branches above. And she didn't land neatly on her toes, either. Her feet flew out from under her on millennia of leaf mold and she skidded on her rear end for maybe three feet, before she could dig her fingers and feet in and stop.

"Elena! Are you all right?" She could hear Stefan and Bonnie calling from behind her, and a quick, impatient: *Are you crazy?* from Damon.

"I was trying to figure out where we were by testing the gravity," she said, standing up on her own and brushing leaves off the seat of her jeans, mortified. Damn! Those leaves had gone up the back of her T-shirt, had even gotten inside her camisole. The group had left most of their furs behind at the Gatehouse, where Sage could guard them, and Elena didn't even have spare clothes. That had been *stupid*, she told herself angrily now. Embarrassed, she tried to walk and shimmy at the same time, to get the crumbled leaves out of her top. Finally she had to say, "Just a second, everybody. Guys, could you turn around? Bonnie, could you come back here and help me?" Bonnie was glad to help and Elena was astonished at how long it took to pick gunk away from her own flinching back.

Next time you want a scientific opinion, try asking, Damon's scornful telepathy commented. Aloud, he added, "I'd say it's about eighty percent Earth's gravity here and we could well be on a moon. Doesn't signify. If Sage hadn't helped us with this compass, we'd never be able to find the tree's trunk—at least not in time."

"And remember," Elena said, "that the idea that the star ball is near the trunk is just a guess. We have to keep our eyes open!"

"But what should we look for?" Once, Bonnie would have wailed this. Now she simply asked quietly.

"Well . . ." Elena turned to Stefan. "It will look bright, won't it? Against this horrible half-light?"

"This horrible camouflage-green half-light," Stefan agreed. "It should look like a slightly shifting bright light."

"But put it like this," Damon said, walking backward gracefully and flashing his old 250-kilowatt smile for a second at them. "If we don't follow Sage's suggestion, we'll never find the trunk. If we try to wander randomly around this world, we will never find *anything*—including our way back. And then not only Fell's Church, but we will all die, in this order. First, we two vampires will break with all civilized behavior, as starvation—"

"Stefan won't," cried Elena, and Bonnie said, "You're just as bad as Shinichi, with his 'revelations' about us!"

Damon smiled subtly. "If I were as bad as Shinichi, little redbird, you would already be punctured like an empty juice box—or I would be sitting back with Sage, enjoying Black Magic—"

"Look, this is pointless," Stefan said.

Damon feigned sympathy. "Maybe you have . . . problems . . . in the canine area, but I do not, little brother." He deliberately held the smile this time so everyone could see his pointed teeth.

Stefan wouldn't be baited. "And it's holding us up—"

"Wrong, little brother. Some of us have mastered the art of speaking and walking at the same time."

"Damon—stop it! Just *stop*!" Elena said, rubbing her hot forehead with cold fingers.

Damon shrugged, still moving backward. "You only had to ask," he said, with just the slightest emphasis on the first word.

Elena said nothing in return. She felt feverish.

It wasn't all just straight walking. Frequently there were huge mounds of knotted roots in their way that had to be climbed. Sometimes Stefan had to use the axe from his backpack to make footholds.

Elena had come to hate the deep green demi-light more than anything. It played tricks on her eyes, just as the muffled sound of their feet on the leaf-strewn ground played tricks on her ears. Several times she stopped—and once Stefan did—to say, "There's someone else here! Following us!"

Each time they had all stopped and listened intently.

Stefan and Damon sent telepathic probes of Power as far as they could reach, seeking another mind. But either it was so well disguised as to be invisible or it didn't exist at all.

And then, after Elena felt as if she had been walking her whole life, and would keep walking until eternity ended, Damon stopped abruptly. Bonnie, just behind him, sucked in her breath. Elena and Stefan hurried forward to see what it was.

What Elena saw made her say, unsteadily, "I think maybe we missed the trunk and . . . found . . . the edge . . ."

On the ground in front of her and as far as she could see, was the star-studded darkness of space. But washing out the light of the stars was a huge planet and two huge moons, one swirled blue and white and one silver.

Stefan was holding her hand, sharing the wonder with her, and tingles ran up her arm and into her suddenly weak knees, just from his feather-light touch on her fingers.

Then Damon said caustically, "Look *up*."

Elena did and gasped. For just an instant her body was completely unmoored. She and Stefan automatically wound their arms around each other. And then Elena realized what they were seeing, both above and below.

"It's water," she said, staring at the pool spread out before them. "One of those freshwater seas Sage told us about. And not a ripple on it. Not a breath of wind."

"But it does look as if we're on that smallest moon,"

Stefan said mildly, his eyes deceptively innocent as he looked at Damon.

"Yes, well, then there's something *exceedingly* heavy at the core of this moonlet, to allow for eight-tenths the gravity we normally experience, and to hang on to so much atmosphere—but who cares about logic? This is a world we reached through the Nether World. Why should logic apply?" He looked at Elena with slightly narrowed, hooded eyes.

"Where is the third one? The grave one?"

The voice came from behind them—Elena thought. She was—they all were—turning from looking at brilliant light into half-darkness. Everything shimmered and danced before her eyes.

> *"Grave Meredith; laughing Bonnie;*
> *And Elena with golden hair.*
> *They whisper and then are silent . . .*
> *They plot and I no longer care . . .*
> *But I must have Elena,*
> *Elena with the Golden Hair . . ."*

"Well, you're not going to have me!" cried Elena. "And that poem is a complete misquote, anyway. I remember it from freshman English class. *And you're crazy!*" Even through her anger and fear she wondered about Fell's

Church. If Shinichi was *here*, could he bring about the Last Midnight *there*? Or could Misao simply set it off with a languid wave?

"But I *will* have you, golden Elena," the kitsune said.

Both Stefan and Damon had knives out. "That's just where you're wrong, Shinichi," Stefan said. "You will never, ever touch Elena again."

"I have to try. You've taken everything else."

Elena's heart was pounding now. If he'll talk sense to any of us, he'll talk to me, she thought. "Shouldn't you be getting ready for the Last Midnight, Shinichi?" she asked in a friendly tone, inwardly trembling in case he should say, "It's already over."

"*She* doesn't need me. *She* wouldn't protect Misao. Why should I help *Her*?"

For a moment Elena couldn't speak. She? *She?* Other than Misao, what other *She* was involved in this?

Damon had a crossbow out now, with a quarrel loaded in it. But Shinichi just went rambling on.

"Misao couldn't move anymore. She had put all her Power into her star ball, you see. She never laughed or sang any longer—never made up any plots with me. She just . . . sat.

"Finally she asked me to put her into myself. She thought we'd become one that way. So she dissolved and merged right into me. But it didn't help. Now . . . I can barely hear her. I've come to get my star ball. I've been using its energy to travel through the dimensions. If I put Misao into my star ball, she'll recover. Then I'll hide it again—but not where I left it last. I'll put it *farther* up where no one else will ever find it." He seemed to focus on his listeners. "So I guess it's Misao and I who are talking to you right now. Except that I'm so lonely—I can't *feel* her at all."

"You will not touch Elena," Stefan said quietly.

Damon was looking grimly at the rest of the group at Shinichi's words, ". . . I'll put it *farther* up . . ."

"Go on, Bonnie, keep moving," Stefan added. "You too, Elena. We'll follow."

Elena let Bonnie go some feet ahead before saying telepathically, *We can't break up, Stefan; there's only one compass.*

Watch out, Elena! He might hear you! came Stefan's voice, and Damon added flatly, *Shut up!*

"Don't bother telling her to shut up," Shinichi said. "You're mad if you think that I can't just pick your thoughts right out of your minds. I didn't think you were *that* stupid."

"We're not stupid," Bonnie said hotly.

"No? Then did you figure out my riddles for you?"

"This is hardly the time for that," Elena snapped. It was a mistake, for it caused Shinichi to focus on her again.

"Did you tell them what you think about the tragedy of Camelot, Elena? No, I didn't think you'd have the courage.

I'll tell them, then, shall I? I'll read it as you put it in your diary."

"No! You *can't* have read my diary! *Anyway—it's no longer applicable!*" Elena flared.

"Let me see . . . these are your own words now." He assumed a reading voice. 'Dear Diary, one of Shinichi's riddles was what I thought of Camelot. You know, the legend of King Arthur, Queen Guinevere, and the knight she loved, Lancelot. And here's what I thought. A lot of innocent people died and were miserable because three selfish people—a king, a queen, and a knight—couldn't behave in a civilized way. They couldn't understand that the more you love, the more you find to love. But those three couldn't give in to love and just share—all three of them . . .' "

"Shut up!" screamed Elena. "*Shut up!*"

My God, Damon said, *my life just lapped itself.*

So did mine. Stefan sounded dizzy.

Just forget about all of it, Elena told them. *It's not true anymore. Stefan, I'm yours forever, and I always was. And right now we've got to get rid of this bastard, and* run *for the trunk.*

"Misao and I used to do that," Shinichi said. "Talk alone together on a special frequency. You're certainly a good manipulator, Elena, to keep them from killing each other over you."

"Yes, it's a special frequency I call the truth," Elena said. "But I'm not half as good a manipulator as Damon is. Now attack us or let us go away. We're in a hurry!"

"Attack you?" Shinichi seemed to be thinking over the idea. And then, faster than Elena could track it, he went for Bonnie. The vampires, who had been expecting him to try to get to Elena, were caught off guard, but Elena, who had seen the flicker of his eyes toward the weaker girl, was already diving for him. He moved back so quickly that she found herself heading for his legs, but then she realized she had a chance to throw him off balance. She deliberately went for a headbutt with his kneecap, at the same time stabbing deep into his foot with her knife.

Forgive me, Bonnie, she thought, knowing what he would do. It was the same as what he'd had his puppet, Damon, do when he'd held Elena and Matt hostage before—except that he didn't need a pine branch to direct the pain. Black energy erupted directly from his hands into Bonnie's small body.

But there was another factor he hadn't taken into account. When he'd had Damon attack Matt and Elena he'd had the sense to keep away from them while directing agony into their bodies. This time, he'd seized Bonnie and wrapped his arms around her. And Bonnie was a most excellent telepath herself, especially at projecting. When the first wave of agony hit her, she screamed—and redirected the pain toward Shinichi.

It was like completing a circuit. It didn't hurt Bonnie any less, but it meant that anything Shinichi did to her he felt in his own body, amplified by Bonnie's terror. That was the system that Elena slammed into as hard as she could. When her head impacted with his knee, his kneebone was the more fragile of the two, and something inside it crackled. Dazed, she concentrated on twisting the knife she'd stabbed *through* his foot and into the soil below.

It wouldn't have worked if she hadn't had two extremely agile vampires right behind her. Since Shinichi didn't fall over, she would just have been putting her neck at the perfect level for him to snap cleanly.

But Stefan was only a split second behind her. He seized her and was out of Shinichi's reach before the kitsune could even assess the situation properly.

"Let me go," Elena gasped at Stefan. She was determined to get Bonnie. "I left my knife," she added craftily, finding a more concrete reason for forcing Stefan to let her back into the fray.

"Where?"

"In his foot, of course."

She could feel Stefan trying not to laugh out loud. "I think that's a good place to leave it. Take one of mine," he added.

If you've quite finished your little chat, you might get rid of his tails, came Damon's cold telepathy.

At that moment Bonnie passed out, but with her own telepathic circuits still wide open and directed back toward Shinichi. And now Damon had gone into offensive mode, as if he cared nothing about Bonnie's well-being, as long as he could get through her to Shinichi.

Stefan, quick as a striking snake, went for one of the many tails that now waved behind Shinichi, advertising his tremendous Power. Most of them were translucent, and they surrounded his real tail—the flesh-and-blood tail that every fox had.

Stefan's knife went *snick* and one of the phantom tails fell to the ground and then disappeared. There was no blood, but Shinichi keened in fury and pain.

Damon, meanwhile, was ruthlessly attacking from the front. As soon as Stefan had distracted the kitsune from the back, Damon slashed both Shinichi's wrists—one quickly on the upstroke, the other just as fast on the down-stroke. Then he went for a body blow just at the moment that Stefan, with Elena held like a baby on his hip, snicked away another phantom tail.

Elena was struggling. She was seriously worried that Damon would *kill* Bonnie to get to Shinichi. And besides, she herself would *not* be toted around like a piece of lug-gage! Civilization had tumbled down all around her and she was reacting from her deepest instincts: protect Stefan, protect Bonnie, protect Fell's Church. Put the enemy *down*. She hardly realized that in her heightened state she had sunk her unfortunately still-human teeth into Stefan's shoulder.

He winced slightly, but he listened to her. All right! *Try to get Bonnie, then—see if you can ease her.*

He let go of her just as Shinichi whirled to deal with him, channeling the black pain that, back on Earth, had flung Matt and Elena off their feet in seizures, directly toward Stefan.

Elena, just released, found that everyone was making a half turn, as if to oblige her, and suddenly she saw a chance. She snatched at the limp form of Bonnie, and Shinichi dropped the smaller girl into her arms.

Words were echoing in Elena's brain. *Get Bonnie. See if you can ease her.*

Well, she had Bonnie now. Her own sense split Stefan's two orders with another—*get her away from Shinichi. She's the priceless hostage.*

Elena found that she could almost scream with fury even now. She had to keep Bonnie safe—but that meant leaving Stefan, gentle Stefan, at the mercy of Shinichi. She scrambled away with Bonnie—so small and light—and at the same time threw a backward glance at Stefan. He was wearing a slight frown of concentration now, but he was not only *not* overwhelmed with pain, he was pressing forward the attack.

Even though Shinichi's head was on fire. The brilliant crimson tips of his black hair had burst into flames, as if nothing else would express his enmity and his certainty of winning. He was crowning himself with a flaming garland, a hellish halo.

Elena's anger at that turned into chills down her spine as she watched something most people never lived to analyze: two vampires attacking together, perfectly in sync. There was the elemental savagery in it of a pair of raptors or wolves, but there was also the awesome beauty of two creatures working as a single, unified body. The distance in Stefan's and Damon's expressions said that this was a fight to the death. The occasional frown from Stefan or vicious smile from Damon meant that Shinichi was sending his searing dark Power through one or the other of them. But these weren't weak humans Shinichi was playing with now. They were both vampires with bodies that healed almost instantly—and vampires who had both fed recently—from *her*—Elena. Her extraordinary blood was feuling them now.

So I'm already a part of this, Elena thought. I'm helping them right now. That would have to satisfy the savagery this no-holds-barred fight elicited in her. To ruin the perfect synchronicity with which the two vampires were handling Shinichi would be a crime, especially when Bonnie was still limp in her arms.

As humans, we're both liabilities, she thought. And Damon wouldn't hesitate to tell me so, even if all I wanted was to get in one single stroke.

Bonnie, come on, Bonnie, she thought. *Hold on to me. We're getting farther away.* She picked up the smaller girl under the armpits and dragged her. She backed up into the olive dimness that stretched in all directions. When she tripped over a root and accidentally sat down, she decided that she'd gone far enough, and maneuvered Bonnie into her lap.

Then she cupped her hands around Bonnie's little heart-shaped face and she thought of the most soothing things she could imagine. A cool plunge at Warm Springs back home. A hot bath at Lady Ulma's and then a four-handed massage, lying comfortably on a drying couch with the scent of floral incense rising around her. A cuddle with Saber in Mrs. Flowers's informal den. The decadence of sleeping late and waking up in her own bed—with her own mother and father and sister in the house.

As Elena thought of this last, she couldn't help giving a tiny gasp, and a teardrop fell onto Bonnie's forehead. Bonnie's eyelashes fluttered.

"Now, don't *you* be sad," she whispered. "Elena?"

"I've got you, and nobody's going to hurt you again. Do you still feel bad?"

"A little. But I could hear you, in my mind, and it made

me feel better. I want a long bath and a pizza. And to hold baby Adara. She can almost talk, you know. Elena—you're not listening to me!"

Elena wasn't. She was watching the dénouement of the fight between Stefan and Damon and Shinichi. The vampires had the kitsune down now and were squabbling over him like a couple of fledglings over a particularly tasty worm. Or maybe like a pair of baby dragons—Elena wasn't sure if birds hissed at each other.

"Oh, no—yuck!" Bonnie saw what Elena was watching and collapsed, hiding her head against Elena's shoulder. Okay, Elena thought. I get it. There's no savagery at all in you, is there, Bonnie? Mischief, but nothing like bloodlust. And that's *good.*

Even as she thought this, Bonnie abruptly sat up straight, bumping Elena's chin, and pointing into the distance. "Wait!" she cried. "Do you see *that*?"

That was a very bright light, which flared brighter as each vampire found a place to his liking on Shinichi's body and bit simultaneously.

"Stay here," Elena said, a little thickly, because when Bonnie had bumped her chin she'd accidentally bitten her tongue. She ran back to the two vampires and knocked them as hard as she could over the heads. She had to get their attention before they got completely locked into feeding mode.

Not surprisingly, Stefan detached first, and then helped her to pull Damon off his defeated enemy.

Damon snarled and paced, never taking his eyes off Shinichi as the beaten kitsune slowly sat up. Elena noticed drops of blood scattered around. Then she saw it, tucked into Damon's belt, black and crimson-tipped and sleek: Shinichi's real tail.

Savagery fled . . . fast. Elena wanted to hide her head against Stefan's shoulder but instead turned up her face for a kiss. Stefan obliged.

Then Elena stepped back so that they formed a triangle around Shinichi.

"Don't even think of attacking," Damon said pleasantly.

Shinichi gave a weak shrug. "Attack you? Why bother? You'll have nothing to go back to, even if I die. The children are pre-programmed to kill. But"—with sudden vehemence—"I wish we'd never come to your damned little town at all—and I wish we'd never followed *Her* orders. I wish I'd never let Misao near *Her*! I wish we hadn't—" He stopped speaking suddenly. No, it was more than that, Elena thought. He *froze*, eyes wide open and staring. "Oh, no," he whispered. "Oh, no, I didn't mean that! I didn't mean it! I have no regrets—"

Elena had the feeling of something coming at them at tremendous speed, so fast, in fact, that she just had time to open her mouth before it hit Shinichi. Whatever it was, it killed him cleanly and passed by without touching anyone else.

Shinichi fell facedown onto the dirt.

"Don't bother," Elena said softly, as Stefan reflexively moved toward the corpse. "He's dead. He did it to himself."

"But how?" Stefan and Damon demanded in chorus.

"I'm not the expert," Elena said. "Meredith is the expert on this. But she told me that kitsune could only be killed by destroying their star balls, shooting them with a blessed bullet . . . or by the 'Sin of Regret.' Meredith and I didn't know what that meant back then—it was before we had even gone into the Dark Dimension. But I think we just now saw it in action."

"So you can't be a kitsune and regret anything you've done? That's—harsh," Stefan said.

"Not at all," Damon said crisply. "Although, if it had operated for vampires, no doubt you would have been permanently dead when you woke up in the family vault."

"Earlier," Stefan said expressionlessly. "I regreted striking you a mortal blow, even as I was dying. You've always said I feel too guilty, but that *is* one thing I would give my life to take back."

There was a silence that stretched and stretched. Damon was at the front of the group now, and no one but Bonnie could see his face.

Suddenly Elena grabbed Stefan's hand. "We still have

a chance!" she told him. "Bonnie and I saw something bright *that* way! Let's run!" He and Elena passed Damon running and he grabbed Bonnie's hand too. "Like the wind, Bonnie!"

"But with Shinichi dead—well, do we really have to find his star ball or the biggest star ball or whatever is hidden in this awful place?" Bonnie asked. Once, she would have whined, Elena thought. Now, despite whatever pain she felt, she was running.

"We do have to find it, I'm afraid," Stefan said. "Because from what he said, Shinichi wasn't at the top of the ladder after all. He and his sister were working for someone, someone female. And whoever *She* is, *She* may be attacking Fell's Church right now."

"The odds have just shifted," Elena said. "We have an unknown enemy."

"But still—"

"All bets," Elena said, "are off."

36

Matt broke a lot of traffic rules on the way to the Saitous' street. Meredith leaned on the console between the two front seats so that she could see the digital clock ticking down to midnight, and so that she could watch the transformation of Mrs. Flowers. At last her recently sane, sensible mind forced words out of her mouth. "Mrs. Flowers—you're changing."

"Yes, Meredith, dear. Some of it is due to the little present that Sage left for me. Some of it is my own will—to return to the days when I was in my prime. I believe that this will be my last fight, so I don't mind using all my energy in it. Fell's Church must be saved."

"But—Mrs. Flowers—the people here—well, they haven't always been—exactly nice—" Matt stammered his way to a stop.

"The people here are like people everywhere," Mrs. Flowers said calmly. "Treat them as you'd like to be treated, and things will be fine. It was only when I'd let myself become a bitter, lonely old woman, always resentful of the fact that I had had to turn my home into a boarding-house just to make ends meet, that people began to treat me—well, at best as a loony old hag."

"Oh, Mrs. Flowers—and we've been such a bother to you!" Meredith found the words coming without her volition.

"You've been the saving of me, child. Dear Stefan was the start, but as you can imagine, he didn't want to explain all his little differences to me, and I was suspicious of him. But he was always cordial and respectful and Elena was like sunlight, and Bonnie like laughter. Eventually, when I dropped my hidebound barriers, so did you young ones. I won't say more about those who are present so as not to embarrass you, but you've done me a world of good."

Matt ran another stop sign and cleared his throat. Then, the steering wheel wavering slightly, he cleared his throat again.

Meredith took over. "I think what Matt and I both want to say is . . . well, it's that you've become very special to us, and we don't want to see you get hurt. This battle—"

"Is a battle for all I hold dear. For all my memories. Back

when I was a child and the boardinghouse was built—it was just a home, then, and I was very happy. As a young woman, I was very happy. And now that I have lived long enough to be an old woman—well, besides you children, I still have friends like Sophia Alpert and Orime Saitou. They are both healing women, and very good at it. We still talk about different uses for my herbs."

Matt snapped his fingers. "That's another reason I was confused," he said. "Because Dr. Alpert said that you and Mrs. Saitou were such good people. I thought she meant the old Mrs. Saitou—"

"Who is not a 'Mrs. Saitou' at all," Mrs. Flowers said, almost sharply. "I have no idea what her name really is—perhaps she is really Inari, a deity gone bad. Ten years ago, I didn't know what made Orime Saitou suddenly so diffident and quiet. Now I realize that it began just around the time her 'mother' moved in with her. I was quite fond of young Isobel, but she suddenly became—aloof—in an unchildlike way. Now I understand. And I am determined to fight for her—and for you—and for a town that is worth saving. Human lives are very, very precious. And now—here we are."

Matt had just turned onto the Saitous' block. Meredith took a moment to openly stare at the figure in the front passenger seat. "Mrs. Flowers!" she exclaimed.

This made Matt turn to stare in his turn and what

he saw made him clip a Volkswagen Jetta parked by the sidewalk.

"Mrs. . . . Flowers?"

"Please park now, Matt. You needn't call me Mrs. Flowers if you don't want to. I have returned to the time when I was Theophilia—when my friends called me Theo."

"But—how—why—?" Matt stuttered.

"I told you. I felt that it was time. Sage left me a gift that helped me change. An enemy beyond your powers to fight has arisen. I felt this back at the boardinghouse. This is the time that I have been waiting for. The last battle with the true enemy of Fell's Church."

Meredith's heart actually seemed ready to fly out of her chest. She had to be calm—calm and logical. She had seen magic many times. She knew the look of it, the feel of it. But frequently she had been too busy comforting Bonnie, or too worried about aiding Bonnie to take in what she was facing.

Now, it was just her and Matt—and Matt had a stricken, stupefied look, as if he hadn't seen enough magic before. As if he might crack.

"Matt," she said loudly, and then even louder, *"Matt!"* He turned, then, to look at her, with his blue eyes wild and dark.

"They'll *kill* her, Meredith!" he said. "Shinichi and

Misao—you don't know what it feels like . . ."

"Come on," Meredith said. "We have to make sure that it *doesn't* kill her."

The dazed look passed from Matt's eyes. "We *have* to do this," he agreed simply.

"Right," said Meredith, finally releasing him. Together they got out of the car to stand by Mrs. Flowers—no, by Theo.

Theo had hair that hung almost to her waist; so fair that it looked silver in the moonlight. Her face was—electrifying. It was *young*; young and proud, with classic features and a look of quiet determination.

Somehow during the drive, her clothes had changed too. Instead of a coat covered with bits of paper, she was wearing a sleeveless white gown that ended in a slight train. In style, it reminded Meredith a little of the "mermaid" dress she herself had worn when going to a ball in the Dark Dimension. But Meredith's dress had only made her look sultry. Theo looked . . . magnificent.

As for the Post-it Note amulets . . . somehow the paper had disappeared and the writing had grown enormously, changing into very large scrawls that wrapped around the white gown. Theo was literally swathed in haute couture arcane protection.

And although she was reed slender, she was tall. Taller than Meredith, taller than Matt, taller than Stefan, wherever he was in the Dark Dimensions. She was this tall not only because she had grown so much, but because the train of her dress was just brushing the ground. She had entirely overcome gravity. The whip, Sage's present to her, was coiled into a circle attached to her waist, shining as silver as her hair.

Matt and Meredith simultaneously closed the SUV's doors. Matt left the engine running for a quick getaway.

They walked around the garage so that they could see the front of the house. Meredith, not caring what she looked like or whether she seemed cool or in control, wiped her hands, one and then the other, on her jeans. This was the stave's first—and possibly only—true battle. What counted was not appearance, but performance.

Both she and Matt stopped dead when they saw the figure standing at the bottom of the steps in front of the porch. It was no one they could identify from the house. But then the crimson lips opened, the delicate hands flew up to cover them, and wind-chime laughter came from somewhere behind the hands.

For a moment they could only stare, fascinated, at this woman who was dressed all in black. She was fully as tall as Theo, fully as slender and graceful, and she was floating equally high off the ground. But what Meredith and Matt were staring at was the fact that her hair was like Misao's or Shinichi's—but reversed. Whereas they had black hair with a crimson fringe on the bottom, this woman had crimson hair—yards and yards of it, with a black fringe all around it. Not only that, but she had delicate black fox ears emerging from the crimson hair, and a long sleek crimson tail, tipped with black.

"Obaasan?" Matt gasped in disbelief.

"Inari!" Meredith snapped.

The lovely creature didn't even look at them. She was staring at Theo in contempt. "Tiny witch of a tiny town," she said. "You've used nearly all your Power just to stand up to my level. What good are you?"

"I have very small Powers," Theo agreed. "But if the town is worthless, why has it taken you so long to destroy it? Why have you watched others try—or were they *all* your pawns, Inari? Katherine, Klaus, poor young Tyler—were they your pawns, Kitsune Goddess?"

Inari laughed—still that chiming, girlish giggling, behind her fingers. "I don't need pawns! Shinichi and Misao are my bond-servants, as all kitsune are! If I have left them some freedom, it has been so they can get experience. We'll go on to larger cities now, and ravage them."

"You have to take Fell's Church first," Theo said steadily. "And I won't let you do that."

"You still don't understand, do you? You are a human, with almost no Power left! Mine is the largest star ball in the worlds! I am a Goddess!"

Theo lowered her head, then lifted it to look Inari in the eyes. "Do you want to know what I think the truth is, Inari?" she said. "I think that you have come to the end of a long, long, but not immortal life. I think you have dwindled so that at last you need to use a great deal of Power from your star ball—wherever it is—to appear this way. You are a very, very ancient woman and you have been setting children against their own parents, and parents against children across the world because you envy the children's youth. You have even come to envy Shinichi and Misao, and let them be hurt, as revenge."

Matt and Meredith looked at each other with wide eyes. Inari was breathing rapidly, but it seemed she couldn't think of anything to say.

"You've even pretended to have entered a 'second childhood' to behave girlishly. But none of it satisfies you, because the plain, sad truth is that you have come to the end of your long, long lifetime—no matter how great your Power. We must all take that final journey, and it is your turn now."

"Liar!" shrieked Inari, looking for a moment more glorious—more radiant than before. But then Meredith saw why. Her scarlet hair had actually begun to smolder, framing her face in a dancing red light. And at last she spoke venemously.

"Well, then, if you think this is my last battle, I must be

sure to cause all the pain I can. Starting with *you*, witch."

Meredith and Matt both gasped. They were afraid for Theo, especially as Inari's hair was braiding itself into thick ropes like serpents that floated around her head as if she were Medusa.

The gasps were a mistake—they attracted Inari's attention. But she didn't move. She only said, "Smell that sweet scent on the wind? A roast sacrifice! I think the result will be *oishii*—delicious! But perhaps you two would like to speak to Orime or Isobel one last time. I'm afraid they can't come out to see you."

Meredith's heart was pounding violently in her throat, as she realized that the Saitous' house was on fire. It seemed as if there were several small fires burning, but she was terrified at the implication that Inari had already done something to the mother and daughter.

"No, Matt!" she cried, grabbing Matt's arm. He would have charged straight at the laughing black-clad woman and tried to attack her feet—and seconds were invaluable now. "Come help me find them!"

Theo came to their aid. Drawing up the white bullwhip, she whirled it once around her head and cracked it precisely on Inari's raised hands, leaving a bloody gash on one. As a furious Inari turned back to her, Meredith and Matt ran.

"The back door," Matt said as they careered around the

side of the house. Up ahead they saw a wooden fence, but no gate. Meredith was just considering using the stave to pole-vault, when Matt panted, "Here!" and made a cradle of his hands for her to step into. "I'll boost you over!"

Meredith hesitated only an instant. Then, as he skidded to a stop she jumped to place one foot in his interlocked fingers. Suddenly she was flying upward. She made the most of it, landing, catlike, on the fence's flat top, and then jumping down. She could hear Matt scrambling up the fence as she was suddenly surrounded by black smoke. She jumped backward three feet and yelled, "Matt, the smoke is dangerous! Get low; hold your breath. Stay outside to help them when I bring them out!"

Meredith had no idea whether Matt would listen to her or not, but she obeyed her own rules, crouching low, breath held, opening her eyes briefly to try to find the door.

Then she almost jumped out of her skin at the sound of an axe crashing into wood, of wood splintering, and of the axe crashing again. She opened her eyes and saw that Matt *hadn't* listened to her, but she was glad because he'd found the door. His face was black with soot. "It was locked," he explained, hefting the axe.

Any optimism Meredith might have felt splintered like the door as she looked inside and saw only flames and more flames.

My God, she thought, anyone in there *is* roasting,

is probably dead already.

But where had that thought come from? Her knowledge or her fear? Meredith couldn't just stop now. She took a step into searing heat and shouted, "Isobel! Mrs. Saitou! Where are you?"

There was a weak, choking cry. "That's the kitchen!" she said. "Matt, it's Mrs. Saitou! *Please* go get her!"

Matt obeyed, but threw over his shoulder, "Don't you go farther in."

Meredith had to go farther in. She remembered very well where Isobel's room was. Directly under her "grandmother's."

"Isobel! Isobel! Can you hear me?" Her voice was so low and husky from smoke that she knew she had to keep going. Isobel might be unconscious or too hoarse to answer. Meredith dropped to her knees, crawling on the ground where the air was slightly cooler and more clear.

Okay. Isobel's room. She didn't want to touch the door handle with her hand, so she wrapped her T-shirt around it. The handle wouldn't turn. Locked. She didn't bother to investigate how, she simply turned around and mule-kicked the door right beside the handle. Wood splintered. Another kick, and with a wooden scream the door swung free.

Meredith was feeling dizzy now, but she needed to see the entire room. She took two strides in, and—there!

Sitting up on the bed in the smoky, hot, but otherwise scrupulously tidy little room was Isobel. As Meredith neared the bed she saw—to her fury—that the girl was tied to the brass headboard with duct tape. Two slashes of the stave took care of that. Then, amazingly, Isobel moved, raising a blackened face up to Meredith's.

That was when Meredith's fury peaked. The girl had duct tape across her mouth, to prevent her from making any cry for help. Wincing herself to show that she knew this was going to be painful, Meredith grasped the duct tape and stripped it off. Isobel didn't cry out; instead she took in lungful after lungful of smoky air.

Meredith stumbled toward the closet, snatched two identical-looking white shirts, and swerved back to Isobel. There was a full tumbler of water right beside her, on the nightstand. Meredith wondered if it had been put there deliberately to increase Isobel's agony, but she didn't hesitate to use it. She gave Isobel a quick sip, took one herself, and then soaked each shirt. She held one over her own mouth and Isobel mimicked her, holding the wet shirt over her nose and mouth. Then Meredith grabbed her and guided her back to the door.

After that it simply became a nightmare journey of crawling and kneeling and choking, pulling Isobel with her all the time. Meredith thought it would never end, as each inch forward became harder and harder. The stave was an unbearable weight to heave along with her, but she refused to let go of it.

It's precious, her mind said, but is it worth your life?

No, Meredith thought. Not *my* life, but who knows what else will be out there if I get Isobel into the cool darkness?

You'll never get her there if you die because of—an object.

It's not an object! Painfully Meredith used the stave to clear some smoldering debris from her path. It belonged to Grandpa in the time when he was sane. It fits my hand. It's not just a *thing*!

Have it your own way, the voice said, and disappeared.

Meredith was beginning to run into more debris now. Despite the cramping in her lungs, she was sure that she could make it out of the back door. She knew there should be a laundry room on her right. They should be able to feel a space there.

And then suddenly in the dark something reared up and struck her a blow on the head. It took her dimming mind a long time to come up with a name for the thing that had hurt her. Armchair.

Somehow they'd crawled too far. This was the living room.

Meredith was flooded with horror. They'd gone too far—and they couldn't go out the front door into the midst of magical battle. They would have to backtrack, and this time make sure to find the laundry room, their gate to freedom.

Meredith turned around, pulling Isobel with her, hoping the younger girl would understand what they had to do.

She left the stave on the burning living room floor.

Elena sobbed to get her breath, even though she was allowing Stefan to help her now. He ran, holding Bonnie by one hand and Elena by the other. Damon was somewhere in front—scouting.

It can't be far now, she kept thinking. Bonnie and I both saw the brightness—we *both* did. Just then, like a lantern put into a window, Elena saw it again.

It's big, that's the problem. I keep thinking we should reach it because I have the wrong idea of what size it is in my mind. The closer we get, the bigger it gets.

And that's *good* for us. We'll need a lot of Power. But we need to get there soon, or it could be all the Power in the universe and it won't matter. We'll be too late.

Shinichi had indicated that they *would* be too late—but Shinichi had been born a liar. Still, surely just beyond that low branch was . . .

Oh, dear God, she thought. It's a star ball.

37

Then Meredith saw something that was not smoke or fire. Just a glimpse of a door frame—and a tiny breath of cool air. With this hope to sustain her, she scuttled straight for the door to the backyard, dragging Isobel behind her.

As she passed the threshold, she felt blessedly cold water somehow showering down onto her body. When she pulled Isobel into the spray, the younger girl made the first voluntary sound she had during the entire journey: a wordless sob of thanks.

Matt's hands were helping her along, were taking away the burden of Isobel. Meredith got up to her feet and staggered in a circle, then dropped to her knees. Her hair was on fire! She was just recalling her childhood rehearsal of stop, drop, and roll, when she felt the cold water turned on it. The hose water went up and down her body and she turned around, basking in the feeling of coolness, until she heard Matt's voice say, "The flames are out. You're good now."

"Thank you, Matt. Thank you." Her voice was hoarse.

"Hey, you were the one who had to go all the way to the bedrooms and back. Getting Mrs. Saitou out was pretty easy—there was the kitchen sink full of water, so as soon as I cut her free from the kitchen chair we just got all wet and dashed outside."

Meredith smiled and looked around quickly. Isobel had become her responsibility now. To her relief, she saw that the girl was being hugged by her mother.

And all it had taken was the nonsense choice between a thing—however precious it was—and a life. Meredith gazed at the mother and daughter and was glad. She could have another stave made. But nothing could replace Isobel.

"Isobel said to give this to you," Matt was saying.

Meredith turned toward him, the fiery light making the world crazy, and for one moment didn't believe her eyes. Matt was holding the fighting stave out to her.

"She must have dragged it with her free hand—oh, Matt, and she was almost dead before we started . . ."

Matt said, "She's stubborn. Like someone else I know."

Meredith wasn't quite sure what he meant by that, but she knew one thing. "We'd all better get to the front yard.

I doubt the volunteer fire department is going to come. Besides—Theo—"

"I'll get them moving. You scout the gate side," Matt said.

Meredith plunged into the backyard, which was hideously illuminated by the house, now fully engulfed in flames. Fortunately, the side yard was not. Meredith flicked the gate open with the stave. Matt was right behind her, helping Mrs. Saitou and Isobel along.

Meredith quickly ran by the flaming garage and then stopped. From behind her she heard a cry of horror. There was no time to try to soothe whoever had cried, no time to think.

The two fighting women were too busy to notice her—and Theo was in need of help. Inari was truly like a fiery Medusa, with her hair writhing around her in flaming, smoking snakes. Only the crimson part burned, and it was that part that she was using like a whip, using one snake to wrest away the silver bullwhip from Theo's hand, and then another to wrap around Theo's throat and choke her. Theo was desperately trying to pull the blazing noose from her neck.

Inari was laughing. "Are you suffering, petty witch? It will all be over in seconds—for you and for your entire little town! The Last Midnight has finally come!"

Meredith glanced back at Matt—and that was all it

took. He ran forward, passing her, all the way up to the space below the fighting women. Then he bent slightly, cupping his hands.

And then Meredith *sprinted*, putting everything she had left into the short run, leaving her just enough energy to leap and place one foot into Matt's cupped hands, and then she felt herself soaring aloft, just within distance for the stave to slice cleanly through the snake of hair that was choking Theo.

After that Meredith was in free fall, with Matt trying to catch her from below. She landed more or less on top of him and they both saw what happened next.

Theo, who was bruised and bleeding, slapped out a part of her gown that was smoldering. She held out a hand for the silver bullwhip and it flew to meet her outstretched fingers. But Inari wasn't attacking. She was waving her arms wildly, as if in terror, and then suddenly she shrieked: a sound so anguished that Meredith drew in her breath sharply. It was a death-scream.

Before their eyes she was turning back into Obaasan, into the shrunken, helpless, doll-like woman Matt and Meredith knew. But by the time this shriveled body hit the ground it was already stiff and dead, her expression one of such unrepentant malice that it was frightening.

It was Isobel and Mrs. Saitou then who came forward to stand over the body, sobbing with relief. Meredith looked at them and then up at Theo, who slowly floated to the ground.

"Thank you," Theo said with the faintest of smiles. "You have saved me—yet again."

"But what do you think happened to her?" Matt asked. "And why didn't Shinichi or Misao come to help her?"

"I think they all must be dead, don't you?" Theo's voice was soft over the roar of the flames. "As for Inari—I think that perhaps someone destroyed her star ball. I'm afraid I was not strong enough to defeat her myself."

"What time is it?" Meredith abruptly cried, remembering. She ran to the old SUV, which was still running. Its clock showed 12:00 midnight exactly.

"Did we save the people?" Matt asked desperately.

Theo turned her face outward toward the center of the town. For nearly a minute she was still, as if listening for something. At last, when Meredith felt that she might shatter from tension, she turned back and said quietly, "Dear Ma*ma*, *Grand*mama, and I are one, now. I sense children who are finding themselves holding knives—and some with guns. I sense them standing in their sleeping parents' rooms, unable to remember how they got there. And I sense parents, hiding in closets, a moment ago frightened for their very lives, who are seeing weapons dropped and children falling onto master bedroom floors, sobbing and bewildered."

"We did it, then. *You* did it. You held her off," Matt panted.

Still gentle and sober, Theo said, "Someone else—far away—did much more. I know that the town needs healing. But *Grand*mama and Ma*ma* agree. Because of them, no child has killed a parent this night, and no parent has killed a child. The long nightmare of Inari and her Last Midnight is over."

Meredith, grimy and bedraggled as she was, felt something rise and swell inside her, bigger and bigger, until, for all her training, she couldn't contain herself any longer. It exploded out of her in a yell of exultation.

She found that Matt was shouting too. He was as grubby and unkempt as she was, but he seized her by the hands and whirled her around in a barbarian victory dance.

And it was *fun*, whirling around and yelling like a kid. Maybe—maybe in trying to be calm, in always being the most grown-up, she had missed out on the essence of fun, which always felt as if it had some childlike quality to it.

Matt had no trouble in expressing his feelings, whatever they were: childlike, mature, stubborn, happy. Meredith found herself admiring this, and also thinking that it had been a long time since she'd really looked at Matt. But now she felt a sudden wave of feeling for him. And she could see that Matt felt the same way about her. As if he'd never really looked at her properly before.

This was the moment . . . when they were meant to kiss. Meredith had seen it so often in movies, and read about it in books, that it was almost a given.

But this was life, it wasn't a story. And when the moment came, Meredith found herself holding Matt's shoulders while he held hers, and she could see that he was thinking *exactly* the same thing about the kiss.

The moment stretched . . .

Then, with a grin, Matt's face showed that he knew what to do. Meredith did too. They both moved in, and hugged each other. When they drew back, they were both grinning. They knew who they were. They were very different, very close *friends*. Meredith hoped that they always would be.

They both turned to look at Theo, and Meredith felt a pang in her heart, the first since she had heard they'd saved the town. Theo was changing. It was the look on her face as she watched them that gave Meredith the pang.

After being young, and while watching youth at its peak, she was once again aging, wrinkling, her hair going white instead of moonlit silver. At last, she was an old woman wearing a raincoat covered with bits of paper.

"Mrs. Flowers!" *This* person, it was perfectly safe and right to kiss. Meredith flung her arms about the frail old woman, lifting her off her feet in excitement. Matt joined them, and they boosted her above their heads. They carried her like this to the Saitous, mother and daughter, who were watching the fire.

There, sobered, they put her down.

"Isobel," Meredith said. "God! I'm so sorry—your home . . ."

"Thank you," Isobel said in her soft, slurred voice. Then she turned away.

Meredith felt chilled. She was even beginning to regret the celebration, when Mrs. Saitou said, "Do you know, this is the greatest moment in the history of our family? For hundreds of years, that ancient kitsune—oh, yes, I've always known what she was—has been forcing herself upon innocent humans. And for the last three centuries it has been my family line of samurai mikos that she has terrorized. Now my husband can come home at last."

Meredith looked at her, startled. Mrs. Saitou nodded.

"He tried to defy her and she banished him from the house. Ever since Isobel was born, I have feared for her. And now, please forgive her. She has trouble expressing what she feels."

"I know about that," Meredith said quietly. "I'll go have a little talk with her, if it's all right."

If ever in her life she could explain to a fellow traveler what fun having fun was, she thought, it was now.

38

Damon had stopped and was kneeling behind an enormous broken tree branch. Stefan pulled both girls to him and caught them so that they all three landed just behind his brother.

Elena found herself staring at a very large tree trunk. Still as big as it was, it was nowhere near as large as she had been expecting. It was true; the four of them certainly couldn't have held hands around it. But in the back of her mind had been lurking images of moons and trees and trunks that were as tall as skyscrapers, in which a star ball could be hidden on any "floor," in any "room."

This was simply a grand oak tree trunk sitting in a sort of fairy circle—perhaps twenty feet in diameter on which no dead leaf had strayed. It was a paler color than the loam they had been running on, and even sparkled in a few places. Overall, Elena was relieved.

More, she could even see the star ball. She'd feared—among other things—that it might be up too high to climb, that it might be so entangled with roots or branches that today, certainly after hundreds or even thousands of years, it would be impossible to chop out. But there it was, the greatest star ball that had ever been, fully the size of a beach ball, and it nestled freely in the first crutch of the tree.

Her mind was racing ahead. They'd done it; they'd found the star ball. But how much time would it take to get it back to where Sage was? Automatically, she glanced at her compass and saw to her surprise that the needle now pointed southwest—in other words, back to the Gatehouse. That was a thoughtful touch of Sage's. And perhaps they didn't have to go through the trials backward; they could simply use their Master Key to go back to Fell's Church, and then . . . well, Mrs. Flowers would know what to do with it.

If it came to that, maybe they could just blackmail *Her*, whoever *She* was, to go away forever in exchange for the star ball. Although—could they live with the thought that she might do this again—and again—and again to other towns?

Even as she planned, Elena watched the expressions of her comrades: the childlike wonder on Bonnie's heart-shaped face; the keen assessment in Stefan's eyes; Damon's dangerous smile.

They were viewing their hard-won reward, at last.

But she couldn't look for too long. Things had to be *done.* Even as they watched, the star ball brightened, showing such brilliant, incandescent colors that Elena was half-blinded. She shielded her eyes just as she heard Bonnie inhaling sharply.

"What?" Stefan asked, a hand in front of his eyes, which, of course were much more sensitive to light than human eyes.

"Someone's using it right now!" Bonnie replied. "When it went bright like that, it sent out Power! A long, long way out!"

"Things are heating up in what's left of poor old Fell's Church," said Damon, who was staring intently upward at the branches above him.

"Don't talk about it like that!" Bonnie exclaimed. "It's our home. And now we can finally defend it!" Elena could practically see what Bonnie was thinking: families embracing; neighbors smiling at neighbors again; the entire town working to fix the destruction.

This is how great tragedies sometimes happen. People with a single goal, yet who are not in sync. Assumptions. Presumptions. And, maybe, most important of all, the failure to sit down and talk.

Stefan tried, even though Elena could see that he was still blind from the brilliance of the star ball. He said quietly, "Let's talk this over for a while and brainstorm ways to get it—"

But Bonnie was laughing at him, though not unkindly. She said, "I can get up there as fast as a squirrel. All I need is someone strong to catch it when I knock it down. I know I can't climb down with it; I'm not that silly. Come on, you guys, let's go!"

That's how it happened. Different personalities, different modes of thinking. And one laughing, light-headed girl, who didn't have a precognition when it was needed.

Elena, who was envying Meredith the fighting stave, didn't even see the beginning. She was watching Stefan, who was blinking rapidly to get his eyesight back.

And Bonnie was scrambling as lightly as she had boasted, up on top of the dead tree branch that sheltered them. She even gave them a little laughing salute just before she leaped into the barren, sparkling circle around the tree.

Then microseconds stretched infinitely. Elena *felt* her eyes slowly getting wider, even though she *knew* they were flying open. She *saw* Stefan leisurely reach across her to try to twine his fingers around Bonnie's leg, even though she *knew* that what she was seeing was a lightning-fast grab for the petite girl's ankle. She even heard Damon's instantaneous telepathy: *No, little fool!* as if he were speaking the words in his accustomed lazy tones of superiority.

Then, still in slow motion, Bonnie's knees bent and she

launched into the air above the circle.

But she never touched the ground. Somehow, a black streak, stunningly fast even in the slow-motion horror film that Elena was watching, landed where Bonnie would have landed. And then Bonnie was being *thrown*, being hurled too fast for Elena's eyes to track, outside of the barren circle and then there was a dull thud—too fast for Elena's *mind* to track as being Bonnie's landing.

Quite clearly, she heard Stefan cry "Damon!" in a terrible voice. And then Elena saw the thin dark objects—like curving lances—that were already shooting downward. Another thing her eyes couldn't follow. When her vision adjusted, she saw that they were long, curved black branches, spaced evenly around the tree like thirty spider legs, thirty long spears that were meant to either imprison someone inside them like the bars of a cell, or to—pin them into the strange sand beneath her feet.

"Pin" was a good word. Elena liked the sound of it. Even as she was staring at the sharp recurved barbs on the branches, meant to keep anything caught by them held permanently in the ground, she was thinking of Damon's annoyance if a shaft had pierced his leather jacket. He would curse at them, and Bonnie would try to pretend he hadn't—and . . .

She was close enough by now to see that it wasn't as simple as that. The branch, which was proper javelin size, had gone through Damon's shoulder, which must hurt like hell, in addition to having splattered a blood drop right at the corner of his mouth. But far more annoying than that was the fact that he had closed his eyes against her. That was how Elena thought of it. He was shutting them out deliberately—maybe because he was angry; maybe because of the pain in his shoulder. But it reminded her of the steel wall feeling she'd gotten the last time she'd tried to touch his mind—and, damn, couldn't he *tell* he was scaring them?

"Open your eyes, Damon," she said, flushing, because that was what he wanted her to say. He really *was* the greatest manipulator of all. "Open your eyes, I said!" Now she was really irritated. "Don't play possum, because you're not fooling anyone, and we've really had *enough*!" She was about to shake him hard when something lifted her into the air, into Stefan's line of vision.

Stefan was in pain, but surely not as badly as Damon, so she was looking back to curse Damon when Stefan said harshly, "Elena, he *can't*!"

For just the tiniest fleeting instant the words sounded like nonsense to her. Not only garbled, but meaningless, like saying someone couldn't stop their appendix from doing—whatever it was an appendix did. That was all the respite that she got, and then she had to deal with what her eyes were showing her.

Damon wasn't pinned by his shoulder. He'd been *staked*, just slightly to the left of center of his torso.

Exactly where his heart was.

Words drifted back to her. Words that someone had once said—although she couldn't remember who right now. *"You can't kill a vampire so easily. We only die if you stake us through the heart. . . ."*

Die? Damon *die*? This was some kind of mistake . . .

"Open your eyes!" "Elena, he can't!"

But she knew, without knowing how, that Damon wasn't dead. She wasn't surprised that Stefan didn't know it; it was a hum on a private frequency between her and Damon.

"Come on, hurry, give me your axe," she said, so desperately, and with such an air of knowledge that Stefan handed it over wordlessly, and obeyed when she told him to steady the curving spider-leg branch from above and below. Then with a few quick strokes of the axe she cut through the black branch that was thick enough in circumference that she couldn't have clasped her fingers around it. It was done in a spurt of pure adrenaline, but she knew it awed Stefan and allowed him to let her continue doing it.

When she was finished, she had a loose spider-leg branch that drooped back to the tree, anchored to nothing—and something that looked more like a proper stake in Damon.

It wasn't until she began pulling upward on the stake that a horrified Stefan made her stop.

"Elena! Elena, I wouldn't lie to you! This is just what these branches are for. For intruders who are vampires. Look, love—*see*." He was showing her another of the spider legs that was anchored in the sand, and the barbs on it. Just like the backward-facing tines of a primitive stone arrowhead.

"These branches are meant to be like this," Stefan was saying. "And if you pulled up on it hard enough, you'd just—just end up pulling out chunks of—his heart."

Elena froze. She wasn't sure she really could understand the words—she couldn't allow herself to, or she might picture it. But it didn't matter.

"I'll destroy it some other way," she said shortly, looking at Stefan but not able to see the true green of his eyes because of the olive light. "You wait. Just wait and watch. I'll find a Wings power that will dissolve this—this—*damned abomination*." She could think of many other words to call the stake, but she had to stay in some sort of control.

"Elena." Stefan whispered her name as if he could barely get it out. Even in the twilight she could see the tears on his cheeks. He continued, nonverbally, *Elena, look at his closed eyes. This Tree is a vicious killer, with wood like nothing I've ever seen, but I've heard about it. It's . . . it's spreading. Inside him.*

"Inside him?" Elena repeated stupidly.

Along his arteries and veins—and his nerves—everything connected to his heart. He's—oh, God, Elena, just look at his eyes!

Elena looked. Stefan had knelt and gently pulled up the lids of Damon's eyes and Elena began screaming.

Deep in the fathomless pupils that had held endless night skies full of stars, there was a glimmer—not of starlight, but of green. It seemed to glow with its own hellish luminescence.

Stefan looked at her with agony and compassion. And now, with one gentle pass, Stefan was closing those eyes—forever, she knew he was thinking.

Everything had become strange and dreamlike. Nothing made sense anymore. Stefan was carefully laying Damon's head down—he was letting Damon go.

Even in her fuzzy world of nonsense Elena knew she could never do that.

And then, a miracle happened. Elena heard a voice in her mind that wasn't hers.

All this is rather unexpected. I acted, for once, without thinking. And this is my reward. The voice was a hum on their private frequency, Damon's and hers.

Elena ripped herself away from Stefan, who was trying to restrain her, and fell, grasping Damon's shoulders with her hands. *I knew it! I knew you couldn't be dead!*

It was only then that she realized that her face was dripping wet, and she used her soft leather sleeve to wipe it. *Oh, Damon, you gave me such a scare! Don't you ever, ever do that again!*

I think I can give my word on that, Damon sent—in different tones than his usual ones—sober but at the same time whimsical. *But you have to give me something in return.*

Yes, of course, Elena said. *Just let me get some of my hair off my neck. It worked best like* this *when Stefan was lying down—when we were carrying him out on his pallet from the prison—*

Not that, Damon told her. *For once, angel, I don't want your blood. I need you to give me your most solemn word that you will try to be brave. If it helps at all, I know that females are better than males at this sort of thing. They're less cowardly at facing—what you have to face now.*

Elena didn't like the tone of these words. The dizziness that was making her lips numb was traveling all over her body. There was nothing to be brave about. Damon could stand pain. She would find a Wings power that would obliterate all that wood that was poisoning him. It might hurt, but it would save his life.

Don't talk to me like that! she snapped harshly, before she could remember to be gentle. Everything had begun to float, and she couldn't even remember why she had to be gentle, but there was a reason. Still, it was difficult, when she was using every ounce of her concentration and strength to search for a Wings power she had never heard of. Purification? Would that take away the wood or would it just leave Damon without his wicked smile? There was no harm in trying it, anyway, and she was getting desperate—because Damon's face was so pale.

But even the stance for *Wings of Purification* eluded her.

Suddenly, a huge shudder—a convulsion—went through Damon's entire body. Elena heard broken words behind her.

"Love, love—you really have to let him go. He's living in—in intolerable pain, just because you're keeping him here," the voice said, and it was Stefan's. Stefan, who would never lie to her.

For just an instant Elena wavered, but then a blazing rage came rushing up through her body. It gave her the strength to cry hoarsely, "I . . . *won't*! *I won't ever let him go!* Damn you, Damon, you have to fight! Let me help you! My blood—it's special. It'll give you strength. You *drink* it!"

She fumbled for her knife. Her blood was magical. Maybe if she gave enough, it would give Damon the strength to fight off the wooden fibers that were still spreading through his body.

Elena slashed at her throat. Maybe subconsciously she avoided doing more than nicking her carotid artery, but if so it was *entirely* subconsciously. She simply reached down, found a metal knife, and with one sweep set the blood to gushing out. Bright red arterial blood, that even in the semi-darkness was the color of hope.

"Here, Damon. Here! Drink this. As much as you want—all you need to heal yourself." She got into the best position that she could, hearing but not hearing Stefan's horrified gasp behind her at the recklessness of her slashing, not heeding his grip on her.

But—Damon didn't drink. Not even the heady blood of his Princess of Darkness—and how did the phrase go? It was like rocket fuel compared to the gasoline found in other girls' veins. Now it just ran out of the sides of his mouth. It flowed onto his pale face, soaking his black shirt and pooling in his leather jacket.

No . . .

Damon, Elena sent, *please. I'm—begging you. Please. I'm begging you for me, for Elena. Please drink. We can do this—together.*

Damon didn't move. Blood spilled into the mouth she'd opened and it filled and spilled out again. It was as if Damon were taunting her, saying, *"You wanted me to give up human blood? Well, I have—forever."*

Oh, dear God, please . . .

Elena was dizzier than ever now. Outside events passed dimly around her, like an ocean that only slightly bobbed a person out deep in the swells. She was entirely focused on Damon.

But one thing she did feel. Her bravery—Damon had been wrong about that. Huge sobs were rising from somewhere deep inside her. She had made Stefan let go of her and now she couldn't hold herself up any longer.

She fell right on top of her blood and Damon's body. Her cheek fell against his cheek.

And his cheek was cold. Even under the blood, it was cold.

Elena never knew when the hysterics began. She simply found herself shrieking and sobbing, beating on Damon's shoulders, cursing him. She had never properly cursed him before, not directly to his face. As for the shrieking, that wasn't just a sound. She was once again screaming at him to find some way to fight.

And finally, she began the promises. Promises that deep in her heart, she now knew were lies. She was going to find a way to fix him in a moment. She already felt a new Wings power coming to save him.

Anything so as to not face the truth.

"Damon? Please?" It was an interlude in the shrieking, when she was talking softly in her new husky, hoarse voice. "Damon, just do one thing for me. Just squeeze my hand. I know you can do that. Just squeeze one of my hands."

But there was no pressure on either of her hands. Only

blood that was turning sticky.

And then the miracle happened and she once again heard Damon's voice—very faintly—in her head.

Elena? Don't . . . cry, darling. It's not . . . as bad as Stefan said. I don't feel much of anything, except on my face. I . . . feel your tears. No more weeping . . . please, angel.

Because of the miracle, Elena steadied herself. He'd called Stefan "Stefan" and not "little brother." But she had other things to think about right now. He could still feel things on his face! This was important information, valuable information. Elena immediately cupped his cheeks with her hands and kissed him on the lips.

I just kissed you. I'm kissing you again. Can you feel that?

Forever, Elena, Damon said. *I'll . . . take that with me. It's part of me now . . . do you see?*

Elena didn't want to see. She kissed his lips—icy cold—again. And again.

She wanted to give him something else. Something good to think about. *Damon, do you remember when we first met? At school, after the lights went out, when I was measuring for the Haunted House decorations. I almost let you kiss me then—before I even knew your name—when you just came drifting out of the darkness.*

Damon surprised her by answering immediately. *Yes . . . and you . . . you astonished me by being the first girl I couldn't Influence right away. We had . . . fun together—didn't we? Some good times? We went to a party . . . and we danced together. I'll take that with me too.*

Through her daze, Elena had one thought. Don't confuse him anymore. They'd gone to that "party" only to save Stefan's life. She told him, *We had fun. You're a good dancer. Imagine us waltzing!*

Damon sent slowly, fuzzily, *I'm sorry . . . I've been so horrible lately. Tell . . . her that. Bonnie. Tell her . . .*

Elena steadied herself. *I'll tell her. I'm kissing you again. Can you feel me kissing you?*

It was a rhetorical question, so she got a shock, when Damon only answered slowly and sleepily. *Did I . . . take a vow to tell you the truth?*

Yes, Elena lied instantly. She needed the truth from him.

Then . . . no, to be honest . . . I can't. I don't seem to have . . . a body now. It's comfortable and warm, and nothing hurts anymore. And—I almost feel as if I'm not alone. Don't laugh.

You're not alone! Oh, Damon, don't you know that? I'll never, ever let you be alone. Elena choked, wondering how to make him believe her. Just for a few more seconds . . . now.

Here, she sent in a telepathic whisper, *I'll give you my precious secret. I'll never tell anyone else. Do you remember the motel we stayed in on our road trip, and how everyone—even you—wondered what happened that night?*

A. . . motel? A road trip? He was sounding very unsure now. *Oh . . . yes. I remember. And . . . the next morning—wondering.*

Because Shinichi took your memories, Elena said, hoping that hateful name would revivify Damon. But it didn't. Like Shinichi, Damon was done with the world now.

Elena leaned her cheek against his cold and bloody one. *I held you, darling, just like this—well, almost like this. All night. That was all you wanted, to not feel alone.*

There was a long pause and Elena began to panic in the few parts of her that were not numb or already hysterical. But then the words came slowly to her.

Thank you . . . Elena. Thank you . . . for telling me your precious secret.

Yes, and I'll tell you something even more precious. No one is alone. Not really. No one is ever alone.

You're with me . . . so warm . . . nothing to worry about anymore . . .

Nothing more, Elena promised him. *And I'll always be with you. No one is alone; I promise it.*

Elena . . . things are beginning to feel strange now. Not pain. But I have to tell you . . . what I know you already know. . . . How I fell in love with you . . . you'll remember, won't you? You won't forget me?

Forget *you? How could I* ever *forget you?*

But Damon was speaking on and suddenly Elena knew

that he couldn't hear her, not even by telepathy anymore.

Will you remember? For me? Just that . . . I loved once—just once, really, in my whole life. Can you remember that I loved you? That makes my life . . . worth . . . something . . . His voice faded.

Elena was so dizzy now. She knew she was still losing blood fast. Too fast. Her mind was not sharp. And she was suddenly shaken by a fresh storm of sobbing. At least she would never yell again—there was no one to yell at. Damon had gone away. He had run away without her.

She wanted to follow. Nothing was real. Didn't he understand? She could not imagine a universe, no matter how many dimensions there were, without a Damon in it. There was no world for her, if there was no Damon.

He couldn't do this to her.

Neither knowing nor caring what she was doing, she plunged deep, deep into Damon's mind, wielding her telepathy like a sword, slashing at the wooden connections that she found everywhere. And, at last, she found herself plunging into the very deepest part of him . . . where a little boy, the metaphor for Damon's unconscious, had once been loaded with chains and set to guard the great stone that Damon kept his feelings locked in.

Oh, God, he must be so frightened, she thought. Whatever the cost, he must not be allowed to go away frightened. . . .

Now she saw him. The child-Damon. As always, she could see in the sweetly rounded face, the sharp-cheekboned young man that Damon would become, in the wide black eyes, the potential for his look of fathomless darkness.

But although he was not smiling, the child's look was open and welcoming, in a way that Damon's older self had never been. And the chains . . . the chains were gone. The great stone was gone too.

"I knew you'd come," the boy whispered, and Elena took him into her arms.

Easy, Elena told herself. Easy. He's not real. He's what's left of Damon's mind, the deepest part of his hindbrain. But still, he's even younger than Margaret, and he's just as soft and warm. No matter what, please God, don't let him know what's really happening to him.

But there was knowledge in the wide, dark child eyes that turned up to her face. "I'm so glad to see you," he confided. "I thought that I might never talk to you again. And—*he*—you know—he left some messages with me. I don't think he could say anything more, so he sent them to me."

Elena understood. If there was anywhere the wood had not reached, it was into this last part of the brain, the most primitive part. Damon still could speak to her—through this infant.

But before she could speak herself, she saw that there were tears in the child's eyes and then his body spasmed and he bit his lip very hard—to keep from crying out, she guessed.

"Does it hurt?" she asked, trying to believe that it didn't. Desperate to believe it.

"Not so much." But he was lying, she realized. Still, he hadn't shed any tears. He had his pride, this child-Damon.

"I have a special message for you," he said. "He told me to tell you that he'll always be with you. And that you're never alone. That no one is really alone."

Elena clutched the child to her. Damon had understood, even in his dazed and confused state. Everyone was connected. No one was alone.

"And he asked something else. He asked if you would hold me, just like this—if I got sleepy." Velvety dark eyes searched Elena's face. "Would you do that?"

Elena tried to keep steady. "I'll hold you," she promised.

"And you won't let go ever?"

"And I won't let go *ever*," Elena told him, because he was a child, and there was no point in frightening him if he had no fear. And because maybe this part of Damon—this small, innocent part—would have some kind of "forever." She had heard that vampires didn't come back, didn't reincarnate the way humans did. The vampires in the top Dark Dimension were still "alive"—adventurers or fortune-seekers, or condemned there as a prison by the Celestial Court.

"I'll hold you," Elena promised again. "Forever and ever."

Just then his small body went into another spasm, and she saw tears on his dark eyelashes, and blood on his lip. But before she could say a word, he added, "I have more messages. I know them by heart. But"—his eyes begged her forgiveness—"I have to give them to the others."

What others? Elena thought at first, bewildered. Then she remembered. Stefan and Bonnie. There were other loved ones.

"I can . . . tell them for you," she said hesitantly, and he gave a tiny smile, his first, just the corner of one lip up.

"He left me a little telepathy, too," he said. "I kept it in case I had to call to you."

Still fiercely independent, Elena thought. All she said was, "You go ahead, then."

"The first one is for my brother, Stefan."

"You can tell him in just a moment," Elena said. She held on to the small boy in Damon's soul, knowing that this was the last thing she had left to give him. She could sacrifice a few priceless seconds, so that Stefan and Bonnie could say their own good-byes. She made some sort of enormous adjustment to her real body—her body outside Damon's mind, and found herself opening her eyes, blinking and trying to focus.

She saw Stefan's face, white and stricken. "Is he—?"

"No. But soon. He can hear telepathy, if you think clearly, as if you were speaking. He asked to talk to you."

"To me?" Stefan bent down slowly and put his cheek against his brother's. Elena shut her eyes again, guiding him down through the darkness to where one small light was still shining. She felt Stefan's wonder as he saw her there, still holding the little dark-haired boy in her arms.

Elena hadn't realized that through her link to the child, she would be able to hear every word spoken. Or that Damon's messages would come in the words of a child.

The little boy said, "I guess you think I'm pretty stupid."

Stefan started. He'd never seen or heard the child-Damon before. "I could never think that," he said slowly, marveling.

"But it wasn't much like . . . *him*, you know. Like . . . *me*."

"I think," Stefan said unsteadily, "that it's terribly sad—that I never really knew either of you very well."

"Please don't be sad. That's what he told me to say. That you shouldn't be sad . . . or afraid. He said it's a little bit like going to sleep, and a little bit like flying."

"I'll . . . remember that. And—thank you—big brother."

"I think that's all. You know to watch over our girls. . . ."

There was another of the terrible spasms that left the child breathless. Stefan spoke quickly.

"Of course. I'll take care of everything. You fly."

Elena could feel the grief slash at Stefan's heart, but his voice was calm. "Fly away now, my brother. Fly away."

Elena felt something through the link—Bonnie touching Stefan's shoulder. He quickly got up so that she could lie down. Bonnie was almost hysterical with sobbing, but she had done a good thing, Elena saw. While Elena had been in her own little world with Damon, Bonnie had taken a dagger and cut off a long lock of Elena's hair. Then she had cut one of her own strawberry curls, and placed the locks—one wavy and golden, one curling and red-blond—on Damon's chest. It was all they could do on this flowerless world to honor him, to be with him forever.

Elena could hear Bonnie, too, through her link with Damon, but at first all Bonnie could do was sob, "Damon, please! Oh, please! I didn't know—I never thought—that anyone would get hurt! You saved my life! And now—oh, please! I can't say good-bye!"

She didn't understand, Elena thought, that she was talking to a very young child. But Damon had sent the child a message to repeat.

"I'm *supposed* to tell you good-bye, though." For the first time the child looked uneasy. "And—and I'm supposed to tell you 'I'm sorry,' too. He thought you'd know what that meant and you'd forgive me. But . . . if you don't . . . I don't know what will happen—oh!"

Another of the hateful spasms went through the child. Elena held on to him hard, biting her own lip until the blood came; at the same time trying to shield the little boy completely from her own feelings. And deep in Damon's mind, she saw Bonnie's expression change, from tearful penance to astonished fear to careful control. As if Bonnie had grown up all in an instant.

"Of course—of course I understand! And I forgive you—but *you* haven't done anything wrong. I'm such a silly girl—I . . ."

"*We* don't think you're a silly girl," the child said, looking vastly relieved. "But thank you for forgiving me. There's a special name I'm supposed to call you, too—but I . . ." He sank back against Elena. "I guess—I'm . . . getting sleepy . . ."

"Was it 'redbird'?" Bonnie asked carefully, and the little boy's pale face lit up.

"That was it. You knew already. You're all . . . so nice and so smart. Thank you . . . for making it easy . . . But can I say one more thing?"

Elena was about to answer, when abruptly she was jarred completely out of Damon's mind and back into reality. The Tree had slammed down another spider's-leg set of branches, trapping them and Damon's body between two circles of wooden bars.

Elena had no plans. No idea how to get to the star ball that Damon had died for. Either the Tree was intelligent, or it was wired to have such efficient defenses that it might as well have been. They were lying on the evidence that many, many people had tried for that star ball—and left behind their bones ground to sand.

Come to that, she thought, I wonder why it hasn't gone for us, too—especially for Bonnie. She's been in, and then out, and back in again, which I should never have let her do except that we were all thinking about Damon. Why didn't it go for her again?

Stefan was trying to be strong, trying to organize something out of this disaster that was so stunning that Elena herself simply sat. Bonnie was sobbing again, making heart-wrenching sounds.

Between both circular sets of bars a wooden network was spreading—too close-knit for even Bonnie to squeeze through. Elena's group was efficiently separated from anything outside the sand pit, and just as efficiently separated from the star ball.

"The axe!" Stefan called to her. "Throw me—"

But there was no time. A rootlet had curled around it and was swiftly dragging it into the upper branches.

"Stefan, I'm sorry! I was too slow!"

"It was too fast!" Stefan corrected.

Elena held her breath, waiting for the last crash from above, the one that would kill them all. When it didn't come, she realized something. The Tree was not only intelligent, but sadistic. They were to be trapped here, away from their supplies, to die slowly of thirst and starvation, or to go mad watching the others die.

The best that they could hope for was that Stefan would kill both Bonnie and her—but even he would never get out. These wooden branches would come crashing down again and again, as often as the Tree felt necessary, until Stefan's crushed bones joined the others that had been milled to fine sand.

That was what did it, the thought of all of them, trapped with Damon, making a mockery of his death. The *thing* that had been swelling inside Elena for weeks now, at hearing the stories about children who ate their pets, at creatures who delighted in pain, had, with Damon's sacrifice, finally gotten so big that she could no longer contain it.

"Stefan, Bonnie—don't touch the branches," she gasped. "Make sure you're not touching any part of the branches."

"I'm not, love, and Bonnie isn't either. But why?"

"I can't keep it in anymore! I have to stand like this—"

"Elena, no! That spell—"

Elena could no longer think. The hateful demi-light was driving her mad, reminding her of the pinpoint of green in Damon's pupils, the horrible green light of the Tree.

She understood exactly about the Tree's sadism to her friends . . . and in the corner of her eye she could see a bit of black . . . like a rag doll. Except that it was no doll; it was Damon. Damon with all of his wild and witty spirit broken. Damon . . . who must be gone from this and all worlds by now.

His face was covered with her blood. There was nothing peaceful or dignified about him. There was nothing the Tree had not taken from him.

Elena lost her mind.

With a scream that peeled raw and bleeding from her backbone and came hoarsely out of her throat, Elena grabbed a branch of the Tree that had killed Damon, that had murdered her beloved, and that would murder her and these two others she loved as well.

She had no thoughts. She wasn't capable of thinking. But instinctively she held a high bough of the Tree's cage and let the fury explode out of her, the fury of murdered love.

Wings of Destruction.

She felt the Wings arch behind her, like ebony lace and black pearls, and for a moment she felt like a deadly goddess, knowing that this planet would never harbor any life ever again.

When the attack flared out, it turned the twilight all around her to matte black. What a fitting color. Damon will like this, she thought in confusion, and then she remembered again, and it slammed blistering out of her again, the Power to destroy the Tree all over this small world. It shattered her from the inside but she let it keep coming. No physical pain could compare with what was in her heart, with the pain of losing what she had lost. No physical pain could express how she felt.

The huge roots in the ground underneath them were bucking as if there was an earthquake, and then—

There was a deafening sound as the trunk of the Great Tree exploded straight upward like a rocket, disintegrating to fine ash as it went. The spider's-leg bars around them simply disappeared along with the canopy above. Something in Elena's mind noted that very far away the same destruction was going on, racing to turn branches and leaves into infinitesimal bits of matter that hung in the air like haze.

"The star ball!" Bonnie cried in the eerie silence, anguished.

"Vaporized!" Stefan caught Elena as she sank to her knees, her ethereal black wings fading. "But we'd never have gotten it anyway. That Tree had been protecting it for thousands of years! All we'd have gotten would have been a slow death."

Elena had turned back to Damon. She had not been touching the stake that ran through him—in seconds it would be the only remnant of the Tree on this world. She could hardly dare hope that there was a spark of life left in him now, but the child had wanted to speak with her and she would make that possible or die trying. She scarcely felt Stefan's arms around her.

Once again, she plunged into the very depths of Damon's mind. This time she knew exactly where to go.

And there, by a miracle, he was, although obviously in hideous pain. Tears were rolling down his cheeks and he was trying not to sob. His lips were bitten raw. Her Wings had not been able to destroy the wood inside him—it had already done its poisonous damage—and there was no way to reverse that.

"Oh, no, oh God!" Elena caught the child in her arms. A teardrop fell on her hand. She rocked him, scarcely knowing what she was saying. "What can I do to help?"

"You're here again," he said, and in his voice, she heard the answer. This was all that he wanted. He was a very simple child.

"I'll be here—always. Always. I'm never letting go."

This didn't have the effect that she wanted. The boy gasped, trying to smile, but was torn with a horrible spasm that almost arched his body out of her arms.

And Elena realized that she was turning the inevitable

into slow, excruciating torture.

"I'll hold you," she modified her words for him, "until you want me to let go. All right?"

He nodded. His very voice was breathless with pain. "Could you—could you let me shut my eyes? Just . . . just for a moment?"

Elena knew, as perhaps this child did not, what would happen if she stopped badgering him and let him sleep. But she couldn't stand to see him suffering any longer, and nothing was real again, and there was no one else in the world for her, and she didn't even care if doing it this way meant she would follow him into death.

Carefully steadying her voice, she said, "Maybe . . . we can both shut our eyes. Not for a long time—no! But . . . just for a moment."

She kept rocking the small body in her arms. She could still feel a faint pulse of life . . . not a heartbeat, but still, a pulsing. She knew that he hadn't shut his eyes yet; that he was still fighting the torture.

For her. Not for anything else. For her sake only.

Putting her lips close to his ear, she whispered, "Let's close our eyes together, all right? Let's close them . . . at the count of three. Is that all right?"

There was such relief in his voice and such love. "Yes. Together. I'm ready. You can count now."

"One." Nothing mattered except holding him and

keeping herself steady. "Two. And . . ."

"Elena?"

She was startled. Had the child ever said her name before?

"Yes, sweetheart?"

"Elena . . . I . . . love you. Not just because of him. *I* love you too."

Elena had to hide her face in his hair. "I love you, too, little one. You've always known that, haven't you?"

"Yes—always."

"Yes. You've always known that. And now . . . we'll close our eyes—for a moment. *Three.*"

She waited until the last faint movement stopped, and his head fell back, and his eyes were shut and the shadow of suffering was gone. He looked, not peaceful, but simply gentle—and kind, and Elena could see in his face what an adult with Damon's features and that expression would look like.

But now even the small body was evaporating right out of Elena's arms. Oh, she was stupid. She'd forgotten to close her eyes with him. She was so dizzy, even though Stefan had stopped the bleeding from her neck. Closing her eyes . . . maybe she would look as he had. Elena was so glad that he'd gone gently at the end.

Maybe the darkness would be kind to her, too.

Everything was quiet now. Time to put away her toys

and draw the curtains. Time now to get in bed. One last embrace . . . and now her arms were empty.

Nothing left to do, nothing left to fight. She'd done her best. And, at least, the child had not been frightened.

Time to turn off the light now. Time to shut her own eyes.

The darkness was very kind to her, and she went into it gently.

40

But after an endless time in the soft, kind darkness, something was forcing Elena back up into light. Real light. Not the terrible green half-light of the Tree. Even through shut eyelids she could see it, feel its heat. A yellow sun. Where was she? She couldn't remember.

And she didn't care. Something was saying inside her that the gentle darkness was better. But then she remembered a name.

Stefan.

Stefan was . . . ?

Stefan was the one who . . . the one she loved. But he'd never understood that love was not singular. He'd never understood that she could be in love with Damon and that it would never change an atom's worth of her love for him.

Or that his lack of understanding had been so wrenching and painful that she had felt torn into two different people at times.

But now, even before she opened her eyes, she realized that she was drinking. She was drinking the blood of a vampire, and that vampire wasn't Stefan. There was something unique in this blood. It was deeper and spicier and more heavy, all at once.

She couldn't help opening her eyes. For some reason she didn't understand, they *flew* open and she tried immediately to focus on the scent and feeling and color of whoever was bending over her, holding her.

She couldn't understand, either, her sense of letdown when she slowly realized that it was Sage leaning over her, holding her gently but securely to his neck, with his bronze chest bare and warm from the sunlight.

But she was lying down flat, on grass, from what her hands could feel . . . and for some reason her head was cold. Very cold.

Cold and wet.

She stopped drinking and tried to sit up. The light grip became firmer. She heard Sage's voice say, and felt the rumbling in his chest as he said it, "*Ma pauvre petite*, you must drink more in a moment or so. And your hair has still some of the ashes in it."

Ashes? *Ashes?* Didn't you put ashes on your head for . . .

now what had she been thinking about? It was as if there was a block in her mind, keeping her from getting close to . . . something. But she wasn't going to be told what to do.

Elena sat up.

She was in—yes, she was very sure—the kitsune paradise, and until a moment ago her body had been arched back, so that her hair had been in the clear little stream that she had seen earlier. Stefan and Bonnie had been washing something pitch-black out of her hair. They both were smudged with black as well: Stefan had a big swath across one cheekbone, and Bonnie had faint gray streaks below her eyes.

Crying. Bonnie had been crying. She was still crying, in little sobs that she was trying to suppress. And now that Elena looked harder she could see that Stefan's eyelids were swollen and that he had been crying too.

Elena's lips were numb. She fell back onto the grass, looking up at Sage, who was wiping his eyes furtively. Her throat ached, not just inside, where sobbing and gasping might make it hurt, but outside, too. She had a picture of herself slashing at her own neck with a knife.

Through her numb lips, she whispered, "Am I a vampire?"

"*Pas encore*," Sage said unsteadily. "Not yet. But Stefan and I, we both had to give you massive amounts of blood.

You must be very careful in the next days. You are right on the brink."

That explained how she felt. Probably Damon was hoping that she would become one, wicked boy. Instinctively, she held out her hand to Stefan. Maybe she could help him.

"We just won't do anything for a little while," she said. "You don't have to be sad." But she herself still felt very wrong. She hadn't felt this wrong since she'd seen Stefan in prison and had thought that he would die at any moment.

No . . . it was worse . . . because with Stefan there had been hope and Elena had the feeling that now hope was gone. Everything was gone. She was hollow: a girl who looked solid, but whose insides were missing.

"I'm dying," she whispered. "I know it . . . Are you all going to say good-bye now?"

And with that Sage—Sage!—choked up and began to sob. Stefan, still looking so oddly mussed, with those traces of soot on his face and arms and his hair and clothes soaking wet, said, "Elena, you're not going to die. Not unless you choose to."

She had never seen Stefan look like this before. Not even in prison. His flame, his inner fire that he showed to almost no one but Elena, had gone out.

"Sage saved us," he said, slowly carefully, as if it cost him great effort to speak. "The ash that was falling—you and Bonnie *would* have died if you'd had to breathe any more of it. But Sage put a door back to the Gatehouse right in front of us. I could barely see it; my eyes were so full of ashfall, and it's only getting worse on that moon."

"Ashfall," Elena whispered. There was something at the bottom of her mind, but once again her memory failed her. It was almost as if she'd been Influenced to not remember. But that was ridiculous.

"Why were ashes falling?" she asked, realizing that her voice was husky, hoarse—as if she'd cheered too long at a football game.

"You used *Wings of Destruction*," Stefan said steadily, looking at her with his swollen eyes. "You saved our lives. But you killed the Tree—and the star ball disintegrated."

Wings of Destruction. She must have lost her temper. And she'd killed a world. She was a murderer.

And now the star ball was lost. Fell's Church. Oh, God. What would Damon say to her? Elena had done everything—everything wrong. Bonnie was sobbing now, her face turned away.

"I'm sorry," Elena said, knowing how inadequate this was. For the first time she looked around miserably. "Damon?" she whispered. "He won't speak to me? Because of what I did?"

Sage and Stefan looked at each other.

Ice went down Elena's spine.

She started to get up, but her legs weren't the legs she remembered. They wanted to unlock at the knees. She was staring down at herself, at her own wet and smudged clothes—and then something like mud came down her forehead. Mud or congealing blood.

Bonnie made a sound. She was still sobbing, but she was speaking, too, in a new husky voice that made her sound much older. "Elena—we didn't get the ashes out of the top of your hair. Sage had to give you an emergency transfusion."

"I'll get the ashes out," Elena said flatly. She let her knees bend. She fell onto them, jarring her body. Then, twisting, she leaned down to the little brook and let her head fall forward. Through the icy shock she could dimly hear exclamations from the people above water, and Stefan's sharp, *Elena, are you all right?* in her head.

No, she thought back. *But I'm not drowning, either. I'm washing out my hair. Maybe Damon will at least* see *me if I'm presentable. Maybe he'll come with us and fight for Fell's Church.*

Let me help you up, Stefan sent quietly.

Elena had come to the end of her air. She pulled her heavy head out of the water and flipped it, soaking but clean, so that it fell down her back. She stared at Stefan.

"Why?" she said—and then, with a sudden panic—"Has he left already? Was he angry . . . with me?"

"Stefan." It was Sage, speaking tiredly. Stefan, who was

staring out of his green eyes like a hunted animal, made some faint sound.

"The Influence, it is not working," Sage said. "She *will* remember on her own."

Stefan didn't move or speak for long moments. Elena's heart swelled. Suddenly she was as afraid as he clearly was. She went to him and took both his hands, which were shaking.

Darling, don't cry, she sent. *There must still be time to save Fell's Church. There* must. *It can't end this way. And besides, Shinichi is gone! We can get to the children; we can break the conditioning* . . ." She stopped. It was as if the word "conditioning" echoed in her ears. Stefan's green eyes were filling her vision. Her mind was getting . . . it was getting fuzzy. Everything was becoming unreal again. In a minute she wouldn't be able to . . .

She wrenched her eyes away, breathing hard.

"You were Influencing me," she said. She could hear the anger in her own voice.

"Yes," Stefan whispered. "I've been Influencing you for half an hour."

How dare you? Elena thought, just for him.

"I'm stopping it . . . now," Stefan said quietly.

"As am I," Sage added, sounding exhausted.

And the universe did a slow spin and Elena remembered what it was that they were all keeping from her.

With a wild sob, she rose, scattering droplets, coming to her feet like an avenging goddess. She looked at Sage. She looked at Stefan.

And Stefan proved how brave he was, how much he loved her. He told her what she already knew. "Damon is gone, Elena. I'm so sorry. I'm sorry if . . . if I kept you from being with him as much as you wanted to. I'm sorry if I came between you. I didn't understand—how *much* you loved each other. I do now." And then he dropped his face into his hands.

Elena wanted to go to him. To scold him, to hold him. To tell Stefan that she loved *him* just as much, drop for drop, grain for grain. But her body had gone numb, and the darkness was threatening again . . . all she could do was hold out her arms as she crumpled onto the grass. And then somehow Bonnie and Stefan were both there, the three of them all sobbing: Elena with the intensity of new discovery; Stefan with a lost sound that Elena had never heard before; and Bonnie with a dry, wrenching exhaustion that seemed to want to shatter her small body.

Time lost all meaning. Elena wanted to grieve for every moment of Damon's painful death, and for every moment of his life, too. So much had been lost. She couldn't get her head around it, and she didn't want to do anything but cry until the kind darkness took her mind again.

That was when Sage broke.

He grabbed Elena and pulled her up, and shook her by the shoulders. It snapped her head back and forth.

"Your town is in ruins!" he shouted, as if this was her fault. "Midnight may or may not bring disaster. Oh, yes, I saw it all in your mind when I went in to Influence you. Little Fell's Church is already devastated. And you won't even fight for it!"

Something blazed through Elena. It melted the numbness, the iciness. "Yes, I'll fight for it!" she screamed. "I'll fight for it with every breath in my body, until I stop the people who did it, or until they kill me!"

"And how, *puis-je savoir*, will you get back in time? By the time you walk back the way you came, it will all be over!"

Stefan was beside her, bracing her, shoulder to shoulder. "Then we'll force you to send us some other way—so that we *can* get back in time!"

Elena stared. No. No. Stefan couldn't have said that. Stefan didn't force his way—and she *wouldn't* have him changing himself. She whirled back on Sage. "There's no need to fight! I have a Master Key in my backpack, and magic works here inside the Gatehouse!" she cried.

But Stefan and Sage were staring each other down, each fierce and intent. Elena wanted to go to Stefan but the world was doing another of its slow somersaults. She was afraid that Sage would attack Stefan, and that she couldn't even fight for him.

But instead, suddenly, Sage threw back his head and laughed wildly. Or perhaps it was something between thunderous laughing and crying. It was as eerie as the sound of a wolf baying, and Elena felt Bonnie's small, trembling body hug her—to comfort both of them.

"What the hell!" Sage bellowed, and now there was a wild look in his eyes, too. "*Mais oui*, what the *Hell*?" He laughed again. "After all, I am the Gatekeeper, and I have already broken the rules by allowing you through two different doors."

Stefan was still breathing hard. Now he reached out and grabbed Sage by his broad shoulders and *shook* him with the strength of a vampire gone mad. "What are you talking about? There's no time for talk!"

"Ah, but there is, *mon ami*. My friend, there *is*. What you need is the firepower of the heavens to save Fell's Church—and to undo the damage that has already been done. To wipe it out, to make it as if it had never happened.

And," Sage added deliberately, looking directly at Elena, "perhaps—just perhaps—to undo this day's events, also."

Suddenly every inch of Elena's skin was tingling. Her whole body was listening to Sage, leaning toward him, yearning, while her eyes widened with the only other question that mattered.

Sage said, very softly, very triumphantly, "Yes. They can bestow life upon the dead. They have that Power. They can bring back *mon petit tyran* Damon—as they brought you back."

Stefan and Bonnie were holding Elena up. She couldn't stand on her own.

"But *why* would they help?" she whispered painfully. She wouldn't allow herself even a breath of hope, not until she understood everything.

"In exchange for what was stolen from them millennia ago," Sage replied. "You are in a fortress of Hell, you know. That is what the Gatehouse is. The Guardians cannot enter here. They cannot storm the gate and demand back what is inside . . . the seven—*pardon*, now six—kitsune treasures."

Not a breath of hope. Not a breath. But Elena heard herself give a wild laugh.

"How do we give them a park? Or a field of black roses?"

"We give them the rights to the land that the park

and the field of roses lie upon."

Not a breath, even though the bodies on either side of Elena were shaking now. "And how do we offer them the Fountain of Eternal Youth and Life?"

"We do not. However, I have here various containers, waiting to be collected as garbage. The threat of a gallon bottle of *La Fontaine* randomly spread all over your Earth . . . that would devastate them. And, of course," Sage added, "I know the kinds of gems with enchantments already upon them that they would *most* desire. Here, let me open the doors all at once! We take all we can—the rooms, strip them bare!"

His enthusiasm was contagious. Elena half-turned, breath held, eyes widened to catch the first glowing of a door's light.

"Wait." Stefan's voice was hard suddenly. Bonnie and Elena turned back and froze, embracing each other, trembling. "What is your—your father—going to do to you when he finds out that you allowed this?"

"He will not kill me," Sage said brusquely, the wild tone back in his voice. "He may even find it as *amusant* as I do, and we will be sharing a belly laugh tomorrow."

"And if he doesn't find it amusing? Sage, I don't think . . . Damon wouldn't have wanted—"

Sage whirled around and for the first time since she had met him, Elena could believe with her whole soul that he was the son of his father. His eyes had even seemed to change color, to the yellow of a flame, with diamond pupils like a cat's. His voice was like steel splintering, harder even than Stefan's. "What is between my father and me is my own business—mine! Stay here if you want. *He* never bothers himself about vampires, anyway—he says they're cursed already. But *I* am going to do everything I can to bring *mon chéri* Damon back."

"Whatever the cost to you?"

"The hell with the cost!"

To Elena's surprise, Stefan gripped Sage's shoulders for a moment and then simply hugged as much of him as he could hold.

"I just wanted to make sure," he said quietly. "Thank you, Sage. Thank you." Then he turned and strode over to the Royal Radhika plant, and with one yank, pulled it out of its bower.

Elena, heart beating in her lips and throat and fingertips, ran to gather the empty containers and bottles Sage was tossing out of a ninth doorway that had appeared in between the mine shaft and the field of black roses. She snatched up a gallon container and an Evian water bottle, both with secure caps intact. They were made of plastic, which was good, because she dropped them both just going across the room to the bubbling fountain. Her hands were shaking that badly; and all the time she was sending up a monotonous prayer, Oh, please. *Oh, please. Oh, please!*

She got water into both containers at the Fountain and capped them. And then she realized that Bonnie was still standing in the middle of the Gatehouse. She looked bewildered, frightened.

"Bonnie?"

"Sage?" Bonnie said. "How do we get these things to the Celestial Court to bargain with them?"

"Have no worries," Sage said kindly. "I am certain that Guardians will be waiting just outside to arrest us. They will take us to the Court."

Bonnie didn't stop trembling, but she nodded and hurried to help Sage get bottles of Black Magic—and break them. "A symbol," he said. "*Un signe* of what we will do to this area if the Celestials don't agree. Be careful not to cut your pretty hands."

Elena thought she heard Bonnie's husky voice then, and that it was not a happy tone. But Sage's rumbling murmur was reassuring. And Elena would neither allow herself to hope nor despair. She had a task in hand, a scheme. She was making private Plans for the Celestial Court.

When she and Bonnie had all the plunder they could carry, and their backpacks were full as well, when Stefan had two narrow black boxes that held deeds, and when Sage looked like a cross between Santa Claus and a bronzed, gorgeous, long-haired Hercules, as he carried two sacks made of pillowcases, they gave one last look around at the ravaged Gatehouse.

"All right," Sage said then. "Time to face the Guardians." He smiled reassuringly at Bonnie.

As usual, Sage was right. The moment they came out with their booty, Guardians from two different dimensions were ready for them. The first type were the ones who looked vaguely like Elena: blond hair, dark blue eyes, slender. The Guardians of the Nether World seemed senior to these, and were lithe women with skin so dark it was almost ebony, and hair that curled tightly in a cap over their heads. Behind them were brilliant golden air cars.

"You are under arrest," one of the dark ones said, not looking as if she enjoyed her job, "for removing treasures that rightfully belong to the Celestial Court out of the sanctuary where it was agreed that they would be kept, under the laws of both our dimensions."

And then it was only a matter of hanging on to the golden air cars while hanging on at the same time to their unlawful booty.

The Celestial Court was . . . celestial. Pearly white with a faint hint of blue. Minarets. It was a long distance from the heavily guarded gate—where Elena had seen a third type of Guardian, one with short red hair and slanted, piercing green eyes—to the actual palace, which seemed to encompass a city.

But it was when Elena's group was guided to the throne room that the real culture shock hit. It was far larger and far more glorious than any room Elena had ever imagined. No ball or gala in the Dark Dimensions could have prepared her in the least for it. The cathedral ceiling seemed to be made entirely of gold, as were the double line of stately columns that marched vertically across the floor. The floor itself was of intricately patterned malachite and gold-threaded lapis lazuli, with gold seemingly used as grouting—and with a heavy hand at that. The three golden fountains in the middle of the room (the central one was the largest and most elaborate) threw into the air not water, but delicately perfumed flower petals that sparkled like diamonds in turning at their apex and then floated down again. Stained-glass windows in brilliant colors that Elena couldn't remember ever having seen before threw rainbow light like a benediction from high on every wall, giving warmth to the otherwise cool engraved gold.

Sage and Elena and Stefan and Bonnie were seated in small comfortable chairs just a few feet back from a great dais, draped with a fantastically woven golden cloth. The treasures were spread out in front of them, as attendants dressed in flowing blue and gold took the objects one by one up to the current ruling triumvirate in back.

The rulers comprised one each of the groups of Guardians—fair, dark, redheaded. Their seats on the dais ensured that they were far from—and high above—their petitioners. But with Power sent to her eyes, Elena could see perfectly well that they each sat on an exquisitely jeweled golden throne. They were speaking softly together, admiring the Royal Radhika flower—blue delphiniums at the moment. Then the dark one smiled and sent one of her attendants running for a pot with soil for the plant to survive in.

Elena stared sightlessly at the other treasures. A gallon of water from the Fountain of Eternal Youth and Life. Six bottles of unbroken Black Magic wine, and the shards of at least that many around them. A blazing rainbow to rival the stained-glass windows in fist-sized gems, some raw, some already faceted and polished, but most of them not only faceted, but also hand-carved with mysterious gold or silver inscriptions. Two long, black, velvet-lined boxes with yellowing cylinders of papyrus or paper inside them, one with a pure black rose lying next to it, and the other with a simple spray of light springtime-green leaves. Elena knew what the yellowed documents with their cracked waxen seals were. The deeds to the field of black roses and the kitsune paradise.

When you saw all the treasures together like this, it almost seemed too much, Elena thought. Any one object from any one of the Seven—no, now Six—kitsune Treasures was enough to trade worlds for. One sprig of the Royal Radhika, which was even now being returned, (pink larkspur changing to a white orchid) properly potted again, was immeasurably precious. So was a single velvety black rose, with its power to hold the most powerful of magics. One jewel from the hoard in the mining cavern, maybe a double-fist-sized diamond that put the Star of Africa and the Golden Jubilee to shame. One day in the kitsune paradise, where a day could seem like a perfect lifetime. One sip of that effervescent water that could make a human live as long as the oldest Old One . . .

Of course there should also have been the largest star ball in existence, full of eldritch Power, but Elena was hoping that the Guardians would overlook that.

Hoping? She wondered and shook her head at nothing, causing Bonnie to squeeze her hand tightly. Not hoping. She didn't dare hope. Not a breath yet.

Another attendant, red-haired, flashing them a cold green-eyed look, picked up the plastic gallon bottle that said *Sector 3 Water* on the label. Sage rumbled as she left, "*Qu'est-ce qui lui prend?* I mean, what is her problem? I like the water in the vampire sector. I don't like the pump water in the Nether World."

Elena had already figured out the color code for the Guardians. The blond ones were all business, impatient only with delays. The dark ones were the kindest—maybe there was less work for them to do in the Nether World. The green-eyed redheads were just plain bitchy. Unfortunately, the young woman on the central throne up there on the dais was a redhead.

"Bonnie?" she whispered.

Bonnie had to gulp and sniff before she could get out, "Yes?"

"Have I ever told you how much I like your eyes?"

Bonnie gave her a long brown-eyed gaze before beginning to shake with laughter. At least it started out like laughter, and then Bonnie burrowed her head into Elena's shoulder and simply shook.

Stefan squeezed Elena's hand. "She's been trying so hard—for you. She—she loved him too, you see. I didn't even know that. I guess . . . I guess I've just been blind on all sides."

He ran his free hand through his already-tousled hair. He looked very young, like a little boy who had been suddenly punished for doing something he hadn't been told was wrong. Elena remembered him in the backyard of the boardinghouse, dancing with her feet on his feet, and then in his attic room, kissing her hands, her knuckles bruised with hammering, the pulsing inside of her wrists. She wanted to tell him that everything was going to be all right, that the laughter would come back to his eyes, but she couldn't stand the chance of lying to him.

Suddenly Elena felt like a very, very old woman, who could hear and see only dimly, whose every movement caused her terrible pain, and who was cold inside. Her every joint and every bone was filled with ice.

At last, when all the treasures, including a sparkling, diamond-set, golden Master Key, had been taken up for the young women on the thrones to handle, heft, examine, and discuss, a warm-eyed dark-skinned woman came to Elena's group. "You may approach Their High Judgments now. And," she added in a voice as soft as the stroke of a dragonfly's wing, "they are very, very impressed. That doesn't often happen. Speak meekly and keep your heads low and I think you shall have your hearts' desires."

Something inside Elena gave a bound that would have sent her leaping to clutch at the retreating attendant's robe, but fortunately Stefan had her in an embrace of iron. Bonnie's head came off Elena's shoulder, and Elena had to restrain her, in turn.

They walked, the very portrait of meekness, to where four scarlet cushions blazed against the golden weave of the floor cloth. Once, Elena would have refused to abase herself. Now, she was thankful for a soft resting place for her knees.

This close, she could see that the rulers each wore a

circlet of some metal, from which a single stone hung on to her forehead.

"We have considered your petition," the dark one said, her white-gold circlet with its diamond pendant dazzling Elena with pinpricks of lilac and red and royal blue. "Oh, yes," she added, laughing. "We know what you want. Even a Guardian on the street would have to be very bad at her job not to know. You want your town . . . renewed. The burned buildings rebuilt. The victims of the malach pestilence re-created, their souls swathed again in flesh, and their memories—"

"But, first," interrupted the fair one, waving a hand, "don't we have business at hand? This girl—Elena Gilbert—may not be eligible to be a spokesman for her group. If she becomes a Guardian, she doesn't belong with the petitioners."

The redhead tossed her head like an impatient filly, causing the rose gold of her circlet to flash, and its ruby to shimmer. "Oh, go on then, Ryannen. If your recruitment levels are so low—"

The businesslike fair one ignored this, but bent forward, some of her hair held back from her face by her circlet of yellow gold with its sapphire pendant. "What about it, Elena? I know our first encounter was—unfortunate. You must believe that I am sorry for that. But you were well on your way to becoming a full Guardian when we had orders from Above to weave you into a new body so that you could take up your life as a human again."

"You did that? Of course you did." Elena's voice was soft and low and flattering. "You can do anything. But—our first encounter? I don't remember—"

"You were too young, and you saw just a flash of our air car as it passed your parents' vehicle. It was meant to be a minor accident with one apparent casualty—you. But instead . . ."

Bonnie's hands flew to her mouth. She was clearly getting something Elena wasn't. Her parents' "vehicle" . . . ? The last time she'd driven with her father and mother—and little Margaret—had been the day of the crash. The day she'd distracted her father, who'd been driving . . .

"Look, Daddy! Look at the pretty—"

And then had come the impact.

Elena forgot about being meek and keeping her head low. In fact, she raised her head, and met gold-splattered blue eyes very much like hers. Her own gaze, she knew, was piercing and hard.

"You . . . *killed my parents*?" she whispered.

"No, no!" the dark one cried. "It was an operation gone sour. We only had to intersect with the Earth dimension for a few minutes. But, quite unexpectedly, your talent flared. You saw our air car. Instead of a crash with only one apparent casualty: *you*, your father turned to look and . . ."

Slowly her voice trailed off as Elena's turned unbelieving eyes on her.

Bonnie was staring sightlessly into the distance, almost as if she were in trance. "Shinichi," she breathed. "That weird riddle of his—or whatever it was. That one of us had murdered, and that it was nothing to do with being a vampire or a mercy killing . . ."

"I'd always assumed it was me," Stefan said quietly. "My mother never really recovered after my birth. She died."

"But that doesn't make you a murderer!" Elena cried. "Not like me. *Not like me!*"

"Well, that was why I was asking you now," the businesslike blond woman said. "It was a flawed mission, but you understand that we were only trying to recruit you, yes? It's the traditional method. Our genes have honed us to be the best at managing powerful, irrational demons, who don't respond to traditional strength but require on-the-spot recalculation—"

Elena choked back a scream. A scream of wrath—agony—disbelief—guilt—*she didn't know what.* Her Plans. Her schemes. The way she had handled boisterous boys in the bad old days—it was all genetic. And . . . her parents . . . what had they died for?

Stefan stood up. His jaw was hard, his green eyes were burning brilliantly. There was no gentleness in his face.

He clasped Elena's hand and she heard, *If you want to fight, I'm in.*

Mais, non. Elena turned around and saw Sage. His telepathic voice was unmistakable. She was compelled to listen. *We cannot fight them on their own territory and win. Even I cannot. What you* can *do is make them pay! Elena, my brave one, your parents' spirits have undoubtedly found new homes. It would be cruel to drag them back. But let us demand of the Guardians anything you desire. For a year and a day in the past, demand whatever you wish! I think that we all will back you.*

Elena paused. She looked at the Guardians and she looked at the treasures. She looked at Bonnie and Stefan, who were waiting. There was permission in their eyes.

Then she said slowly to the Guardians, "This is *really* going to cost you. And I don't want to hear that any of it is impossible. For all your treasures back and the Master Key too . . . I want my old life. No, I want a *new* life, with my real old life behind me. I want to be Elena Gilbert, exactly as if I'd graduated with my high school class, and I want to go to Dalcrest College. I want to wake up in my aunt Judith's house in the morning and find that no one realizes I've been gone for almost ten months. And I want a 4.5 grade point average for my last year in high school—just in case of emergencies. And I want Stefan to have lived in the boardinghouse peacefully all that time, and to have everyone accept him as my boyfriend. And I want every single thing that Shinichi and Misao and whoever they were working for did *undone* and forgotten. I want the person they were working for *dead*. And I want everything that Klaus did in Fell's Church undone as well. I want Sue Carson back! I want Vickie Bennett back! *I want everyone back!*"

Bonnie said faintly, "Even Mr. Tanner?"

Elena understood. If Mr. Tanner had not died—mysteriously drained of blood—then Alaric Saltzman would never have been called to Fell's Church. Elena remembered Alaric from the out-of-body experience: sandy hair, laughing hazel eyes. She thought of Meredith and his almost-engagement to her.

But who was she to play God? To say, yes, this person can die because he was unlovely and unloved, but this one has to live because she was my friend.

42

"It's not a problem," the fair ruler, Ryannen, said unexpectedly. "We can make it so that your Mr. Tanner repelled an apparent vampire attack and the school called in Alaric Saltzman to take his place and investigate. All right, Idola?"—to the redhead, and to the dark one—"All right, Susurre?"

Elena wasn't all right. Despite the example she'd just had of turn-on-a-dime plotting and scheming, she was scarcely listening. All she knew was that her voice had gone husky and that tears blurred her eyes. "And . . . for the Master Key—I want—"

Stefan squeezed her hand. Elena suddenly realized that they were all standing, all three of them, beside her. And the look on every face was the same. Dead resolve.

"I want Damon back." Elena hadn't heard quite this

note in her voice since the day she'd been told both her parents had died. If there had been a table, she would have put her clenched fists on it and did her best to loom over the women. As it was, she simply leaned toward them, speaking in a low and grating voice. "If you do that—bring him back, exactly as he was before he walked into the Gatehouse—then you get the Master Key and the treasures. You say no—and you lose everything. *Everything.* This is non-negotiable, get it?"

She kept staring into Idola's green eyes. She refused to see dark Susurre drop her forehead onto three fingertips and begin to rub it in small circles. She wouldn't give a glance to blond Ryannen, who was looking at her steadily, having gone into people-management mode. She stared directly into those green eyes under their willful eyebrows. Idola gave a little huff and shook her gorgeous head.

"Look, someone clearly has screwed up in preparing you for this interview." A glance at Susurre. "The other things you've asked for—all together, it forms a very heavy ransom. Do *you* understand that? Do you understand that it involves changing the memories of all the people for miles around your town, and changing them for every day of ten months? That it means changing everything in print about Fell's Church—and that there is a *lot* in print—not to mention other media outlets? It means begging for three human spirits and weaving flesh around them again. I'm not sure we even have the *personnel* for this—"

Blond Ryannen put a hand on the redhead's arm. "We have it. Susurre's women have little to do in the Nether World. I can lend you perhaps thirty percent of mine—after all, we're going to have to send up a petition to a higher Court for those spirits—"

Idola the redhead interrupted. "All right. What I was saying is that we might just be able to manage—if you throw in the Key. However, your vampire companion—we can't give life back to the lifeless. We can't work with vampires. Once they're gone—they're gone."

"That's what you *tell* us!" Stefan cried, trying to get in front of Elena. "But why are we so particularly damned, of all creatures? How do you know it's impossible? *Have you ever even tried?*"

Red-haired Idola was making a disgusted gesture, when Bonnie interrupted, her voice shaking. "It's ridiculous! You can rebuild a town, you can kill the person who's really behind all Shinichi and Misao did, but you can't bring one little vampire back? You brought *Elena* back!"

"Elena's death as a vampire allowed her to become the Guardian she was originally meant to be. As for the person who gave orders to Shinichi and Misao: It was Inari Saitou—Obaasan Saitou, as you knew her—and she is already dead, thanks to your friends in Fell's Church, who weakened her—and to you, who destroyed her star ball."

"*Inari?* You mean Isobel's grandma? You're saying it was *her* star ball in the Great Tree's trunk? That's impossible!" Bonnie cried.

"No, it's not. It's the truth," blond Ryannen said simply.

"And she's *dead* now?"

"After a long battle which nearly killed your friends. Yes—but what actually *killed* her was having her star ball destroyed."

"So," dark Susurre said quietly, "if you follow the curve . . . in a way your Damon *did* die to save Fell's Church from another massacre like the one on that Japanese island. He kept saying that was what he'd come to the Nether World to do. Do you not think he would be . . . satisfied? At peace?"

"At *peace*?" Stefan spat bitterly, and Sage growled.

"Woman," he said, "you obviously have never met Damon Salvatore before." The tone in his voice—more resonant, more threatening somehow—made Elena finally break off her staredown with the red-haired Idola. She turned and looked—

—and saw the enormous room filled with Sage's outspread wings.

They weren't like any of her ephemeral Wings Powers. They were clearly part of Sage. They were velvety and reptilian, and, unfurled like this, they stretched from distant wall to wall, and touched the grand, golden ceiling. They also demonstrated why Sage didn't usually wear shirts.

He was beautiful this way, bronze skin and hair against those giant, leathery soft-looking arches. But Elena, after one look at him, knew that the time had come to play the ace up her sleeve. She turned around to meet Idola's green gaze squarely.

"All this time we've been bargaining for a Gatehouse full of treasures," she said, "and—one Master Key."

"A Master Key, stolen by the kitsune ages upon ages ago," Susurre explained quietly, lifting her dark eyes.

"And you've said that it's not enough for you to bring Damon back." Elena forced her voice not to waver.

"Not even if it were your only request." Ryannen tossed a golden lock of hair over her shoulder.

"So you say. But . . . what if I throw into the pot . . . another Master Key?"

There was a pause, and Elena's heart began to pound in sick terror. Because it was the wrong kind of pause. There were no shocked gasps. No astonished glances from one Guardian ruler to another. No looks of disbelief.

After another moment Idola said smugly, "If you mean the other stolen key that your friends had on Earth—it was confiscated as soon as they hid it. It was stolen property. It belonged to *us*."

She's been here too long, in the Dark Dimensions, Elena thought with one part of her mind. She's enjoying herself.

Idola leaned toward her, as if to confirm Elena's guess. "It—simply—is not—possible," she said emphatically.

"Really, it isn't," the fair Ryannen added briskly. "We don't know what happens to vampires. But they don't pass through our purview. We never see them after death. The simplest explanation is that they just—go out." She snapped her fingers.

"I don't believe that!" Elena was aware that her voice had risen in volume. "I don't believe that for one moment!"

Voices, not attached to anyone in particular, burst into a clamor of argument around Elena, forming a sort of poem:

Not possible. It's simply not possible! (*But please . . .*) No! Damon is gone, and to ask where is like asking where a candle flame goes when it's blown out. (*But shouldn't you try to bring him back, at the least?*) Whatever has happened to gratitude? You four should be grateful that the other things you asked for *can* be done. (*But in exchange for both Master Keys—*) No Power we can command could bring Damon back! Elena must try to reconcile herself to reality. She has been pampered too much already! (*But what harm can it do to try again?*) All right! If you must know, Susurre has already forced us to try. And nothing came of it! Damon . . . is . . . gone! His spirit was nowhere to be found in the ether! That is what happens to vampires, and everyone knows it!

Elena found herself looking down at her own hands, which were very clean but with broken nails and every knuckle bleeding. The outside world had become unreal again. She was inside herself, struggling with her grief, struggling with the knowledge that Idola, the central ruler of Guardians, hadn't even mentioned before that they had looked for Damon's spirit. And that it was . . . gone.

Suddenly, the room was pressing in on her. There wasn't enough air. There were only these women: these powerful, magical Guardian women; who still did not have enough power or magic to save Damon—or at least didn't even care enough to try twice.

She wasn't sure what was happening to her. Her throat felt puffed out, her chest was both huge and tight. Each heartbeat sounded through her as if trying to shake her to death.

To death. In her mind's eye, she saw a hand hold up a glass of Clarion Loess Black Magic.

And then, Elena knew that she had to stand a certain way, and hold her arms a certain way, and whisper certain words in her own mind. But the last, the naming of the spell, had only to be said aloud at the end.

At the end—when things slowed. When green-eyed Idola—what a perfect name for someone who idolized herself, Elena thought—and fair businesslike Ryannen and nurturing Susurre—all stared at her with open mouths, too shocked to move even a finger as, quietly and calmly, Elena said, "*Wings of Destruction—*"

It was a soldier, just an ordinary one of the rank and file, one of the dark women, who stopped it. She leaped up onto the dais, and, with inhuman speed, slapped her hand over Elena's mouth, so that the final syllable was a mumble, and the golden, green, and blue hall did not explode into fragments with hot metal running in rivulets like lava, and the flower-fountain did not vaporize, and the stained-glass windows didn't shatter into atoms.

Then there were more arms around Elena, holding her down, scarcely letting her breathe, even when she went limp for lack of air. Elena fought like an animal, with her teeth and nails, to escape. But she eventually was completely restrained, pinned to the floor. She could hear Sage's deep voice raging and Stefan, in between desperate telepathic bursts to her, pleading and explaining, "She's still not in reality! She doesn't even know what she's doing!"

But louder, she could hear the voices of the Guardians. "She would have killed us all!" "Those Wings—I've never seen anything so deadly!" "A human! And with just three words, she could have wiped us out!" "If Lenea hadn't tackled her—" "Or if she had been another few feet away—"

"She destroyed a moon, you know! No life on it at all now, and ashes still falling from the sky!" "That isn't the point. The point is that she shouldn't have Wings powers at all. She's got to be clipped of them." "That's right—clip her Wings! *Do it!*"

Elena recognized Ryannen's and Idola's voices at the end there. She was still trying to fight, but they held her so tightly and piled on her so ruthlessly that it had become a fight simply to get air and all she did was exhaust herself.

And then they clipped her Wings. It was quick, at least, and Elena felt very little. What hurt most was her heart. Some proud, stubborn streak had been brought out with the fighting, and now she was ashamed to feel each pair cut off. First went *Wings of Redemption*, those great rainbow-hued arches. Then *Wings of Purification*, white and iridescent as frosted cobwebs. *Wings of the Wind*, like honey-colored thistledown. *Wings of Remembrance*, soft violet and midnight blue. And then *Wings of Protection*—emerald green and gold, the Wings that had saved her friends from Bloddeuwedd's frenzied attack on them the first time they had entered the Dark Dimensions.

And, finally, *Wings of Destruction*—high, ebony arches with edges as delicate as black lace.

Elena tried to keep silent as each power was taken. But after the first one or two had fallen at her sides, in shadows that perhaps only she could see, she heard a small gasp, and realized that it was her own voice. And with the next cut, an involuntary little cry.

For a moment there was silence. And then suddenly there was overwhelming noise. Elena could hear Bonnie keening and Sage roaring, and Stefan, gentle Stefan, shouting blasphemies and curses at the Guardians. Elena guessed from the stifled sound of his voice that he was fighting them, fighting to get to her.

He reached her, somehow, just as the deadly, delicate *Wings of Destruction* were sheared from her shoulders and mind, and fell like tall shadows to the ground. It was good that he did reach her then, because at last, when Elena was the least dangerous she had been since the Powers of Wings had begun awakening in her, suddenly the Guardians seemed afraid. They stepped back from her, these strong and dangerous women, and only Stefan was there to catch her and hold her in his arms.

Stunned, dazed, she was an eighteen-year-old girl who was ordinary. Except for her blood. They wanted to rob her of her blood as well . . . to "purify" it. The three rulers and their attendants had already gathered in a determined, multihued triangle around her and were working their magic when Sage bellowed, "Stop!"

Elena, drooping over Stefan's shoulder, could see him vaguely, his velvety black wings still spread from wall to wall, still touching the golden ceiling. Bonnie clung to him like a bit of stray dandelion fluff. "You have already diminished her aura to almost nothing," he growled. "If you 'purify' the blood of this *pauvre petite* completely, she will die—and then she will awaken. You will have created *un vampire*, *Mesdames*. Is that what you wish?"

Susurre reeled back. For the ruler of such a harsh and unyielding realm, she seemed almost too gentle—but not too soft to shear off my Wings, Elena thought, wriggling her shoulders to ease them. Maybe she didn't know how much it would hurt, another part of her mind offered vaguely.

Then all her mind came together in an emergency meeting. Something warm and cooling was sliding down the back of her neck, in tiny droplets. Not blood. No, this was infinitely more precious than what the Guardians had taken away. Stefan's tears.

She rocked hard, trying to take her own weight on her feet. Somehow, shakily, she managed it. She only realized just *how* shaky she was when she tried to lift a hand and wipe the tears off Stefan's cheeks with her thumb. Her whole hand wobbled as if she were making a childish joke. Her thumb struck his cheek with enough force to make anyone else wince. She looked at him with dumb apology, too shocked to try to speak.

Stefan was speaking. Over and over. "It doesn't matter," he was saying. "It's all right, love. Oh, lovely love, it will be all right." He wiped her eyes with a hand that was rock steady, and all the time he was looking only at her, and—she knew—thinking only of her.

She knew that because she also knew the moment when it changed.

Red hair was in her line of sight, blurred through new tears. Red hair and narrow green eyes, too close to her. That was when Elena felt Stefan remember that there was anything other than Elena in the world.

His face changed. He didn't snarl or stick out his chin. The change was an entire alteration, but it centered around his eyes, which became deadly hard while everything else became sharp and fierce.

"If you touch her again, you vicious *bitch*, I will rip out your throat," Stefan said, and each word was like a chip of ice-cold iron dropped onto the floor.

Elena's tears stopped with the shock of it. Stefan didn't talk that way to women. Even Damon didn't—hadn't. But the words were still echoing in the sudden silence of the cathedral-like room. People were backing away.

Idola was backing away too, but her lip was curled. "Do you think that because we are Guardians that we cannot harm you—?" she was beginning, when Stefan's voice cut through hers cleanly.

"I think that *because* you are 'Guardians' you can kill sanctimoniously and get away with it," Stefan said, and his lip made a far more compelling—and frightening—line of scorn than Idola's had. "You would have killed Elena if Sage hadn't stopped you. *Damn* you," he added softly, but with such utter conviction that Idola took another step backward. "Yes, you'd better rally all your little friends around," he added. "I might just decide to kill you anyway. I killed my own brother, as I'm sure you realize."

"But surely—that was only after taking a mortal blow yourself." Susurre was between the two of them, trying to intercede.

Stefan shrugged. He looked at her with the same contempt as he had the other ruler. "I still had the use of my arm," he said deliberately. "I could have decided to drop my sword, or to merely wound him. Instead I chose to put a blade straight through his heart." He showed his teeth in a distinctly unfriendly smile. "And now I don't even need a weapon."

"Stefan," Elena managed at last to whisper.

"I know. She's weaker than I am and you don't want to see me kill her. That's why she's still alive, love. It's the only reason." As Elena lifted half-frightened eyes to him, Stefan added in a voice only she could hear, *Of course, there are some things about me you don't know, Elena. Things I'd hoped you'd never have to see. Knowing you—loving you—made me almost forget about them.*

Stefan's voice in her head woke something inside

Elena. She lifted her head and looked at the blurry mass of Guardians around them. She saw strawberry-blond curls suspended in midair. Bonnie. Bonnie fighting. Doing it weakly, but only because a pair of the fair Guardians and another pair of dark ones were holding her in the air, one to each limb. As Elena stared at her she seemed to regain energy and fought harder. And Elena could hear . . . something. It was faint and far away, but it almost sounded like . . . her name. Like her name spoken by whispering branches or the whirring of passing bicycle wheels.

lay . . . nah . . . eee . . . lay . . .

Elena reached inwardly for the sound. She tried desperately to grasp whatever came after, but nothing happened. She tried a trick she would have found easy yesterday—channeling Power to the center of her telepathy. It didn't work. She tried her telepathy.

Bonnie! Can you hear me?

There wasn't even the slightest change in the smaller girl's expression.

Elena had lost her link to Bonnie.

She watched as Bonnie realized the same thing, watched the fight go out of the small body. Bonnie's face, upturned in blank despair, was indescribably sad, and somehow indescribably pure and beautiful, all at once.

That will never happen to us, Stefan's voice in her mind told her fiercely. *Never! I give you my—*

No! Elena thought back, superstitiously terrified of a jinx. If Stefan swore, something might happen—she might have to become a vampire or a spirit—to ensure that he didn't break his word.

He stopped, and Elena knew that he had heard her. And somehow this knowledge, that Stefan had heard a single word from her, stilled her. She knew he wasn't spying. He'd heard because she'd sent the thought to him. She wasn't alone. She might be ordinary again; they might have taken her wings and most of the Power of her blood, but she wasn't alone. She leaned toward him, her forehead against Stefan's chin.

"No one is alone." She'd told Damon that. Damon Salvatore, a being who no longer existed. But who still called forth from her one more word, one final cry. His name.

Damon!

He'd died four dimensions away. But she could feel Stefan backing her, amplifying her transmission, sending it like one last beacon through the multitude of worlds that separated them from his cold and lifeless body.

Damon!

There wasn't the slightest glimmer of an answer. Of course not. Elena was making a fool of herself.

Suddenly something stronger than grief, stronger than self-pity, even stronger than guilt, took hold of her. Damon wouldn't have wanted her to be carried out of this hall—even by Stefan. Especially by Stefan. He would have wanted her to show no sign of weakness to these women who'd shorn her and humiliated her.

Yes. That was Stefan. Her love, but not her lover, willing to love her chastely from now until the end of her days. . . .

The end . . . of her days?

Elena was suddenly glad that she couldn't project to strangers telepathically and that Stefan had set shields around them when he'd taken her into his arms. She turned to Ryannen, who was watching . . . warily, but still with business in her eyes.

"I'd like to go now, if you don't mind," she said, picking up her backpack and slinging it over her shoulder with a gesture as arrogant as she could make it. There was a bolt of agony as the weight of the strap hit the place from which most of her wings had sprung, but she kept her face contemptuous and indifferent.

Bonnie, back on the ground since she wasn't fighting any longer, followed Elena's lead. Stefan had left his backpack in the Gatehouse, but he gently cupped a hand around Elena's elbow, not guiding her, but showing that he was there for her. Sage's wings folded back into themselves and were gone.

"You understand that for the return of these treasures which are ours by right—but which we were barred from retrieving—you will be granted your requests with the exception of the imposs—"

"I understand," Elena said flatly, just as Stefan said, much more brusquely, "She understands. Just *do* it, will you?"

"It is already being organized." Ryannen's eyes, dark blue splashed with gold, met Elena's with a look not entirely unsympathetic.

"The best thing," Sussure added hastily, "would be for us to put you to sleep and send you to your—your old, new dwellings. By the time you awaken, all will have been accomplished."

Elena forced her face not to change. "Send me to Maple Street?" she asked, looking at Ryannen. "Aunt Judith's house?"

"In your sleep, yes."

"I don't want to be asleep." Elena moved even closer to Stefan. "Don't let them put me to sleep!"

"No one's going to do *anything* to you that you don't want," Stefan said, and his voice was like the edge of a razor. Sage rumbled his support, and Bonnie stared at the fair woman hard.

Ryannen bowed her head.

Elena woke up.

It was dark, and she'd been asleep. She couldn't

remember exactly how she'd fallen asleep, but she knew she wasn't on the palanquin, and she knew she wasn't in a sleeping bag.

Stefan? Bonnie? Damon? she thought automatically, but there was something odd about her telepathy. It felt almost as if it were confined to her own head.

Was she in Stefan's room? It must be pitch-black outside, since she couldn't even see the outline of the trapdoor that led to the widow's walk.

"Stefan?" she whispered, while various bits of information pooled in her mind. There was a smell, at once familiar and unfamiliar. She was lying on a comfortable double bed, not one of Lady Ulma's silken-and-velvet extravaganzas, but not any lumpy featherbed from the boardinghouse, either. Was she in a hotel?

As these various thoughts came together in her brain, there was a soft quick rapping. Knuckles on glass.

Elena's body took over. She tossed off the bedspread and ran to the window, mysteriously avoiding obstacles without thinking about them at all. Her hands wrenched aside curtains that she somehow knew were there and her skyrocketing heart brought a name to her lips.

"Da—!"

And then the world stopped and did its slowest somersault of all. The sight of a face, fierce and concerned and loving and yet strangely frustrated, just on the other side of the second-story window, brought Elena's memories back.

All of them.

Fell's Church was saved.

And Damon was dead.

Her head bent slowly until her forehead touched the cool pane of glass.

"Elena?" Stefan said quietly. "Could you ask me to come in? You have to invite me in if you want to—to talk—"

Invite him *in*? He was already in—inside her heart. She had told the Guardians that everyone would have to accept Stefan as her boyfriend of almost a year.

It didn't matter. In a low voice she said, "Come in, Stefan."

"The window's locked from your side, Elena."

Numbly, Elena unlocked the window. The next moment she was encompassed by warm, strong arms in a desperate, fervent embrace. But the moment after *that,* the arms dropped, leaving her frozen and lonely.

"Stefan? What's wrong?" Her eyes had adapted and by the starlight through the window she could see him hesitating before her.

"I can't— It isn't— It's not me you want," he said in a rush that sounded as if it came through a constricted throat. "But I wanted you to know that—that Meredith and Matt are holding Bonnie. Comforting her, I mean. They're all okay and so is Mrs. Flowers. And I thought that you—"

"They put me to sleep! They said they wouldn't put me to sleep!"

"You fell asleep, lo—Elena. While we were waiting for them to send us home. We all watched over you: Bonnie, Sage, and I." He was still speaking in that formal, unusual tone. "But I thought—well, that you might want to talk tonight, too. Before I—I left." He put a finger up to stop his lip from shaking.

"You swore you wouldn't leave me!" Elena cried. "You promised, not for any reason, not for any length of time, no matter how noble the cause!"

"But—Elena—that was before I understood . . ."

"You still don't understand! Do you know—"

His hand flew to cover her mouth and he put his lips to her ear. "Lo—Elena. We're in your house. Your aunt—"

Elena felt her eyes widen, although of course subconsciously she had known this all along. The air of familiarity. This bed—it was *her* bed, and the spread was her beloved gold and white bedspread. The obstacles she'd known how to avoid in the dark—the tapping at her window . . . she was *home*.

Like a climber who has negotiated an impossible-seeming section of rock, and almost fallen, Elena felt a tremendous rush of adrenaline. And it was this—or, perhaps, simply the power of the love that flooded through her—that achieved what she had been so clumsily trying to reach. She felt her soul expand and come out of her body. And meet Stefan's.

She was appalled by the hastily swept-away desolation in his spirit, and humbled by the surge of love that flooded every part of him at the touch of her mind.

Oh, Stefan. Just—say that—that you can forgive me, that's all. If you forgive me I can live. Maybe you can even be happy with me again—if you just give it a little time.

I'm already happy with you. But we have all the time in the world, Stefan reassured her. But she caught the shadow of a dark thought whisked quickly out of the way. *He* had all the time in the world. She, however . . .

Elena had to choke back a laugh but then clutched at Stefan suddenly. *My backpack—did they take it? Where is it?*

Right beside your nightstand. I can reach it. Do you want it? He reached in the darkness and pulled up something heavy and rough and none too pleasant-smelling. Elena thrust one frantic hand inside it while still holding on to Stefan with the other.

Yes! Oh, Stefan, it's here!

He was beginning to suspect—but he only *knew* when she drew out the bottle labeled Evian Water and held it to her cheek. It was icy cold, although the night was mild and humid. And as it effervesced violently, it glowed in a way that no ordinary water did.

I didn't mean to do it, she told Stefan, suddenly worried that he might not like to associate with a thief. *At least—not at first. Sage said to get the water from the Fountain of Eternal Youth and Life into bottles. I dug up a big bottle and this little one, and somehow I stashed the smaller one in my backpack—I'd've put the big one in, too, but it didn't fit. And I didn't even think about the little one again until after they took away my Wings and my telepathy.*

And a good thing, Stefan thought. *If they had caught you—oh, my lovely love!* His arms squeezed the breath from Elena's lungs. *So that's why you were suddenly so eager to leave!*

"They took almost everything else supernatural about me," Elena whispered, placing her lips close to Stefan's ear. "I have to live with that, and if they'd given me a chance I'd have agreed—for the sake of Fell's Church—if I'd been logical—" She broke off as she suddenly realized that she had been literally out of her mind. She'd been worse than a thief. She'd tried to use a lethal attack on a group of—mostly—innocent people. And the worst thing was that a part of her knew that Damon would have understood her madness, while she wasn't sure Stefan ever could.

"But you don't have to change me into—you know," she began whispering frenetically again. "A sip or two of this and I can be with you forever. Forever and—for—forever—Stefan—" She stopped, trying to get her breath and her mental balance.

His hand closed over hers on the cap. "Elena."

"I'm not crying. It's because I'm happy. Forever and ever, Stefan. We can be together, just . . . just us two . . . forever."

"Elena, love." His hand kept hers from twisting open the bottle.

"It—isn't what you want?"

With his other arm, Stefan pulled her tightly to him. Her head fell forward onto his shoulder and he rested his chin on her hair. "It's what I want more than anything. I'm . . . dazed, I guess. I have been ever since—" He stopped and tried again. "If we have all the time in the world, we have tomorrow," he said in a voice muffled by hair. "And tomorrow is time enough for you to start to think it through. There's enough in that bottle for maybe four or five people. *You're* the one who's going to have to decide who drinks it, love. But not tonight. Tonight is for . . ."

With a sudden rush of joy Elena understood. "You're talking about—Damon." Amazing how difficult it was to simply say his name. It almost seemed a violation, and yet . . .

When he could talk—like this—for a moment to me, he told me what he wanted, she sent. Stefan stirred a little in the darkness, but said nothing. *Stefan, he only asked for one thing before he . . . went. It was not to be forgotten. That's all. And* we're *the ones who remember the most. Us and Bonnie.*

Aloud she added, "I will never forget him. And I will never let anyone else who knew him forget him—for as long as I live."

She knew she'd spoken *too* loudly, but Stefan didn't try to quiet her. He gave one quick shudder and then held her tightly again, his face buried in her hair.

I remember, he sent to her, *when Katherine asked him to join her—when we three were in Honoria Fell's crypt. I remember what he said to her. Do you?*

Elena felt their souls intertwine as they both saw the scene through the other's eyes. *Of course, I remember too.*

Stefan sighed, half-laughing. *I remember trying to take care of him later in Florence. He wouldn't behave, wouldn't even Influence the girls he fed on.* Another sigh. *I think he wanted to get caught at that point. He couldn't even look me in the face and talk about you.*

I made Bonnie send for you. I made sure she got both of you out here, Elena told him. Her tears had begun to flow again, but slowly—gently. Her eyes were shut and she felt a faint smile come to her lips.

Do you know—Stefan's mental voice was startled,

astonished—*I remember something else! From when I was very young, maybe three or four years old. My father had a terrible temper, especially right after my mother died. And back then, when I was little, and my father was furious and drunk, Damon would deliberately get in between us. He'd say something obnoxious and—well, my father would end up beating him instead of me. I don't know how I could have forgotten about that.*

I do, Elena thought, remembering how frightened she had been of Damon when he'd first turned human—even though he'd put himself in between her and the vampires who wanted to Discipline her in the Dark Dimension. *He had a gift for knowing exactly what to say—how to look—what to do—to get under anyone's skin.*

She could feel Stefan chuckle faintly, wryly. *A gift, was it?*

Well, I certainly couldn't do it, and I can manage most people, Elena replied softly. *Not him, though. Never him.*

Stefan added, *But he was almost always kinder to weak people than to strong ones. He always did have that soft spot for Bonnie . . .* He broke off, as if frightened he'd ventured too near something sacred.

But Elena had her bearings now. She was glad, so glad, that in the end Damon had died to save Bonnie. Elena herself needed no more proof of his feelings about her. She would always love Damon, and she would never allow anything to diminish that love.

And, somehow, it seemed fitting that she and Stefan should sit in her old bedroom and speak of what they remembered of Damon in hushed tones. She planned on taking the same thing up with the others tomorrow.

When she finally fell asleep in Stefan's arms, it was hours after midnight.

44

On the smallest moon of the Nether World fine ash was falling. It fell on two already ash-covered bodies. It fell on ash-choked water. It blocked the sunlight so that an endless midnight covered the moon's ash-coated surface.

And something else fell. In the smallest imaginable droplets, an opalescent fluid fell, colors swirling as if to try and make up for the ugliness of the ashes. They were tiny drops, but there were trillions upon trillions of them, falling endlessly, concentrated over the spot where they had once been part of the largest container of raw Power in three dimensions.

There was a body on the ground on this spot—not quite a corpse. The body had no heartbeat; it did not breathe, and there was no brain activity. But somewhere in it there was a slow pulsing, that quickened very slightly as the tiny drops of Power fell upon it.

The pulsing was made up of nothing but a memory. The memory of a girl with dark blue eyes and golden hair and a small face with wide brown eyes. And the taste: the taste of two maidens' tears. *Elena. Bonnie.*

Putting the two of them together they formed what was not exactly a thought, not exactly a picture. But to someone who only understood words, it might be translated:

They are wiating for me. If I can figure out who I am.

And that sparked a fierce determination.

After what seemed like centuries but was only a few hours, something moved in the ash. A fist clenched.

And something stirred in the brain, a self-revelation. A name.

Damon.